THE
BLOODLINE
WAR

TRACY TAPPAN

THE BLOODLINE WAR

Cover Design by Laura Morrigan
Interior Formatting by Author E.M.S.

ISBN-13: 978-0-9912613-0-7

Published in the United States of America.

ACKNOWLEDGMENTS

I would like to thank two of the best editors on the planet, Jessa Slade from Red Circle Ink and Faith Freewoman from Demon for Details, for their invaluable help on the manuscript. I couldn't have asked for two more grammar smart, plot savvy, and honest women. An additional hug goes to Faith for the useful advice she offered on any topic I threw at her (of which there were many), and for our lively Sunday cyber chats.

To Bruce McAllister, writing coach, father figure, and friend, your advice has always been spot-on and genius; I thank the cosmos for whatever serendipity allowed me to run into you that day on the cliffs of Cinque Terre, Italy.

To Juliette Sobanet, gal pal and author friend, I have no doubt that I'd still be far from the starting line in publishing if not for your generous guidance. It is no exaggeration to say that you changed my life, and for that, I'll be forever grateful.

Thanks also to Trish McCallan for her tireless mentoring and wisdom. You believed in me from not much more than an excerpt off my website, which is pretty darned cool.

And to David and Kelly, who've allowed me to embrace the joy of writing simply by being the two greatest kids ever.

Note to Readers

The symbols that appear above some of the characters' names don't affect pronunciation. They are used only to indicate breed (Om Rău, Half-Rău, Fey, or Fey-Rău). This will make sense to you as you enter the story world.

Om Rău also operates like the word *moose*—the same form for both singular and plural.

The lyrics of the song "White Rabbit" by Jefferson Airplane are reprinted by gracious permission of Hal Leonard Corporation.

THE
BLOODLINE
WAR

To my husband, Jeff,
the love of my life and real-life romantic hero,
Not a day has gone by that you
haven't given me my dreams.

CHAPTER ONE

The house loomed out of the darkness like a hulking beast, its windows black eyes, the front door left gaping wide in a permanent scream. Yellow *Crime Scene Do Not Cross* tape was strung around the perimeter, announcing to the world that bad stuff had happened here, just in case anybody had missed the stink of burned flesh and the eerie silence hanging over everything. Only the occasional crackling dispatcher call from one of the police cruisers parked out front broke the stillness.

A shiver crawled up Toni Parthen's spine, and she had the embarrassing urge to turn around and run. She *really* didn't care for creepy stuff. She dutifully headed for the house anyway, cutting through the red and blue police lights flashing rhythmically across the brick walkway. A uniformed officer was posted at the front door.

She lifted the ID badge hanging around her neck and showed it to him. "I'm your blood expert out of Scripps Memorial. Dr. Toni Parthen." A *real* doctor of hematology, not a mere intern, but still a lowly Fellow. Which meant that when the San Diego Police Department needed a blood specialist, she was the one who got yanked away in the middle of watching *How To Lose A*

Guy In 10 Days to whatever gory scene needed her scientific expertise.

The officer glanced at her badge, then down at the medical bag she was carrying, and then inevitably—she nearly sighed—his eyes landed on her boobs. The Girls were bundled up in a winter coat, nice and tight against the cold January weather, but they were of a size that defied concealment.

She cleared her throat, quashing the urge to quip, *Eyes up here, pal.*

"Uh…yeah, go on in." To his credit, the officer blushed a little. "They're waiting for you upstairs."

She entered the house, passing through a dimly lit foyer and a deserted, well-kept living room. The stink of burned flesh was stronger in here, like a cannibal barbecue gone terribly wrong, and her esophagus tightened. God, but she hated forensics. She arrived at the bottom of a flight of stairs and stopped. Waiting for her at the top was a man with a badge on his belt and a gun in a shoulder holster.

She exhaled sharply. "Crap, not *you.*" The night just got worse.

Detective John Waterson arched a single brow at her, one corner of his mouth climbing upward. "I'm going to stand here and pretend I'm *not* insulted by that, if it's all the same to you."

Toni rolled her eyes. "No offense intended, Detective, but your cases stink." Waterson and his partner, Pablo Ramirez, were on the Occult Crimes Unit, and their crime scenes always ran high on creepiness. Too high.

Waterson's smile widened, the curve of his mouth masculine and sexy, his amazing blue-green eyes warming with amusement.

Trumpets went off in her head. And here was the real reason she didn't like working with this man: John Waterson was hot.

Dressed in cowboy boots, blue jeans, and a dark brown long-sleeved shirt that was folded up at the cuffs to reveal strong forearms, he had the tall, athletically lean build of a swimmer or a tennis player. He had…yes, a very nice mouth, despite the fact that an unlit cigarette was dangling from his lips. He was handsome, self-assured, probably in his early 30's, like her, and in possession of that most alluring of all qualities: intelligence. She was drawn to John in a way she'd never been with any other man. But herein lay the trouble: John was, in point of fact, a *man*, and she'd given up on interacting with their gender—other than professionally—a long time ago.

Sighing, she trudged up the stairs. Nothing else for it. She was here on business. A low rumble of voices was coming from somewhere, a softly crying voice. *Wonderful.* "All right, what am I in for?"

Waterson's eyes danced. "Feeling a bit squeamish again, are we?"

Heat rose into her cheeks. She wasn't squeamish about most things—she was a doctor, for Pete's sake—but she hated the aforementioned creepy stuff. No doubt the result of her older brother dragging her to too many horror films when she was a kid. She narrowed her eyes on Waterson. "Last case we worked on, Detective, some cult freaks had stripped *all of the skin* off the corpse's body."

He held up a hand. "It's nothing like that this time, I swear." Fishing a pack of matches out of his breast pocket, he went on to explain, "A couple of bad guys climbed in through the bedroom window of the fifteen-year-old daughter and tried to snag her." He opened the pack and tugged out a match. "Her father heard her screams, rampaged in with a shotgun, and filled one of the perps with a load of buckshot."

She groaned softly. "Lovely."

"Don't worry." He struck the match and held the flame to the tip of his cigarette. "The scene is surprisingly *un*bloody. That's why you're here."

She plucked the cigarette out of his mouth and mashed it into a plant. "You do know that you're the only person left in California who smokes, don't you?" She headed down the hall and entered a room that was clearly a girl's, and a girl who for once hadn't gone the way of the Goth: lacy lampshades, white eyelet bedspread, posters of Taylor Swift, Taylor Lautner, and, *ah*, second place to Matthew McConaughey: Brad Pitt. Against the backdrop of all this innocence, the black-clad body sprawled out under the window was a grotesque stain.

Two other men were in the room. Pablo Ramirez, a Padres baseball cap perched backward on his head, and a skinny kid—okay, an adult, but one who looked fresh out of science camp for a day of dress-up in his daddy's navy blue suit.

Waterson gestured to him. "This is Silas Thornton, CSI."

She nodded to the CI and moved over to the corpse, stopping at its feet to—

What the hell? She'd never seen anything like this. The guy was a wreck, half a dozen bullet-sized craters in his chest, a few more peppering his thighs, and yet...there wasn't a single drop of blood on him—not anywhere, for that matter. Odder still, the front of the guy's black shirt was completely eaten away, the fabric of his pants nearly in the same condition, and there were holes dotting the carpet beneath him, as if something acidic had dripped off of him and onto it. Jesus, this wasn't just an *un*bloody scene, it was impossibly blood*less*.

She looked at Waterson. "The body was drained?" For what sick purpose, she didn't want to know. Cult freaks were such psychos.

"Evidence suggests it wasn't."

She arched her brows at him in a *what now?* expression.

Waterson gestured, a hint of wryness slanting his mouth. "You want to take a look?"

"At what? You are aware that I deal in actual, physical blood, right, Detective? The kind of stuff that can be viewed under a microscope and put in a centrifuge?"

Another smile tried to make it onto Waterson's mouth. "Just give it your best guess, Doc."

Sighing, she marched over to the body and crouched down. The dead guy was young, maybe only nineteen or twenty, his features smooth and adolescent despite a stern chin and cruel-looking lips. He had a tattoo on his face, black flames crawling

4

up his left jaw like rotten ivy. Biting back an *ugh*, she opened her medical bag and snapped on a pair of latex gloves, then dug out a scalpel. She grabbed the body's wrist.

"Watch out," Waterson warned.

She glanced up.

Waterson nodded at the corpse's hand. "The ring on the perp's finger will give you one helluva shock if you touch it."

"You're kidding." Who in the world booby-trapped a ring? She turned the corpse's wrist to get a better view of it, catching the sparkle of a strange red crystal in the center. Shimmering and undulating, the thing looked like it was filled with some sort of boiling liquid—or as if it lived and breathed. God. This night was reaching new levels of creepy.

Steering clear of the ring, she carefully cut into the corpse's wrist. The vein was empty, not even a trace of blood in it. *Absolutely nothing.* She sat back on her heels and slowly peeled off her gloves. Weirder and weirder. "I can't think of anything that would leave a vein totally stripped. Maybe some chemical...? But I really don't know. You need to get the body on a table and have an ME do a thorough autopsy plus a full chem panel."

The CSI pounced on that. "That's exactly what I said."

She looked at Silas. "Did you?" She shifted her eyes over to Waterson.

Waterson met her gaze without expression.

A flush of heat rolled up the back of her neck. "I see." She threw her scalpel and gloves into her medical bag and snapped it closed. "I'm sorry I couldn't have been more help." She came stiffly to her feet. "Good luck with the case." She spun on her heel and headed through the door, her strides clipped. *Of all the unbelievable—*

"Toni!" Halfway down the stairs, Waterson caught up with her. "Wait—" He took hold of her elbow.

She twisted her arm out of his hold, her pulse kicking up a notch. "Don't touch me, John."

Waterson stepped back, both hands raised, palms out.

"Tonight's call was bogus," she accused, her voice sharp with anger. "This case couldn't be analyzed onsite and you *knew* that."

"All right, you got me." He dropped his hands. "I called you here somewhat unnecessarily. But how else am I going to get to see you? You won't go out with me."

"So stop asking!" she flashed.

Exhaling a long breath, John glanced away. He took a moment, then shook his head and looked back at her. The color of his eyes deepened. "I can't," he said softly.

She pinched the bridge of her nose, drawing a breath to calm herself. "Look, John, just...please just try to understand this has nothing to do with you personally. Okay? I've just had a long string of bad dates, lately."

A really long string, starting all the way back in high school with Brad Flannigan, the super-popular jock star who'd asked her to Homecoming Dance when the head cheerleader had come down with the flu. That night, he'd convinced Toni to give him her virginity, only to broadcast that fact all over school by first period bell come Monday.

Since then it'd been one after another of men who'd start out dating her for her bra size and then get scared off by her IQ size. Or who'd date her for her face, expecting her to be as "perfect" on the inside as they thought she was on the outside, then discover that she most definitely was *not*, and, God, she was so sick of being a disappointment.

The miserable dating run had thankfully come to an end last year when Robert what's-his-name, an anesthesiologist, had loudly announced in front of a movie theatre full of people that she had about as much feeling as a "Dr. House with tits." And after all the faking in bed she'd done for him, too.

Waterson's voice lowered. "I'm not like the rest of the men you've dated, Toni, I can guarantee it. I work on the Occult Crimes Unit, and I wouldn't do that if I liked normal. So, you know, you can be weird, and it's fine."

A spasm of laughter unhinged inside her chest. "That's a

relief." He was probably an all-around nice guy and a great kisser, too. But if she did something stupid like go out on a date with this man, she might then do something even stupider, like crack open the door to her heart. And once again she'd just end up facing down the vast and consuming loneliness which always got worse whenever she was—paradoxically enough—with a man.

Thank God the meat wagon boys started up the stairs just then.

She and John stepped apart to allow the two men hauling a stretcher to pass. "I appreciate the offer, Detective. But I'm afraid the answer's still no."

She left the house, crossing the street at a near run. She fumbled in her purse for her keys, making a noise in her throat, then unlocked her car door with a sharp twist of her wrist. She jerked hard on the handle, throwing her purse and medical bag onto the—

"*One* date," he said behind her.

She froze, her breath catching in her throat.

"That's all I'm asking for," he went on quietly, "then I'll leave you alone forever, I swear. Is that really so unreasonable?"

She closed her eyes, the logical part of her mind saying, "No, it's not unreasonable." What was one night out of her life in the larger scheme of things? Except that it was painful as hell to keep discovering, over and over, that she had some uncanny knack for repelling men.

He moved closer, apparently interpreting her pause as acquiescence. A masculine hand appeared on top of her door, another one bracing itself on the roof of her car. The warmth of his male body stole up right behind her. She inhaled a slow, even breath, recognizing his scent at once, that metallic hint of handcuffs and handgun, tobacco, of course, and just a trace of Drakkar Noir cologne. Heat snaked through her limbs, a surprising jolt of yearning landing in her belly.

"I'm thinking The Fish Market restaurant would be a great place to go." His breath caressed the back of her neck, sending a shudder down her spine. "Toni—" His hand dropped to the curve of her waist and he turned her around. "Please don't keep us dancing around this thing that's been between us for months."

He dipped his head, and her heart skipped a beat when a lock of hair fell across his brow. He hesitated, no doubt waiting for her to do her usual and reject him, but…. His tempting lips were so close to hers, his body warm and smelling so damned masculine that her *nucleus accumbens*—the pleasure center of her brain—just took over and started making decisions. Her chin lifted on its own, offering him her lips.

No more dilly-dallying now. John settled his mouth on hers. She exhaled a small sigh through her nose. His lips were soft and warm and moist, and he tasted surprisingly good, just the slightest suggestion of tobacco covered up by a flavor that was all man. The kiss was light, no more than gentle and reassuring…until she linked her arms around his neck and pressed her breasts against his chest.

A rough groan rushed out of him, and he instantly deepened the kiss, angling his head to the side and opening his mouth over hers. His arms pulled her so close she could feel his heart thundering against her breasts. Her own heart surged into a faster beat. God, he felt wonderful. Everything a man should be, strong and solid, all the things that could make a woman want. With a breathy moan of her own, she slipped her tongue into his mouth and felt his shoulders stiffen. He met her tongue hungrily with the wet heat of his own, and while their tongues dueled, her stomach did a funny gyration. She waited for that little something more…and then there it was: a nice, slow-burning quickening, down low.

She pulled her lips away from his with a gasp, nudging him back a step before her *nucleus accumbens* could really take over and make her plop down right there on the asphalt and to hell with the show she and John would give Officer Bug-Eyes over by the front door.

John stood staring at her through the shadows, his eyes

8

glittering hotly in the silver moonlight, his lungs working in short pants.

"Well, that was convincing," she breathed out, her own chest laboring. She turned toward her purse on the driver's seat of her car and pulled out a business card. She was a fool to give him her number, knowing full well that she was setting herself up for heartbreak again. But damn it, she was also a woman who hadn't had a man's hands on her in over a year, and that kiss had been a doozy. "This is my work number"—she held it out to him—" but it connects to a message system that texts my personal cell phone."

He moved to take it, looking slightly stunned.

She quickly angled it out of his reach. "*Which* Fish Market? Del Mar or Harbor Island Drive?"

He blinked once, at half speed, then his lips spread into a slow smile. "Harbor Island Drive, of course, with that view of the Coronado Bay, the Beach Boys hopefully playing in the background, and us cracking crab legs." His eyes sparkled mischievously. "I happen to think you'd look dynamite in a large plastic bib."

"Right." She snorted and rolled her eyes. "If that's the *only* thing I was wearing."

"Ho!" John clutched his chest and stumbled backward as if he'd been shot.

She laughed. *Oops. Wrong imagery, there.* She handed him the card, still laughing. He really was irresistible.

He tucked it into his breast pocket next to his cigarettes, his eyes remaining steady on hers, his mouth still too dangerously inviting.

She quickly hopped into her car and buckled up. He closed the door for her, and she unrolled the window. "I only ask that you don't smoke around me, okay?"

He nodded once. "Fair enough." He leaned through the window and snatched a quick kiss. "Get home safe, Doc."

She met his eyes with a warm smile. "I will."

He slapped the roof of her car.

She pulled away, watching in her rearview mirror as he headed over to a blue Chevy and jumped inside next to Pablo. She caught her own reflection and saw that she was grinning like an idiot. She was an idiot. An all too familiar twist of panic shot through her belly, and she shut down her smile. She needed to be prepared going into this thing for it not to work out…. For her to like him more and more, and then for him to eventually leave because that's—

Her cell beeped the arrival of a text message. Frowning, she tugged her IPhone out of her purse and glanced at the screen.

So how desperate is it that I'm already messaging you? I'm really looking forward to our dinner…:o) J.

Pleasure entered her chest. Okay, maybe this was going to be—

A horn blared a warning. She jerked her eyes up. *Oh, my God!* The headlights of another car were swerving toward her. With a gasp, she yanked her steering wheel hard to the right, her cell phone jettisoning from her grip. Her car shrieked into a sideways skid, tires smoking and screeching, and—

The cars collided.

She cried out as her body lurched forward violently. The exploding airbag punched her back in the seat and sent her head snapping against the headrest. A searing pain tore through the backs of her eyeballs. Glass tinkled, steam hissed, and….

There was only blackness.

CHAPTER TWO

It started out like a normal enough mission. Then again…all missions do, don't they?

Jaćken Brun stood braced for action next to his other two operatives, all three of them riding up the Scripps Memorial Hospital elevator in focused silence. Their fourth operative, Cleeve, had already been dropped off at Admin. There, as per their usual MO, the young computer dweeb would hack into the hospital's system and enter transfer orders for their target female, giving this abduction a nice, official stamp of approval.

On Jaćken's right was Vinz Mihnea, decked out in a Brooks Brothers suit and lab coat for the role of doctor he'd be playing, reeking of Elvis appeal with those thick black sideburns. On Jaćken's left was Thomal Costache in a pair of scrubs. Thomal's flattop blond hair might've made him look too much like the soldier he really was, but his face would distract from that; he had the kind of unreal good looks most women found fertility-inspiring. Having Thomal along pretty much guaranteed a whole lot of babbling, "Of course, sir. Anything you want, sir."

Jaćken had no way of knowing that in less than fifteen minutes one of these men would have a knife planted in his chest. And not just any knife. A Bătaie Blade.

Yeah, *that's* what the real goatfuck turned out to be. Jačken hadn't even remotely considered that there might be competition for the woman at the hospital, especially from someone who carried a Bătaie Blade. They'd never faced opposition before, not in their six previous, immaculately executed abductions. For a short second, Jačken had worried his team had gooned something up. It'd been two long years, after all, since the data-filtering spyware they'd embedded in the laboratory computers of various hospitals around San Diego had spotted a woman's blood containing the coveted Peak 8 in it. But no. Their only mistake had been getting caught with their pants down.

The elevator dinged its arrival on the fifth floor.

Game on.

Vinz broke right and headed for the doctor's lounge, where he'd wait for the go-ahead from Jačken once the transfer orders were complete. Thomal went left, a syringe filled with 250 mgs of Ketamine tucked in his breast pocket next to a fountain pen—really a mini camera and microphone—and headed for his destination: Room 506, temporary living quarters of their target.

One Dr. Antoinetta Parthen.

Jačken found the nearest deserted waiting room, and stationed himself there—as good a place as any to conceal himself from the general public. Sunny Californians seemed to get all jumpy around the distinct Rambo vibe he gave off. He bought a Styrofoam cup of coffee from the vending machine, planted his butt on an uncomfortable couch, then set his laptop on the coffee table and flipped it open.

The main screen instantly lit up into three smaller screens: video inputs from each operative's fountain pen camera. Two quadrants were on top—one for Vinz, one for Cleeve—and a half-screen on the bottom for Thomal. From this point on, Jačken would serve as the team's communications center. Even though his men could hear and speak to each other through earpieces, he was the only one who could see the whole picture.

Cleeve's voice crackled into his ear. "Transfer orders are in, cha-*ching*." The kid angled his fake fountain pen toward his face and tossed Jaćken a pleased-as-punch smile. "Who d'ya love, huh?"

Jaćken twisted his lips. That was damned fast. "I owe you a beer at Garwald's Pub, runt. Now shut up and get out of there. Vinz—show time."

"Aw, man, I just grabbed a jelly donut." The image in Vinz's quadrant changed, a long hallway appearing, at the end of which was a nurse's station.

Jaćken sipped his coffee as he marked Vinz's progress; Thomal's, too. The lower screen showed that Thomal-the-male-nurse was just arriving at Antoinetta's room. Passing by the door, Thomal continued down the hall about ten more feet and stopped beside a gurney.

Jaćken narrowed his eyes at Thomal's half-screen. What the hell was the man doing?

"Good morning, I'm Dr. Bernard," Vinz was saying to a busty nurse with the name Barbara Hollowitz stamped on her ID tag.

"Um, Jaćken," Thomal said in a low tone. "The subject's awake."

Jaćken furrowed his brow. "At 3:45 in the morning?"

Vinz cleared his throat pointedly. "Yes, Miss Hollowitz, I see by the patient's chart that Dr. Parthen has a concussion and is being awakened periodically according to proper procedure."

"Ahhhh"—Thomal elongated the sound in understanding—"that explains it. You want me to go in there and charm her, chief?"

Jaćken plunked his coffee cup down. "It's why I put up with your annoying personality, Costache."

Thomal half-stifled a laugh. "Well, no prob on this one. I caught a whiff of the lovely Miss Parthen on the way past and…damn, she smells hot."

The busty nurse tsk-tsked sympathetically. "My, Dr. Bernard, you're certainly getting an early start this—"

"Just get moving before I call in Arc to replace your ass."

Arc was Thomal's older brother, taller and longer-haired but with the same blond "dreamboat" attractiveness. He was currently hanging out in the downstairs parking garage with the other backup team members, probably chewing gum and playing hacky sack, not a worry in their heads about this mission. Jaćken grunted. "He's better looking than you are, anyway."

"That hurts me, man." Thomal strode into Room 506, switching to a cheery, "Good morning, Dr. Parthen." He moved over to Antoinetta's bedside, giving Jaćken his first glimpse of her: the soft lines of an elegant profile, shimmering strawberry blonde hair spread out across the pillow. The muscles in his stomach tightened. Even with her image pixelized by the computer screen—not to mention she probably wasn't at her best in a hospital—she was a knockout.

Then things got moving. He shifted his gaze back and forth between screens as he kept track of his two main players, the babble of multiple voices filling his earpiece.

"...sure you'll find everything complete, Miss Hollowitz," Vinz assured the nurse, "with the transfer request...."

"...change in doctor's orders, Dr. Parthen," Thomal was saying in a chipper tone. "He'd like you to get some solid sleep now." Thomal's hands reached for Antoinetta's IV.

"Wait, what are you doing?" Antoinetta interceded.

"If you'd sign here, Dr. Bernard," Nurse Hollowitz crooned, "then we'll just head down to Room ...."

"I have a concussion, Nurse. I'm not supposed to sleep deeply." Antoinetta's voice turned authoritative. "I'd like to see your badge."

Ah, shit. "You need to throttle back, Vinz," Jaćken hissed. "The target isn't knocked out yet."

Vinz's voice suddenly mellowed into warm honey. "You know, Barbara, that's a very beautiful necklace you're wearing. Do you mind if I take a closer look at it?"

Jaćken saw Thomal plunge the syringe of Special K into Antoinetta's IV tube.

"My God!" Antoinetta blasted. "What did you just give me?" She started to yank the IV needle out of her arm.

Thomal grabbed her wrist.

A loud *crack* rang out as she slapped Thomal across the face with her free hand. "Let go of me!" She reached for her needle again, and they started to struggle.

"Oh, ho, my fun meter is pegged now," Thomal panted out.

"…a lovely stone, Barbara. Is it an opal…?"

Jaćken gritted his teeth. "For Chrissake, Thomal, is this what you call charming the target? Get moving!"

"Ah!" Thomal exhaled, straightening from a limp Antoinetta. "Target is sacked out, gentlemen."

Jaćken released a pent breath. "You hear that Vinz?"

Apparently, yes. Vinz's video image started down the hall again. "Well, I should probably see to my patient," he said to the nurse, both of them entering Room 506. "Don't want to get stuck in San Diego rush hour traffic if—oomph!" The picture in Vinz's quadrant fell to the floor, blanking to fuzzy snow. A second later, the nurse screamed once, then went abruptly silent.

Jaćken stiffened on the couch. *What the—*?! "Costache!?" he barked.

But the image in Thomal's quadrant was jiggling wildly, the sounds of scuffling and cursing exploding into Jaćken's earpiece. *Holy shit!* He jumped over his laptop and the coffee table in one leap and ran from the waiting room, moving down the hall with absolute silence in his heavy boots. Pressing his back flat against the wall just outside of Room 506, his breathing tight, he peered around the jamb.

A low curse snarled past his lips. Vinz's body was sprawled out on the floor in a stain of spreading blood, a knife sticking out of his chest, that busty nurse flopped over the top of him with her ass in the air. Two other men were in the room, both large, both dressed in the type of metal-accessorized aggressive black leather usually saved for BDSM parties. One had a shaved head with black flame tattoos curling up from his temples to the top of his skull. The other guy had spiked black hair and the same tattoos, his climbing the length of his neck.

It was this asshole, Spike Boy, who was clutching a blue-faced Thomal by the throat.

Louder alarm bells went off in Jaćken's head. Whatever power these men were wielding was something outside the norm. Thomal was one of the fastest of his kind, and Jaćken had never seen anyone get a firm grip on the man unless he allowed it in training.

Hissing under his breath, Jaćken reached to the back of his belt and eased a long knife out of its sheath. He stepped through the doorway and, keeping to his maxim of *fuck up an enemy first, ask questions later*, he threw the weapon with a sharp snap of his wrist. Aiming for a point as far away from a collision with Thomal as possible, he sent the blade thwacking into the meaty part of Spike Boy's shoulder.

With a scream, Spike Boy stumbled backward into a medical cart, sending metal drawers clattering, scissors, gauze, forceps tumbling to the floor. Thomal crumpled out of the man's hands, and then Spike Boy himself dropped.

Jaćken turned on the other one, Skull—just as that peckerhead let fly his own knife. Jaćken hit the deck and rolled, hearing the knife swoosh just past his head, then thunk into the floor. A moment later, it exploded, geysering up ragged pieces of linoleum. Holy Christ. Only one type of knife exploded. A Bătaie Blade! Who the hell *were* these assholes? There wasn't time for a Q&A. Powering to his feet in front of the bed, Jaćken plowed a hard right cross over the mattress into Skull's face, landing the punch dead center. Skull's head snapped back, the bones in his nose splintering beneath Jaćken's fist. The man hit the wall, bounced forward, then grabbed Jaćken by the shirtfront.

Jaćken shouted as Skull hauled him off the floor with impossible strength, tossing all 215 pounds of him over Antoinetta's bed and into the far wall. His shoulder rammed out a hole in the drywall, the plaster blasting apart into a dense white cloud around him. Landing unsteadily on his feet, he struck out blindly and missed, his head spinning. His upper gums throbbed ruthlessly in primitive reaction to the violence.

Spike Boy was on his feet now, too, Jaćken's knife still sticking out of his shoulder, white liquid oozing from the wound. White…?

Spike Boy slammed a fist into Jaćken's gut.

Air whooshed out of Jaćken's lungs. Jesus Christ, these guys were strong. "I need backup!" he yelled, hoping like hell Thomal's fountain pen would pick up his shout, his own mic being inconveniently attached to his laptop back in the waiting room.

Skull and Spike Boy exchanged looks.

"Bloody fuck!" Skull whirled and snatched up Antoinetta.

Jaćken bolted forward, but Spike Boy's fist flying into his peripheral vision stopped him. Ducking the punch, he came up with a brutal uppercut that evidently sloshed Spike Boy's brain in his skull; the asshole made a second trip down to the linoleum, this time in an unconscious heap.

Jaćken grabbed Antoinetta out of Skull's arms, pulling so hard he fell backward onto the bed with her.

Skull jumped on top of him, toppling Antoinetta to one side of the mattress, her body wedging against the bedrail. Skull grabbed Jaćken by the collar and cranked back a fist.

Two things pinged Jaćken's senses in rapid succession: one huge holy-shitter was that Skull's eyes were as black as his own. Not just very dark brown, but as black as if the pupils had eaten up the irises—and only one breed of man owned black eyes. Second, Skull stank…like corroded metal or transmission fluid. Not at all like blood. Not at all like the way he should've smelled with the black eyes of an Om Rău.

Jaćken dodged the punch Skull threw at him. Skull countered by trying to put him in a headlock. Jaćken grappled with the man, grunting and cursing, their arms and legs tangling. Muscling Skull underneath him, Jaćken hit the fucker hard enough to split the skin on his knuckles. Skull rolled Jaćken back over, both men landing on Antoinetta's feet, and punched

Jaćken in return, a ring on his finger tearing a line of flesh out of Jaćken's cheek in a streak of pain.

Jaćken snarled, grabbing Skull by the throat and—

"Well, heck, looks like I'm missing all the fun."

Jaćken and Skull stopped fighting and snapped their eyes up to the door in unison. Relief jackhammered Jaćken's heart. Nyko!

His older brother was standing in the doorway, looking super bad-assed *huge* with his tall, broad, muscular body filling the entire frame. Eyes as cold and dark as black glaciers peered out from a tumble of shaggy black hair, and a savage array of black interlocking teeth tattoos ran the length of his forearms and ringed his neck. Nobody would guess that on the inside Nyko was pure marshmallow, because on the outside, he looked one hundred percent psycho serial killer.

Thank crap for that. "About damned time," Jaćken growled.

Eyebrows lifting, Nyko started into the room, but made it only one step inside when there was a blur of motion off to the left.

From out of nowhere, Skull suddenly had a pair of medical scissors sticking out of his neck, a disgusting gurgling sound coming from him.

Thomal stood next to the bed, a nasty sneer on his face. "Sorry, guys, but I owed these bitches a spanking."

A white foamy substance like shaving cream oozed from Skull's wound. Some of it blopped onto Jaćken's chest and began to eat through his shirt. "Jesus!" He heaved Skull off, letting the man crash unaided to the floor, and shot to his feet, tearing his shirt off and hurling it aside. "What the *hell?*"

Nyko shook his head, his expression troubled as he crouched down next to Vinz and checked for a pulse. Nyko rolled the nurse off the fallen warrior, her removal exposing a unique sunflower burst of blood on the wall.

A startled curse came out of Thomal's mouth.

Nyko carefully pulled the knife out of Vinz's upper chest and held it up with one hand, the other jammed to Vinz's wound.

The hilt was carved with intertwining black flames, not like the interwoven black teeth they were used to seeing on their pain-in-the-ass Om Rău neighbors' knives, but still with the boiling red crystal on it that marked it a Bătaie Blade.

"Yeah, I saw it," Jacken said grimly.

Thomal hissed a breath. "What the hell are these jagoffs doing with an Om Rău blade?" The man already looked like warmed-over shit, both eyes red from blown capillaries and dark bruises forming around his throat.

"Maybe because they *are* Om Rău," Jacken returned.

Thomal's blond brows arched high. "The only Om Rău in existence live next door to us."

Jacken tossed Nyko a roll of gauze. "These slimeballs have black eyes, Bătaie Blades, tribal tattoos, and were strong as fuck."

"They also bleed acid," Thomal pointed out.

"Then we need to look into the possibility that they're a different genetic branch of Om Rău."

Nyko looked up from bandaging Vinz. "A branch that just so happens to be after our women, too?"

Thomal made a guttural noise in his chest, his protective hackles going up.

Women like Antoinetta carried a bloodline that was key to the salvation of their race. Jacken and his men of the Warrior Class protected and guarded any they found like the rare and precious commodity they were.

"We'll debrief further when we get back to Țărână." Jacken grabbed a bag and started shoving Antoinetta's personal effects into it. "We've got to get out of here. Sunrise is riding up our asses, and we don't want to get stuck in the safe house with Vinz needing to see Dr. Jess right away." He looked at Nyko. "What's the SITREP?"

"No more bad guys are en route," Nyko replied. "I put the backup team on the stairwell to keep an eye on that. Couple of nurses heard some noise coming from this room, but Arc is pulling a flirt 'n divert." Nyko pushed to his feet, tossing Vinz over his shoulder as if the warrior weighed no more than a CPR dummy. "Still, we should get going PDQ."

"Agreed." Jaćken reached for Antoinetta. "Let's get our target safely down to— Whoa!" He jerked back a step.

Thomal stepped up beside him. "Told you she smells really good."

Really good? That was a massively enormous understatement. He hadn't been able to tell before, what with so much of Vinz's blood masking her scent, but...*Jesus.*

Thomal glanced at Jaćken's bare chest. "You sure you want to be the one carrying her, chief?"

Jaćken exhaled a short breath. Right, the feel of this woman's fragrant body pressed close to his, with only her thin hospital gown as a barrier between them, would probably make it right to the top of the Bad Idea Column. "You take her," he ordered.

But as soon as Thomal scooped up Antoinetta and settled her snugly against his chest, Jaćken had the sudden, savage—and totally irrational—urge to tear out Thomal's perfect blond entrails.

CHAPTER THREE

"Mürk and Rën bodged up the mission."

Raymond stopped writing in his ledger and looked up, squinting through the glare of his desk lamp at the young blonde woman standing just inside his study, a clipboard propped on her hip.

She was dressed like a blooming tart, as was her habit, wearing four-inch pointies on her feet and a miniskirt not much wider than a belt. Her blouse showed as much cleavage as it did midriff, displaying a jeweled belly button ring, along with a black flame tattoo that curled from her navel down into parts unknown. Well, not entirely unknown from what he understood of his daughter's escapades when she went out pubbing with the girls.

"I beg your pardon," he asked coolly, even though he'd heard her.

Pändra hesitated, spinning the immortality ring on her finger with her thumb, the eerie red stone reflecting light like blood flecked with diamonds.

The blasted thing was more often a curse than a salvation these days, all of the progeny seeming to think they had *carte blanche* to rampage around like blootered bulls.

"Mürk and Rën failed to nab Toni from the hospital."

Raymond narrowed his eyes, anger burning through his head and into his nostrils. *The* most important part of his plan was the attainment of Toni Parthen, and after that, her brother, Alex. Mürk and Rën were fully aware of that. "I see," he replied acidly. "And what, pray tell, occurred?"

"I don't know all the crack," she said, "but the gist is that our lads got into a punch-up with some other blokes, who ended up nicking Toni from—"

He slammed to his feet, knocking the metal arm of his desk lamp into a crazy swing. "*Other men* have taken her?" A wave of his power burst off his body and thumped into Pändra.

She staggered backward a couple of paces, her black eyes flaring wide.

He took an immediate breath and composed himself, locking his power into a low simmer. There was no need to be uncivilized, no matter how extreme his anger. "Where are Mürk and Rën?" Those two needed to give him a full report on this catastrophe, posthaste. He felt a muscle in his jaw flicker as he added, "In jail, I presume?"

"Um...." Pändra moved forward to her former position. "No. They escaped before the police arrived."

"I see," he drawled. "So the lads were too frightened to face me and went on a bender instead. Why am I not surprised." He crossed to his cherrywood sideboard and poured himself a Courvoisier. Mouth tight, he stared down at his drink, the cut crystal of the double old-fashioned glass biting into his palm.

The devil take Mürk and Rën. Raymond had been preparing for this next step for *twenty-six years*. He and his partner, Boian—the last two pure Fey men on earth—had kept their Om Rău female, Ɏavell, churning out children during that entire quarter of a century and more, sometimes one baby a year, usually one every two years to prevent her womb from clapping out completely. Now they had eighteen progeny between them, and more planned for the future. But this year, the year Rën and

22

Mürk, born eleven months apart, came of age at twenty-six, was the year to set his scheme in motion.

If women with the correct bloodlines could be acquired.

More easily said than done, apparently, what with the way their missions had been going pear-shaped of late. First, Tëer and Däce had failed to obtain that fifteen-year-old girl, and now Mürk and Rën had made a dog's dinner out of nabbing Toni. Taking her should've been a doss of a task, as well, since she'd been nearly unconscious in a hospital bed. When the detectives Raymond kept on permanent assignment watching Toni had informed him of the poor girl's unfortunate car accident, Raymond decided straight away that this was the perfect time to take her. And now Mürk and Rën had bodged it. By God, Raymond would be a bloody codger before he saw his first grandchild born.

He looked up from his drink at Pändra again, the skin across his cheeks taut. "What do my detectives have to say about this? I imagine my chaps saw something."

"Yes," Pändra said. "I checked with Mr. Perkins and Mr. Rathburn before coming to speak with you."

Raymond arched a single eyebrow. *Smart girl.* "And?"

Pändra glanced down at her clipboard. "Perkins said there were seven men total at the hospital, although it appears only four actually got into a row with Mürk and Rën; one man was dragged out injured and unconscious, I imagine due to our lads. Two men," she glanced up "—and here's the important part— had black eyes and tribal tattoos." She lowered her clipboard. "By the way Perkins and Rathburn described the tats, they sound like the same as Mum's."

Raymond snorted elegantly. "That would make the two men Om Rău."

Pändra shrugged noncommittally.

Raymond frowned over that. "Ÿavell is supposed to be the last of that breed." The rest of the Om Rău race, it was rumored, had killed each other off. Hardly surprising, that. They were such ghastly creatures.

"I can't be sure, of course. I didn't see the tats myself." Pändra shifted from foot to foot.

He took a sip of his drink. His daughter's feet must be near wrecked in those ridiculous shoes.

"Mürk and Rën will have to confirm it."

"Well, I shan't be waiting for those two dimmocks." He set down his glass. "Best I go have a little chat with your mum." Lord, the very thought soured his stomach. He preferred to have contact with that woman only when it was his turn to impregnate her, and that was about as much of a lark as doing the business with a leaf shredder. And probably gave him about as many injuries. "Am I correct in assuming that your neglect to mention Toni's whereabouts indicates that no one has the remotest idea where she is?"

Pändra fidgeted again; maybe she was wearying of her role as the bearer of bad news. "Perkins said he and Rathburn followed the getaway van for a good half hour, but the blokes eventually lost them."

As I suspected. He was surrounded by incompetents. He headed for the study door. "When the lads get home," he told his daughter as he passed her, "send them to me straight away."

Pändra blank-faced the request.

She must have realized that the poor chaps would be enjoying one of his more inventive castigations.

Kimberly Stănescu jammed her thumb into the remote control button, flipping channels quickly and aggressively, her jaw set. She wasn't watching anything on the television, just waiting for her husband to *finally* get his butt home. Outside her living room window sunlight was fading into dusk—or rather, the huge stadium lights mounted on the cave ceiling that passed for this underground community's version of sunlight were dimming.

At last! She heard the distinctive clomp of her husband's Timberland hiking boots on the walkway outside.

The front door swung open and Sedge came inside, tossing his duffle bag negligently into a corner of the foyer. "Hey," he said.

She hey'd him back, flipping to the next channel with a hard jerk of her hand.

He paused a moment. "Is something wrong?"

"Really?" She slammed the remote onto the coffee table. "You're going to ask me that after you've just come home from *kidnapping* another woman?"

"Jesus, please don't start, Kimberly, okay?" He moved through the foyer into the kitchen. "Today's mission sucked and I feel like crap." Opening the refrigerator, he pulled out a Heineken. "Vinz got stabbed, you know."

She surged to her feet and marched into the kitchen after her husband. "Yes, I do know." It'd been one of those moments of sheer, unadulterated terror when she'd opened her front door and found Roth Mihnea, the leader of the community, standing on her doorstep with a grim look on his face. She'd thought Roth had come to tell her that it was Sedge who'd been killed. Which would've fit in perfectly with her life to date. Because things were going about as right for her as if she'd spent all of her days spilling salt, breaking mirrors, and walking under ladders.

She plunked her hands on her hips. "If you're waiting for me to feel sorry for Vinz, then you're going to stand there till you petrify, Sedge. Because here's the thing. Vinz wouldn't have been injured in the first place if you warriors hadn't been out kidnapping another woman!"

Sedge didn't respond. He twisted the Heineken cap and she heard it *siss* open.

"Damn it, Sedge, I can't believe you took another one! Have you heard nothing I've had to say about this?" How ridiculously naïve she'd been to think that Gwyn Billaud, the woman who'd been taken after her, would be the community's last kidnap victim. How completely idiotic to assume that anyone in this barbaric town had actually listened to Kimberly or learned one single thing from forcing Gwyn down here into danger and then *losing* her.

"Oh, I've heard," Sedge returned, tipping the beer to his mouth and drinking it down.

She seamed her lips together. *Well, that's just great.* She loved it when men chugged beer around her. It was, like…memories galore. "You men of the Warrior Class think you're such heroes, saving your people from possible extinction with what you're doing. But do you know what you really are? Criminals! No better than a bunch of thugs."

Sedge lowered his beer and pinched the bridge of his nose. "Yes, thank you. You've made that abundantly clear in the past." He set his beer on the kitchen island. "This is the same argument we've been having for two years, Kimberly, and it gets us nowhere. There's nowhere *to* go with it. I wish there were, but I'm in an impossible situation here. I have a job that requires me to follow orders, so I follow them, but that means I end up doing something you hate." His gaze darkened. "That I hate."

She curled her hands into fists. "If you hate it, then stand up to Roth."

Sedge shook his head. "You know I don't have the power to change anything around here. But even if I could get Roth to stop sending warriors topside on kidnap missions, how in the world is that going to help you, Berly? It won't. *Nothing* will change for you. You're stuck down here with me, no matter what." The muscles around his throat tightened and a raw thread of pain entered his voice. "I know you're miserable. That's more than clear. I wish I could send you topside daily to your lawyer job—you have no idea how much I want that—but security issues make that impossible. Too many comings and goings risk exposure, and Roth is really paranoid about it. You know that, Berly, okay, so…. I'm truly sorry for how unhappy you are. I mean that from the depths of my heart. But I don't know what I can do about it."

She just stared at him, her chest hitching as she fought back tears. It was more or less the same speech she'd heard for the two years of their marriage, and, as always, Sedge was right. There wasn't anything he could do to free her, barring killing himself. She was well and truly trapped, and the worst part was that she'd colluded in her own entrapment by marrying him. Worse still, her marriage had handed a victory to Roth, who'd abducted her down here for the very purpose of hooking her up with one of the men. It was the stupidest thing she'd ever done in a long list of stupid things in her life, letting herself fall in love with Sedge.

He wasn't even particularly her type. She didn't like big men, not since her ex-boyfriend, Tim, anyway, and Sedge was huge, nearly six foot four and as wide as the side of two barns. His long mane of blond hair, spread in thick waves across his shoulders, only served to enhance the sheer breadth of him and emphasize his muscular power.

But behind all the muscle he was sweet and doting, and had a pair of puppy-dog brown eyes that spoke of a good soul. Those qualities in themselves had been difficult enough to resist, but men of his kind also fiercely protected their women, and the allure of the safety Sedge could provide her had ended up proving too tempting. Unfortunately, she also hated herself for that. In her logical mind, she told herself she should be strong enough to look out for herself—she was, damnit! She didn't need a man! Of course, this fueled the conflict inside her head which invariably had her performing a push-pull dance with Sedge that was far from healthy. She knew it, saw herself doing it, but just couldn't seem to stop.

"There's got to be something meaningful you can do down here," Sedge insisted. "Then—"

"Ha! Like what? Build rock gardens?" She braced her hands on the kitchen island and leaned toward him. "Do you know what I did before you people stole my life? I worked for the Peace Corps for two years before I went to law school. After I graduated, I was in-house counsel for an environmental group, saving trees and ocean and air, and right before you kidnapped me, I'd just won a case where I helped to uphold the First Amendment rights of the United States Constitution." She straightened and threw out her arms. "I used to save the world, Sedge. After that, what the unholy hell do you think I can find to do in this stupid little town that would feel meaningful?"

Sedge bowed his head. "Tell me," he implored hoarsely. "Just tell me what I need to do to make you happy, and I'll do it. Anything."

She took a step back from him, torn between how moved she was by his obvious love for her and yet how clearly ineffectual he was at making her happy. She felt nearly consumed by an acute disappointment in her husband, because she believed he really would stop the kidnappings if he weren't so damned indoctrinated into the community's system of sole leadership.

And really, why *would* anyone question King-frigging-Roth? Why should *he* question it, when he never suffered any of the long-term consequences of his fucked-up repopulation program? Sure, the abducted women were upset and angry when they first got dragged into the town of Ţărână, but the dawning amazement of finding a community where they could truly belong, when most had faced nothing but rejection in their former lives, and the supremely gorgeous and attentive men who were wandering the streets around here, were pretty damned powerful tools for winning them over. All the women caved eventually.

Just as she had.

Her face flushed with heat. Well, not this time. Acquisition number seven, whoever that new kidnap victim might be, was the last straw. "You want me to find something meaningful to do around here? Well, all right. I've got something in mind." She spun around hard on her heels and marched for the stairs. She was damn well going to save the new woman.

"Ah, hell." Sedge raced up the stairs after her. "Kimberly, please, you've got to stop stirring the pot around here."

She kept trudging. "Somebody's got to."

"You're going about it all crazy, Berly."

She didn't say anything.

"I mean, Jesus, you tried to get equal rights for the Stânga Town kids."

"You bet I did. Your system of hierarchy around here is prejudicial and asinine."

He threw out his arms. "You complained that there wasn't a health inspector for the *two* places in town there are to eat out."

"Three," she shot back. "Besides Garwald's Pub and The Diner, you can buy snacks and drinks at the movie theatre. And Roth hired one, didn't he?"

"For the love of God, you lobbied for a longer lunch recess for the school kids."

"So?"

"They're *preschoolers*," he told the side of her face as she came to the top of the stairs; she was refusing to look at him. "The stuff you do doesn't make any sense. It's completely off the wall."

She planted herself in their bedroom doorway, her hand on the doorknob. "Oh, you ain't seen nothin' yet, buster." She slammed the door in her husband's face.

CHAPTER FOUR

Toni peeled open one eyelid, swept the room with a glance, then closed her eye again. *Wonderful.* She was hallucinating. Damn, she'd known something like this was going to happen the moment that strange male nurse had come into her hospital room. *Strange,* not as in strange-looking. No, actually he'd been gorgeous: stylish flattop blond hair, cheekbones that could cut steel, and a double scoop of sculpted butt that even hospital scrubs hadn't been able to camouflage. But strange in that he hadn't known what the hell he was doing.

Change in doctor's orders, he'd said, *get some solid sleep now.* Ludicrous. She knew her doctor, for Pete's sake, and Steven wouldn't have altered her treatment plan without first discussing it with her. Not only that, but what kind of change in orders would knock her out right before she was supposed to be discharged?

She'd just been tee'ing up for a good harangue when Incompetent Nurse...Nurse Goodbody or...Ratched, or whoever he was, had sedated her. And now whatever medication he'd given her had screwed up her poor concussed brain. When she'd cracked open her eyelid just now, she'd found herself not in her hospital room, but in some extravagant bedroom decorated in Louis XVI furniture...which just upped the weird factor even more because if she was ever going to hallucinate, she imagined it'd be in Country French.

Not that she had any idea what it was like to trip out. She wasn't straight-laced or anything, just focused and determined. She'd had to be to get where she'd wanted to go in life; the bio undergrad program at UCSD had been brutal, and med school at UCLA even harder, but she'd graduated at the top of her class in both.

Her mother had responded to these achievements by dubbing her a blonde-haired, blue-eyed, D-cup'ped, over-achiever. Basically, *straight-laced* in mother parlance, although Toni didn't do more than secretly roll her eyes over it. Comments from her mother came few and far between these days, and Toni didn't want to risk putting any more distance between them than already existed.

Odd thing about her mother. Shannon Parthen had been a fantastic parent when Toni and her older brother, Alex, were growing up. Toni's Mom and Dad got divorced when Toni was about six, and after that—no doubt *because* of that—Shannon had thrown herself into the job of motherhood with all her heart. As soon as Toni had gone away to college, though, it'd been like, *bam!* No need for further involvement now that her daughter was launched into the world. A grown woman. Raised.

Although the truth was, none of Toni's female relationships had ever been all that close. Single girls were threatened by her looks, homemakers treated her like an alien from the Planet Zorg because she was thirty-two and still didn't have any children, and professional women were...well, threatened by her.

Boyfriends hadn't exactly proved fertile ground for intimacy, either.

So it was her brother, Alex, who got an earfull of her woes whenever she had them. In fact, she really needed to talk to Alex about that cabbage-headed maneuver she'd pulled by giving her phone number to Detective John Waterson. She'd hadn't had a chance to talk to him before the accident and—

The soft chiming of a clock brought her back to her current situation. She snapped her eyes open, both of them this time. *Damn. Same Louis XVI head trip going on.* Right. She needed to get her fuzzy brain on task here.

Sitting up slowly, she swung her legs over the side of the mattress and sat on the edge of the bed. A wave of dizziness overtook her, but it passed quickly, leaving a dull ache behind her eyes. She waited another minute, but the swanky bedroom refused to change back into the hospital room at Scripps. Crap, this was real.

She looked around and found the clothes she'd worn into the hospital the night of her car accident neatly folded on a bedside table, piled next to one of those fancy white-and-gold French Contessa-style phones. And her purse? She reached out carefully to look through her belongings. No purse; no cell. *Perfect.* She eyed the Contessa phone. There weren't any numbers on it, but, well…. She picked up the receiver.

There was a soft *hum*, then a woman's voice came on the line. "Operator."

Operator? Weird. Had she somehow landed herself in a hotel? "Um…hello, yes…uh…." How did one go about asking *Where am I?* without sounding like a complete nincompoop? "Could you dial a number for me, please?" Her brother was probably the best option. "It's a 619 area—"

"Ah, Dr. Parthen," the operator interrupted. "It's good to hear you're awake. I'll send the doctor in to see you right away."

The…? *Wait*—The line went dead.

She pulled the phone away from her ear and eased the receiver back into its cradle. *Doctor?* Was she at a—? She shot to her feet, her heart thundering. Dear God, whatever drug Nurse Fine Ass had given her had put her into a coma and now she was in some high-class treatment facility for…for *how long*?! Holy crap!

Her head started to spin, and she gripped her forehead, forcing herself to take slow, even breaths. *Okay, calm down, Toni. Be logical.* She wasn't hooked up to an IV or a feeding tube, and her muscles were in working order. Weren't they? She took a few experimental steps. *Yes...yes.* Okay, then.

There was probably a simple explanation for this.

She spied a set of long, gold velvet curtains across the room. The San Diego skyline would be just outside that window, or some landmark which would clear up this *where am I?* mystery, and then she could stop worrying. She walked over and parted the curtains.

Bong. She could almost hear her own jaw drop.

A sliding glass door led out onto a wrought iron balcony...and that's where all semblance of normalcy ended. About twenty feet beyond the end of the balcony were prison bars. Each steel post was about as big as a birch tree, no more than a couple of feet of space between them, and appeared to surround the entirety of whatever building she was in. As ease of escape-ability went, the place ranked about a Houdini.

Beyond the prison bars was the real freak-show. Rock above, rock below...she was inside a cave! And a cave that'd been converted into a small town. . At the beginning of a long street that continued into the distance she saw a coffee shop called Aunt Ælsi's, a clothing store named The TradeMark, and around the corner and just visible from the building she was in, there was a movie theatre where Transformers blinked on the marquee, with plenty more of the same, plus people bustling about, doing their everyday business. This was unbelievable. She dropped her forehead into her palm. How concussed was her brain, anyway?

Jesus, knowing her luck, she was probably—

Male voices approached her door. She whirled around, her heart speeding again. The raucous voices grew louder, laughing about somebody named Cleeve, then passed her doorway and faded. She dove for the nightstand and started hauling on her clothes: bra and panties, a pair of navy slacks, a turquoise cotton blouse, and Italian leather flats. She'd be damned if she was meeting some stranger, regardless if he or she was a doctor, in a show-your-crack-to-the-world hospital gown. This place was giving her a major case of the creeps.

She finished dressing and darted her gaze around, searching for a hair brush or comb. Nothing. There wasn't time to go hunting for one, either. The lock clicked and the door swung open.

She didn't know who she'd expected to come striding in, but somehow it wasn't this tall, lean gentlemen. He was elegant and stylish, if a bit too "cleanliness is next to Godliness" in his hygiene standards. His black hair was groomed down to the last follicle, and his Armani suit had been pressed to within an inch of its life. His age was indeterminate. There seemed to be a wisdom and maturity in his turquoise eyes that suggested substantial life experience, yet there wasn't a single wrinkle on his face.

"Oh, you're on your feet," the man observed delightedly. "Splendid." He crossed to her, holding out his palm. "I'm Dr. Jess."

She didn't shake his hand, instead pointing to the balcony window. "Excuse me, but where am I?" So much for pleasantries.

"Yes, I imagine you have many questions. If you'll come with me, the head of the department will explain everything." The doctor offered her a close-lipped smile.

That was probably meant to reassure her, but it didn't. A guy who gave a girl a big, toothy grin, now *that* was a man who could be trusted. "Head of *what* department?"

Dr. Jess moved to stand by her bedroom door. "I'm sorry, I know this must be unsettling, but the head prefers to give these explanations himself." He politely waited for her to precede him, that enigmatic smile still on his face.

She exhaled sharply. *Unsettling* was putting it mildly. She didn't trust this Dr. Jess, but what choice did she have but to meet this "head" if she wanted to find out what was going on.

"Very well." She crossed through the bedroom door and into a wide, balconied hallway thickly carpeted in burgundy Berber.

Dr. Jess moved past her and led the way down an even wider staircase.

Wow. Whatever this place was, it was clearly backed by a great deal of money. It was almost overwhelmingly palatial and lavishly decorated, with large oil paintings on the walls, mostly landscapes, life-sized Greek and Roman statues, and gold-fitted, shiny wood banisters. At the bottom of the stairs, they cut through what could only be The Grand Entrance Hall. The floor of the room was tiled in checkered mauve and white marble, with potbellied brass vases standing sentinel next to soaring white marble pillars, a sparkling gold-and-crystal chandelier lording over the entire room.

Dr. Jess took her down another smaller staircase, this one leading into a long hallway lined with doors. Passing one of the doors, she heard male voices again, their bantering and cursing punctuated by the distinct *thud* of fist meeting flesh.

She slanted a look at Dr. Jess.

He smiled pleasantly at her.

They came to a large set of double doors at the end of the hall. Dr. Jess pressed an intercom button. "Dr. Parthen and I are here, sir."

"Ah, excellent," came the affable reply. "Come in, of course." A buzzer sounded and the double doors *snicked* open.

Dr. Jess again politely stood back for her to enter first. She stepped into a room that appeared to be a combination library and office. Tall mahogany bookshelves lined three of the walls, and an arrangement of plush, dark leather chairs of the kind one might find at an Oxford men's club was set around a coffee table of polished oak.

All of this received no more than three seconds of her attention. As magnificent as the décor was, her eyes couldn't help but rivet on the two black-haired men across the room.

One was rising from behind a desk, unfolding himself to a height of well over six feet. He was dressed with understated wealth, pleated gray silk slacks and a v-necked cashmere sweater in cobalt: a completely respectable look that should've offered reassurance, except that there was just something about this man. Something…that whispered danger.

Yet, even *he* only received about one second of her attention. As much as this man demanded notice, the man who was standing statue-still off to the side of the desk, his hands clasped behind his back in a stance that pushed his enormous shoulders forward and made them look even more enormous, demanded it more.

He was, without doubt, the most frightening man she'd ever seen outside of the movies. No whispering here; this man's danger came at a person like a wrecking ball. He was dressed in clothes directly out of a Gangstas Я Us catalog, steel-toed biker boots with thick silver buckles at the ankles, black leather pants that hugged a pair of powerfully built thighs and lean hips, and a black lycra T-shirt that similarly clung to his torso in a way that displayed every delineated muscle the man owned, of which there were *a lot*. The scary dude look was made complete by a pair of dark sunglasses that hid his eyes, and a jaw so hard she'd bet she could take a crowbar to it and never crack a smile out of him. Maybe someone had already tried that maneuver; there was a line of scabbed flesh streaking the man's cheek.

"Dr. Parthen, welcome," the man behind the desk said in that same affable tone she'd heard over the intercom. "My name is Roth Mihnea. I'm the leader of this community. Please, come and sit down. We have much to discuss."

Community? Had she…oh, crap, had she been committed to a mental hospital by mistake? Jesus, she'd probably completely wigged out on Nurse Bun's drug and…

But then…these men didn't exactly look like psychiatrist dweebs, did they?

Roth Mihnea indicated one of the antique black Renaissance chairs set before his desk and smiled. No big, toothy grin here, either.

She rounded on Dr. Jess. "What's going on here?"

The doctor's expression turned sheepish as he shut the double doors, and she heard another *snick*. This time it was the lock reengaging.

Adrenalin surged through her body, tripping her heart into a runaway beat and suffusing her flesh with heat. She was usually pretty quick on the up-take, but it was only now reaching her concussed brain that perhaps she'd been knocked unconscious for reasons other than incompetence.

CHAPTER FIVE

"Am I being held against my will?" Toni asked tightly. Probably a *real* stupid question, all things considered.

"I should think not," Roth answered mildly. "We're hoping you'll willingly help us, Dr. Parthen, once you've heard of our plight." Roth's smile remained in place. "I admit that drugging you and then abducting you is hardly likely to have put you in a helpful frame of mind. I do apologize for that. But this is a top-secret community, and such methods were necessary to maintain security."

Top secret? As in...? *What?* A research institute for nuclear weapons...? Chemical warfare...? Cloning...? Stem cells? Again, she didn't think so. Whatever else these two men might be, they definitely weren't think-tank dweebs, either. She rapidly ran through a list of other possibilities, her mind landing on the most probable, at least based on the presence of Hard Face over there, who looked every inch a "goon" bodyguard, and the Drug Lord security system. These guys were Mafia. An icy prickle raised the fine hairs on her skin. *Oh, shit.*

"I understand how disconcerting this is," Roth inserted into her elongated silence. "Please, Doctor, I just ask that you listen to what we have to say. If you don't agree to our offer after that, then you're free to go."

Did she have another option? Most likely not. But she wasn't going to let herself get in a panic about it. A member of the "family" was probably a hemophiliac or maybe had a Myeloproliferative disorder, and she'd been brought in to offer a second opinion for Dr. Jess's diagnosis. Whatever the case, the sooner she cooperated and treated the patient, the sooner she could get out of here.

"All right," she said, moving over to the Renaissance chair Roth had indicated and sitting down.

"Thank you." Roth sat down, too, a hint of relief showing on his face. "Let me start by explaining our need for secrecy. This community is home to a very special race of people, Dr. Parthen. All of us who live here"—he made a wide gesture—" must remain in hiding because we have a unique genetic…variance, if you will, that the outside world doesn't understand or accept." He folded his hands over his desk blotter, his long, tapered fingers braiding. "We all have unusual bone marrow, you see. Ours makes predominately white blood cells and very little red. This condition has its advantages. We have heightened powers of healing and, as such, a much longer lifespan than people of your race, but it has also left us with our curse: a blood-need, we call it, which requires us to get our red blood elsewhere."

"Oh?" Toni kept her expression neutral. What hay cart had this man fallen off of? There was no bone marrow disorder that functioned that way.

"Unfortunately, as will often happen with people who are different and misunderstood, we've suffered extreme prejudice, thought of as diseased and dangerous, rather than simply…unusual. Our kind used to prevail in Romania, but our enemies spread lies about us over a hundred years ago—1877, to be exact—which led to a wave of mass hysteria and killings."

Toni frowned. Romania? Not Italian Mafia?

"We were hunted savagely and without mercy, nearly all of

our kind slaughtered. This forced us to flee our homeland and go into hiding or else be wiped out." Roth's knuckles whitened briefly.

Toni shifted in her seat. Something about this didn't ring true. She couldn't imagine any group being persecuted to the point of forced seclusion and near extinction, not in this day and age. The ACLU would have a fit.

"By the time we finally made it to California," Roth continued, "and were safely hidden away here in this secret underground community, our numbers had dwindled severely. We tried to rebuild our people, but reproducing within such a small gene pool eventually took its toll. Our bloodlines weakened to the point that we ceased being able to produce viable offspring." His voice quieted. "That was thirty years ago. After more than ten years of these stillbirths, I finally forbade any more procreation within the race. We tried reproducing with the general population, but once again that brought us nothing but stillborn children. It seemed we were truly lost." Roth's eyelids swept down, as if concealing a private pain.

She waited, then exhaled silently. "I'm sorry, Mr. Mihnea, but I'm a bit confused. Is this a genetic problem you're having, or a blood disorder?" She switched her gaze between Roth and Dr. Jess, who was seated in the Renaissance chair next to hers. "Because as terrible as I feel for your predicament, genetics isn't really my forté."

"Ah, but Dr. Jess here knows a great deal about our genetics." Roth brightened. "The good doctor finally found a solution to our problem. You see, in the process of mapping the blood components of both the general population and our kind, Dr. Jess stumbled upon a rare element in the makeup of some of your race which would mix well with our DNA. Reproducing with this unique offshoot of people allows us to have children with all of our characteristics, and with renewed vitality, health, and strength. Peak 8, he called the element, named for its placement on the blood graph."

Toni nearly rolled her eyes. Jesus Christ, the man had a gift for talking around an issue; she still had no idea what he wanted. "There's no technique for mapping blood that would result in anything called Peak 8, Mr. Mihnea, at least none that I'm aware of."

"Not with your methods, no. Dr. Jess's analyses are unique."

She shot a narrow glance at Jess. Just what sort of doctor was he, anyway?

"Peak 8," Roth went on, "is representative of an element from a very ancient lineage, Dr. Parthen. In an earlier age, both of our cultures used to interbreed with a now-extinct race called Dragon. *Not* because they're actual dragons, of course," he hastened to add, "but because the people of this species were born with an extravagantly winged creature of brilliantly colored scales on their backs, almost like a tattoo. Of a dragon."

She smiled thinly. Right. As far as weird went, they'd sort of just left the playing field. "Okay," she went along, "did someone contract hepatitis from one of these dragon tattoos, is that what you're getting at? Or HIV, maybe, because if that's the case, then—"

"The tattoos are hereditary, Dr. Parthen, but that's hardly the point."

"Then what *is*?" she snapped. She was getting really sick of *The Munster Family Story Hour*. "I've been waiting forever for you to get to the punch line."

Roth sat back in his chair and drew a deep breath. "You have this special ancestry I've just described, Dr. Parthen. *You* carry the Dragon bloodlines we so desperately need bred into our population."

"I—" She slammed her mouth shut, then opened it again. "I *what*?" What was this guy talking about? "I most certainly do not, Mr. Mihnea."

"I'm afraid you do, doctor."

"I'm a hematologist, for Pete's sake. I think I'd know if I have a blood anomaly."

"You just haven't been able to see it with the type of tests you use. With the right analyses, you could." Roth pushed his chair back and opened his desk drawer, taking out a manila folder and placing it on his blotter. He pulled a sheet of paper out of it. "Here's the blood graph Dr. Jess drew up on you based on the CBC Scripps ran while you were in the hospital. It clearly shows Peak 8 as a part of your makeup." He set the graph on the edge of the desk facing her.

She glanced dismissively at the unfamiliar hills and valleys spread out across the page. "I've never seen a chart like this before in my life." Her patience growing thinner by the minute, she made a flip gesture at the paper. "For all I know, you generated this using an Etch A Sketch. Not only that, but my CBC wouldn't exactly have been available for public scrutiny."

"Dr. Jess would be happy to show you how he performs his tests. I have no doubt you'll find his methods adhere to all of the most rigid scientific standards." Roth pulled out another sheet from the folder: an 8x10 photograph. "You also have the mark." He spun the photo around and set it next to the graph. "Although you had it lasered off several years ago."

She looked down at the picture of her bare back, and gasped. It was from her confidential medical records!

"It's a dragon's foot, you see." Roth pointed to the left side of her spine, where a brown, irregular blotch marred her skin. "And claws: if you look closely, you can see them. The mark isn't made up of colorful scales as it is with our race, and the majority of your dragon is missing, but that's typical for someone of your—"

"It was a *birthmark*," she cut him off coldly. This conversation was rapidly moving from ridiculous to downright irritating.

Roth retracted his finger and slowly arched his brows. "Precisely."

"Oh, for the love of God." She pressed two fingers to the middle of her brow. She might as well stick her head in a car door and slam it a couple of times rather than try to make this man see reason. "Okay. Fine. For the sake of argument, let's just say I can suspend disbelief and *common sense* long enough to accept the idea that I have some fantastical ancient 'dragon' blood anomaly. What's your point?"

"My point, as I said from the beginning, is that we need your help." Roth spread his hands. "You're the only type of woman the men of our race can have children with."

"Children? You mean for...." Her breath hissed out of her in sudden understanding. "Oh, my God, you want to...you want to have a baby with me!?"

"Well, not me in particular." Roth chuckled, sounding embarrassed. "Actually, I've selected three—"

"Him?!" She pointed at Hard Face, alarm burying her anger as she imagined that brute pushing between her thighs.

Roth coughed lightly. "No, not Jacken, either. Actually, I've selected three men from our Warrior Class for you to choose from."

She gripped the armrests of her chair, panic pushing acid into her throat as another realization hit her. "And if I refuse," she whispered horribly, "I'm not free to go, am I?"

Roth's gaze dropped briefly. "You'll adjust and eventually be happy, I assure you. The others have."

She sucked in an appalled breath. "You've done this to other women?"

"There are five other Dragon females," Roth informed her. "Women who've found men to love here, who have homes of their own, fulfilling careers, and a caring community to raise their children in—everything we're offering you."

Her heart was pounding so hard she was starting to feel sick. Jesus Christ, somebody needed to put Haldol, Thorazine, Navane, or any of the choicer antipsychotics into the water supply around here. This man Roth was a bona fide lunatic.

"You'll meet the others soon," he said. "They'll be of tremendous help to you during your adjustment. They know exactly what you're going through right now."

She shook her head numbly, as if the mere act of moving her head from side to side could deliver her from this nightmare.

She couldn't believe this was happening. "My God," she rasped out, "who *are* you people?"

Roth held her gaze for a long moment. "Our race is called Vârcolac, Dr. Parthen." He came to his feet and strode to the middle bookshelf where a crystal decanter sat. He poured out a measure of Scotch, then crossed back over to offer it to her.

She remained very still, swallowing with a hard *click* of her throat. The amber liquor sparkled through the cut glass. Roth's eyes turned to gray smoke.

"People of your race devised the name vampire for us." He smiled at her, his expression making a valiant attempt at sympathy even as he showed her a set of pointed canines. "But we're Vârcolac."

CHAPTER SIX

Jaċken kept his eyes locked on Antoinetta Parthen through his sunglasses, every muscle in his body held rigid as he waited for her to flip her lid, pretty much par for the course when a new acquisition heard the V-word. If she kept to the usual script, there'd be a whole lot of screaming and hysteria coming out of her any minute, *definitely* begging, then after that, the worst part. She'd start to cry.

Only Hannah, the very first Dragon woman they'd ever brought into Ţărână, hadn't had a total meltdown. But then Hannah was a librarian with a master's degree in fables and myths, and she'd been instantly captivated by them. It hadn't hurt that she'd also been instantly taken with Nice Guy Vârcolac, Willen Crişan, the two of them falling in love in that cupid's-arrow-in-the-ass kind of way. In the six years since the repopulation program at Ţărână had been set into motion, Hannah and Willen had already had three kids and another was on the way. Everyone loved Hannah, although she'd misled them all into thinking that their acquisitions would always run so smoothly. They hadn't.

Ellen and Beth had come next, numbers two and three, one

right after the other. Both had been very pissy about being ripped from their lives and forced into the program. Considering that they had a solid point there, they'd adjusted reasonably quickly. Ellen was a dentist who'd become fascinated by a whole new species of dentistry, and Beth was a fashion designer who'd opened her own clothing store, The TradeMark, and become *the* word on all matters of style in Ţărână. She'd hooked up with Arc Costache, and they now had two kids, while Ellen had somehow cracked the surface of brooding Pedrr and landed him, also getting herself a couple of squirts.

Then had come number four, Magnolia, aka Maggie, a pampered former Southern belle and trained horticulturist, a totally useless profession in a cave, and a year later, number five, Kimberly, a workaholic, ladder-climbing, and also useless—at least to this particular community—lawyer. Both had been real trouble cases when it came to adjusting.

Luken, an indisputable *saint* of patience, had finally calmed down high-maintenance Maggie enough to get her underneath him and pregnant. Which had left Kimberly. Who knew Sedge would end up taking care of that little problem. But one day the badassed Mixed-blood Warrior had jacked her up against the wall outside of Garwald's Pub and balled her brains out. Presto! Problem solved. No kids out of those two, yet, though.

The community had been way ready for another easy case like Hannah when number six had come along: sweet-as-chocolate pediatric nurse, Gwyn, who'd immediately taken to the eight Mixed-blood children in Ţărână. Gwyn had definitely been on the road to adjusting well, but....

Jacken's stomach wrenched on a pang of regret. No one would ever know how that might've turned out.

Gwyn was the only acquisition who'd been stolen by their nasty Om Rău neighbors.

Şarvan had been in charge of guarding Gwyn that fateful day, but the dingus warrior had let himself get distracted flirting with Trinnía, the community hairdresser, who was, granted, a total babe. To add insult, Trinnía was also a fellow Vârcolac, which meant that they'd both been breaking all kinds of fraternization laws with their bonehead actions. Meanwhile, Gwyn had darted off to chase after one of the children who'd headed into Stânga Town, Ţărână's slum. She'd come too close to the Outer Edge, the main entrance to the Om Rău Hell Tunnels, and been grabbed.

Jacken had fired Şarvan's ass and tossed the fuckup in jail for a week. But that couldn't bring Gwyn back. Nothing could. Not when it was impossible for a Vârcolac to enter the extreme heat of the Hell Tunnels.

Losing Gwyn had been Jacken's worst day as a warrior, not counting those six other days when he'd had to abduct an innocent woman, knowing full well how much he was about to screw up her life. Each time he did that, the part of him that believed in protecting women, not messing them up, suffered a blow. In his mind, there had to be a better way to bring these Dragons into their community, but when he'd questioned Roth privately, his boss had been snappish on the subject.

"What would you have us do, Jacken? Just ask them?" Roth had flung a hand out. "Yes, let's imagine a delegation of our race shows up on a Dragon woman's doorstep and says, Excuse me, Miss So-and-So, would you mind giving up, (A) seeing your family on a regular basis, (B) your career objectives, and (C) any love interest you might currently have? And, oh, yes (D) would you also mind living underground, in permanent hiding, so that you might have babies with a vampire? I wonder what she would say? Or, no, perhaps I already know." Roth exhaled impatiently. "We have to get the women down here to win them, Jacken. There *isn't* another way."

And Roth had the final word in these matters.

Besides, Jacken wasn't in any position to make demands regarding Ţărână's way of life, having lived here these last thirty-seven years subject to the generosity of the community. Besides, Roth had a point. People pretty much shut down at the first mention of the V-word, and wouldn't give them chance one.

So, yeah, now here they were with number seven: recent acquisition, Antoinetta Parthen, doctor of hematology and all-around hot chick.

All Dragons were blonde and incredibly beautiful, a fortunate side-effect of their Dragon bloodlines, but Antoinetta was exceptional. Her hair was a flaxen waterfall streaked with fire flowing just past her shoulders, her eyes sapphire gemstones, and her body was a heart attack, the kind of leggy and busty combination that required a nearby drool cup to handle. On top of that, her scent was...had a.... Jesus, there was an added sweetness to her fragrance that had him working as hard to keep his pants on as his fangs choked back.

She was an unmated female, yeah, and all unmateds gave off a strong scent, a kind of a primitive pheromone which to a Vârcolac male smelled like she'd spritzed herself down with Eau de Screw Me.

Human females were more aromatic than Vârcolac females, and the Dragons were downright heart-stopping. But smelling this woman was like freebasing adrenaline and lust in one big fucking eight ball. He'd bet sweet blood like hers coated the tongue like a velvet orgasm. Squeezing his eyes shut behind his sunglasses, he pictured Antoinetta with her head thrown back, the graceful curve of her throat exposed, inviting him to take his fill. Or the creamy length of her thigh laid bare to him. Yeah, taste her essence, then go straight for the femoral....

Jacken clenched his teeth, grinding them together until the bones in his head sounded like rocks tumbling down a cliff. He would *never* taste this woman...not in any way, ever, so he needed to shut his brain the hell up and pay attention. Not that there was anything much to pay attention to. Dr. Antoinetta Parthen had been silent for quite some time now.

He knotted the hands he had clasped behind his back into fists, and looked from Roth, who was seated behind his desk again, to Jess, then over to Antoinetta. The wait was killing him. *Damn it, do something already, lady.*

And then she did.

To his utter shock, she came out of her chair, snatched a letter opener off the desk, and pointed the nasty end of it at Roth. Jačken stiffened as the expression on her face clicked from shocked horror to hostility as fast as someone pushing the button on a slide show.

"You'll excuse me if I must decline your invitation, Mr. Mihnea," she said between gritted teeth. "But having turkey basters filled with 'vampire' sperm stuck up inside of me isn't particularly my idea of a good time."

Roth looked mortified by the very idea. "I *assure* you, Doctor, that's not at all what—"

"Don't move," she commanded sharply.

Roth stopped coming to his feet and sat back down, placidly placing both hands palms down on top of his desk. "We have no intention of hurting you."

"You don't move, either." She aimed fierce blue eyes at Jačken, obviously sensing that he was about to go Medieval on her ass. "I know how to use a knife," she warned, switching her grip on the letter opener with a flip of her wrist, now holding it in perfect throwing position. "And I'm telling you, if you take one step toward me, I'm going to plant this thing in your chest."

He sneered at her. What a crock of shit. Just because the lady could probably wield a scalpel didn't mean she could go *Kill Bill* with any blade she happened to pick up.

"P-please," Dr. Jess stammered, his face white. "I think everyone just needs to—"

"And that would kill you, right?" She laughed, a bit of hysteria edging the sound.

Well, hell, looked like Jačken was going to get that meltdown he'd been waiting for, after all.

"I mean, you being a 'vampire' and all, and this being the proverbial stake in the heart. Or are you a zombie?" She backed up a step, keeping everyone within her sight line. "Maybe The Creature from the Black Lagoon, or—or, wait!—The Terminator. Yes! You look that part, don't you?"

Roth shot him a droll look. "Well, this is new."

"Put the letter opener down, now," Jaćken ordered her, pitching his voice to a lethal tone. "If I have to take it from you, Dr. Parthen, I can guarantee you won't like my methods." He came out of his stance, his arms swinging forward and his legs spring-coiling in readiness.

Antoinetta let out a startled cry, her eyes widening on his forearm tattoos. "Holy crap! You're one of those cult freaks!" Leaping at Jess, she seized the doctor by the top of his hair and cranked his head back, setting the tip of the letter opener at his throat.

Jess squeaked in alarm.

Roth roared to his feet as if he'd been goosed in the ass by an ice pick. "No!" he shouted. "Please, I beg you to take care, Dr. Parthen." He held out a staying hand. "Blood is sacred to us, and if you draw Dr. Jess's that...that will be an act of claiming him."

Unfortunately, in her humanness, she couldn't give Roth's warning the weight it warranted. "Then I *suggest*"—she dug in the tip of the opener deeper to emphasize her point—"you unlock that door and let me out of here right now!"

"Dear heavens!" Roth gestured emphatically at Jaćken. "Stop her before she does something irrevocable."

Finally, *action*. Jaćken stepped forward—

It might not be said he could move as fast as a Dragon warrior, but he could definitely get his ass in gear when necessary. Fast enough, at least, to stupefy the hell out of Antoinetta. Her eyes rounded when she found him suddenly standing right in front of her, his fingers wrapped around her weapon hand. Locking eyes with his target, he forcibly pulled the letter opener clear of Jess's throat.

The doctor scrambled out of the way, smoothing a manicured hand down the front of his silk paisley tie.

Antoinetta's blue eyes blazed furiously, the heat of her gaze sending blood pounding against Jaćken's temples and into his ears. He applied steady pressure to her hand, but she wouldn't give up the letter opener. *Stupid woman.* He twisted her arm down and behind her, then realized his own stupidity when the move brought her jerking up against him, her full breasts squashing into his chest. An electrical charge went through him, a burning heat landing right in his groin.

Antoinetta's cheeks flushed a brilliant red, the plump softness of her breasts rising and falling unsteadily against the underside of his pecs.

His balls tightened at the feel of her. Her powerful scent tunneled into the ventricles of his brain. A noise came out of him, a deep, guttural *something*. It rolled up from his gut and rumbled from his chest, sending a warning vibration through his fangs. Antoinetta clearly found the animal quality of it convincing. Her arm went slack. He took the invitation and tugged the letter opener from her grasp, then stepped back and jammed it into his belt. Without missing a beat, he grabbed her by the shoulders, propelled her back over to her chair, and ass-planted her into the seat.

Air spilled out of her in a heavy rush, her cheeks leaching of color as her eyes went stark with fear.

Yeah, he'd guess it was finally sinking into her brain pretty damned firmly that she was completely at their mercy. That part of him that didn't like to mess up women? It was an all over body-throb.

Easing back into his own chair, Roth gave her a look of genuine regret. "I apologize for the necessity of that, Doctor. We truly don't want to hurt you."

She swallowed visibly, casting an apprehensive glance over her shoulder at Jaćken.

Roth, ever the peacekeeper, gave him a discreet back-off nod.

Jaćken moved out from behind Antoinetta's chair and took up his usual position next to Roth's desk.

Roth offered Antoinetta a sympathetic smile. "I understand your fear, I really do, what with all the lore and legend that has traditionally surrounded vampires. Let me unequivocally assure you, doctor, that Vârcolac are not monsters. We're *not* undead creatures who sleep in coffins and transform humans with our bites. We *can* see our reflections in mirrors. We *aren't* driven off by garlic or crucifixes, although," he added dryly, "a sharp object like a letter opener being driven into our hearts will kill us." Roth let out a sigh. "Those are just hyped-up lies invented by our enemies years ago. We're quite human, doctor, just a different...species of human, if you will. Look at us and you'll agree there're many similarities between our races." He gestured broadly. "We laugh, we cry, we—"

"Suck blood?" The question was asked in no more than a whisper.

Jaćken nearly rolled his eyes. Guaranteed she was imagining some pasty-faced fiend swooping down on her and plunging stalactite-looking fangs into her neck. Dracula 101 crap all the way.

"That...." Roth cleared his throat. "Yes. That's something we do. We call it feeding, but we don't do it for any sinister purpose, rather because of a limitation to our physiology, that blood-need I described earlier. It's a weakness, certainly, as is our inability to go out into the sunlight; we're severely allergic to vitamin D, I'm afraid. But our breed also has many strengths. We're physically stronger than regular humans, we can move faster, and our senses are more highly attuned in many areas. Can you imagine the benefits we could've brought to the human race had we been allowed to do so? What kind of soldiers we would've made, or detectives or researchers or—"

"Please, Mr. Mihnea." She held up a hand. "I'm sorry, but I don't believe any of this. I'm a scientist, and none of what you're saying fits in with my knowledge of how the world works."

"Ah, yes." Roth stood up and strode around to her. "People of science tend to need concrete proof. I remember that with Ellen, our dentist." He settled his hip on the edge of the desk, gesturing at the blood graph and photo next to him. "Something more tangible than these, I imagine?"

"No. I—Really. I'd just like for us to agree to accept our

differences and go our separate ways."

Roth looked over at Jacken as if she hadn't spoken. "Where are Dr. Parthen's mate-choices at present?"

Jacken glanced down at his watch. "In the gym training."

"Excellent. They're right down the hall. Jess, my good man, would you mind bringing them here?" Roth smiled. "I believe now would be a good time for Dr. Parthen to meet her future husband."

CHAPTER SEVEN

Somewhere along the way, Toni's brain had come unplugged. There wasn't much going on inside her mind except a lot of white noise, backed by a repetitive *holy crapping* chant which seemed to be caught in an endless loop. No grand plans about how to get herself out of this disaster, that was for damned sure.

Okay, time to regroup. Line up her thoughts into a manageable row.

Right. The main thing was to Stay Calm. Panicking could only lead her into more acts of stupidity, like threatening three men who were in top-notch condition—one who looked to be set on permanent wanna-kick-your-ass mode—with little more than a letter opener. Not the best of ideas.

Behaving idiotically wasn't her usual style, but in her own defense, this was the first time a group of individuals had drugged her, kidnapped her, told her they wanted to use her as a brood mare because she was a "dragon," and then claimed to be "vampires." *Uh huh*. Here's what was really happening; she'd woken up on the TV show Scare Tactics, and any minute now Shannen Doherty was going to jump out and jeer, "Ha, ha, you fell for it, you boob." See, because the last she'd checked, there was, you know, *no such thing as vampires.*

She fidgeted in her chair, her fingers flexing and releasing around the armrests. Okay, door number two, Bob. This wasn't a reality TV hoax. She was being held hostage by a bunch of schizoid delusional freaks who appeared to have formed a cult—or, ahem, "community"—for all of their schizoid delusional followers. *Oh, God....* Her throat shut off. *A* cult. What she wouldn't give to go back to these guys being Mafia.

The moment she'd seen the tattoos on that Jacken creature's forearms was pretty much the moment her self-control had gone bye-bye. The marks were almost exactly the same as the tattoo she'd seen on that corpse's jaw the night of the crime scene, although Jacken's were more like black interlocking lines, rather than flames...no, not lines: long, swooping teeth of the kind on a saber-toothed tiger. Seeing them had instantly filled her mind with nightmare images of having her skin stripped off her body in a ritual satanic killing.

Tension coiled across her shoulders as she tried to imagine what these sickos planned on doing to her. The possibilities, especially those of a sexually deviant nature, were endless. Just her luck that she'd ended up being kidnapped, not just into some vampire cult, but into a vampire *sex* cult.

"Ah, here they come." Roth rose smoothly to his feet at the sound of male voices approaching. He pushed a button and the double doors buzzed open.

Dr. Jess reentered with three men trailing him, a blond, a brunette, and a black-haired one.

She came stiffly out of her own chair, schooling her face into an indifferent expression. The last thing she'd wanted from her challenge of Roth's claims of vampirism was a meet-and-greet with the "vampires" she was expected to do the nasty with. Whatever concrete proof he planned to show her using them, she didn't even want to try and imagine.

The three drew up in front of her, and only her years trained in the art of keeping bad diagnoses from her face allowed her to deadpan her reaction to them, because, Jesus, they were all ridiculously gorgeous.

To a man, they had physiques to die for, their powerful builds only enhanced by the dark workout gear they were wearing. Each was dressed in black wrestling shoes, a black lycra T-shirt, and black shorts styled after Calvin Klein boxer-briefs. The trim cut of the shorts emphasized each man's...er, potency in a manner that gave the impression of straining seams and near-popping front laces.

Heat crept into Toni's cheeks, and she forced her eyes away. How long had it been since she'd had sex, that she'd be staring goggle-eyed at the packages of men who were no better than Jim Jones wannabes?

Roth set right to the explanation of how matters stood. "Dr. Parthen and I have been discussing some of the distinctive traits of our breed, but, as one might expect, she's having a bit of difficulty accepting the authenticity of everything without some proof. Ergo, I thought this might be a good opportunity for her to meet all of you and familiarize herself with your unique qualities."

"Familiarize?" The blond, who had enough innate sex appeal to melt iron, despite some fading bruises on his throat and bloodshot eyes, cocked a single brow. "You mean, like...she wants to give us a medical examination?"

"Works for me." The one with black hair, matching goatee, and a small Bad Boy gold hoop earring dangling from his left earlobe, glanced around the room. "Where do you want us to undress?"

Her face burned hotter. "I don't think—"

"No, no, it's nothing like that," Roth jumped in.

"Cut the shit, Nichita," Jacken snapped.

"Yes, sir." Bad Boy winked at her.

"You see, Dr. Parthen, there are different breeds of Vârcolac," Roth explained, "within the entirety of the species, and each one has an extraordinary ability." He laid a hand on Bad Boy's shoulder. "Devid Nichita here can—"

"Excuse me, but please, it's Dev," Bad Boy corrected. "I hate Devid."

Well, she could relate to that sentiment. She'd always thought her mother had been suffering from a severe case of postpartum dementia to have named her Antoinetta. But Shannon had always claimed she'd just been compelled to give her children majestic-sounding names, and to this day she was grumpy that Alexander went by Alex, and Antoinetta, by Toni.

"Dev's a Pure-bred Vârcolac," Roth continued, "like myself and Dr. Jess. You can always tell a Pure-bred by their black hair and their ability to grow facial hair. A Pure-bred can also see in the dark and light up his eyes. You'll be impressed by that, surely."

Dev bobbed his eyebrows at her and grinned broadly, displaying a mean set of canines.

She took a step back. She couldn't believe someone would purposely file down his teeth like that. It had to have hurt like hell. But then again, none of these men was altogether *there* in the sanity department, were they?

"This is Thomal Costache and Kasson Korzha," Roth introduced the other two.

Kasson, the brunette, had a boyish-looking cowlick in the front of his hair, and what appeared to be a serious case of the fidgets.

"They're what we call Mixed-bloods," Roth said, "meaning they have both Dragon and Vârcolac ancestry in their bloodlines. Dragons always have light hair: blonde, just like *yours*," he made sure to emphasize, "or varying shades of brown. The blonder they are, the more Dragon they have in them. Dragons can move with blurring speed. They also have a full dragon tattoo on their backs, but their creatures—unlike the washed-out tattoo that Dragon humans such as yourself have— are made of colorful scales. I thought we'd start by showing one to you."

"Ho, really?" Thomal's face brightened while Bad Boy Dev turned his eyes to the ceiling and muttered a curse.

"Kasson." Roth gestured Cowlick forward. "Come here, let's have you—"

"God, no way!" Kasson jerked backward, his eyes rounding.

A frown tugged at Roth's mouth.

"I-I'm sorry, sir, but I can't get close to her. She...she...." Kasson closed his eyes and moaned. "She *smells.*"

Toni tucked in her chin. *I what?*

"I'm afraid I might...." Kasson shook his head. "Oh, this is bad."

Roth looked nonplussed. "I don't understand. Are you saying she's more pungent than the other Dragons?"

Jacken answered that. "Definitely."

Flushing, Toni self-consciously squeezed her arms against her ribcage, closing off her armpits. Steeped in hospital *yuk* for a day and two nights, she probably did smell like an unpleasant combination of rubbing alcohol, latex, and orange Jell-O, but there hadn't exactly been time to take a shower.

"Interesting." Roth turned to Dr. Jess. "Are you picking up on it?"

"No."

"You two are mated males," Jacken said tightly. "For an unmated, it's pure torture." He gestured at the other men. "Trust us on that."

Dr. Jess crossed his arms, the finger of one hand pressed contemplatively against his lips. "What does she smell like?"

Dev snorted. "Nothing that can be described politely." He glanced at Thomal. "Was it this strong at the hospital?"

"Vinz's blood was around, so—"

Hospital! "Oh, my God!" Toni burst out. "You're Nurse Fine Ass!" Glaring, she pointed an accusing finger at Thomal. "You drugged me, you big jerk!"

Thomal's expression flared wide with astonishment. "Hey, whoa!" He threw up his hands. "I was just doing my job, okay? Don't get mad."

"Nah, get as mad as you want, Doc." Dev slung an arm around Thomal's shoulders. "And feel free to have this jerk bounced off your list of mate-choices. You have other options, you know."

Thomal shoved Dev off him. "She doesn't want to get rid of me, Nichita. Weren't you listening?" Thomal settled a pair of stunning blue eyes on her. "She just said I have a *fine ass*."

"All right, enough of this," Roth intervened. "Let's move on to the demonstrations. Dr. Parthen, if you would take a seat...."

She closed her eyes. Demonstrations? Oh, this day was turning into a regular party.

CHAPTER EIGHT

The computer clicked, then whirred its way into the boot process, making noises that were as familiar to Alex Parthen as his own heartbeat and always oddly relaxing. He propped his feet up on the desk and took a sip of morning coffee from his UC Berkley mug.

He smiled as he thought back to his student days. He'd been such a rage-against-the-machine hippie at that liberal school, shuffling around in flip-flops, cut-off shorts, and a tie-dyed tank top with a peace symbol like a bull's eye smack in the middle of it. He and his computer buddies used to get into one hacker war after another to see who could topple the government's "tower of power."

Alex swung his feet off the desk as his computer settled into a low, friendly hum. It was kind of ironic to think about those rabidly anti-government days now, especially since the main contract for his at-home business was the DoD. He glanced down at himself and chuckled. He supposed he did look a bit like a stuffed shirt, too, what with his fondness for khaki Dockers, plaid button-downs, and gold-rimmed glasses. But, hey, at least he wasn't strangling himself with a damned necktie every day.

Grabbing the mouse, he opened his Gmail account and scanned for news from his sister. Ah! He clicked on her email.

Had dinner at Wasabi's last night, good, but overpriced. Off to another seminar...Sorry to be in such a rush these days. Love you.

Alex frowned. Since when did their conversations revolve around restaurant choices? And Toni didn't like sushi.

The doorbell rang.

Great, the FedEx guy. Setting down his mug, Alex hopped up and grabbed the disc he was sending off for Beta testing. He headed out of his office, sliding the disc into a preaddressed envelope as he cut across the brightly lit jungle that passed for his living room. He loved plants: ferns, palms, Pothos.... He opened the front door and—

Hey, *not* the FedEx courier. The man on his porch looked like a pretty regular guy, though, dressed in Levi's, cowboy boots, and a collared maroon shirt under a navy windbreaker. He was about Alex's height, though brown-haired instead of blondish-reddish, and sans glasses. He had an athletically lean body and eyes that were green or blue, kind of turquoise, maybe. Alex had never met the dude.

"Hello, may I help you?" he asked, setting the disc aside on an empty plant stand, whose occupant was currently draining in the kitchen sink.

"I hope so," the guy responded pleasantly. "Are you Alexander Parthen?"

He was tempted to come back with *depends on who's asking*, but the guy didn't look like a missionary or an insurance salesman, so he just said, "Yes."

The dude reached into his windbreaker and pulled out a wallet. "I'm Detective John Waterson, SDPD." He flipped it open. Not a wallet, after all, but a badge.

"Wow, shit, really?" This was an unexpected drag. "Is there a problem?"

"I'm hoping there's not, actually."

Alex tilted his head. *Funky answer.*

"I'm here about your sister, Mr. Parthen."

"Toni?" Alex blinked.

"Have you had any contact with her since early Wednesday morning?"

"I...wait. Is something wrong?"

"That's what I'm here to find out from you." Waterson tucked his badge away. "Your sister and I worked on a case together Monday night. A blood specialist was needed to consult on a murder scene I was investigating."

A murder scene? Hell, Toni must've drawn the short straw on that one. She hated them.

"She gave me her phone number afterward, because, uh...." The detective patted the breast of his windbreaker, as if searching for something. "We were supposed to keep in touch, so when she didn't answer any of my text messages, I started to worry. I know it's only been a few days, but she doesn't seem like the type to blow me off." Waterson shoved a hand into his jeans pocket and pulled out a rubber band. "You can imagine my concern when I showed up at Scripps Memorial Hospital early Wednesday morning to investigate a violent crime, only to find out it'd been committed in your sister's hospital room."

Alex startled. "What? You're kidding?"

"Unfortunately, I'm not." Waterson circled the rubber band around his two index fingers like a pulley. *Snappity-snappity.* Over and over. "Toni wasn't anywhere to be found, and none of the damned nurses working that morning could remember if the crime had been committed before or after Toni was transferred to Sharp Rehabilitation Hospital, so I—"

Alex frowned. *Huh?*

"—immediately hauled my butt out to Sharp to check on her there. And guess what?" *Snappity-snappity.* "They have no record of her whatsoever. By now, of course, my detective alarms are clanging like crazy. I don't like it when things don't add up. So I head back to Scripps to find out what the F about your sister, and this time I talk to the folks up in Admin. They now inform me that Dr. Parthen has had to leave town suddenly on a personal family emergency, return date unspecified. But, hey, lo and behold, here I am talking to you, her brother, who's clearly *not* off on a family emergency and seems fine and dandy."

"Holy cow, man." Alex ran a hand through his hair. "Sounds like a screw up of the highest order. You can mellow out about Toni, though, okay. She's at a hematology seminar in St. Louis. She emailed me just today."

Waterson's brows flew up. "Really?" Then he blew out his cheeks. "Jesus Christ, what a relief." He shoved the rubber band back into his pocket. "Hey, do you mind if I come inside for a minute? It's colder than a witch's tit out here."

"Oh, sure." Alex stepped aside to allow Waterson to walk past him, smiling apologetically. "California's sun can be deceiving." He closed the door. "You want some coffee? It's hot."

"Thanks, that'd be great." Waterson followed Alex into the kitchen. "I'm going to need Toni's contact information. She's not answering her cell, and I have to question her about what she might've witnessed in or near her hospital room Wednesday morning. But, mostly, hell, I just want to hear her voice and make sure she's truly okay."

Alex pulled his *Yes, I practice safe text* mug out of the cupboard and crossed to the coffee pot. After this conversation, he needed the same. "Sure, man, as soon as I get her number, I'll pass it on to you." He handed the steaming mug to Waterson. "Cream and sugar?

"Black's fine." Waterson took the mug, cupping his hands around it. "You don't know her hotel info?"

"No." Alex leaned back against the kitchen counter.

A flicker of surprise crossed Waterson's face. "Have you asked her for the information?" He sipped the coffee.

"Of course. Several times. But she keeps forgetting to tell me. This seminar's keeping her super busy, and I think she's just exceptionally distracted because of that."

Waterson took another sip. "This is really good coffee, by the way." He was silent for a moment, just drinking. "Is that…unusual for your sister not to give you any contact information?"

"Um…." Alex's stomach felt funny all of a sudden. "Yeah, actually, it's extremely unusual."

Waterson peered down into his mug for a long moment, then looked up. "My detective alarms are clanging again," he said quietly.

"Aw, c'mon, man." Alex pushed off the counter. "Don't say that."

Waterson set his coffee cup on the kitchen table. "Would you mind if I take a look at her emails?"

"Shit." Alex exhaled. "All right, yeah." He led the way out of the kitchen.

His office was nothing special, simply furnished with everything IKEA could provide, and his computer looked like any other PC to the average consumer, little fishy screen savers bobbing across the monitor. On the inside, though, his tower was jacked to the hilt with such a choice collection of high-tech software, any propeller-head worth his salt would go sloppy-faced over it: CSAP database system, Automated Security Incident Measurement software, intrusion detection, triple data encryption standard, a myriad of filters, and enough firewalls to stop the best of hackers. All comfortably tucked into a terabyte of RAM and kept humming along in a liquid-cooled interior.

Alex wiggled his mouse to make the fishies swim away. Toni's last email was still up on the screen. "You should be able to see the entire email stream between us for the last couple of days. It's not much."

"Okay." Waterson gestured to the desk chair. "May I?" At Alex's nod, the detective sat, first pulling the rubber band out of jeans pocket. As he read, he circled it around his index fingers again with that *snappity-snappity* noise. Over and over. *Snappity-snappity.*

Alex couldn't help grimacing. "I know you're a cop and all, but, dude, if you don't stop doing that, I'm going to have to hit you."

The rubber band stilled. "Sorry. I'm, uh, trying to cut down on smoking and sometimes I have to do something with my hands or go nuts." He swiveled toward Alex. "These emails aren't personal at all, general newsy stuff for the most part. Is that normal?"

Alex shrugged. "We usually keep the real personal stuff out of cyberspace and talk about it over dinner." He and his sister maintained a standing Friday night date.

Waterson nodded, accepting that. "She's definitely evading your questions, though: where she's staying in St. Louis and when her seminar ends. Whether she's doing that because she's distracted or for some other reason is the big question."

Alex stilled. "What other reason could there possibly be?"

"I don't know," Waterson answered honestly, "that's what I'm trying to figure out." He stroked a thumb along his jaw. "When was the last time you actually *saw* your sister?"

"Um, Monday night, right after her car accident. My mother and I both went to see her in the hospital. Wednesday I was supposed to pick her up when she was discharged, but I got a text from her, telling me that she was heading to St. Louis. The hospital was providing transportation directly to the airport."

Waterson frowned. "So soon after an accident?"

Alex spread his hands. "Toni's generally a hard charger, so, you know...."

"You didn't talk to her on the phone about it, though?"

"No."

"So you haven't heard the sound of her voice since...when?"

"Shit...Tuesday, I guess. I called her at the hospital to check in."

"Did anything strike you as strange about the conversation?"

"No." He shoved his hands into his pocket. This conversation was really beginning to blow chunks. "She was just anxious to get out, doctors making the worst patients and all."

Waterson went silent. He stared at the computer screen for what seemed like a small eternity, stroking his jaw again. "Is there any way to determine if these emails are actually coming from St. Louis?"

"Yeah, I can do that." Alex took over his desk chair. "Even though Toni would be using her own laptop, she'd most likely be hooking into her hotel's WiFi." As he spoke, he clicked on *details* at the top of Toni's email. A full message header popped up. He scanned down until he found the *received from* line, then ran the IP code and checked the location. "It's the Crowne Plaza Hotel in St. Louis."

Relief spread over Waterson's face. "Well, that's good news. Now I can track—"

"Not necessarily." Alex's throat squeezed down to a narrow cable as he read further. "This might just be a proxy server."

"A what?"

"A forged IP address. In other words, even though the email *looks* like it came from St. Louis, it could've actually originated from someplace else. See"—he pointed to a row of numbers on the screen—"the time stamps are off...they don't match."

Waterson bent and squinted at the monitor. "I don't understand."

"There's a significant time delay between when Toni's message was sent and when it arrived here, meaning that it bounced through several servers before coming out as the Crowne Plaza."

Waterson straightened. "Why would it have done that?"

Alex scooted his chair back and looked up at the detective. "Somebody programmed it to do that."

Waterson's face stilled. "To hide the email's true starting point?"

"That's the usual reason, yes." Alex's stomach was *really* feeling funny now.

A tic pulsed in Waterson's jaw. "Can you determine the actual place of origin?"

"Probably not. The sender most likely used an anonymizer to create their proxy server, and those are almost impossible to trace." Maybe he'd just get it over with and throw up already.

"Damn," Waterson breathed.

"Tell me...." Alex had to swallow twice before he c͟
continue. "What does all this mean, Detective? Is Toni ͟
trouble?"

"I'm not sure," Waterson answered, at least still being honest
about it. "I don't like this, though."

Alex didn't, either. "Do you think any of this has to do with
that murder you guys investigated together? It just seems like all
this convoluted crap started right after Toni consulted with
you."

"That occurred to me, too, but I've wracked my brain and
can't come up with any connection." Waterson sighed. "This is
probably just one of those stupid situations that will turn out to
be nothing. Toni's probably consumed by work, like you said,
and hasn't realized how much time has passed since she last
called you. I'm sure there's—"

"Yo, John!" A voice hollered from the front of the house.

"Here!" Waterson shouted back. "Excuse me," he added to
Alex, "that's my partner."

Waterson headed out of the office and into the living room.

Alex followed, slowing in the hallway at the sound of the
other cop's voice.

"—just got word from Matthews," he was saying. "He's at
the Medical Examiner's office."

"Hell, finally," Waterson came back. "The ME got a report
on our acid corpse yet?"

"No, amigo, that's the thing."

There was a weird note in the partner's voice, and Alex
stopped walking completely.

"The corpse is gone."

"What do you mean *gone*?" Waterson demanded.

"Gone, like in, *poof*! Like it just got up and walked out of the
morgue."

CHAPTER NINE

Kimberly sat in a chair on one side of the mansion's long, elegantly set dining room table, with the other four Dragon women, Maggie, Ellen, Hannah, and Beth, seated next to her.

A marvelous spread was artistically arranged before them: Ladyfingers on crystal plates, petit fours and daintily iced cookies on tiered stands, a gaudy silver tea service with delicately flowered china cups and small plates. All of it to celebrate the Fab Five's first meeting with the "new acquisition."

The guest of honor was seated across from them, her hands folded on top of the table and her expression closed. She hadn't spoken a word.

Kimberly had been tempted to greet the new girl with a *Rah! Rah! Way to stick it to Roth, sistah.* Word had it that Toni, as she preferred to be addressed, and Roth were locked in a showdown: Toni had refused to date any of her mate-choices the whole week she'd been here, and Roth had countered by not allowing Toni out of the mansion until she did.

Toni's hutzpah brought warmth to Kimberly's heart, oh, yes it did. Such gumption made Toni a perfect candidate for

Kimberly's Evil Plans of Doom, although with all this showdown stuff going on, Kimberly hadn't been able to approach Toni about it. Yet.

That left her with here and now, in front of the other Dragons, to set her scheme of mutiny in motion. But since all of the Dragons had to get on board with the plan eventually to make it work, anyway, now was actually good timing.

"Would you like a cookie?" Maggie of the short curly blonde hair and pastel-colored clothes peeled tinfoil off the top of a fluted tray. "Homemade Oatmeal Butterscotch," she coaxed Toni in her soft southern drawl.

Kimberly nearly rolled her eyes. To Maggie, there wasn't any problem that couldn't be solved with a pinch of Southern hospitality. Not that such a thing had worked for her own adjustment. From what Kimberly understood, Maggie had spent her first six months in Țărână crying. Hopefully, those memories would put Maggie firmly in Kimberly's camp.

"I brought you some books as well." Hannah's golden blonde hair was in pigtails today, her big belly close to popping with her fourth pregnancy. She sat straight in her chair, holding herself with the royal composure that came with being Țărână's premier reproducer; Hannah Crişan was pretty much treated like the Town Princess on any given day.

She was the one Kimberly had to worry about. Ask Hannah Banana about Țărână, and she'd swear they all lived in MunchkinLand.

"I run the library in town," Hannah told Toni, "so if you want a specific book, just let me know."

Still mute, Toni gave Hannah a flat stare.

Ellen took a swing. "You're a doctor, right? I'm a dentist, so whenever you're ready, I'd love to share my observations with you." Today, like every day, Ellen's shoulder-length light brown hair was in serious need of doing battle with a comb. "I think you'll find my research about Vârcolac dentistry fascinating." As a logical thinker, Ellen could be counted on to keep a level head about Kimberly's plan, whether she agreed with it or not.

More silence.

Beth Costache, owner of The TradeMark and the most stunning of all of them—which was really saying something—let out a long sigh. "She thinks we're a bunch of brainwashed bimbos." Beth was the wild card. She was sweet and caring, yes, but so gaga over her heartthrob of a husband that she might not want to go against him, even for the greater good.

Ellen nodded. "Suffering from Stockholm Syndrome or full-on Patty Hearst hopefuls."

"From where I'm sitting," Toni finally spoke, her tone crisp, "all of you are pretty much poster girls for the Stockholm Syndrome. If not that, then you're cult devotees. Either choice means you're brainwashed."

Kimberly laughed. "Sounds about right."

Hannah shot her a repressive look. "This community is not a cult," she corrected. "I assure you, Dr. Parthen, every one of us began our time here the same way you have—taken from our lives and forced into a strange place with unfamiliar people, feeling scared, angry, and frustrated." She smoothed a hand over the mound of her belly. "But we all ended up giving this place a chance, and if you're willing to let us tell you about this community's incredible benefits, maybe you'll decide it's worth a chance, too."

Toni arched her brows. "Benefits like contracting Black Lung from days on end of breathing cave dust?"

Ellen's brows drew together. "Oh, we don't—"

"I think we should clear up the Ființă issue right away." Maggie took one of her own cookies and placed it on a napkin before her. "I really hate it when the new girls think we're addicts."

Toni looked curious, probably despite herself. "Ființă?"

Ellen slid a cucumber sandwich off one of the crystal trays. "That's the elixir that comes out of a Vârcolac's fangs when he or she feeds. It serves several important medical functions you might find interesting; it mixes with the blood of the Vârcolac's host to create a more useable blood for them, and it has a repairing and clotting function so that when he pulls out his fangs, the punctured vein closes instantly." She took a bite of her sandwich. "But mostly Fiinţă is Mother Nature's way of making sure hosts never balk at being fed upon. The elixir gives incredible pleasure." She smiled as she chewed. "Suffice it to say, most Vârcolac couples make love and feed at the same time."

Toni didn't react—which had to have been an effort.

"But," Maggie added adamantly, "even though Fiinţă does have addictive properties, our husbands only feed on us about every three days to avoid that issue. Okay?"

Toni let out a sigh, the exhale sounding like *what-ever.* "FYI, this is exactly why all of you sound like cult crazies. The whole idea of Vârcolacs or "vampires" or whatever they claim to be is ludicrous."

"Understood," Kimberly said quickly. Toni's predictable skepticism actually worked better for her plans. Kimberly's ability to get Roth by the short and curlies would die fast if Toni was seduced the same way the rest of them had been. And with Toni being a Dragon, with a Dragon's inevitable history of distant relationships and rejection, the question wasn't a matter of *if,* but *when.* "However, the issue isn't *who* brought you here, but *how.* You were kidnapped, and I think each of us owes you an apology for that."

Kimberly glanced around at the surprised expressions of her Dragon comrades. "Yes, ladies, we have to own up to our part in this. Since we 'gave this place a chance,' as Hannah described it, and then became oh-so-hunky-dory with our circumstances, we didn't make Roth pay for his actions. By doing so, we aided and abetted the perpetuation of his crime. I believe that until Roth experiences consequences for his actions, he'll continue abducting women." She gestured to Toni. "Case in point. On top of that," she went on, pouring herself some tea, "Roth makes us come here and try to convince the new girl how privileged she is to have been brought into this wonderful new life, when every single one of us knows that what Toni's going through right now is really damned awful." She dumped a teaspoon of sugar in her tea and stirred. "The whole thing is sick."

Maggie scrunched a napkin in her hand. "Oh, my God, how come we've never talked about this before? I, for one, have always felt really wrong about being so complacent."

"Because we *are* brainwashed." Ellen dragged her fingers through her unkempt hair. "Complaints rise in my mind, I'll admit that, but then my husband kisses me in that way that lets me know how much I mean to him—to the entire race!—or I go to book group and have a blast with friends, *true* friends, or my kids do something so utterly adorable that I can't help thinking how lucky I am." She sighed. "I'm going to bet you all have the same experiences."

Everyone went silent for a moment.

Maggie let out a long sigh. "We couldn't do anything even if we wanted to, anyway. We don't have any power here."

Kimberly pounced on that. "We do in one area. We could all agree to cut off our husbands from feedings until Roth promises to cease and desist all kidnappings." She smiled narrowly. "We could call it a Hunger Strike."

Maggie snorted. It sounded a bit like a laugh.

"That isn't funny," Hannah snapped, her face pink. "What you're proposing is *appalling*, Kimberly. Feeding is one of *the* most intimate acts that occur within the Vârcolac relationship. Our husbands depend on our blood for their very lives. We can't just use that in a power play."

"Plus," Ellen put in, "you're thinking too much like a lawyer, Kimbo. Topside, you could've written up an iron-clad contract against Roth reneging once the danger of the Hunger Strike had passed. But here, that won't hold water, not with Roth being the only law."

Kimberly cursed. That's exactly what she'd been thinking.

Toni's eyebrows lifted. "Is this man Roth a dictator?"

"Almost." Kimberly twisted her lips. "In the old days, the Vârcolac system of government operated as a monarchy, and they just can't seem to get away from that culture. Roth, as supreme emperor, doesn't—"

"Everyone is making Roth sound like a monster," Hannah interrupted with clear annoyance, "when he's not." She pinned a heated gaze onto Toni. "I happen to know that he cares very much about our well-being. He hates how unhappy we are when we first arrive, and he's only doing what he does to save his species."

"Boo-fucking-hoo." Kimberly rolled her eyes.

Hannah's face stained a livid shade of red. She kept her eyes on Toni, though. "I ask you to please understand their history, Dr. Parthen. After the Vârcolac fled Romania, they settled in England for a time. For about...I don't know, thirty years. They lived among Regulars again, careful to hide their true selves, but they were discovered anyway and forced, once again, to flee for their lives. So Roth *has* to be adamant about keeping everyone securely hidden down here. He's not purposely trying to cause unpleasantness with his strict attitude. It's just life or death for them."

Toni's brows came together. "Are you saying you *never* get to go back up?"

"Have a baby," Kimberly drawled. "Then you'll be allowed topside to visit family for birthdays and Christmas."

Toni took a moment to digest that, then she glanced around at the other faces. "Do you all have children?"

"Everyone except for me." Kimberly turned her teacup in its saucer. "I haven't seen the light of day in three years. But, God, no, Roth's not a monster."

Hannah's body went rigid enough to crack in half.

"Have any of you ever tried to escape while you're up top?" Toni pressed.

"Our husbands come, too." Ellen shrugged helplessly.

"Where would we go, anyway?" Maggie added. "What would we do?"

"What you'd *do*," Toni declared, "is shake things up around here. Because it sounds to me like no one's listening to you."

"We can't be sure of that," Ellen countered in a reasonable

tone. "We haven't been complaining, as I said, at least besides some initial kicking and screaming."

"I have," Kimberly qualified, "for *two straight years* of marriage. And I think my husband speaks for all of the men in Ţărână when he says that he doesn't have the power to change anything."

"Yeah," Ellen conceded, "that's actually true. They believe that to be true, anyway."

"Which means none of them," Kimberly kept going, "will take a stand against Roth about the repopulation program."

Ellen nodded.

"So the kidnappings will continue unless *we*"—Kimberly banged her fist on the table—"make the stiffs around here sit up and take notice. I'd say a mass exodus of Dragons from the community would be just the ticket."

"Oh, for crying out loud," Maggie exasperated. "If it was possible to escape from down here, don't you think we would've done that back when we were new and miserable? This is all just talk. We don't have any power, as I keep reminding you."

Ellen sipped her tea, looking at Kimberly over the rim. "Unless either you or Beth could finagle a key code card out of your warrior husbands. Then we could get past the secured exits."

Kimberly snorted. "No way in hell on my end. But Beth might be able to charm one out of Arc. He's totally smitten with her. One look at her boobs," Kimberly teased, glancing at the fashion designer, "and he'll go so sloppy-stupid Beth could slip a nuclear bomb into his pants and he wouldn't know it."

A blush rode up Beth cheeks. Her mouth opened, then closed. "But I...I...."

Hannah quickly pressed her hand over the top of Beth's. "You don't need to respond to that, Beth." She glared at Kimberly. "We're not going to get drawn into this ill-behaved scheme, Kimberly."

"Ill-behaved?" Kimberly repeated incredulously. "Well, golly,

Funshine Bear, it seems to me that it's a mite *ill-behaved* to go around abducting women." She glared back at Hannah through narrow lids. In her old life, she used to consume fusty librarians like her in a single yummy bite. "As happy as you are in this community, Hannah, can you honestly sit there and tell me that you support the abduction of women? Because if you can, then you and Beth are excused from the rest of this meeting."

A profound silence descended over the room, the very air seeming to shudder with it. For a long, tense moment Hannah's eyes clung to Kimberly's, then she looked away, her lips trembling. "I just don't want our husbands to get hurt," Hannah said hoarsely.

"We don't, either," Maggie said gently, then she sighed loudly. "And that's the problem: Roth knows that. If we escape topside, so what? Roth realizes that as soon as any one of our husbands plunges too deep into his blood-need, we'll come running. All he has to do is wait it out."

"Let him wait." Kimberly hardened her jaw. "In a game of chicken, we have the upper hand."

"Why, because we're the holders of life-sustaining blood?" Maggie shook her head. "No. As I said, Roth *knows* that we love our men too much to allow them to truly get hurt. Being married to a Vârcolac makes it impossible for us ever to have any real power."

Kimberly threw her hands up. Maggie was like a dog on a piece of meat about this issue. "Well, I think it's pretty freaking clear that we absolutely don't have *any* negotiating power down here. Escaping topside would at least put us in a position to play chicken." She leaned back in her chair and crossed her arms over his chest. "And I happen to be a damned good bluffer."

"So how do we get our hands on a key card?" Toni asked.

Kimberly exhaled a breath. "Only the warriors carry them." She glanced once at Beth. No help would be coming from that quarter. "The warriors live in the mansion on the same floor as you do, Toni, so you might be able to get access to a key card. Give it a try."

Toni looked slightly taken aback by the suggestion, but after a moment's pause, she nodded. "All right."

"Once we have a card, we'll figure out the rest." Kimberly's heart jumped ahead a beat. They were really going to do this! She cast a smile over the group. "Meanwhile, ladies, mum's the word."

CHAPTER TEN

Beth Costache couldn't sleep. Curled on her side under one of her grandmother's crocheted afghans, her thick honey blonde hair still damp from the shower she'd taken an hour ago, she stared at the mechanical clock on her nightstand. *Shh-flip*, another number flapped over to the next. She blinked slowly, her eyes gritty from her recent crying jag. God, *why* did she have to be such a baby about confrontations. The whole time Kimberly had been stirring up mutiny at the tea party, Beth's throat had been tight, leaving her unable to do much more than sit in place and not talk.

She might as well have been back in high school.

Unlike most of the other Dragon women, Beth had had tons of friends growing up, but the relationships had been shallow, which was *just* like a typical Dragon story, kids hanging out with her because she was The Best Looking and Most Popular Girl. Whenever she'd opened her mouth to say anything, her so-called friends would invariably look at her like her head had turned into a cauliflower. To this day, she wasn't sure if she'd said stupid things or not, but she'd soon learned it was better to act like a pretty ornament rather than risk it.

She was sick of still being worried about that. In her heart, she knew she wasn't just some dumb blonde, but—

The door to the bedroom eased open and Arc stepped inside, pausing to watch her sleep, even though she wasn't. From the corner of her eye, she saw that he was still dressed in his all-black warrior gear, which meant he'd just come off duty. He was running late tonight, but then the warriors always went on super high alert whenever there was a new acquisition in town. Until a woman was marked through mating to a Vârcolac, she was up for grabs as a potential reproducer by their Om Rău neighbors, making her dangerously vulnerable to capture.

Arc headed into the master bathroom, shut the door, and turned on the shower. She tucked her hand beneath her cheek as she pictured him undressing, his clothes falling away to reveal the broad shoulders, solidly sculpted chest, and ripped abs of a natural born soldier. He had a fantastic body, hands down *the* best of any man she'd ever been with. Which was saying a lot, because, modesty aside for a moment, she'd never lacked for some seriously handsome boyfriends in her dating years.

The shower turned off and she heard Arc moving about, brushing his teeth and such.

She continued to stare at the clock. *Shh-flip*...another number.

The bathroom door opened, releasing a cloud of steam. Arc padded over, fiddled with his alarm clock, then climbed under the covers on his side of the bed.

Two warriors out on the street exchanged quiet greetings as they changed the watch.

Shh-flip....

Her husband edged over and slipped his arm around her waist, pulling her close against his hips.

"Arc!" She jabbed an elbow into his abdomen. "Quit it!"

Laughing softly, he nuzzled her neck. "You *are* awake. I knew it." The hard length of him prodded her rump.

"Yes, but *not* in the mood."

"Hmm, no? Well, why don't we see about getting you in the

mood." Setting a hand on her hip, he rolled her onto her back and smiled that smile of his which always turned her belly to sugar. Oh, God, why did he have to be so handsome?

Moonlight—well, really specialized stadium lighting—was leaking in through a crack in the curtains, cutting across the hard contours of his bare chest and turning his blond hair silvery white. His body heat wrapped around her like a cocoon of intimacy and his scent washed over her. Freshly showered male. Was there anything sexier?

He trailed a hand under her nightie, skimming over her belly toward her—

She slapped his hand away and lurched to a sitting position, clutching the afghan to her breasts to hide nipples that had gone erect with laughable speed. "Honest to Pete, Arc, stop it, would you? I've had a rotten day."

"Tell me about it, baby." His fingers danced over her knee. "Your clothing order arrive messed up or something?"

She scooted away, giving him her best glare. Not a very good one, since glaring wasn't one of her specialties. He just widened his smile, not taking her seriously at all. "The five of us Dragons met with Toni today, Arc, and it was awful."

Arc levered himself up on an elbow, discreetly inching back toward her. "It's always tough at first, but things eventually smooth out."

"This time they won't. I'm warning you, Arc."

His eyes glimmered out of the shadows. "Sassiness. Now I'm really getting turned on." He wrapped a brawny forearm around her waist and hauled her back over to him.

She shoved away again.

He sighed. "You have two wonderful children, a rewarding career, a community that adores and supports you, no financial concerns, and a husband who's *absolutely* crazy in love with you. What's the complaint here, Beth?"

"This community takes women against their will, Arc. I'd think that'd be sort of a big *duh* of an answer."

His lids hooded.

She bit her bottom lip. "The Dragons are really upset that you've taken another woman, Arc." She didn't want to betray the secret meeting, but maybe if she just *talked* to Arc and got him to understand the Dragons' position, then life could return to being peaceful. "There was a big hullabaloo about it at Toni's tea today. They want to…. It's time to…take a stand about it." She flung a hand out, and the afghan sagged away from one of her breasts.

Arc's gaze latched onto the sight like a beacon. "Um…yes…." He crept forward and kissed her shoulder. "Take a stand…."

She fumbled with the afghan. "You're not listening to me, Arc—"

He slid closer still, his hand coming to rest on her belly.

"There's going to be trouble."

"Right, right." With the hand on her stomach, he urged her down onto the mattress.

"Hannah and Kimberly got really nasty with each other, and—"

Her husband tugged on her panties.

"Arc!" she gasped. She wriggled against his efforts to strip her, but he just laughed low in his throat and before she knew what had happened, he had her panties and nightie off.

With a ragged groan, he rolled on top of her and settled between her thighs.

"Stop it, Arc, you pain in the butt!" She slammed her palms against his shoulders to push him off.

"I'll talk to Roth," he panted, "first thing in the morning, okay." His shaft throbbed against her thigh.

She froze, a kernel of hope sparking to life in her chest. "Really?"

"Absolutely." He slanted his lips over hers, his kiss open and devouring, his tongue sliding inside her mouth like sweet fire.

Never trust what a man says when he's focused on putting his schlong into your cookie, dear. Her mother's oft-stated warning, with her one-of-a-kind genitalia descriptions, clanged through Beth's ears, then flew straight out of her head at the feel of her husband's powerful body on top of her, his well-defined chest warming her breasts. A thrill skipped through her body, sending embers of feeling lighting off along every inch of her skin. She entangled her tongue with Arc's, sifting her fingers into the back of his silky hair to hold him in place. God, he was such a great kisser, never a hard-thrusting, gagging-tongue type.

His fingertips trailed up the side of her ribcage, all the while his mouth teasing and tasting, then he cupped her breast. She squirmed eagerly beneath him as he grazed his thumb across her nipple, caressing the rosy bud into an even harder point, then tugging gently on it with his fingers. She bowed off the mattress, moisture surging into her core.

Arc tore his mouth from hers with a harsh sound, his nostrils flaring. No hiding the scent of lust from a Vârcolac.

She spread her legs wider and bent her knees, making room for his large body, inviting him inside.

"Oh, yeah," he moaned, grabbing his length in his fist and positioning himself at her entrance. He pushed inside her body, a smooth easy thrust, always so careful of her. A growl wrenched from his lips.

She gripped his shoulders as he began to move inside her, tension steadily building in her womb, tightening, growing. He never skimped on penetration, each surge of his hips burying his shaft deep inside her. Exquisite ripples of ecstasy tumbled through her body.

"Arc," she gasped in helpless pleasure.

"Come on, baby." He increased his tempo as he bent his head to her neck, latching his lips onto her skin and sucking. The sharp tip of an elongated fang grazed her, and she pressed her head back into the pillow, stretching her throat out to him. His lips continued only to suckle her, though, his breath puffing in quick, hot bursts against her skin. He wouldn't feed on her tonight.

No matter. She preferred a Ființă-backed orgasm, but didn't need it. She flexed her legs tightly around Arc's pumping flanks and dug her fingers into the valley that bisected his back, the scales of his dragon tattoo cool beneath her touch. Heat spiraled to the boiling point, her privates aching with the need for release. She gritted her teeth. Only...a few more...strokes, and...*oh!* She flung her head back and cried out as her sex squeezed and squeezed and *squeezed*. A shout rose in her throat that surely would've woken the kids had she not locked it behind her teeth. *Oh! God!*

A guttural noise erupted from Arc's chest as the tight, rhythmic pulsing of her sheath sent him racing toward his own release. The muscles in his body stiffened...and then he was clutching her to him with impossible strength, a deep animal noise rumbling out of him that no human could've ever made. His sex pulsed inside her as he came within her body, and he hugged her even tighter.

This part of his orgasm had been so strange to her the first few times they'd made love, this fierce, almost desperate embrace he gave her. The men she'd had sex with before had reared off her in the final throes of their ecstasy, body braced on straight arms, head craned back as they made all of their *oh-this-feels-so-great* noises. But not Arc. In the last intense moments of his climax, he held her to him as if he feared she might disappear back into a dream if he didn't keep a firm grip on her. And it was...the most romantic thing ever.

His climax spent, Arc slackened on top of her, gasping for breath, his heart hammering against her breasts. She kept her arms wrapped loosely around him while they both calmed their breathing and let their heart rates settle. His member throbbed with the occasional aftershock inside her, his fangs gradually pulling back into his upper jaw. Contentment enveloped her. In the ensuing quiet she heard the clock flap its number over, *shh-flip*.

Her husband nuzzled her throat, rose up and kissed her lightly on the nose, then withdrew himself and gently covered her naked body with the afghan.

She sighed quietly. *Sweet and gorgeous.* How was she

supposed to resist him, really? "I'm such a pushover," she murmured.

"Hmm, baby?" His voice sounded drowsy. He was already flopped onto his back, his jaw loosening with sleep.

She pushed up on an elbow and gave him a quick peck on the cheek. "I love you is all. Go to sleep."

With his eyes closed, he smiled lazily. "Love you, too, beautiful wife."

She swung her legs over the side of the mattress and got out of bed, towing her afghan with her as she headed into the bathroom.

She took more time than she'd originally planned, deciding to take a quick shower to clean up the wetness between her legs. She brushed her teeth again for good measure and finally plopped down on the toilet. Out of habit, she grabbed an ovulation stick from the nearby cup. It was probably a waste of an O-stick—not that there weren't millions around the community—seeing as she wasn't due to ovulate for another couple of—

What the *heck*? She squinted down at the stick. Good God, there were *three* hash marks on it. Not just one or two as a warning of impending fertility.

"Oh, no," she breathed, glancing anxiously at the bathroom door. What was she going to do now? On the other side of that door lay a bonded male Vârcolac who'd take one whiff of his mate in her fertile time and instantly turn into an instinct-driven machine. His sole objective would be to impregnate her and he wouldn't stop having sex with her until he'd achieved that end.

She grimaced. The two times she'd gone through it to get pregnant with Lysha and then Brynt had completely worn out her vagina. Plus, her neck got really sore because Arc kept sampling her blood for the telltale taste of the pregnancy hormone. Only when he tasted that would a neuron get triggered in his brain that signaled Mission Accomplished and he'd collapse into a three-day hibernation state, and finally free her from his incessant attentions.

Frankly, after the rough day she'd had, she wasn't particularly psyched up for that.

Somehow she had to get out of here. She tiptoed over to the bathroom door and lifted her robe off the hook, shrugging it on, then stepped into her slippers. She was just going to have to make a run for it and get herself into lockdown. A funny thing to call the female-only secured rooms in Roth's mansion, considering that the suites were outfitted with every imaginable luxury, and barring herself in one of the rooms for the two or three days of her fertile time was like a mini-vacation from life's responsibilities. But, anyway, one of the Dragon women, probably Kimberly, had coined the term and it'd stuck.

Placing her hand on the doorknob, she drew a fortifying breath and prayed for speed, then…. She didn't move. Her eyes drifted closed as she imagined carrying one of Arc's babies beneath her heart again, her chest aching with longing. *No. Stop this.* She had plans to expand her store this year. She wanted to start carrying a grunge line for the Stânga Town kids, among other things. Some jewelry maybe.

All right, then. She quickly twisted the knob, jerked open the door, and dashed into the—

She yelped as her husband jackknifed out of a sound sleep and growled at her. She ran like the dickens, her slippers flapping as she raced for the bedroom door. Lord, this was going to be close! It wasn't *even* close. Her athletic god of a husband came at her like a nuclear-powered freight train, tackling her to the floor before she'd barely made it into the hall.

"Arc," she squeaked as she found herself squashed beneath her husband's unrelenting body.

He powered to his feet and stood over her, his legs spread wide and his hands curled into loose fists at his sides, an enormous erection jutting out from his body. His nostrils were flaring rhythmically with the inhalations of her fertility he was drawing into his lungs, his eyes rapidly glazing over. *Yikes, Elvis has pretty much left the building.* She had about two seconds, maybe less, to issue him a firm *no*-command and get away before he was lost completely to the primal state of a Vârcolac male in full procreation mode.

With a feral grunt, Arc bent over and grabbed her ankle, turning and dragging her back into the bedroom. Her robe bunched around her waist, her hair trailing out behind her. She opened her mouth to stop him and then....

Didn't.

CHAPTER ELEVEN

Toni propped a shoulder against the sliding glass door of her third-story bedroom balcony and gazed through the prison bars at the town of Ţărână, home to 429 "followers": 229 males and 200 females—married, single, young, and old. She was so damned sick of the view. Same-old-same-old every day for the last *week*. She curled her lip at it. Such a cheery scene down there, the whole setup made to look like Main Street in Anytown, USA. But, it wasn't, was it? No, that down there was the freaking Batcave or Count Chocula's 'hood or...*or* if a woman was going to buy Dr. Jess's explanation, then she was looking at one of the many undiscovered spurs of tunnels naturally created by movement of tectonic plates in the San Andreas fault.

That first night after her meeting with Roth, Dr. Jess had puttered about in her room, preparing her a tidy cocktail of medications: Motrin for a headache she'd had the size of Jupiter, big surprise; vitamin D, a regular supplement for those of them who needed *real* sunlight down here; and a sleeping pill to help her adjust to Ţărână's automated light-dark cycle, which ran opposite to the real one topside. And as Jess had puttered, he'd chatted all about her new "home."

Apparently, oxygen flowed into the community through a honeycomb of wormholes formed by the same process of plate shifting that had created the tunnels themselves; the town's closer position to the earth's core maintained a constant temperature of 68 degrees Fahrenheit—they were a surprising one-half mile deep; water was piped in from topside, and TV and Internet came into the town through a secret network of cables; electricity was self-generated; the rocky earth was mined for diamonds and other precious minerals to provide the community with financial resources, which were obviously substantial; food and other supplies were transported in by non-reproducing, non-"dragon" human females called Travelers. These were the women who'd been brought in nearly twenty years ago for the first failed repopulation experiment between Vârcolac and "regular" humans.

All in all, it was quite the well-oiled machine of efficiency and production, a system well worth admiring had it not been a haven for a bunch of wackos who could stand with a bit of screw-tightening. She had to give credit where credit was due, though. Even during her psych rotation in med school, she'd never encountered a more complexly constructed fantasy world than this one. Or a group of people who were so deeply committed to adhering to said fantasy world, all the while appearing and sounding reasonably intelligent and rational, especially the so-called "dragons" she'd met at the tea.

Case in point was the day each Vârcolac breed demonstrated his extraordinary ability. The special effects they'd used to uphold their illusion of vampirism had been extremely impressive, some of the best she'd seen. She knew every trick in the book from her brother's horror filmmaking stage back in high school. Dev could've put drops of something called Fluorescein into his eyes to make them glow. Although, yes, a black light was generally required for activation. There were also Scleral contact lenses. Thomal could've used any number of unique glues to affix the scales of his dragon tattoo onto his back in order for them to look so real. Hell, he could've gone so far as to have had them surgically attached. And when Thomal ran so fast that he'd disappeared before her eyes, he could've...well, um.... She'd decided to blame her concussed brain for that one.

Truthfully, the scientist in her might have been fascinated, had these people not been so completely screwing up her life.

The latest outrage was that these freaks had broken into her topside house and packed up her stuff. Stuff, as in all of her clothes and most of her personal items: photos, jewelry, books, bathroom products. Then they'd brought it all down here for her, the idea being to make her feel more at home. Yes, thank you so much, she felt *so* much cozier now. Behind that generosity was the scarier idea that they obviously planned to keep her here for quite some time.

On top of that, some goober named Cleeve was answering emails *in her name*; her hospital had been informed that she was on emergency personal leave, and her mother and brother were being fed some crock about Toni being out of town at a hematology seminar. So no one even knew she was missing. No one was searching for her. The Cavalry wasn't going to charge to her rescue any minute. She truly was on her own if she intended to escape this lunatic asylum.

If that meant she had to employ the help of a group of "dragon" women who thought they were married to "vampires," then so be it.

The warriors live in the mansion on the same floor as you do, so you might be able to get access to a key card. Give it a try.

Here they came now, in fact. Toni heard the first group of warriors returning from their mid-morning training session.

Pushing away from her balcony, she crossed her bedroom and listened at the door.

"...should've seen the dump I just took, man. It came out like a small, greased-down squirrel, I kid you...."

"...just have to drain the main vein, then we'll grab the football and...."

"Dude, you're an idiot. The length of a woman's legs doesn't determine the size of her...."

"Oh, I'm sorry, do you have to check with your wife before you can scratch your balls, too?"

As the warriors' voices faded and the last of their bedroom doors closed, Toni cracked open her own door. *All clear?* She poked her head out. *Yes.* She slipped into the hallway and took a deep breath, forcing herself to remain calm. If anybody asked, she was just out for a stroll. She had been given free run of the mansion, after all; a big bonus that had turned into a little bonus as soon as she'd discovered that any room worth entering was kept locked, including the warriors' bedrooms. Because of that whole pesky locked door situation, she was going to have to search for a key card while one of the men was actually *in* his room.

She crept to the bedroom across the hall, her heartbeat racing despite her efforts to remain calm, and pressed her ear against the Colosseum; in this mansion, the doors were painted with murals of famous European cities to distinguish one room from another. This one was Rome. Hers, to go along with her French décor, was Paris, replete with a soaring Eiffel Tower.

She leapt back, nearly crying out as she was hammered by some kind of raging rock music cranked to near eardrum-bursting volume. Jesus! Hurrying away from the pounding, howling cacophony, she moved on to check Oslo and then London. No luck, until finally she heard a shower running at Dublin. She inhaled-exhaled. *Okay, here goes.*

She opened the door and darted inside, making sure to—

Wow. Whose room was this, anyway? The décor was extraordinarily tasteful, done in warm and inviting earth tones, hunter green, mauve, and chocolate brown predominating, the bedspread a patchwork combination of all three. A CD of the Cowboy Junkies was spinning on a state-of-the-art sound system, filling the room with soft, bluesy music. Even more surprising, a floor to ceiling wine rack stood against the far wall, large enough to house more than a hundred bottles and nearly full. In front of it was a small table laden with all of the paraphernalia an expert sommelier would need. *Well.* Whoever lived here had taste and class, and she couldn't imagine which warrior that could possibly be.

Not that she had time to figure it out.

She stole over to the dresser and started to rummage through the drawers. Only clothes, damn it, and a...Penthouse magazine. So much for taste and class. *Ugging* silently, she shoved the magazine back underneath a stack of shirts and moved over to a chest, lifting the lid to see if—

The shower shut off.

Crap! She sprinted soundlessly across the room, grabbing the doorknob and quickly and quietly yanking it—

Ho, shit! Her breath rammed into her throat, log-jamming right next to her heart as a large hand shot out over her head and slammed the door shut again. It'd taken the occupant of this bedroom exactly one millisecond to open the bathroom door behind her and then arrive at her back.

"Looking for something?" a dark, smoky voice drawled into her ear.

She groaned out loud, recognizing that voice. Of all the warriors who could've possibly caught her, why did it have to be Devid who.... Hold on. *This* was Dev's room? She spun around and—

Immediately she wished she'd kept her face pasted to the back of the door. The man was stark naked, dripping wet, and standing right in front of her. One hand was still planted on the door by her head, the awesome breadth of his shoulders eclipsing her view of the rest of the room. Her pulse spiked, and it took every ounce of resolve she owned to keep her eyes from sproinging out at him like a Bug-Out Bob doll.

"Curiosity finally got the better of you, did it? Out of your room at last...." His silver eyes brightened with a teasing light. "Maybe you'd like to give me that medical examination now?"

Was the room shrinking? She cleared her throat and pointed a remarkably steady finger at the bathroom behind him.

"There's a towel right in there, Mr. Nichita. Perhaps you'd be good enough to make use of it."

A thoroughly masculine smile curved his lips. "I'm sure I don't have anything you haven't seen before, right, Doctor?"

Riiiiiight. She would challenge any female physician in the Western Hemisphere to pull off viewing this man's body with solely a clinical eye. Not that *she* was looking at it.

"Or maybe not." He took a step back, his smile growing as he held his arms out from his body, presenting himself to her in all of his naked glory. "See anything new?"

Her eyes latched directly onto the area between his legs. Impossible to stop herself. It was...*that* was quite a sight. Clinically speaking, it pretty much shot directly past racehorse dimensions and right into elephant-penis status.

Tearing her eyes away, she made what she hoped was an offhand gesture. "You're right," she agreed, "you don't have anything I haven't seen before."

He lowered his arms, the air seeming to sweeten and thicken as he asked softly, "Maybe a set of fangs, then? That'd be new, I bet."

She crossed her arms firmly beneath her breasts, secretly clutching herself. "Actually, no, it wouldn't be. I've seen plenty of those teeth which you people call 'fangs.'" Everyone in this town had their canines filed down into sharp points. *Ouch.*

His deep laugh reverberated through the room, sending a shiver through her. "Ah, but you haven't seen them elongated, honey, that's the thing. But never fear, Dev is here." The gleam in his eyes sharpened as he took a step toward her.

She jerked backward, dropping her arms and pressing her spine against the door.

A single black eyebrow arched upward. "I have to get close to you to show you, sweetheart. Fangs can only be provoked to lengthen when the Vârcolac himself is...stimulated."

Her lungs grew tight, the air suddenly burning inside them.

"By the smell of blood," he went on as if she'd asked, "aggression, or sexual arousal." A brow arched again, devilishly.

"That's a rather convenient set of parameters for you, isn't it, Mr. Nichita?" And no wonder none of her mate-choices had shown her a set on demonstration day.

He chuckled. "Well, I guess you could always ask Jaćken. He and his brothers are the only ones who can control their fangs voluntarily." Dev's eyes danced with amusement. "You want to go see if he'll give you a demo?"

"Thanks, but no." Maybe if she pressed her back to the door hard enough she'd be able to rearrange her molecules and slip right through. "And although I do appreciate that lesson in Vârcolac taxonomy, Mr. Nichita, I think I'll also have to decline your offer. I have no desire to slice my wrist open or," she snorted, "do a lap dance just to see you *elongate*." His eyes flew up, and she smiled tartly into his startled expression. "Or are you offering to get into a fist fight with me?"

His answering smile was a knee-melter. "Ah, honey, all I need to do is tuck my face right in here," he pressed his thumb lightly to the artery in her throat, his fingers curling around the back of her nape, "and I'll be able to smell your blood just fine."

Her pulse reacted crazily to his touch, the wild drumbeat of it pounding from her vein into the pad of his thumb.

His pupils dilated, a feral darkness seeping into his gaze. "Don't be afraid." His voice was thick velvet over her skin, a palpable sensation of warmth and seduction, stirring a singeing heat to life in her blood.

She pressed her palms flat against the door. *Dear God, what...what...?* She had the alarming desire to throw back her head and present her throat to him. And if he wanted to fondle her breasts that would be just fine, too.

He shifted closer, his nostrils quivering. "You smell so damned good, Toni." He caressed his thumb along the length of her artery.

Her eyes sagged in their sockets. *Hmm, really, you don't say? Maybe we can....*

Forcing her teeth together, she blinked past her dizziness and shook the spellbinding fog from her brain. "Stop it, Devid.

Whatever you're doing." She grabbed Dev's wrist, jerking his hand from her throat. Then she made use of the YMCA Self Defense Training Course she'd taken a few years back. She gripped the sensitive area between his thumb and forefinger and pressed her own thumb in, hard.

His eyebrows soared in surprise. "Ow."

She hauled his arm down, throwing him off balance, then gave him a shove. As he stumbled backward, she spun around and shot out the door. Not putting it past a man like Dev to chase after her without benefit of clothing, she didn't even try to make it back to her own bedroom. She dashed directly into Berlin next door.

Shutting the door hurriedly behind her, she gulped in deep breaths as she listened for—

"What the hell do you think you're doing?"

She whirled around. *Oh, damn.* Deflating back against the door, she cursed the universe. Couldn't she ever catch a break?

Jacken.

CHAPTER TWELVE

Big, Dark and Murderous was standing over by a black entertainment center, his hands planted on his hips and a scowl knitting his eyebrows into a fierce vee. The proverbial tower of manhood and menace. He was dressed in that super sexy all-black workout gear the warriors wore for training, and although he was still his usual scary self, he also looked surprisingly...well...super sexy.

Toni's stomach gave a start and then a funny flutter at the sight of him. Powerful muscles stood out in rigid relief against the tight fabric of his gear, his body so clearly articulated with grooves and crevices he could've been held up in anatomy class as an example of the perfect male specimen. *These are the quadriceps, class, this, the tibialis anterior, and* this *part right here between his legs is the...oh, my. Let's just all make a 'yum' noise, shall we.*

Toni briefly closed her eyes. She really needed to get some help.

"Well?" he pressed in a peeved tone. "I asked you a question."

"Yes, I'm...uh...." *I'm here to steal a key card so that I can instigate an escape plan.* She covertly scanned the room for inspiration on another excuse, figuring the truth wouldn't go over well with a man of Jaćken's temperament. It was then she noticed just how black his bedroom was: black wooden dresser and entertainment center, sleek black lacquered wet bar, black bedspread with a dark gray geometric design on it. *Sheesh.* If her bedroom was Louis XVI, Dev's like a cozy room out of a château, then this bedroom—in keeping with the whole French theme—was Marquis de Sade all the way. Well, at least the bedroom fit the man this time.

"I just came to see if, um...." Her gaze zeroed in on a stack of DVD's in his entertainment center. "If you wouldn't mind if I borrowed a movie."

"You ever hear of knocking first? I was about to get into the shower. I could've been standing here naked, lady."

That gave her pause. Despite all logic, the thought of Jaćken naked wasn't a wholly unpleasant prospect. Not at all, in fact. Clearing her throat, she started forward. "I'm a doctor, Mr. Brun," she said in the kind of overly patient tone she knew would annoy him. "You surely don't have anything I haven't seen before." Mmm, *that* was about as big a joke as it had been with Dev.

She drew up right in front of him, and startled as a tingle of sensual awareness lit off a short burst of heat in her belly. She was close enough to smell him now, clean male sweat and a hint of Old Spice deodorant and Irish Springs soap; everything that was completely masculine and just about curled all the fine hairs on her body. An immense power radiated off of him, like the force of a tornado barely held in check, along with determination and confidence and ruthless intelligence, and something...strangely raw.

Her lips parted on a small breath, all that was feminine in her helplessly reacting to him. What was it about this man? How was it that she was even more aware of all the glorious differences between men and women while standing here with Jaćken than she had been with Dev, when he'd been naked as a jaybird?

"Would you mind backing the fuck up?" Jacken ground out, his nostrils flaring white at the rims. "Being this close to your smell is about as much fun as a fork in the eye."

Cured, instantly, of all wayward thoughts. Bristling, she plunked her hands on her hips. "Up yours, Jacken. You're such a misogynist, I swear to God."

His eyes slitted.

He had the darkest eyes she'd ever seen, so deep a brown they looked almost black…Jesus, they *were* black.

"A what?" he snapped.

"A woman-hater." She *pished* a breath. "What's your problem, anyway? Your mommy neglect to breastfeed you?"

His face tinged red. "You don't know jack shit about me, lady."

"No?" She slanted an insolent brow at him. "I've been watching you from my bedroom balcony this past week, you know."

He stiffened, the color in his face deepening.

"Yes, *spying* on you," she needled, "and I've seen how you are with women. Every morning you stand in front of Aunt Ælsi's and hand out muffins or pastries to the warriors going on duty, but when Beth strolls by to go to work, you don't give her a single thing."

"She's someone else's wife!"

"You barely even say hello to her!" she lashed back. "And what about the school teacher? When she came by with her students, you didn't say *one word* to her, you just gave her a curt nod. But you sure as hell had the decency to squat down and talk to the kids, didn't you, even going so far as to ruffle their hair, and—miracle of miracles!—crack the tiniest smile." She flung out her hands. "So what's it about women, Jacken, you scared of us or something? You one of those types who's threatened by the multiple female orgasm because you think it makes you—"

"Get out!" he growled, grabbing her elbow. "Nothing about me is any of your damned—"

"Keep your paws off me, you meathead!" She wrenched her arm out of his grasp, pulling so violently against his hold she knocked into his entertainment center, sending his stack of DVDs tumbling off the shelf. "I'm not one of your warrior peeps who you can just boss..."

She froze as her peripheral vision caught sight of the DVDs at her feet: *The Hunchback of Notre Dame*, *It Happened One Night*, *Singing in the Rain*. Her jaw loosened, shock chasing the anger out of her. She couldn't believe it. Hard-faced, foul-mouthed Jacken liked old movies? Humphrey Bogart flicks appeared to be his favorite. *The Maltese Falcon*, *The Treasure of the Sierra Madre*, the incomparable *Casablanca*. She bent to pick one up.

She straightened, holding one of her favorites. "*The African Queen*," she whispered. She looked up at Jacken, a nostalgic smile pulling at her lips. "I love Katherine Hepburn, she's always so—"

He snatched the movie out of her hand.

"Oh, for Pete's sake!" She exhaled sharply. "You're really the most foul-tempered person I've ever met."

"I'm going to take a shower now." He flung *The African Queen* back on its shelf. "I recommend you get the hell out." He turned around, yanking his lycra shirt off over his head as he stalked toward the bathroom. "Unless you have some demented need to see my pecker." He stopped and reached for the laces at the front of his black boxer briefs, his eyes narrowed in challenge.

She didn't budge. She just stood there and stared, utterly dumbfounded by the sight of his bare chest. It was covered with more of those black, interlocking saber-toothed tattoos, the design starting just above his nipples and climbing up the brutal slabs of his pecs to his collarbone. A strange uneasiness curled through her belly. Something didn't seem right about them. The skin underneath the marks was dented in places, pockmarked in others. Damaged.

"Shit." He bowed his head, losing his bravado in the face of her gawping refusal to leave.

She walked toward him, and his head instantly snapped back up, his expression guarded.

"Those tattoos aren't normal," she said quietly, stopping in front of him. Her stomach cramped with another wave of disquiet. She stared at him for a long moment, the uneasy tension building inside her until it was painful. "Somebody hurt you, didn't they?"

Jaċken's lip quivered on the verge of a sneer as his black gaze met hers in ruthless defiance, silence his only answer. The room suddenly felt stifling. The pounding rock music switching to more pounding Nickelback down the hall was the only noise to invade their mute battle of wills. They stood there for a full minute, just staring at each other. She could've stood for many more minutes. The most stubborn girl alive, her brother had called her many times, and although Alex hadn't meant it as a compliment, the trait served her well this time. Jaċken finally caved.

"My father did this to me." A muscle in his jaw spasmed viciously. "The bastard hammered ink-soaked tacks into my skin to mark me as his son and turn me into a man. Tack after tack after tack," he gritted between his teeth, "and I wasn't allowed to make a single sound. You fucking happy now?"

Bile lurched into her throat and horror invaded her chest. He was trying to shock and hurt her by telling her his story so brutally, to make her wish she'd never pressed him about it. It did all those things and more, planting a picture in her mind of Jaċken as a boy—scared, lost, vulnerable, just trying to survive—and she wasn't sure how to reconcile that image with the stony-faced man before her.

She turned her head to the side, staring across the room with distant eyes. Was this the something raw she'd sensed in him earlier? Was there a hurt child inside him who mirrored her own, simply a boy who didn't want to feel so alone? God, did she really share a connection with this man? It felt oddly...right.

Nickelback switched to something else. The entertainment

center shimmied before her gaze as memories unfolded across her mind.

"My own father," she said softly, "packed only a single small duffle bag on the day he left. I remember that very clearly because even though I was only about six at the time, it still struck me as very weird he'd take so little. I think it also gave me the vague hope he wouldn't really leave. But no...." She pressed her lids closed as the memories sleeted over her. "He stopped in the doorway, leaned down to kiss me on the forehead, and said, 'Goodbye, Antoinetta.' That's it. No, 'Hey, see you this weekend for an ice cream, kid' or even 'I love you.' Just, 'Goodbye, Antoinetta.'" She paused as she came to the part of the story that always hollowed her out. "I never saw him again."

She turned to look at Jacken. His eerily dark eyes had gone strangely intense, pinned on her in a way that made her think an earthquake could rock the room and he would've stayed just as he was. "What father never sees his kids again just because he divorces their mother?" she asked earnestly, almost expecting him to answer. "Other divorced fathers saw their children, right? Weekends and every other Christmas, half of summer vacation. So it must've been *me*, don't you see. I'd done something to drive him away."

Some kind of emotion flickered across Jacken's face. She couldn't tell what it was, and then it was gone.

"So I, uh...." She swallowed thickly, and pulled her eyes away, unable to bear the intensity of his dark gaze anymore. "I went out into my back yard one day and gathered a bag of small rocks and pebbles, then spread them under the sheets in my bed." She half shrugged. "I guess I figured that maybe if I punished myself severely enough, my father would somehow know how sorry I was and come back.

"God, I must've slept on those rocks for a good week before my mother discovered them and went bonkers. Well, she stayed calm on the outside, but she sent me to a child psychologist all the same. I don't remember much about those sessions, except there were a lot of puppets involved." She laughed humorlessly. "But I suppose in the end I came to realize my father's departure wasn't my fault."

She turned to him again, her throat working convulsively as she looked at Jacken's tattoos. "What you experienced was so much worse than what I went through. I know that. I don't mean to invalidate your dreadful experiences. I just…I know what it's like to live a childhood feeling pretty lost."

His face remained absolutely still, not a single muscle moving, bones set in place. Only the rhythmic flexing of his hands at his sides revealed that he wasn't made of stone. *Except for his heart, that is.*

She took a single step backward on unsteady legs, feeling exposed down to the depths of her soul. Why in the world had she let some weird, disturbing—and, please God, temporary— connection with this man inspire her to regurgitate *the* most agonizing experience of her childhood? He had about as much ability to respond to her pain as a 2x4.

"I'll leave you to your shower now." She practically sprinted for the door.

"Start dating your mate-choices."

She froze with her hand on the knob, astonished that he'd spoken to her.

His voice was as gritty as a rusted out 10-speed. "They'll…I think one of them could make you very happy, a kind of happy you'll never find topside, Toni, and…you deserve it."

A choking lump of emotion lodged in her throat. Unable to speak, she pulled open the door and hurried out. Once inside her own room, she crossed to her bed and crumpled down onto the mattress. Tears gathered in her eyes as emptiness swept over her like a cold wind, spreading numbness through her extremities. She wanted to run; run down the hall; run out of this building; run back home and throw herself into her brother's arms and never let go.

She hugged her middle and looked around the room with bleary eyes. This wasn't *her* room. She didn't belong here.

She'd spent a week straight in this rotten bedroom and had never felt as alone and out of place as she did now.

A kind of happy you'll never find topside, Toni.

Damn that man. Gulping a breath, she scooted over to the French Contessa phone on her nightstand and picked up the receiver.

There was the usual soft *hum*. "Operator."

"Yes, this is Dr. Toni Parthen. I'd like to speak to Mr. Roth Mihnea, if I may."

A single tear traced a path to her jaw. She'd start dating, all right. Her mate-choices were warriors, and somehow, damn it, she was going to finagle a key card off one, and then get the hell out of this place.

CHAPTER THIRTEEN

Alex absently strummed his guitar, the instrument feeling like an old friend in his hands. He hadn't played in a while, not since his band's bass player had gone into treatment for colon cancer, if four computer geeks could even be called a band. Toni had given him this guitar for Christmas years ago: a handmade mahogany/spruce Sorbera acoustic. He'd just about killed her for going so over budget that year, but she'd wanted to encourage his music, seeing real talent in what to him had just been another rebellion: his electric guitar rocker phase.

He picked out the first few chords of *Hotel California* as he gazed at his computer with enough force to bore a hole through the screen. He was seated stiffly on the edge of the couch in his office, the light of a dying sun filtering in through the west facing window, coloring the room a mellow gold. The ice in an untouched gin and tonic *chinked* softly on the table next to him. On the computer monitor, the mouse cursor blinked where he'd left it stalled out on Toni's latest email, or actually the email from whoever was pretending to be her.

He was absolutely sure now that whoever was sending those emails wasn't his sister. The emails sounded *almost* like her to anyone who didn't know Toni as well as he did, but it all came down to the fact that over a week had gone by and Toni still hadn't called or given him any contact information. No way would Toni keep him out of the loop this long. He and his sister were just too close these days. They'd always been tight, even as kids, but in the last few months—hell, years—with neither of them dating much or going out with friends, they'd really come to rely on each other for big time sanity checks. For companionship. A couple of days without calling was pushing it. A week was…impossible.

Alex and Detective Waterson had been working the fake Toni theory together, but the detective wasn't having any luck running down information. Neither was Alex, for that matter; just as he'd predicted, that forged IP address was proving impossible to trace.

He'd been attacking the problem with his best stuff, too. The moment Waterson and his partner had driven off seven days ago, Alex had brought his no-no hacker programs out of mothballs and reinstalled them: sniffer, crack, malicious logic, cryptographic checksum, DNS and IP spoofing, daemons. He'd been sending emails to Fake Toni ever since, with various Trojans attached to try and probe out system information, but whoever was working on Toni's end had access control encrypted tighter than a virgin's honey pot. Just when Alex would manage to follow a signal a few steps, the footprints would cross a stream, so to speak, then just vanish. He knew they were there, but hell if he could see them.

Damn, but he was so friggin' sick of feeling helpless. Bowing his head, he switched from the Eagles on his guitar to Eric Clapton, gently plucking out *Tears in Heaven*, a song he only played when he was mega depressed. A sudden rush of tears startled him, and he stopped playing to press his eyelids. "C'mon, sister mine," he whispered, "where are you?" God, this sucked. He had to do something, man.

He glanced at his closet door. What was hidden inside there could…

No, don't even go there, Alex. Using the "piggy-backer" was a bad idea.

The program, called a piggy-backer for its ability to ride any signal undetected, was too unpredictable. On a good day, it was a brilliant device, allowing him to hack into a system he had no business messing with. Fabulous on the surface, yes, except that when he'd invented the software back in his Berkeley days, he hadn't had the time or the talent to rid the thing of all its bugs. So on a bad day, his piggy-backer had a nasty habit of spazzing out and obliterating everything within the very system it'd breached. A real downer. In fact, it was such a serious negative that if he used the program to hunt down Fake Toni, he could just as easily end up slamming shut the only open door he had into information about her. He'd spent this entire last week avoiding the damned thing, even though time was rapidly ticking by while his sister remained missing. Possibly in serious danger. Or dead.

"Ah, hell," he breathed, anguish burning into his temples like a soldering iron. *Screw it.* Surging to his feet, he carefully set the Sorbera on its guitar stand, then crossed to his office closet. Hunkering down on his hands and knees, he rummaged through the junk inside, cursing and grunting. The small chest was way in the back, purposely buried under a crapload of stuff to keep it away from easy reach. With a final huff, he pulled the chest out, flipped open the lid, and...just about fell back on his ass.

Holy Christ, *The Book.*

He'd all but forgotten about the thing. He hadn't opened it in years because...well, whenever he did, it was kind of a bizarre-o trip-out for him; for several nights afterward, his dreams would be filled with strange, fantastical pictures.

It was an amazing book, though. The cover itself was striking, sandy-colored and grainy in texture, the center decorated with a dark blue crescent moon and star that shimmered almost supernaturally. On the pages inside were wondrous and detailed drawings of dragons, fairies, kings and queens, labyrinths, and...a people so magnificently stunning, he couldn't quite figure out who they were. Or *what* they were. Because he had a strange sense beauty like that didn't come without a mystical element attached to it.

He'd originally thought The Book was a fairy tale written in some extinct language. The lettering looked like a mixture of ancient hieroglyphs, Runic markings, and, hell, something J.R.R. Tolkien might've invented. But when he'd taken it to the language department at UCSD for analysis, the linguist had told him it was utter gibberish, nothing at all readable. Although the thing was...*he* could read it. Sometimes, at least. Or more like, "see" pictures in the lettering, although he didn't know how. And, well...it was no fairy tale, he'd figured out that much. More like a history of sorts, a prophesy, maybe, somehow a commentary on his own life, which was the really freaky part.

Temptation pulled at him to open The Book, but he forced himself to set it aside. He didn't need that kind of distraction right now. He rooted deeper in the chest and found the piggy-backer. Sitting back on his heels, he stared at the disc. Maybe he should try fixing it first.... But beta testing generally took a long time, and time was exactly what he didn't have right now. No, that precious commodity was rapidly ticking away.

He crossed to his desk and sat down, pulling the piggy-backer out of its sleeve. He filled his lungs with a long, deep breath, then slid the disc into his computer tower.

Time to set a trap.

CHAPTER FOURTEEN

Beth Costache hauled open the gymnasium door and planted herself inside, her face schooled as best she could into an expression of displeasure. The grunts of men exerting themselves flowed over her at about the same moment as the humidity of six sweaty bodies training.

Gábor was working out at the punching bag, the bull skull tattoo on his arm flexing with each hit; Nyko was at the weight rack, bench pressing what looked to be the poundage of a Hyundai; Thomal and Sedge were sparring in the boxing ring; and her husband was wrestling with Dev across the room, the two going at it relatively easily since Arc had just woken from his hibernation state today.

Gábor noticed her first. "Yo, Arc," he called out, backing off from the bag. "Looks like trouble in paradise, Bro."

Arc peered up from his pretzeled position on the mats. "Beth!" He untangled himself from Dev and jumped to his feet, snatching up a small towel as he crossed to her. "Hey, honey, what's up?"

"I tried to arrange a lunch date with Toni for tomorrow, but couldn't." She scowled at her husband, but his lack of reaction made her feel, as usual, like some low rent actress hired for her looks and not her ability to pull off anger with any believability. "Apparently, I have to get my husband's approval before I'm allowed to be alone with her."

"Aw, no worries, baby." He scrubbed the towel over his sweaty blond hair. "You can go. I'll let Roth know everything's cool."

She grrred beneath her breath. "Oh, well, thank you *so* much for your *permission*."

Arc flipped the towel over his shoulder. "Don't get all bunched up, Beth. It's just that Roth knows there's some discontent among the wives right now, so he wants all requests to see Toni to go through the husbands."

"Don't get bunched up?!" she repeated hotly. "You're controlling my actions, Arc." She crossed her arms beneath her breasts. "Frankly, I don't appreciate it."

His mouth turned down slightly as he skimmed his eyes over her. "What's up with you?"

Oh, yes, God forbid I should ever complain about an unfairness...or anything else! "You wouldn't have to ask me that if you ever bothered to listen to me."

"What are you talking about?"

She couldn't believe this! "The other night I tried to tell you how unhappy the Dragons are about the kidnappings. It's more than just *discontent*, Arc, but you didn't pay any attention. You just started kissing me, and...and.... Honest to Pete...sex, sex, sex! That's all you ever think about or want to do."

Arc opened his mouth...then just left it hanging open.

"Dude, Arc," Thomal snickered from a few feet away, "you dawg."

Arc blushed a mottled shade of red. "Shut the fuck up, would you, Thomal. Maybe nearly thirty years of not getting laid after reaching physical maturity took a big toll, all right." He swept a glower across the other warriors.

"Hey, man," Dev threw up his hands, "no need to explain it to me."

Arc turned back to her. "Can we talk about this later, *please?*"

"You mean alone in our bedroom?" She made a *hah* noise. "I'm not falling for that again."

Arc passed a hand over his face. "Beth, I'm sorry, okay. You're...God, an incredibly beautiful woman, and I...just can't help myself sometimes."

"I'm glad you're attracted to me, Arc, of course. But you're my husband, and I'm supposed to be able to talk to you about anything." A tight feeling caught in her throat.

"You can, baby."

She was tempted to leave it at that. He looked and sounded so genuine, and it'd be the easiest thing in the world to allow her husband to tell her "everything's fine," then just go home and pretend it was. To let the other Dragon women burn their bras and instigate change so that she wouldn't have to spend a single moment feeling uncomfortable. God, she was pitiful; she wasn't even sure she knew how to confront her own feelings anymore. Had she really wanted to get pregnant? She loved the child growing inside her, of course, now that the baby was there, but she hadn't thought the matter through much more than to acknowledge that being pregnant would please Arc and the community at large. And being the girl who pleased people was the skin she felt safest in. Trouble was, she was also getting fed up with how pathetic that made her feel.

The tightness slid into her chest. Her next breath strained out of her. "For five years we've been married and I've hardly ever argued with you. I hate to fight, so I...I've never told you certain things, like how much it hurts me that you don't share the details of your work with me or that we don't talk about anything deep, about books or the news or culture. It makes me feel like you think I'm weak or stupid."

"C'mon, honey. I don't think that."

"Really? Did you ever talk to Roth like you said you would?" She saw his expression. "No. Of course you didn't. Because you didn't think I'd call you on it; you didn't take me seriously! Heck, you probably didn't even mean it. You just said it because you wanted to put your thingy in me."

There was a muffled snort from one of the warriors.

"Jesus, Beth." Arc's face went up in smoke. "What the hell do you want me to say to Roth, anyway? Excuse me, sir, but the Dragons don't agree with the method you're using to try to *save our entire race from extinction*."

"It'd be a start."

Arc looked toward the ceiling for help. "Would you please be reasonable."

"As soon as you stop being *un*reasonable and start speaking out against something you recognize is wrong."

"You know," Sedge butted in, "Kimberly says the same thing to me, Beth, and it's frustrating, because this isn't our decision to make. We're not the men in charge."

"Exactly," Arc agreed enthusiastically, obviously glad for the support. "What you're asking me to do would be like me asking you to tell the President of the United States that he needs to fucking shape up."

Her stomach fluttered nervously. Facing down more than her husband hadn't been in the plan. And it wasn't just Sedge on Arc's side; all of the warriors were. She could see it on their faces. "Y-yes, well, at least in America we have a say, a vote, about matters that affect our lives, and...and we have certain freedoms. The President of the United States sure as heck doesn't get to tell me who I can or can't have lunch with. Or when I can or can't use the Internet. Here in Ţărână, Roth has way too much power, and the Dragons are sick of it. We need a voice, and if you can't stand up to the leadership for us, if...if...." She made herself push the words out, "if you're too damned weak to do that, then *we* will."

Arc's cheeks flushed a dull, furious red.

One of the warriors made a low sound in his throat that resounded into a weighted silence.

Her eyelashes started to quiver uncontrollably, and she fought to keep her stomach where it belonged.

"You know what—" Arc yanked open the gym, door. "Go ahead, then." He invited her to leave with a sweep of his hand. "Do your worst, Beth."

Her lips parted. She gaped at him for several erratic pulse beats, unable to believe he was being so cavalier about her—or any of the Dragon's—ability to wreak havoc on Roth or the community. It was insulting beyond measure, and it put steel in places she'd never had it before, like her spine.

Snapping her mouth shut, she moved stiffly into the doorjamb. "In five years of marriage, I think I'm seeing you clearly for the first time, Arc." Tears surged into her eyes, but she fought them back.

A muscle quivered in Arc's jaw.

"You Vârcolac males like to make us Dragons think we're so special to you, but the truth is," she lowered her voice to a hiss, "we're not even worth the effort for you to fight for us."

Arc opened his mouth, but she was done arguing.

She whirled and stormed down the hall, her heart beating as fast at her feet.

CHAPTER FIFTEEN

Toni opened her bedroom door and popped her eyebrows up. "Jesus, what's going on?" There were half a dozen warriors standing on her doorstep.

The group of them looked like a communal nightmare, dressed from neck to boots all in black, their chests and backs crisscrossed with leather straps and holsters for a dozen wickedly sharp knives.

"Is there a problem?" She swept the group with a questioning gaze, recognizing all of them from the "family" meals she shared with the residents of the mansion in Roth's lavish dining room. A huge, scary man called Nyko, who was Jaċken's older brother; Vinz, a dark-haired hottie despite his 70's sideburns, now fully recovered from some injury she'd heard he'd suffered; Gábor, whose left biceps sported a tattoo of a bull skull that was "attached" to his arm by a thickly braided ink rope; two others whose names escaped her, and then...

The King of Nightmares himself, Jaċken, planted right in front, wearing a headset, like the other men, and, unlike the others, dark sunglasses. His jaw was set in its typical default mode, steely and immobile.

She narrowed her eyes on him, wanting to smack the hard right off his face, the urge no doubt intensified by five days of nursing her embarrassment over their last run-in. She crossed her arms beneath her breasts and leaned one shoulder against the doorjamb. "Let me guess, Mr. Brun, you've finally managed to unclench your sphincter enough to offer a kindness. You're here to lend me *The African Queen*."

Vinz rubbed a hand over his mouth to hide a smile, while Jacken's eyebrows disappeared behind his shades, a sure sign he was—here was a shocker—scowling at her. Guess he didn't like being reminded about their last run-in, either.

"You're being allowed outside of the mansion," Jacken informed her tautly.

She straightened abruptly. "What? But I thought I was only being permitted out tonight?" She had a date with Buns of Steel Thomal at the ever-popular Garwald's Pub. It could've been at a butcher shop for all she cared, as long as she was getting out of this hateful building.

"Last night you proved you were serious about dating your mate-choices," Jacken went on, still tight-lipped as somebody with a corn husker up his butt.

Ah, yes, her romantic dinner with Dev in a cozy corner of the mansion's Garden Parlor. Roth's chef had cooked the meal and Dev had brought a bottle of wine from his collection, an outstanding Tuscan red. To her surprise, she'd actually enjoyed some parts of the evening. Dev's lively anecdotes and unexpected level of intelligence had proved entertaining. His ability to make her feel naked with the merest glance had not.

"Dr. Jess has requested some time with you." Jacken crossed his arms over his chest full of knives, one corner of his lip curling. "But hey, lady, if you'd rather stay in your room and flick the bean all day, or whatever it is you do in there, be my guest."

Gábor made a huff noise that sounded suspiciously like a stifled laugh.

Her face warmed, but she regrouped quickly. "And you need

five other men to help escort me? Sheesh, 'fraidy cat! A girl brandishes a letter opener one time...."

The small town of Țărână was full of activity at this time of "day," people bustling about with their chores and on errands, although without any real sense of urgency. There was always time to pause and chat, call out a greeting and wave. Toni, of course, received plenty of stares. But then, how was a girl supposed to pass unnoticed when she was towing an entourage of Xbox 360 characters with her?

She spied the first older folks she'd yet to see in the town when they passed Aunt Ælsi's. Several clusters of gray-haired men and women were sipping cappuccinos and lattes at small tables and laughing. One group of women was engaged in a lively game of canasta. A lady dressed in a frilly apron with her grayish-blonde hair swirled into an extravagant French knot, strode back and forth from the counter to the tables, clearly the owner and Grande Dame of the place.

"That's Ælsi, Kasson's mom," Vinz provided from off to her right. "Your future mother-in-law if you play your cards right." He chuckled.

She didn't join in. She was too busy trying not to fall further down the rabbit hole into this surreal Alice in Wonderland experience. How could everything and everyone look so damned normal, for Pete's sake? These people thought they were "vampires." Shouldn't they look like Trekkie conventioneers or squint-eyed after-hours clubbers? Shouldn't the town be some sort of cross between Transylvania and the movie *Blade Runner*?

Not *Pleasantville*.

One pill makes you larger and one pill makes you small....

At the end of Main Street the road forked, the right fork expanding into a gigantic cavern. The left continued into a dimly lit tunnel, making it impossible to see what was further down. An exit, maybe? One of her guardsmen probably had a

113

key card on him right now.

They headed to the right, strolling past an aluminum-sided diner with pink awnings, a grocery store with a banner of happy faces strung in the window, and a schoolhouse that could've been peeled right off the screen of a *Little House on the Prairie* episode. Jesus, just...*über* weird. She didn't know how she'd ever manage to describe this place to the police and capture its true essence: *yes, officer, just try to imagine a bunch of Dracula wannabes living on the Good Ship Lollipop.*

Go ask Alice when she's ten feet tall....

The hospital came into view, and *wow*. It was a beautiful four story building, glass-fronted on the upper stories, with a pristine white façade and arched portico on the bottom floor. She couldn't believe how many impressive buildings she was finding inside a *cave*. Further up the road, she glimpsed the beginnings of a residential neighborhood, brightly painted houses lined up in a neat row, each with a cheery white picket fence and a lawn of AstroTurf.

Okay, whoa. Somehow they'd switched to the set of the 1950's *Leave it to Beaver* sitcom.

And any minute the Mad Hatter was going to jump out and invite her to tea.

No, just a young boy riding by on a Big Wheel. Dear God, she was going to weep from the sheer insanity of it all.

And if you've just had some kind of mushroom and your mind is moving slow....

Once inside the hospital, Jacken led her to a lab while the other five warriors took up positions at various points in the building. For the most part, the laboratory was furnished like any other she'd spent too many hours in over the course of her career: incubator, centrifuges, microscopes, autoclave.... Ah, but here, too, the concept of normal failed her. There were also several newfangled models of apparatus she'd never seen before. How on earth was there a piece of lab equipment she didn't recognize?

When logic and proportion have fallen sloppy dead, and the

White Knight is talking backwards and the Red Queen's 'off with her head'....

Dr. Jess was standing near a metal cabinet, his lab coat bleached to near sun-blinding whiteness. He was talking to two other people: another lab-coated fellow and a cute brunette. He broke off as she entered to come welcome her. "Dr. Parthen!" He gave her hand a warm shake and smiled broadly, all big, toothy grin now that he didn't have to hide his fangs. "What a delight to have you here finally."

She returned his smile with a crooked one of her own. She hadn't expected him to be so genuinely happy to see her. "I appreciate your gallant reception, doctor, especially in light of the fact that I threatened to cut your throat the last time we were together."

"Oh, pish posh!" Blushing charmingly, Jess brushed that aside with a wave of his hand. "That's already long forgotten and forgiven. You were in a stressful situation." He cleared his throat. "Still are, I imagine. Come, I'm excited to give you a tour of the facility and show you some of our methods and machines." He first introduced her to the other two people in the lab, his assistant, Mekhel, and the brunette, Syrian. He then went on to outline his plans for their time together. She only half-listened to him, her attention craning toward a conversation that'd started up between Syrian and Jaćken.

"...missed your appointment yesterday," Syrian was saying. "Can you come see me now?"

"I'm working," Jaćken snapped at her, ever the gentleman.

Syrian released a measured sigh. "I moved around several others to fit you in today because I knew you'd be overdue. Look, you're wearing your sunglasses." No response. "I can only take one man a day, Jaćken, so you really shouldn't be messing with my schedule like this."

"...brand new MRI machine," Jess was gushing, "upstairs in the...."

"Chrissake," Jaćken grumbled. He pressed the "speak" button on his headset. "Vinz, you copy? Yeah, I need to step away for about five minutes. Take up position at the lab door for me."

Toni felt the brand of Jaćken's eyes land on her for a moment, then he spun on his heel and stalked off with Syrian. Next, Mekhel left, off to gather supplies, and then Dr. Jess was handing her a white lab coat of her own.

"Shall we begin now?" the doctor asked pleasantly. "I want to show you how the Sigmund-phase works."

"Yes, of course." She shrugged on the coat, and followed Jess over to a work station, intrigued by what a Sigmund-phase was and how it…"Who was that woman?" Okay, maybe she was *more* intrigued by that right now. "That, um, Syrian?" And what was she planning on doing with Jaćken? *I can only take one man a day….*

"Ah, yes. Syrian Popovici's one of our blood donors." Dr. Jess pulled over a small red machine that had four tubes on the top of it and a valve on the side. "Jaćken has gone off to feed."

Soooooo, Jaćken was engaging in a little bite-the-neck with that cute brunette was he? She almost snorted. Right, a euphemism for sex if she'd ever heard one. Because, really, she didn't know what the men and women did around here when they played vampire, but she'd bet it got hot and heavy pretty quickly. Bodies would inevitably press close with all that neck nibbling, breasts rubbing against a thickly muscled chest, legs entangling, and—

Her stomach clenched suddenly as an image of Jaćken making love to that woman hurtled into her mind: his powerful body moving rhythmically over her, buttocks flexing taut at each rise and fall of his hips, muscles in his back and shoulders undulating with every…. The tightness in her belly sharpened into a feeling that would've been jealousy had such an emotion been possible with a man like Jaćken.

"The blood donors are a valued group of widowed spouses in Țărână," Dr. Jess continued to explain. "They are both men and women who've volunteered to let unmated Vârcolac feed on them. It's a much-needed service, seeing as our genetic predicament has left us with so many singles who need to feed but can't form a bond."

That sounded rather antiseptic, not at all like a tightly knit cult. "Vârcolac aren't allowed to get close to one another?"

Jess smiled. "Oh, Vârcolac become very close, my dear, but in this case you misunderstand the term 'bond.' When an unmated Vârcolac feeds on and then makes love to a mate of equal unmated status, he physically bonds to her. Actual *biological* changes occur within him." Jess started cleaning the red machine with an alcohol wipe, even though the thing already looked immaculate. "After that, he can only feed on his mate's blood; he's dependent on it. His wife in turn will be rendered infertile to any male other than her husband."

Wow, she had no idea the community was so strict. "I guess it's 'till death do you part' for real around here, huh?"

Jess chuckled. "Very much so." He pushed a pipe cleaner into the machine's valve and swished it around. "This blood-bond is *permanent*, Dr. Parthen. There can be no going back once you've chosen your mate. You need to be clear about that."

Toni smiled archly. "I'll make sure to remember." Aw, shucks, and here she'd had her heart set on hooking up with two. "I overhead Syrian mention that she can only take one man a day yet the other, uh, 'dragon' women said that their husbands only...um," God, she hated talking like this, "'feed' on them every three days so they won't get addicted."

"The donors are addicted."

She blinked. "Oh." She paused, waiting for more. Apparently, that was all Dr. Jess had to say about that. "Are donors always widows?"

"Yes." Jess tossed the pipe cleaner into a trashcan and grabbed another, going to work on the valve again. "Widows were already bonded to someone else in the past, you see, so their blood is resistant to further bonding."

She tugged out a wet wipe and used it to sterilize her hands, a move which Dr. Jess seemed to appreciate. "And...the same goes for sex?" She glanced at the door through which Jacken had disappeared. "Only with a donor?"

"Stars, no. Donors and their clients never make love. It's true," Jess added when she gave him a dubious look. "In fact, they *can't*. Vampires aren't physically capable of performing sexually until they're bonded."

"So they have to—" She stilled in the process of snapping on a pair of latex gloves. "Wait. Holy crap. No sex. Are you telling me all the single men and women in this community are *virgins*?"

Another chuckle rippled out of Dr. Jess. "My goodness, it's not a disease."

"No, no, of course not, it's just...." *I don't believe it.* "For one, the men in this town exude more masculinity and sex appeal than an entire squad of Navy SEALS."

Jess slanted a look at her. "Can't a man be both? Sexually appealing *and* a virgin?"

She shrugged. Frankly? Not to her mind, no. She just couldn't imagine some girl not getting her mitts on a guy who was as hot as the ones around here.

Jess threw away the second pipe cleaner. "The concept of male virginity is only strange to you humans. For us, it's quite ordinary. It's the norm."

The norm, right. She almost laughed; she could just imagine how *that* Classified Ad had run.

Have you seen 'Interview with a Vampire' more than ten times? Would you like to escape the harsh realities of life without drinking the Kool Aid? Well, then, join our club! (those who've already experienced hot monkey love need not apply).

"From what I've seen," she said, "the men around here act just as horny as any other guy." An image flashed into her mind of Dev, naked in his bedroom, eyes smoldering. "Hell, *more*."

"Of course they do, and it makes sense if you consider how many years the single men and women have had to suppress their urges and live in a state of deprivation." Jess opened a drawer and pulled out a couple of syringes. "They can't even masturbate."

Oooo-kay. That was kind of TMI.

Mekhel re-entered the lab with a rack of blood-filled test tubes. "I have the samples, doctors," he announced with a smile.

Jess clasped his hands together. "Excellent. All right, Dr. Parthen, I'm going to show you how to use the Sigmund-phase now, and you'll see how to create a Vârcolac blood graph." He started to neatly cuff up his left sleeve. "We'll also experiment with the blood graphs stored in the hospital computer. Everyone in the community has one on file."

"Mmm, yes," she murmured, making all of the correct *I'm listening* noises as out of the tail of her vision she saw Jačken return to the lab door. He exchanged a few words with Vinz, then took the man's post.

"When you draw my blood," Jess instructed as he handed her a syringe and an alcohol swab. "I want you to keep the sample in your possession at all times. That way you can be certain I don't add anything to it or make a switch of some sort."

"Right." She absently slipped the plastic cap off the hypodermic needle and pretended to listen to Dr. Jess's further explanations. Surreptitiously, she let her gaze wander over Jačken, checking out the column of corded muscles in his neck, the mounds of twin biceps bulging out from his short-sleeved T-shirt, and the way his crisscrossed knife-holster emphasized the breadth of his back. She lifted her gaze to his profile, and took a deep breath. He really had an incredibly chiseled face when a girl let herself see past how disagreeable his expression was much of the time. Cult fanatic or not, the man really was a damned hot bastard.

As if feeling her stare, Jačken swiveled his head in her direction, his sunglasses no longer hugging his stony face. She almost startled when his eyes met hers. *So impossibly dark....* They locked gazes and held, remaining bound in a game of stare-down long enough for crickets to chirp and tumbleweeds to roll by.

She pulled her eyes away at last, her lashes lowered, heat flushing her cheeks.

She'd never understood the male obsession with virginity. How it was that the moment a guy found out a girl was a virgin, the first thing he wanted to do was take it.

She turned to Dr. Jess with the syringe and tried to keep her hands from trembling.

Now she did.

CHAPTER SIXTEEN

Garwald's Pub looked like any bar directly out of Good Ol' Boy Americana: sawdust and peanut shells on the floor, dimly lit green-shaded lamps suspended over mauve vinyl upholstered booths, and tall cushioned barstools at a long, shiny bar. Coors and Budweiser neon signs blinked from the wooden walls, hanging next to hubcaps and license plates, and some fishing paraphernalia. The requisite pool table was in the back, lorded over by a huge elk head on the wall.

The juke box was pumping out a Doobie Brothers oldie as Jaćken entered, Nyko close on his heels. The two of them threaded between the tables in the center of the room, heading toward a booth in the back, Jaćken bumping recklessly into a couple of empty chairs. That earned a few glances, but otherwise everyone kept to their own drinks and conversations. Thirty-seven years ago, when the three Brun Brothers had first arrived in Țărână, that wouldn't have been the case. Then, one of Jaćken's dark moods would've sent many people slipping rapidly, if discreetly, out the back door. But the townsfolk had long since learned that, although Jaćken was far from a chummy person, he did know how to control the...baser aspects of his unique bloodlines, as did Nyko. Shon was a different matter.

Speaking of his younger brother.... "Where's Shon?" Jacken asked, scanning the bar as he sat down in the empty booth.

Nyko claimed the seat opposite to him. "My guess would be at The Shank Tooth."

"What?" Jacken scowled. "You're fucking kidding me."

"You want him *here* when he's in one of his moods?" Nyko grabbed a handful of peanuts out of the bowl and started cracking them open.

Jacken gave his brother a heated look. "Shon's a member of the Warrior Class, Nyko. He shouldn't be hanging in Stânga Town at The Shank Tooth. He patrols that town, for Chrissake."

Nyko shrugged. "It's where Shon goes when he feels bad. C'mon, Jacken, you know that." He tipped his head back and trickled the shelled peanuts into his mouth from his fist, the tattoos on his neck rippling.

Jacken exhaled hard, rubbing a hand over his brow. Well, hell, he didn't want Shon beating himself up over what had happened with Toni today. Okay, yeah, it *was* Shon's fault that Jacken and Nyko were here at Garwald's on some unscheduled R & R when they didn't want to be. The youngest Brun had caught an up-close-and-personal whiff of Toni today and gone apeshit, which had prompted Roth to insist that *all* the Bruns take a night off from guarding the exceptionally fragrant women. Roth had been trying to do them a solid by giving them this break; for men who'd taken the vow the Bruns had, it was especially torturous being around Toni. But it would've been nice if the man just let them do their fucking jobs.

"Howdy, boys." Luvera Nichita sashayed up to their table, pulling a notepad from her apron and a pencil out of her black-haired bun. "What can I get you two princes tonight?"

Nyko smiled at her. "Couple of longnecks ought to do it."

"Well, heck, I don't need to write that down." Luvera shoved her notebook back in her apron. "I shoulda figured, anyway."

The Bruns generally only drank beer; hard alcohol, and just about any other chemical stimulant or intoxicant, was never a good idea for men of their unique bloodlines.

Luvera winked at them. "Be back in a jiff'."

Nyko watched her go, his smile turning wistful. "Luvera's real sweet, you know. She'd make a guy a great mate."

Jacken hiked a brow. "You saying you want the job?"

Nyko whipped his gaze back over to Jacken. "No, of course not. I mean, uh...if it were possible, I certainly wouldn't kick her out of my, um...." His cheeks reddened as he stumbled about on unfamiliar ground. They rarely talked about women...sex, children, family, a home, the future. What would be the point? "I'm just *saying* it'd be nice if we could get some human Dragon males down here. The women of our breed deserve a chance at a family, too."

Jacken shrugged. "Soon as a guy pops up with Peak 8, we'll go get him." Kidnapping a male would be interesting; more so trying to keep control of him down here.

Luvera plunked down two longneck Budweisers on their table. "Here ya go, boys."

"Hey, that was fast." Nyko smiled at her again.

"You're my favorite customer, Nyko Brun." Luvera tweaked his nose, then bustled off.

Blushing, Nyko picked up the bottle and took a swig of—

He choked halfway through the sip.

Jacken felt it, too, like a ramrod straight up his spine.

His back was to the door, but Toni's entrance hit the entire place like a sonic boom, rolling through the bar like a punch to each man's gut. Some men jerked upright and tightened their jaws, while others slid low in their seats, their eyes rolling up into their skulls.

It slammed into Jacken in such a physical wave of ball-clenching sex vapor, he almost bit his tongue from clamping his teeth hard enough to keep from moaning.

Nyko set down his beer with exaggerated care. "*When* will that woman be able to wear the mud?"

Jacken took a hard pull on his beer, contemplating chewing his way through the rest of it. "Dr. Jess tested her today to see if she's allergic." *Please* have the Universe be feeling kind and let her pass that test with flying colors. A few dabs behind Toni's ears of the sulfuric mud which bubbled up in the cave and her scent would be cut in half. Once a woman was mated, her scent diminished, thank Christ, for anyone save her husband, but until then, the smell of an unmated Dragon woman running amok was equal to one long communal, never-ending ball massage…. minus the happy ending, of course. Insanity.

Raucous voices pulled Jaćken's attention over to the pool table. Thomal was introducing Toni to a group of his friends, and she was smiling and shaking hands with everyone. Jaćken's stomach cranked over. She had the kind of smile that made a man want to conquer worlds, if only to see that smile aimed at him in gratitude and awe. Either that, or fuck her silly.

"They make a nice couple," Nyko mused. "She'd do well to choose Thomal, I think."

"Yeah." Jaćken tore at his Bud label. "They're the picture of perfect blond-ness together."

Nyko jerked his eyes back to him, but Jaćken only gave his brother a view of the top of his head.

"Uh, huh." Nyko shoved out of the booth.

Jaćken snapped his head up. "Where do you think you're going?"

"To get Shọn."

Jaćken scowled at him. "Don't be a pussy, Nyko."

"Sorry, but I can't handle it." Nyko pushed his beer over to the salt and pepper shakers. "Why don't you come along?"

Jaćken curled his lip. "The hell if I want to go into Stânga Town on my night off." It was probably absurdly transparent that he really wanted to watch out for Toni without "officially" guarding her.

Nyko blank-faced it, though, which was awfully nice of him. "Be back in a few, then." He tossed off a salute and left.

Jaćken leaned back in his booth and stared at the dart board across the bar, trying to talk himself into leaving Toni to the care of her Protection Team. Breen and Gábor were posted in the pub, Jeddin would be outside. Jacken managed the incredible feat of keeping his eyes glued to the board for a full count of ten before he shifted his gaze back to her. He gripped his Bud and took another long pull. Jesus, she looked fantastic tonight.

Not that he didn't doubt somebody could tie Toni to the back of a Jeep and drag her through horseshit for two days straight, and he'd still want her with a kind of hunger that bordered on crippling. But tonight...she looked like something out of a dream. The jeans she wore shaped her ass perfectly and rode provocatively low on the sweet curve of her hips. Low enough that a peek of her slim waist showed beneath a short-sleeved red sweater that was *just* tight enough across her tits to make his eyes want to boing out of their sockets.

It only upped his torture that he'd fed on Syrian a few short hours ago, putting his strength at its highest and his senses at their most finely honed. Every little detail about Toni was magnified a hundredfold to him: the little freckles sprinkling her arms, the way her long, tarnished-blonde eyelashes curled at the tips, the shimmer of certain strands of her hair, as if they were peppered with gold dust, others alight with living flames.

She was wearing it up in a youthful ponytail tonight, exposing the vulnerable sweep of her neck and the downy little hairs there. Even from this distance, he could pick out each one with the same acuity as if he were standing right over her, head bowed to her neck, nuzzling that peachy fuzz in the last breathless moments before driving his fangs in.

He wrapped his hands around his knees and squeezed them hard under the table, saliva filling his mouth. *Damn it all to—*

His whole body jerked as Toni's laughter echoed across the bar, the musical quality of it sending the already twitching mass of barely contained males into a near orgasmic seizure.

Toni clearly found humor in her inability to master the game of pool, even though Thomal was doing his level best to teach her the finer points of it...and finding every opportunity to touch her in the process. The little prick.

Ellen and Pedrr were a part of the group, as were Maggie and Luken, and the two couples couldn't keep their hands off each other, either. Every little piece of byplay seemed to be a reason to laugh up into each other's eyes, to pass some secret message of love and adoration. Grinding out a curse, Jaćken braced his elbows on the table and bowed his head, jamming his thumbs against the bridge of his nose. The hell if he was going to watch one more minute of a scene that held about as much relevance to his life as knitting.

You want some balloons for this pity party, Jaćken? Damn, but he hated it when he got all whiny. Yeah, okay, so he'd been handed a shit deal in the genetics department. No kids for him. Ever. So what. No wife, no love, no nothing. Whatever. He was here in Ţărână with friends, his brothers, and comrades. Gratitude was the only thing he should be feeling. Because by all rights he should still be living among the Om Rău.

Escape from their town had been impossible. Unless a person knew a direct route through the lengthy labyrinth of passageways which stretched from the Om Rău town of Oţărât to Ţărână, he wouldn't get through fast enough. He'd end up cooking inside the tunnels that plunged so deep toward the earth's core they were, quite literally, hot as Hell. If his mother hadn't done the impossible and stolen a map of the Hell Tunnels from Lørke's lair, and then smuggled Jaćken and his brothers out, a sacrifice which had ultimately led to her death, they'd all still be there.

A shudder crawled up the back of his neck. He still had nightmares about the heat they'd endured during their escape, along with life itself in Oţărât: the sparse food and water, the caved-in buildings, the stench of unwashed bodies and running sewage, the violence that had ruled any given day, providing the landscape for the most horrific of his nightmares—the unbridled brutality raging in the streets, men raping the women at will, beating the crap out of each other. Yeah, Om Rău weren't exactly known for their mercy or self-control. He'd lost count of how many times he'd been beaten into unconsciousness over

something as stupid as a chicken drumstick, an
times he'd had to pound someone until his fists w
broken just to survive.

And then there was the unmatched terror of his father's
abuse....

Jacken wrenched his eyelids tighter. In all of his fifty-six
years of life, he'd never told a soul about his father's little tattoo
parties. Even he and his brothers didn't talk about it anymore.
But he'd told Toni. A bolt must've come loose in his brain for
him to have done that, though it might've been worth it if he'd
succeeded in driving the infernal woman away. She was
supposed to have been disgusted by who he was and run like
hell for the door. But instead she'd done this...*thing* where
she'd shared one of her own vulnerabilities to make him feel
better about confessing his.

To mess him up even further, she'd looked all helpless and
sad during the telling of her story, probably just like when she'd
been six-years-old and her bastard of a father had bailed on her.
The sight of her like that had carved out a weird soft spot in the
center of his chest that—

"Do you have a headache?"

He slammed upright at the sound of her voice, knocking his
beer bottle into a wobble across the table.

CHAPTER SEVENTEEN

Fumbling his Bud upright, Jacken stared in appalled shock as Toni slid gracefully into the booth across from him into Nyko's spot, somehow avoiding the usual vinyl farting and butt scooting that went along with such a maneuver.

She set her cocktail glass on the table: a martini, straight up, with olives, probably the drink of choice among all Big Shot doctors when they went to their Big Shot fundraisers or wherever the hell they went.

He stared at her for another astounded three seconds, watching her dig through her purse. "Do you have a death wish?"

"I know." She angled a quick, sardonic glance at him while still searching her purse. "Either I'm a glutton for punishment or the doctor in me just can't stand to see anyone in pain. Ah!" She pulled out a pill box and extracted a couple of capsules. "Ibuprofen." She pushed them across the table at him. "400 mgs ought to be enough to take the edge off."

He thinned his lids. She was being *nice* to him?

She rolled her eyes as she shoved the pill box back into her purse. "They're not poison, for Pete's sake. Just because you have AMI doesn't mean I can't help you."

He narrowed his lids down further. Great, more of her big ass terms. "AMI?"

She smiled innocently. "Anger Management Issues."

He curled his lip. This women lent new definition to the B-word. "Aren't you supposed to be on a *date*?" He searched the vicinity of the pool table, wondering how long it'd take for Thomal to stalk over here and accuse Jacken of poaching Toni.

"Thomal's in the bathroom," she said, "then on a drink run."

"Go away anyway."

She plucked a peanut out of the dish and crunched it open. "I suck at pool."

"Well, my brothers will be back any minute." Petulant as a two-year-old, he jerked the peanut dish out of her reach.

Her eyes slowly narrowed on him, and then she tsked, the noise expressing something along the lines of *stupid, stupid.* "Do you know I once sat on my brother for fifteen minutes to get him to let me play with his red fire truck."

A challenging glint entered her eyes, and then she...

Ah, shit.

She leaned across the table and yanked the peanut dish back, her ponytail *swishing* forward across her cheek, sending her scent *swishing* at him. *You're not going to beat me*, was the obvious message, but he couldn't give an unholy fuck. He was too busy trying not to bulldoze across the table, latch his fangs onto her neck, and ram another part of himself deep inside her.

Jesus, her fragrance had him engulfed in something between excruciating pain and mind-numbing ecstasy. His mouth watered, his gums feeling like they were bulging as a thousand pinpricks of sensation tingled along his skin and detonated a firecracker in his belly. He turned his head aside to gulp in a quick breath. It didn't help much.

She rooted around the dish for another peanut. "So why do you like old movies?"

"You're a real fucking whack job," he growled, "you know that, lady?"

Her brows leapt high for a second in surprise, and then a laugh came out of her, the sound and her accompanying smile hitting his solar plexus with a *whomp*.

He shifted in the booth, his muscles tense and screaming for some kind of action. Somewhere in the vague recesses of his mind he registered that women generally didn't smile at him. Most were pretty good at reading his *stay back, dangerous animal* sign.

Her lips twisted. "I suppose it wouldn't surprise you to hear I've been called worse?"

"Hag?" He drawled the suggestion. "Nagging shrew?"

Her eyes danced with her humor.

He closed his hand into a fist around his Budweiser bottle, his heart banging in his chest. Either it was the lighting or his extra-honed senses, but her eyes seemed impossibly blue tonight.

"Feel better now?" she asked wryly.

He smiled savagely. "Much."

"Wow, look at that." Her brows popped up. "The man has teeth, and a good-looking set, too."

He snapped the smile off his face as fire blazed into his cheeks, his stomach doing some sort of weird back flip.

"I mean, don't go crazy on me or anything. I still think you're a—"

"Thomal's back," he clipped out, jerking his chin at the bar.

She glanced over her shoulder. "He's getting our drinks." She went back to the peanut dish and asked again, "So why do you like old movies?"

"I don't know," he retorted mulishly. Evidently, he was still doing the two-year-old thing.

She went on searching for an acceptable peanut. "Yes, you do."

He scowled down at the top of her head. "Other people eat those nuts, you know."

"See how I'm ignoring your crabbiness, Jacken?" She perkily popped a denuded nut into her mouth. "Are you noticing that?"

He glared at her throat, this time without an eye toward biting it. Maybe he could just squeeze until she shut that gaping maw of hers and not kill her entirely.

She exhaled a long sigh. "Don't make me be a whack job again."

"Did you ever stop?" Ho, *that* put the challenging light right back into her eyes, and as soon as he saw it, he caved, to his utter shock, like a total lightweight. "I just like that everything was simpler back then, all right. *Jesus.*" He gave his shoulders a tight shrug. "I like the happy endings." They were the only ones he'd ever get.

"Ah." She braced an elbow on the table and propped her chin on her hand, her gaze poignant. "Yes, I like that part, too."

He fidgeted, the tender look in her eyes burrowing into his newly formed soft spot. He glanced around the bar for a warrior. He needed someone to beat some Man back into him, like fucking quick. No worries: any minute, Thomal would probably step up to do the job.

"I've probably seen all of Katherine Hepburn's films three times." Straightening, she stirred her martini with the toothpick that was speared through her olives. "Of course, that was before I started on a steady diet of Matthew McConaughey movies."

He jerked his eyebrows up in surprise. "You're kidding me."

"No." She chuckled. "Why not? He's gorgeous."

"The guy's *pretty.*" He snorted. "He might as well be a girl."

"Oh, my God, I can't believe you just said that. Have you taken a look around here, lately, mister? The men in this town give new meaning to the concept of beautiful. There's not one person here, in fact, man or woman, who isn't some level of good-looking, at least not that I've seen." She *clink-clinked* her toothpick against the rim of her glass. "It's kind of spooky, actually."

"*Actually*," he returned, "it's genetics, Doctor, or natural selection, if you prefer. Vârcolac are attractive because they have to be in order to survive." The muscles in his thighs clenched tight as he watched her lean forward to pluck an olive off the toothpick with her teeth. "We're a breed of human who has to take in blood for sustenance. So Mother Nature was generous enough to give our species the kinds of faces and forms that would make it easy to seduce a host into surrendering a vein."

She stopped chewing her olive and swallowed. "Dr. Jess said Vârcolac either feed on a bonded mate or a donor, neither of whom needs a whole lot of seducing."

Well, bowl him over with a feather, she knew something about their breed now. He'd have given her a solid month before she would've opened her mind to that kind of information. "It wasn't always that way. The first Vârcolac could take blood for nourishment without forming a permanent bond, which allowed them to pursue multiple sources. You can pick up on that old way of being if you pay attention around here: Pure-bred's have a predatory edge to them because they used to hunt, whereas the Mixed-blood Dragons, who came later, are the charmers."

"Ah...." She sat back, and her lips twitched. "And which one are you?"

He took a hard swig of his beer, an irrational anger gusting over him. The sparkle in her eyes and the teasing tone of her voice were bad enough, like some kind of damned flirtation, but her comment was also a complete face-shove into exactly why he could never have her. Or any woman.

"Actually," he sneered, "I'm a genetic mutation, Doctor, if you really want to know, not entirely Vârcolac, not quite human, but a creature in every sense of the word." He leaned toward her, jutting his jaw aggressively. "I'm a beast who hovers all of about two inches away from the edge of pure evil and the *last* thing you should be sitting your pretty little hinie across from." He eased back, exhaling through tight lips. "You know, for someone who's probably real smart about most things in life, you have your head particularly far up your ass about staying away from me. See my eyes, lady? They're pure black. Don't you think that ought to tell you something?"

She bit another olive off her toothpick and chewed...chewed

and chewed and stared at him with such casual indifference that he wanted to grab her by the shoulders and shake her until her head tumbled off her neck. What did it take to get rid of this woman?

"Are you trying to scare me, Jacken? Because if you are, you're going to have to come up with something better than that." She lifted a shoulder. "So you're a freak. So what? You're the one who has his head up his ass if you think you've got the market cornered on that." She polished off her drink, then tossed the toothpick into her empty martini glass with a sharp *tink*. "I feel like just as much of a freak as you do, pal, so you can take your holier-than-thou attitude and stuff it." Snatching up her purse, Toni came abruptly to her feet. "But, hey, you want me to keep my hinie away from you? No problem. Consider me *gone*."

"Yo, what's up?" Nyko drew up at the table, as nonchalant as if it was an everyday occurrence to find Jacken chitchatting with a woman.

"Your brother's a psychotic piece of bird crap, that's what."

"Oh, well...." Bobbing his head, Nyko slid his hands into his pockets.

Toni waved at Thomal just as the blond warrior turned from the bar with a drink in each hand, martini in one, draft beer in the other, and headed back to him.

Nyko stood in place for a second, then scooted into the booth, quietly taking a sip of his beer.

Jacken just sat there, his whole body humming as if any minute it would shatter into a thousand pieces. He cleared his throat. "Where's Shon?"

"Back in his room at the mansion. I told him we'd watch a DVD with him. He said any flick but one of yours." Nyko moved his beer bottle around in its wet ring. "You okay?"

"Sure. Why not." Lungs tight, Jacken stared a hole straight through the top of the table. He was so screwed up. Now that he'd finally managed to get rid of Toni, he only wanted her to *come back*. He pressed his eyes closed as a round of boisterous laughter rang out from over by the pool table. *Don't look.*

But he did.

The humming inside him instantly shut off, replaced by a prickly tension that made him feel like his whole body was wrapped in barbed wire. Over by the pool table, Toni was holding Thomal by the hand and pulling him toward the back door, her beautiful eyes sparkling at *him* now. Jacken clenched his jaw so hard, the muscles in his face throbbed. Whatever low words Toni was saying to Thomal had the man nearly stomping a boot mark on his tongue.

Jacken slugged back the rest of his beer as the two blondes disappeared out the back door. It was only by the narrowest margin of control that he didn't throw back his head and howl until the roof caved in.

It wouldn't take long for a horny little shit like Thomal to crowd Toni back up against Garwald's outside wall and start kissing a path up her throat, tasting the softness of her flesh, succumbing to the sweet insanity of her scent. His fangs would unsheathe from the force of his desire, and from there, it'd only take a few whispered words to convince Toni to moan, yes. Next would come the sweet puncture of a vein, then the wash of her blood into Thomal's mouth and down his throat, the intoxicating liquid entering his body like living and breathing warmth, charging up every atom in his body with strength and energy, turning him into a man—a *complete* one, at last.

Then Thomal would take her, pushing inside her body to feel her wet heat close around him, savoring the hot, aroused cadence of her breathing in his ears and the sting of her fingernails at his back. He'd fill her womb with his seed, marvel at her belly growing with his child, cuddle up on a couch with her after dinner to watch *The African Queen*. Or not watch it, as they once again found themselves unable to keep their hands off each other.

But most of all, Thomal's exalted status as Toni's bonded mate would give him the right to ask her the name of her father so that he could hunt down the bastard and go Postal on his ass.

Lurching back in his booth, Jaćken exhaled a raw, cursing breath. He looked across the expanse of table at Nyko. "Fuck it," he said quietly. "I'm not okay."

"Yeah, I know," Nyko said simply.

"What...?" The word got stuck halfway up his throat and he had to start again. "What am I going to do?"

Nyko shook his head. "Don't worry about it, Jaćken. It'll get better once she's mated. Her scent won't be all over the place, making you crazy."

Yeah.... But no. It was way more than just her scent. *She* had him tied up in knots, smart-mouthed, pain-in-the-ass *her*, and seeing her get hooked up with another guy would just do a whole lot of making it worse. He propped his elbows on the table and grabbed his temples between his hands. He really needed to stop this train wreck before he fell completely in love with—

His thoughts jerked to a halt as his gaze fell on the two Ibuprofen Toni had given him, still on the table. His heart wrenched so hard that his eyes actually burned. "I need to get the hell out of here, Nyko. Let's head back to the—"

Thomal stumbled up to their table, his face red and sweat-misted, a hand clutching his belly low down. "Toni just kneed me in the balls," he gasped out, "and ran off."

Jaćken leapt to his feet. "Damn it, what kind of pantywaist are you, Costache?"

"She *really* distracted me, okay."

Jaćken held up a hand to stop any more of *that* shit from coming out of Thomal's mouth. "Just find her," he snapped. He turned and jogged for the door, his stomach twisting into a hard knot of worry. If Toni somehow made it to The Outer Edge and became another Gwyn Billaud, he'd never forgive himself for driving her away.

CHAPTER EIGHTEEN

Toni darted in and out of the buildings along Main Street, keeping close to the shadows as she headed for the fork at the end of the road. The left fork. Breathing heavily, she shot into the low tunnel, the walls closing in around her. Dark, dank, slime climbing the walls, water drip-dripping steadily down slick rock. A prickle of unease touched her nape. Had she actually wanted the town of Țărână to appear freakier in order to fit better into her definition of what a "vampire" lair should look like? *Well, be careful what you wish for.*

Here was a cave, and one that ranked about a million on the creep-o-meter.

She loped along for about three hundred yards, then came to a gasping halt at the end of the tunnel. Just like in the right fork, the cave opened into a large cavern of buildings, although this part of the town was like...*Jesus!* It looked like The Projects times a Third World Country times...she didn't know what—a scene out of *Nightmare on Elm Street*, *Friday the Thirteenth*, *The Texas Chainsaw Massacre* or any one of the choicer slasher films her brother had dragged her to see all those years ago.

Low, misshapen buildings were jammed cheek-to-jowl next

to one another in the center of a u-shaped cut out of rock. Some were boarded up and many were dark. A few showed signs of life in the form of a bulb sputtering in a window, the dim light casting eerie, writhing shadows across the cave floor and up the lumpy walls. A pit of burping mud off to the left added a fitting sulfuric odor to the scene, though the worst smell was the out-and-out human stink.

Hardly an Ozzie and Harriet neighborhood like the right fork. More like Amityville, New York.

The surreal wail of a guitar cried out, and a shiver skittered up her spine. How bad did she want to turn around and run back to Garwald's Pub? *Bad.*

Crap. She hissed a breath as the distant sounds of shouting skipped down the tunnel. Thomal had obviously recovered enough to announce her escape. She craned her neck, spying over the tops of the buildings to her right the opening of another cave tunnel. This entrance was caged off by about a twenty-foot stretch of steel bars, just like the ones surrounding Roth's mansion. Worth investigating, for sure. She forced herself back into a run, heading right, and careened around the rundown building closest to—

She slammed to a halt and quickly ducked back against the building. *Damn it!* There was a crowd of men by the bars, about five on this side, the same number on the other side where the tunnel opening was. The group of them looked like they were gathered at a Hell's Angels mixer, what with all of the torn black clothing, piercings, tattoos, chains and steel accent pieces.

Arc Costache was in the middle of the mess, on Ţărână's side, of course, dressed in his warrior blacks and strapped to the gills with the usual dozen or so knives. "I've had enough of this shit," he was saying in an annoyed tone. "Now break it up. If you assholes start flashing your blades around again, somebody's going to get cut."

Both sides of men lit off over that, complaining and jeering in what sounded remarkably like playground *nana-nana-boo-boo* speak.

"Nilan," Arc barked at a man on his side, "get your friends back into the bar. Tøllar," he snapped at the leader on the other side, "line up nuts-to-butts and march right back into—" He broke off and pressed two fingers to his earpiece. "Yeah, I copy. What's up?" Brows down, Arc listened intently to whoever was speaking to him. "Roger that, I'll start looking for her."

Oh, wonderful. Toni clenched her teeth together. *Damn it*, again.

"Dev," Arc continued into the microphone of his headset, "come down off the wall and give me some backup. I've still got some hairballs down here with their panties in a bunch."

Toni darted into the building she was hiding against and shut the door quietly behind her, suddenly finding herself enveloped in the kind of atmospheric gloom typical of a bar. A neon sign on the wall flickered the name of the joint, The Shank Tooth, while the rest of the lighting was done in a red, ethereal motif that had her blinking her eyes to adjust them. When they did adjust...wow, Twilight Zone, anyone? The creep-o-meter had just been pegged.

Granted, she didn't tend to frequent places that catered to the underbelly of human society. So maybe it was standard to find small groups of people dressed in Alice Cooper garb huddled around tables like edgy nonconformists, mouthing their drinks and murmuring incoherently while a hermaphroditic musician made artistic love to a guitar on stage. Right. To someone used to this scene, it was probably perfectly normal, if a bit felonious, and didn't feel at all like the type of bar where Freddy Krueger might hang out with Leatherface, Michael Myers, and Jason, in keeping with the whole slasher symbolism.

Now how bad did she want to rush back to Garwald's? She closed her eyes and gave herself a mental shake. She really had to stop thinking like that.

Stealing over to the far end of the bar, she caught the bartender's attention. The grubby man came striding over, but barely got to within three feet of her when his eyebrows nearly jumped off his forehead.

"Holy snakes," he gasped, "you're a human." He closed the final gap between them, sucking air through his nostrils so hard his chin jerked back. "And *unmated*," he added in outright horror. "Who the farks brought you here?"

"Some friends," she quickly lied. "May I please use your phone?"

He made a face. "What ass-brain would bring an acquisition to The Outer Edge?"

"It's a local call," she continued in a rush. Heads were starting to turn her way, nostrils quivering. "A 619 area code, I swear."

The bartender looked at her as if she'd just asked him who he thought would win the next Olympic Figure Skating pairs competition. "You can't reach topside by phone, dummy, don't you know that? Only with the Internet."

She fought for calm, her nerves stretching to the breaking point. Someone exhaled sharply up near the stage. The guitar hit an off-key note. "Do you have a computer I can use, then?"

"Get!" he shooed her as if she was a cat. "You don't belong here, missy."

No kidding. Compared to the rest of the patrons, she was a schoolmarm from *The Waltons*. "Please, I'll pay you anything you—"

The door slammed open.

The guitar *twanged* into silence and faces began to turn, one by one, to squint at the open door.

Toni exhaled a sigh that vibrated her lips. She herself didn't need to turn around to know who'd just entered the bar.

"Yeah, I've got her," Jacken said from the doorway, presumably talking into a headset. Footsteps approached, then stopped at her side. "All right, Toni, let's go."

She turned her head to give him an icy stare. "No."

Jacken released a tight-sounding breath, as if his ribcage had shrunk around his lungs. The noise was loaded with impatience and frustration. Poor man, was his kidnap victim being difficult? "It's not safe here." He paused. "I'll toss you over my shoulder if I have—"

"Don't you dare," she seethed, her eyes catching fire. "You touched me in Roth's office the day you took the letter opener from me." She held up a rigid index finger in front of his face. "That was your *one* freebie. There won't be another."

He planted his hands on his belt, his gaze dipping over her. She could see in his eyes that he was assessing her, probably remembering how easily it'd been to overpower her in Roth's office.

The helplessness she'd felt that day flooded over her again, swamping her body, the remembered fear like a knife turning in her. Her soul screamed the unfairness of her situation. She stepped up to Jaćken, teeth gritted, and rammed a forefinger into his hard chest. "I might not be able to throw a knife as well as you, pal." Well, a letter opener. "But I *do* know how to perform some pretty inventive acts on a man's testicles. And I don't mean just kneeing them. Believe me when I—"

"I do believe you," he cut her off, his lips tight.

"Good." She stepped back. "Because I'm. Not. Going. Anywhere." Right outside this bar was a tunnel that probably led someplace very important. She turned back to the bartender, who looked like he'd swallowed a bug. "May I have a Manhattan, please?"

"Cancel that order," Jaćken overrode her. "Dr. Parthen won't be staying."

The bartender moved to the other end of the bar. Who could blame him, but Toni still felt sided against. She pressed taut fists to the top of the bar. Not since she was seven years old had the urge to throw a temper tantrum been so strong.

"Listen…" Jaćken smoothed a horizontal hand through the hair. "We can do this easily if—"

"You're a bully, Jaćken, you know that?"

His face reddened, much to the fascination of their audience.

"And, gee, I'm sorry if I'm not making things *easy* for you." Her breathing sped up. Frustration, anger, and powerlessness collided, churned, rose up and pushed tears to her eyes. "Damn it." She bowed her head and pressed her thumb and forefinger to her eyelids.

"Shit," Jaćken muttered. "Toni...I don't have to take you back to your room, okay. We can go anywhere you want. I know...what it's like to feel trapped, and—"

"Oh, that's rich!" She bolted her head up, her lips trembling. "You don't know anything!" What the hell did Jaćken want from her, anyway? For her to soul-share with him again just so he could push her away like he'd done five days ago? Ten minutes ago! "Aren't you the one who told me to get my hinie away from you? Well, follow your own advice and *leave me alone*!"

She jerked away from him.

"You're in danger here. Please..." He matched her step for step, an emotion she didn't recognize swimming into his eyes. Desperation?

She braced her hands on his muscular chest and shoved, which produced no movement from him whatsoever. "Damn you! I'm so sick of you Masters of the Universe men!" She snatched up an empty beer bottle and swung it at his jaw.

He tilted his head out of the way.

Heat pressed outward against her cheeks. That'd been laughably easy for him to dodge. Growling, she hurled the bottle at him, then ran outside.

Dev was now by the tunnel, dealing with the gathered hoodlums, Arc off somewhere.

Her arrival on the scene brought all speech to an abrupt halt: this side, that side, every man froze. Two beats of silence passed, then the space-time-continuum pressed "play" again, and a redheaded man from the other side, the one Arc had called Tøllar, stuck his head between the bars and sniffed noisily— and, really, quite rudely—in her direction. "Unmated!" he yelled, then the big-bad-mo-fos did the strangest thing. They turned and scurried like bunnies into the tunnel.

"Shit!" Dev swore. "Jaćken!" he shouted as her nemesis came crashing out of The Shank Tooth. "We've got tattle-tailers."

"Ah, fuck," Jaċken spat. "Lørke or Jøsnic will be coming any second, then. I'll deal with them, you get her to the mansion. Now!"

"Roger that." Dev grabbed her by the knees and tossed her over his shoulder in a fireman's hold.

"Hey!" she protested. "Put me down!"

The big lunk ignored her, of course. The earth started to pass before her vision as Dev vaulted into a run, the barred tunnel that could be a means of escape rapidly receding behind her. *Crap!* Reaching between Dev's scissoring legs, she grabbed his testicles through his pants and gave them a good, firm squeeze.

Dev yelped and fell to his knees.

She tumbled off his shoulder, rolled onto her butt, her hair in her face, then scrambled to her feet.

Still kneeling on the cave floor, Dev gave her a look of abject shock. Behind him, all hell was breaking loose over by the bars. Nilan's band of saggy-pants minions was shouting in panic, while a stream of vile curses was seething steadily past Jaċken's bared teeth. What was going—? Then she saw him, or...or.... *It.*

CHAPTER NINETEEN

Toni stood rooted to the spot as a giant's form took shape out of the shadows of the barred tunnel, the black-haired man having to duck to accommodate a height of well over seven feet. Her chin sagged down to her chest. Had her brain been capable of rational thought just then, she might've considered the man's body to be a medical miracle, more like boulders stacked together into human form rather than muscle and flesh. His face likewise resembled stone, or stone age, like something Paleolithic, with its huge, hinged jaws and wide, barbaric forehead. His right temple was marked with a saber-toothed tattoo, some of the black "teeth" stabbing into his eye socket. *Saber-toothed tattoo....* Dear God.

The giant was dressed like the head subjugator in a Medieval torture chamber: black leather pants with spiked kneepads, a shirt of see-through black mesh interwoven with metal links, and steel-toed boots with rings of knives surrounding the calves. Spiked bracers covered his wrists and forearms, and two more large knives were jammed into his belt—knives which he was even now drawing as his black eyes locked onto her with ruthless satisfaction. Her belly went gelatinous.

With what seemed like no more than a casual flick of his wrists, he sent the blades whizzing at Jaćken and…her?

Jaćken dove out of the path of the weapon, hitting the ground and rolling.

Dev surged to his feet and pushed her out of the way just as the knife hit his upper back with a meaty *thunch*. He yelled in pain, staggering forward a step.

She blinked at him in horror, catching a glimpse of the hilt: intertwining black saber-teeth with an undulating red crystal on it. Then—*sch-plop*! Part of Dev's shoulder exploded into her face, warm blood hitting her cheeks and spraying onto the front of her sweater. Dev dropped like a scarecrow that had lost its stuffing.

"No!" She fell down onto her knees beside him, alarm nearly blinding her with a dizzying rush of adrenaline. She jammed both hands over his wound, pressing hard to staunch the flow of blood.

"R-run," Dev croaked at her.

Blood was oozing steadily through her fingers. "We have to get you to the hospital!"

"You're in…danger," Dev gasped painfully. "L-Lørke can get past the key code box."

What? She whipped her eyes up.

The giant had just come to the blockade of steel bars and, without missing a beat, he wrapped one enormous hand around the code box protecting the door and ripped it off its bolts. Sparks flew out from the gnarled metal wreckage, showering over the giant, and a high-pitched siren started to wail.

Toni lurched to a standing position, the earth sloping beneath her feet like a carnival tilt-a-whirl ride. In defiance of every law of physics and science she'd ever learned, all the rules of nature she believed in with every fiber of her being, that giant was enduring what *had* to be a fatal electrical charge. And grinning at her.

His pupils glowed a bright, unnatural red as he flung the gate wide and came at her, his body looking bigger and taller with each step he took.

"*Run*, damnit!" Jaċken was racing to her rescue from over near The Shank Tooth, his legs pumping like a couple of pistons, his boots tearing up the ground. He had two knives already half-drawn....

But Nilan and his friends, who obviously agreed that, yes, running was the best course of action, did just that. As the panicked mob turned and scattered, they bowled Jaċken down and heaped on top of him.

She herself tried to run, she really did. Her neurons were firing all of the necessary fight-or-flight messages, with flight taking huge precedence, but panic had paralyzed her. She could do no more than stand and stare as the giant drew up right in front of her.

Dizzied by his looming presence and the scorching heat coming off his body, she swayed backward. He reached out a hand, but not to steady her. No. He twisted a large paw into the front of her bloody sweater, then balled his other hand into a huge iron mallet and delivered her an unbelievable hammer of an uppercut. The blow snapped her chin back so hard it felt like her head came ripping partially off her neck.

She hurtled backward through the air, her sweater ripping out of the giant's hold, and crashed to the cave floor onto her shoulder blades, flipping a backward somersault and sprawling facedown. A choked sob escaped her as agony blasted through her jawbones and ricocheted around in her skull. A strange buzzing noise shut down her ears and her eyeballs rolled into the back of her head.

The feel of a hand tangling in her hair jolted her back from her momentary slip into unconsciousness. The giant yanked her to her feet, and she cried out at the burning pain in her scalp. More black dots danced before her vision, making it seem like she was hallucinating when she saw Thomal, Nyko, and Arc stampeding toward her from various directions of the cave. *Not close enough*....

The giant tossed her onto his shoulder. Somehow she managed to act through her swimming senses and drive the sharp point of her elbow into the median nerve of her captor's neck. His grip loosened and she threw herself off his shoulder, hitting the rock floor with jarring impact. More birdies did laps around her head, singing her a lullaby, luring her back toward unconsciousness.

The giant locked a fist around her throat and hauled her to her feet. She heard a *whoosh*, and then the giant grunted, the hilt of a dagger suddenly appearing out of his shoulder. He spun in his attacker's direction.

Jacken!

Straight-arming her into immobility, the giant cocked back another knife. Jacken was much closer now, an easy target...*no!* Her vision blurred and narrowed, blackness coalescing over the surface of her eyes. She wrapped a feeble hand around the giant's wrist, the muscles in her neck straining as she fought to pull any amount of oxygen into her lungs.

The giant threw his knife.

Jacken twisted out of the path of the blade, spinning a full 360. The knife screamed harmlessly past, but the attack had done its job. Jacken was diverted long enough for the giant to sling her over his shoulder again and take off for the tunnels. Within seconds, he was passing through the still-smoking gate.

The need to vomit broke over her flesh in a cold sweat. Instinctively, she now knew those passageways weren't the way out, but the way into some—

Whirr, then *clunch-clunch*. Two knife handles were sticking out of the giant's back, protruding on either side of her waist. Her captor roared and flung her to the ground, adding bruised ribs to her rapidly growing list of injuries. He turned and rushed Jacken.

Half-blinded by sweat and tears, she watched from a fetal position on the ground as the two men went at each other with unmatched brutality, fists slamming into flesh in one bone-crushing punch after another, the relentless pounding of their blows echoing off the cave walls like thunder.

She'd never seen such violence in her life. Soon both men's

chests were heaving with exertion, their faces awash with sweat and blood. Jaćken's left eye was rapidly swelling shut, and the giant's nose was smashed out of alignment. The battle seemed to go on forever, although it probably only lasted the twenty seconds it took for Thomal, Nyko, and Arc to pound onto the scene. The three men arrived just as the giant seized Jaćken by the throat and hiked him off his feet. With veins bulging on his forehead, Jaćken still managed to kick the giant in the stomach. The creature flung Jaćken at Nyko.

The two men collided, hit the ground, and rolled across Thomal's path. With a shout, Thomal leapt over the two warriors, barely clearing them. Jaćken was back on his feet in an instant, blasting toward the tunnel.

But the giant had already disappeared.

"Shit!" Boots planted wide, his lungs working furiously, Jaćken stood at the mouth of the tunnel and glared into it. "Fuck!" he shouted into the echoing chamber, frustration and anger apparent in every unyielding line of his body.

Toni pushed onto her hands and knees, coughing weakly, her breath rushing painfully along her tender throat. Her jaw felt as if someone had taken a baseball bat to it. She tried to rise, but couldn't. Her legs had no more substance than overcooked spaghetti.

"Oh, Jesus, Toni." Thomal hunkered down in front of her and took her by the shoulders, his expression clouding with concern. "You're covered in blood." He pressed his lips together as if hiding something in his mouth.

"I-It's not my blood," she stammered. "D-Dev, it's…. Is he…?"

"Nyko's heading over to him now," Thomal said softly. "He'll be all right."

She nodded her head, the movement stabbing pain into the backs of her eyeballs. She couldn't seem to stop crying. Maybe this was what hysteria felt like. She turned and looked for Jaćken.

He was standing several feet away, his bloody face a rigid,

unreadable mask, his dark eyes devoid of emotion. "Jaćken...." Her lips trembled and then her whole body began to shake. "Don't—" She reached out a hand to him, feeling suddenly like he was the only one who could keep all of the monsters of the world under the bed where they belonged. *Don't leave me.*

He stood wooden and unmoving, making no effort to approach her.

You know, for someone who's probably real smart about most things in life, you seem to have your head particularly far up your ass about staying away from me.

She let her hand fall.

Arc placed a palm on Thomal's shoulder. "Let's get Toni to Dr. Jess."

A final tear slipped from her eye. She tilted sideways, and the last thing her conscious mind registered was that it was Thomal who caught her when she fainted dead away.

CHAPTER TWENTY

Jaċken stood in front of Toni's bedroom door and fidgeted with the cold thermos he was carrying. Shit, just how many sandwiches short of a picnic was he? Three hours ago at Garwald's he'd all but planted his size thirteens on Toni's ass to get her away from him, and now here he was standing outside her *bedroom*. Fucking genius.

He should just go. He took a step backward, but then hesitated, staring at the Eiffel Tower on her door. Thing was, he might be a lot of damned things—a hard, difficult man, a real prick sometimes—but he was never undependable. Ask any of his warriors and they'd say he was the most reliable son of a bitch out there, a man anyone would want watching his six. And, no, maybe he didn't know thing one about being there for a woman, but that didn't mean it was sitting well with him that he'd let Toni down.

She'd needed him after that gut-wrenching near-Gwyn reenactment at The Outer Edge tonight. Not Thomal, but *him*. He'd figured out that much in the hours he'd paced his bedroom while Toni was being tended in the mansion's basement clinic. *What* she'd needed was still a bit of a mystery to a man with his limited understanding of females, but whatever it was, he'd been too catatonic with his own fear to give it to her. Yeah, *him*, a guy who faced the possibility of death in battle as easily as he picked out his breakfast cereal. A guy who'd been beaten, stabbed and tortured more times than he cared to count had been scared out of his ever-loving mind when he'd seen Toni on the ground in Stânga Town, banged up and covered in blood.

He swallowed convulsively as he pictured her in Oțărât right now, serving as some Om Rău's party favor. He gripped the thermos in a hard fist. *All right, enough of this crap*. If he kept on like this, he'd end up standing in front of her door doing jack diddly squat, just like in Stânga Town, maybe start in on some blubbering. That'd be real fucking manly.

Drawing in a tight breath, he knocked softly on Toni's door. She didn't answer. Christ, knowing his luck, she'd off'ed herself because he was such an unmitigated bastard. Muttering under his breath, he pushed open the door and stepped into her room. No one was inside...no Toni hanging from a light fixture, either, at least.

He paused to look around, some of his tension easing. The place felt like Toni now. Her delicious scent saturated everything, of course, but more than that, she'd made the room her own with a collection of paperbacks on a corner bookshelf, a different bedspread, kind of a puffy, pale purple comforter, and about half a dozen framed photographs. Most were of an older blonde woman—probably Toni's mother to judge by the resemblance—and of a guy about Toni's age, strawberry-blond like her, but wearing glasses. A brother? Jacken shifted his boots restlessly, feeling oddly like an intruder, yet also suddenly wanting to know everything about her. *Do you know that I once sat on my brother for fifteen minutes to get him to let me play with his red fire truck?* That kind of shit was, you know, really cool to find out about.

He swiveled his head abruptly at the sound of retching coming from the open door of the bathroom. *Ah, hell.*

He crossed into the bathroom and stopped just inside the

doorway, his gut twisting. Toni was slumped against the side of a gargantuan bathtub, her eyes watery and still haunted with the trauma she'd endured, her face colorless except for a vivid bruise on her jaw. His heart took a nosedive into his soft spot at full speed, the way it always seemed to do whenever he saw her looking so damned vulnerable. Fuck him for failing to protect her better.

"Go away," she told him, though not unkindly. "Don't you know that girls don't like anyone to see them barf."

"Here." He stepped forward and offered her the thermos. "Drink this. It'll make you feel better."

She didn't take it. "How's Dev?" she asked thickly, wiping a small towel across her mouth.

"Recovering. More worried about you." A sentiment he could totally relate to. He squatted down on his haunches and pressed the thermos into her hand.

"What is it?"

"A mixture of juices: my own recipe. I, uh, have a bit of personal experience with puking over the things Lørke can do to a person."

"Oh." Her eyes ran over his battered face. "You look like reconstituted hell, by the way."

He propped a forearm on his thigh. "I suppose it wouldn't surprise you to hear I've been called worse?"

She snorted at hearing the words she'd spoken to him at Garwald's repeated back to her. Lowering her eyes, she added, "I owe you my thanks, Jacken. I would've died out there tonight if you hadn't saved me from that fiend. Of course"—her chin came back up—" I'd like to point out that it wouldn't have been an issue if you hadn't kidnapped me in the first place."

He pressed his lips together into something close to a smile. "Noted."

She fiddled with the thermos lid for a moment. "What...happened out there tonight, Jacken? I've never seen a knife do what it did to Dev. It just exploded in his shoulder. And that giant man walked through what looked like a spray of electricity as if it was no more than a field of daisies." She met his gaze. "What's going on?"

He sat back on his heels and sighed. "Are you sure you want to know? I mean, Christ, you're still not entirely convinced you're living among Vârcolac."

She eyed him intently through a long pause. "I think I need to know."

He massaged the back of his neck. "All right, then. Here it is. The man who attacked you is Lørke, one of the leaders of a neighboring town called Oţărât, home to another species of human. Like Vârcolac, their people are incredibly strong and fast, but their Peak 12, their aggression gene, is mutated, escalating their hostility and violent behavior off the charts. They lack impulse control and a sense of morality, they're nearly impossible to kill, and they can create enchanted knives called Bǎtaie Blades, which you saw in action on Dev today. All of that makes them very dangerous beings. We call them Om Rǎu." He paused. *Here comes the fun part....* "Regular human lore and legend would probably refer to them as demons."

She blinked once, then dropped her face into her hand. "Oh, God. Of course. Yes. "Demons" and "vampires" all living in unhappy discord together half a mile below the earth's surface. Why not?"

He glanced aside. Yeah, he'd figured as much.

"Okay...." She opened the thermos and gulped some juice. "Okay, so how do I come into this? Why did that Lørke monster want to kill me? It didn't seem like he was just acting out of simple demonic impulsivity."

"Your death is the last thing Lørke would've wanted. He was trying to knock you senseless enough to kidnap you easily into Oţărât. He wants to breed you, same as we do. Lørke and his kind *can* have children with regular females, but those offspring turn out weaker, and with fewer Om Rǎu traits, so they want your Dragon bloodlines."

Her face reddened and her brows drew down. "And you've

known about this all along," she accused, struggling to a standing position.

He stood, as well, his head down to hide a grimace.

"Why the hell didn't you warn me, Jačken?"

"Roth doesn't like to scare the new acquisitions any more than they already are." Another topic of contention between the two men.

"That's great." She *plunked* the thermos on the edge of the tub. "Have you ever lost a woman? Holy crap," she hissed when his face colored. "Jačken, please." She grabbed his forearm. "You have to get me out of this place before something worse happens. *Please.* I'm in mortal danger here, stuck in the middle of some...some bloodline war between your kind and these Om Rău."

He paused for a moment, struggling to overcome the feel of her hand on his arm so that he could stay in this conversation.

She moved closer, her demeanor changing. Her eyes turned limpid blue. "You said that you know what it's like to feel trapped, remember?"

He became aware of her body heat, warm and feminine, and how it laced with her scent in a way that was entirely too intimate for his well-being and sanity. What she'd said was even more dangerous, forging a connection between them that had no right to be there. Had no place to go. Why had he said that to her at The Shank Took, damn him? The next time he had the brilliant impulse to comfort a woman, he should just stab himself.

He gave his feet a stern command to retreat—*run like hell* would've been even better—but couldn't get any body part to obey. "I'm sorry," he managed to get out, "but sending you to the surface isn't the answer. Not anymore. There's a new faction of Om Rău, a Topside Om Rău, hunting you. They were at Scripps Hospital the same night we were, also trying to kidnap you."

"What?" She let go of him, her lips parting in shock. "What are you saying? That I can't *ever* go back?"

The expression on her face twisted his innards into knots.

"Only under full guard." *Yeah. Lame.* "If you went back to the surface to live, the Topside Om Rău would eventually find you and take you. Your bloodlines are just too valuable. And I can guarantee that, as much as you think you hate it here in Țărână, life with the Om Rău would be a living nightmare. Trust my experience on this."

"Good God," she breathed, her lips bloodless. "This isn't happening." Tears pooled in her eyes.

A bolt of panic shot up his spine. "Toni...please, don't cry. Okay, uh…. Vârcolac males can't handle...we don't do so well with that." Despite his warning, a tear trembled along her lashes, then slid down her cheek. He watched it in outright horror, his knees turning to sand. "Just give Țărână a chance," he said quietly. "I know you can't feel it, yet, but this is where you belong." He shoved a hand through his hair. *What* in *hell* was he supposed to do with a crying woman? "I can keep you safe here," he tried, "I promise. Nothing bad would've happened to you tonight if you hadn't escaped your Protection Team."

"No," she cried, burying her face in her hands. "No." Her shoulders began to shake and little hiccupping noises came out of her.

He stared down at the delicate crown of her head, his arms dangling loosely at his sides, his belly sagging into his boots. Blinking a couple of times, he finally lifted his hand, held it in a hover over her head for a second, then plunked it on top of her hair.

She froze.

He froze. *Now, uh, what?* Her crying quieted a bit. That was good. He began to pet her head. *Whoa.* Her hair felt even softer than it looked. A sinew quivered in his jaw as emotions he couldn't name muscled his chest to the floor and pinned it there. The shape of her head felt so small and vulnerable beneath his large, callused palm.

She stopped crying.

Holy shit, he'd made her stop. *Him!* His lungs expanded. He was King of the World.

Impulsively, he grabbed both sides of her head and gently pulled her forward. She didn't resist, just stepped closer to him. Shutting his eyes, he pressed his nose to the top of her hair and breathed in deeply. *Stupid, stupid, stupid....*

Her scent swirled through the lobes and crevices of his brain, locking inside there with a feeling of absolute rightness. He shuddered.

Angling her head up, Toni caught his gaze. Intimacy warmed the air around them, wrapping their bodies in a private cocoon.

He lost himself in the drowning blue depths of her eyes. *Stupid, stupid, stupid....*

Toni lifted a hand to his bruised cheek, touching him lightly with her fingers.

He inhaled a slow, uneven breath. Two fingers against his skin and he wanted to die.

"Lørke has the same teeth tattoo as you do," she said softly, "but here..." She moved her fingers up to his temple.

His heart stopped, dread squeezing his chest.

She dropped her hand, but never took her eyes off him. "The man who pounded ink-soaked tacks into you," she said, the caring tone of her voice both wonderful and terrible, "the man who made you feel trapped...that was Lørke, wasn't it?"

The moment of intimacy between them evaporated. No, more like—*ka-blooey!*—it exploded, all the old cage doors slamming shut inside him, walls going up, guards put on full alert. He should thank her for it. Long experience had taught him that it was way fucking easier not to feel a thing rather than deal with all the pain and defeat, all of the heart-wrenching disappointment that was surely heading his way from this woman.

"Yeah, you figured it out," he told her flatly. He paused a beat for emphasis, then shoved the three damning words past his lips. "Lørke's my father." He gestured at the thermos. "Drink that," he instructed, then turned hard on his heel and walked out.

CHAPTER TWENTY-ONE

Raymond leaned impatiently on his walking stick, his double-breasted camel hair topcoat buttoned tight against the evening's brassy weather, a pair of Aspinal leather gloves covering his hands like a second skin. Mürk and Rën were standing off to his right, Rën's incessant gum-chewing near driving him around the bend, and Tëer was kneeling on the weedy earth in front of an opening into the rocky cliff. They were all clandestinely gathered behind *The Cave Store* on Coast Boulevard in La Jolla Cove, so close to the Pacific Ocean that Raymond could hear the boom of the surf and feel the occasional mist of sea spray.

He glanced irritably at his Rolex, visible by virtue of the security lighting attached to the back of the store. It was after midnight. "Best you haven't called us out here for naught, son." Raymond had just been about to get a leg over with a lush sort from his polo club when he'd received Tëer's message.

Tëer gestured at the machine on the ground in front of him. "Subterranean vibrations are registerin' on the meter, so the elevator should be movin'."

Hidden just inside the cliff face were elevator doors—

supposedly one of the secret passageways of the Underground Om Rău. So, yes, fancy that, the creatures did exist. It'd been quite the kerfuffle getting that information out of the demonic mother of his children; Ÿavell apparently feared being reacquired by some chap named Lørke, a demon she'd escaped from some years back.

It'd been another scrap persuading the old gal to reveal the whereabouts of the doorways into the Om Rău's underground den. His leg was still feeling a bit out of sorts from that violent confrontation. 'Struth, he found fisticuffs to be dreadfully barbaric, but Ÿavell's pure Om Rău bloodlines lent her a certain immunity to his power. However, that was neither here nor there. The information had been acquired; it just remained to be seen if it was outdated or not. Tëer had been watching this entrance for twelve days and nights, and had seen no comings and goings.

Tëer wearily scratched the black flame tattoo on his left jaw with the backs of his fingers, his young face looking knackered from his long stint of vigilant camping out. "They're probably just comin' from really deep in the—"

There was a metallic *clank* of an elevator coming to a stop, then the *shish* of doors sliding open.

Tëer hopped to his feet and moved to Raymond's left side.

Two men stepped through the rocky doorway, both of them tall, muscled, wretchedly soiled, and dressed in ill-fitting dark clothing. One had fiery red hair and several safety pins stuck through his earlobes. The other had black hair and black teeth tattoos surrounding his enormous biceps *à la* Ÿavell, and like the tattoos of the men who'd kidnapped Toni, apparently. Both had the black eyes which marked them as definitely Om Rău.

Well, bully for Ÿavell. The old broad had been correct.

"Tally-ho, mates," Raymond greeted them.

The two came to a dead halt, their surprise at finding four strangers standing there turning into shock when they noted the black flame tribal tattoos on Mürk, Rën, and Tëer.

"Who the fuck are you?" Red Hair demanded, flashing a

steel tongue stud in the process. "And how the fuck do you know about this portal?"

"A little Om Răú birdie told us." Raymond smiled, sorely tempted to pull out his handkerchief and press it over his nose; the two smelled atrocious.

Red Hair slitted his lids. "What the fuck do you want?"

"Such language, lad." Raymond *tushed*. "But, yes, let's crack on with matters." He planted his walking stick firmly in front of him and leaned on it with overlapped hands. "Nearly a fortnight ago some of you blokes nicked a Dragon female from Scripps Memorial Hospital. Strawberry blonde hair, blue eyes, height about five-five."

Red Hair scratched his crotch. "She got big titties?"

Rën stepped forward, a hot, territorial aggression boiling off him.

Toni was Rën's by right of him being Boian's eldest son, and the lad evidently didn't care to hear his woman's attributes being discussed. Perhaps from this Om Răú's personal knowledge of them? Raymond nearly sighed. Rën's temper could be quite annoying at times. If Raymond had his druthers he'd pair Toni with Mürk instead, but the genetic muck-up such a coupling would produce made that impossible.

Raymond held up a staying hand to Rën. "She would be the one, yes."

"So." Red Hair drew a battered flask out of his jacket pocket. "What about her?"

"You blokes took her erroneously, old tosspot. She's ours." Raymond let another smile curve his lips. "And we want her back."

Red Hair shrugged. "Shit happens, Pops. 'Fraid you're gonna hafta live with the screw up." He took a pull on his flask. "That girl's too much of a fuckable twinkie to give her up."

Rën snarled.

The black-haired Om Răú sniggered and reached for his buddy's flask.

Red Hair jerked it out of his reach.

"*Or*," Raymond countered in a steely tone, "you and I could negotiate a trade for her."

The black-haired Om Ră
u tried to take the flask again. A shoving-slapping-hitting match ensued, which ended in Black giving Red a hard purler to the face and then seizing the coveted flask.

Growling, Red swiped a hand across his bloody mouth. "No way a cum-chugger like you has anything I'd want to trade for."

"No?" Raymond raised his hand, palm out. He generally didn't use such theatrics when activating his power, but he wanted to make right certain these two gobbins understood who had the true negotiating power here. "How about your continued good health?" He blasted a shock of energy off his hand.

The two Om Rău shot backward, hit the rocky cliff, and rebounded. Stumbling forward, they convulsed for several moments, then stood in place, blinking and twitching. The supernatural red light in Black's eyes pulsed in and out steadily, while Red, who Raymond was beginning to discern was more humanoid, tamped down the glow in his own eyes.

"You psychotic dickend," Red hissed, "back the fuck off. We don't have her. It's the Vârcolac who took her. I just *seen* her."

"Vârcolac?" Raymond snapped his brows down. "Are you under the assumption I'm soft in the head, boy? Vampires have been extinct for centuries."

"Well, then, you've been misinformed." Without warning, Red caught Black a perishing smacker on the jaw.

The poor sod, still unsteady on his feet, crashed to the dirt, his arms and legs sprawling.

Red snatched the flask out of Black's hand. "They live underground, same as us, but in their own part. They're just real good at keeping themselves hidden from people up here, is all."

"That's a load o' shite," Rën bit out. "I *saw* the man at the hospital who took our woman. He had black eyes and the same kind of tattoos on his forearms that your knobber friend here has on his arms. That makes him an Om Rău."

"I ain't lying, jizzbeard, so you can go plow yourself up the ass. The cocksucker you saw at the hospital was a Brun, and he's Vârcolac, sure enough. Just a Half-Rău."

Half-Rău? Raymond deepened his frown. How was that possible? "Vârcolac and Om Rău can't interbreed."

Red shrugged. "Guess it's what you'd call an amolly...animally...."

"An anomaly," Raymond provided drolly.

"That's it." Red chugged the rest of whatever was in the flask

Raymond compressed his lips, his patience growing thin under this convoluted run of turnabouts. His own progeny were Half-Rău, but a mixture of *Fey* and Om Rău. He knew what to expect from that combination, but didn't have the foggiest notion what sort of creature would come from pairing an Om Rău with a vampire. "Will *they* negotiate with us?" he pressed.

Red dragged his sleeve across his mouth. "No way, Pops. Those Vârcolac ain't givin' up their pussy for nuttin. They protect their women good, too. Seven Dragons those bloodsuckers have gotten ahold of, and we've only been able to steal one."

Raymond stiffened. These ruddy Vârcolac had succeeded in obtaining *seven* Dragon females? How in botheration had he missed this? He gripped his walking stick in a rigid fist. Well, shame on him for not paying sufficient attention to the possibility of competitors while waiting for the two eldest boys to come of age. His full attention was engaged now, however. "You wouldn't happen to be privy to where the Vârcolac's portals are, would you, dear boy?"

Red stepped warily to the side as Black finally managed to hoist himself to his feet. "Naw, not topside. But there's a way into the Vârcolac side from our town. If you wanted to try and snatch the twinkie yourselves, I could take your dickfucks here"—Red gestured at Rën, Mürk and Tëer—"down into Oţărât. That is," he hooded his eyes, "for a price."

"Dare I ask what that might be?" Raymond drawled.

"Ten Dragon females."

"Exorbitant," Raymond countered. "Ten Dragon females for only *one* in exchange. That wouldn't make sound business sense on my part, would it?"

Red showed his dirty teeth in a smug smile. "But, see, the big tittie one's special to you." He tapped two fingers to his temple, presumably indicating his mind. "My own little birdie told me that."

It seemed that Red's more human lucidity had the potential to be a proper pain in the posterior, too. "Very well," Raymond agreed. Not the best of all situations, but he didn't exactly have an alternative, not short of outright war. These Underground Om Rău controlled the only access to Toni. "We have an accord, lad, save that ten Dragons will take some time to procure, and I want my woman now."

"You wanna pay in installments, okay, but no welshing, Pops." Red shoved the empty flask back into his jacket pocket. "And you *pay* whether you manage to swipe your bitch or not. You don't, and it's Lørke and Jøsnic who'll be coming after you, and your so-called bionic hand there won't do nuttin but make them laugh."

"I'm a man of my word," Raymond returned icily. "No need to tender threats."

"Come back in five days, then," Red said, "things are whack downstairs right now. Be here at midnight. And no guns. Bullets bounce off the walls down there and end up pegging the wrong guy in the uglies." Red turned to smirk at Mürk, Rën, and Tëer. "Hope you ass-pounders like the heat." Cackling, he started off.

Raymond's voice stopped them. "What's your name, boy?"

"I'm Tøllar." He smacked Black on the shoulder. "This is Ejøhn. Oh, and in case you get any ideas about going it alone." Tøllar jerked his chin at the opening in the cliff face. "That elevator will blow a guy's Beaver Cleaver off in nine different directions, he operates it wrong." Tøllar grabbed the black-haired Ejøhn and pulled him toward the street, more of his maddening cackling floating back to them.

"Wretched creatures," Raymond murmured as he watched the two Underground Om Răude saunter off.

Mürk crossed his thick arms over his chest. "They're goin' to try and snuff us down there, you know that."

"Let 'em fuckin' try," Rën bristled. "They can't."

"Yeah, but it'll make for one ballache of a mission."

Raymond fingered the lion's head on his walking stick. "I'd hardly send you three to deal with those blighters without some of my choicer enchantments to aid your endeavors." He glanced at Rën. "You, in fact, will be using one of my most powerful concoctions on Toni. She'll be an obedient and devoted piece under the influence of it, lad. You just make bloody well certain she looks at you, and *only* you, right after you inject her with it. Do you hear?" The lion's head bit into his gloved palm. "By God, if you bugger up this part, Rën, the entire plan will go all to cock."

CHAPTER TWENTY-TWO

Kimberly scribbled frantically on a yellow legal pad, occasionally referring to the four huge law books open in front of her on the library table. Inspiration was really hitting now. The article was going to be great, even if she was more likely to give birth to a Chihuahua, or anything else, for that matter, than ever get it published from down here. Still, the distraction was helpful, allowing a side part of her brain to work the key card problem; Toni had sent word to Kimberly that her first attempt to steal a card had been a bust. And now Toni was laid up in bed from having Lørke go to serious fist-city on her.

That left Kimberly options like, well...

...drugging Sedge, although she only had access to OTC meds that might kill him in overdose.

...or doing some kind of outlandish miner-sixty-niner sexual position to render him stupefied, although that would be suspicious, considering that she hadn't slept with the jerk since Toni had been kidnapped.

...or outright begging, which would be completely transparent, not her style, and probably not worth it, anyway.

None of these options was, in truth. Fact was, she'd never

actually *seen* a key card on her husband's person.

She wouldn't have put it past him to have decided to keep his own card locked up in a safe somewhere, far away from her. Large didn't equal stupid when it came to Sedge. She wasn't sure how she felt about him outsmarting her in this area. Either filled with a boatload of respect or a pathological need to kick his ass. Anyway....

Back to business, working other options. She flipped a page in one of the law books and read intently. She had to hand it to good ol' Pollyanna, Hannah Banana had stocked the library extremely well with volumes that only Kimberly would use.

"I have to talk to you," a voice told Kimberly in an underbreath.

Kimberly popped her head up to find Beth's pretty face only inches from hers.

The clothing designer's blue eyes were alive with excitement. "I need to show you something."

"Oh, really?" Kimberly eased back in her chair, her eyebrows inching upward. "What would that be: your new fall line?"

"No." Beth said the one word succinctly, as if Kimberly were just learning English. "This has to do with what we discussed at the tea party."

A surprise, and then some. The five Dragons had been lying low for the seven days since their first meeting with Toni, all doing the "act casual" thing until someone could produce a key card. Beth was the last person, besides Hannah, that Kimberly would've expected to approach her.

Kimberly looked Beth up and down, not bothering to hide her suspiciousness. "I didn't think you'd found your Zen place about our plans."

"Well, I have." Beth's lips curled inward, her chin tightening slightly: a different look for her. "Thanks to my husband's utter lack of help with the matter."

Kimberly jerked forward, her heart stumbling out of rhythm. "Crap, Beth. You *told* Arc about what we're up to."

"I didn't give him specifics," Beth returned tartly. "But I figured...well, I thought that if we could get our men to approach Roth about our demands, then we could avoid a lot of hullabaloo."

Kimberly snorted. "They're not going to do that."

"No," Beth agreed quietly, her eyelashes floating downward. "Arc and the other men pretty much held the company line about them not having any power, just like you said they would." She pressed a slender hand to her brow. "I'm trying not to feel too disappointed with Arc over that. I understand that the Vârcolac history has been very tragic, and that the people of this community have learned to band together around their leadership because of that, but...." Dropping her hand, she trailed into a sigh.

"Changes are a'comin'," Kimberly murmured.

Beth met Kimberly's gaze, a fierceness in her blue eyes that Kimberly never would've guessed the too-sweet-to-be-true woman could manage. "They just expect *us* to do all the work," Beth accused, her cheeks blooming. "We're expected to adapt to *their* ways, to learn *their* culture. We're forced to give up everything, and they don't give up a danged thing."

Wow, whatever level of asshole'ness Beth's normally devoted husband had sunk to, thank you, stars above. Kimberly now had a definite ally. She smiled at Beth. "Welcome to the light side of the Force, my padawan."

Beth drew a quick breath, a look of satisfaction flashing across her gaze. Planting her hands on the tabletop, she leaned forward, putting her face right into Kimberly's again. "So, do you want to do this thing, or what? Because if you do, then you need to get your butt over to my house right now so I can show you the email I received from *Alex Parthen*, a man claiming to be Toni's brother."

Kimberly shot to her feet so fast she nearly stumbled out of her shoes.

They made it to the Costache residence in under five minutes, Beth locking the front door behind them. "Arc's working and the kids are at preschool. Over here..." She led Kimberly to a desk situated in a cubby off the living room. "Apparently, this Alex Parthen is some sort of computer genius. He hacked into our system to get to me, if you can believe it."

"I can't," Kimberly said as she sat in the desk chair. Cleeve kept the community on a constantly changing network of cables that was—supposedly—impossible to breach. "Maybe someone inside the community sent this email to test how serious we are about raising Cain, you know, to see how we'll respond to it."

Beth surprised Kimberly with a harshly exhaled *Ha!* "Look me in the eye, Kimberly, and tell me that for *one minute* your husband has taken your ability to cause trouble seriously. I know Arc hasn't."

Kimberly twisted her lips. "You make a good point."

Beth reached over Kimberly's shoulder and grasped the computer mouse. "Alex told me a person sending him emails in Toni's name was using the same small, private IP address as mine."

Huh. So Cleeve had failed to keep up his ruse as Toni, had he? Funny, he'd kept Kimberly's family bamboozled for three years by claiming that she'd gone back into the Peace Corps, working in Comoros, Africa, a country that wasn't even as big as Rhode Island. *So, gee, I can't email too often, guys, being in the middle of nowhere and all, but I'm doing such amazing work for these poor unfortunates....*

Beth brought up the email from Toni's brother. "He wants to know if I have any information about his missing sister. He sounds really worried about her."

"I can imagine." Kimberly read the email, but Beth had already summarized the main points.

"So what do you think?" Beth asked breathlessly.

Kimberly swiveled in the chair to look up at Beth. Something about the polite, but urgent tone of the email smacked as very real. "Genius may be understating matters for this Alex guy."

Beth giggled, her expression bright and eager again.

Kimberly bounced the desk chair back on its sturdy springs. "And I'm thinking if Toni's brother can hack Cleeve's computer system, then I bet he can help us circumvent the key code boxes." She waggled her eyebrows. "We need to tell him about—"

"Wait a minute," Beth stopped her. "We can't divulge the community's security system."

Kimberly stopped bouncing. "What did *you* plan on doing with this email? Just tell this Alex fella, 'Hey, pal, don't worry, Toni's okay, she's just locked away in an underground bunker for vampires, but she'll be home for a visit as soon as she squeezes out a puppy, so chill your nuts.'"

Beth's forehead pleated.

Kimberly exhaled a laugh. "I'm kidding—about the vampire part, at least." Who would believe her anyway?

"You know the Vârcolac history of discovery. Being found out would be hugely problematic for the people around here, including my own children."

"No one's going to find out where we are," Kimberly assured Beth. "Even if it turns out Alex can tell us how to crack the code box, he couldn't use the information to breach an entrance himself to get to us. He doesn't know where our entrances are, any more than we do."

Beth mulled that over for a moment. "I suppose you're right," she said, chewing her bottom lip. "One of us needs to stay down here, though."

Kimberly straightened the chair, planting her feet on the floor. "Are you kidding? Do you have any idea how much backlash there's going to be?"

Beth spread her hands. "We promised the other Dragons that none of the husbands would get hurt," she reasoned. "You won't get them to escape topside unless a go-between stays behind to email a message if one of the husbands' blood-need gets too severe."

"Shit." Kimberly clasped her brow between the stretch of her thumb and forefinger. Beth was probably right; if they assured the husbands' wellbeing from the get-go that would help shut down possible complaints. "Okay," she sighed. "I'll stay." So much for the happy reunion she'd planned to have with her parents.

"No. You're the fantastic bluffer, remember? You'll be needed topside to negotiate with Roth." Beth drew in a breath that swelled her breasts. "I'll be the one to do it."

Kimberly dipped her chin, eyeing Beth askance. "Are you sure?" Beth seemed more like the type of woman to get *out* of the kitchen when things got too hot.

Beth's throat worked around a swallow, but her nod was firm. "Yes. This is something I need to do."

Chapter Twenty-Three

Toni barely made it out of Aunt Ælsi's with her hand still attached to her wrist. Everyone in the morning coffee crowd had been determined to grab it, pat it sympathetically, and ask how she was doing, all the while *tut-tutting* over the fading three-day-old bruise on her jaw. She didn't think she'd ever been engulfed in so much genuine niceness and affection before. It'd made her feel glad she'd left her room. She still felt like warmed over hell, but hadn't wanted to put off visiting Dev in the hospital another day.

She was now strolling along Main Street, surrounded by Vinz, Gábor, and the two warriors whose names she'd forgotten before: Jeddin and Breen. Jacken was conspicuously absent, as he had been ever since he'd ordered her to finish her juice, then all but bolted from her bedroom.

She should be glad for it. *Thrilled*, even. Between him manhandling her during the letter-opener incident, his stinginess with *The African Queen*, and his overall rude behavior at Garwald's, she should welcome a break from his oh-so-stellar personality.

But the truth was, she kind of missed him.

She nearly groaned. Dear God, if she was developing feelings for that man, she might as well hike to the highest point in the cave and leap off. It didn't make any sense for her to fall for a man like Jaćken. Dark and smoldering Dev? Yes. Thomal? Christ, who wouldn't with that amazing ass? Detective John Waterson with his sexy smile and even sexier kisses? He was absolutely a sensible candidate. Not an ill-tempered, black-eyed, tank of a man, who, oh, incidentally, claimed to be a half-demon, half-vampire.

If she didn't know better, she'd think she'd suffered permanent brain damage from her concussion.

Or maybe it made *too* much sense to fall for a man like Jaćken, and that scared the crap out of her. There was no denying she wanted to jump his bones and plunder his virginity all to hell like the worst sort of pirate wench. There was also no getting around the connection she kept forging with him whenever they had their run-ins. Each time, she found a new similarity, whether it was knowing what it felt like to be trapped and alone, or always feeling like a freak, or the big one, being raised by rejects for the Father of the Year award, or not raised, as in her case.

If only he hadn't smiled at her at Garwald's; that's what had set off this whole lovesick thing. It hadn't even been a friendly smile, but he'd just looked so…different, the hard angles of his face softening, small lines appearing at the corners of his eyes, years peeling away to reveal the young man he must've been once. Or maybe the man he *would've* been, had he not been raised in such horrific circumstances.

Or maybe…the man he could be…with the right woman.

Yes, excellent. That was exactly what she needed to be thinking right now.

Oh, for Pete's sake. A girl didn't get together with a man in order to save him. A woman fell for a guy who truly understood her on a soul-deep level…a guy who called her things like "whack job" and "nagging shrew" because he knew she wasn't perfect and was totally fine with it. A girl flipped over a man she trusted to do something really sweet like show up in her room with a thermos of juice, even if he'd blown it the first time around, a guy who made her feel safe, even when he looked a little lost himself.

A girl fell in love with a man whose mere presence did a whole lot of saving her.

Fall in love...Oh, God. She pressed a hand to her forehead and moaned. She was in real trouble here.

"Hey, Toni," Vinz set a gentle palm on her shoulder. "You all right?"

She stopped walking. "Yes, I, um, was just thinking...." About what it'd felt like to have Jacken stroke her hair. His touch had been inexpert and unsure, clumsy. In a word, *perfect*.

"Are you having flashbacks about what happened with Lørke?" Vinz's brow furrowed. "I don't want you to worry about that, okay. The men and I aren't going to let anything happen to you. Just stick with us."

Yes, well, that'd been the main stipulation for her to be allowed outside of the mansion again: no more escaping her Protection Team, definitely no more going back into Stânga Town. "Thank you, Vinz." She smiled faintly. "I know."

They continued on to the hospital.

Once inside, Gábor, Jeddin, and Breen took up posts around the building while Vinz led her to Dev's room. Toni stopped in the doorway, shock bringing her up short.

The patient looked remarkably good.

Dev was sitting up in bed and chatting with his sister, Luvera, that sweet-natured waitress from Garwald's, his dark flannel pajama top doing wonders to emphasize his robust frame and healthy complexion. There wasn't a cannula in his nose to give him extra oxygen or even an IV line.

Toni frowned. How bizarre. She'd had a close-up view of the severity of Dev's wound, and he shouldn't be looking this good only three days after his injury. The punch she'd taken to her jaw, as bad as it'd been, had been way less debilitating than Dev's injury, yet he looked a hundred times better than she did.

"Hey!" Dev's eyes brightened when he saw her in the doorway. "Come on in, Toni. Have you met my sister, Luvera?"

Luvera turned to smile at her, her eyes the same dazzling silver as Dev's and her hair a similar rich black. The woman was stunning, even dressed in a baggy sweatshirt and a long, shapeless skirt. *Sheesh*, spend enough time in Ţărână and a normally pretty girl would start feeling like the Thing that had crawled out from under a bridge.

"Yes, we've met. Hi, Luvera." Toni walked forward, stopping at the side of Dev's bed. "She's been campaigning for you."

"Has she?" Dev flashed his sister an affectionate look. "That's cool. Did she mention I can—Whoa." Dev's brows soared. "You smell different."

"Ah, yes, I'm wearing some kind of gross mud now." She hadn't been thrilled about having to slap on that nasty stuff behind her ears. It was both sticky and tingly, but that had been Stipulation Two for going outside the mansion. "Here, I brought you this." She held up the coffee she'd purchased with some credits at Aunt Ælsi's. "A Mocha Frappuccino."

"Hey, thanks." Dev's expression turned wry as he accepted the to-go cup. "I…look like a Mocha Frappuccino guy, do I?"

"I don't know." She shrugged. "I just wanted to do something to thank you for saving my can."

Dev chuckled. "Well, it's such a nice can…." He took a sip. His eyebrows shot up. "This is straight black coffee."

She smiled warmly. "Is it?"

He chuckled again, the sound resonant and smoky. "Here's an idea. Why don't you check out my wound, Doc, and give me a thumbs up for getting out of here." He set his coffee cup on the tray attached to his bed. "Then you and I can go someplace private."

She laughed outright at that. *Get out of here.* The man was delusional. "Still vying for a medical examination from me, are you, Mr. Nichita? Well, you've already *had* one, buddy. Three days ago. In Stânga Town."

Dev frowned over that, then understanding lit his face. He threw back his head and whooped, his gold hoop earring catching the light. "You mean that nut-grab you pulled on me? Hell, I'd hardly call that a...now, wait just a second here.... I might be okay with that."

The group of them laughed together just as Dr. Jess bustled into the room.

"Well, sakes alive," the doctor's eyes danced, "how wonderful to see everyone in such high spirits. Ah! Dr. Parthen, how are you feeling?"

"Better, thank you."

"Excellent." Dr. Jess smiled cheerfully. "Please, stay and observe, then. I was just going to check Devid's injury. This will give you the opportunity to observe a vampire's healing abilities at their finest."

Toni blinked. A vampire's...?

"The Nichitas have some of the purest bloodlines in the community. Their powers of restoration are truly extraordinary." Dr. Jess wheeled over a cart full of medical paraphernalia. "Come closer, Dr. Parthen."

"Yes, come closer," Dev all but purred. His silver eyes latched onto her as he unbuttoned his flannel shirt and shrugged it off, baring the powerful muscles of his smooth chest.

Toni walked around the bed, suddenly feeling like she was moving in a trance, and stopped next to Dr. Jess. Every nerve in her body prickled with a strange anticipation of something huge about to happen.

Dr. Jess tugged on a pair of latex gloves.

"...gotta go," Luvera was saying. "Mom says she'll come by later to...."

The doctor carefully peeled the white square of bandage from Dev's shoulder, then set the dirty gauze on the cart.

Toni sucked in a painful breath.

"You see!" Jess exclaimed triumphantly. "Most Vârcolac would need to wear their stitches for a week, but Devid's can be taken out already."

Toni abruptly felt as if her feet were no longer in solid contact with the floor. Dr. Jess was right; the skin was completely closed beneath Dev's stitches. The wound was still red, yes, and somewhat swollen, but for the most part it looked like a laceration that'd been healing for two *weeks*, not three days. Toni's heart slipped somewhere down into the environs of her feet, and she swallowed so hard her throat made a noise. This had to be a trick, some kind of super-fancy, complicated FX. She'd seen Dev's wound, damn it, and it was a *biological impossibility* for an injury of that magnitude to have mended so quickly.

"Excuse me," she snapped, pushing past Dr. Jess. "I don't know what the hell you think you're trying to pull here, but it's not going to work." Snatching up a pair of latex gloves, she wrenched them on and bent close to Dev, exploring his shoulder with gentle fingers.

"Jesus Christ," Dev hissed.

A disquieting unease pressed the oxygen from her lungs. Dev's skin *was* repaired. Genuinely. Actually. No fake, no special effect. She straightened, hearing a low ringing in her ears.

And what about all of the time she'd spent with Dr. Jess in his lab three days ago? She hadn't been able to find a single fault or error in his methods.

And the unreal glow in Dev's eyes?

Thomal's impossible speed? The dragon tattoo on his back made of living tissue in the form of scales?

The supernatural red light in Lørke's eyes and his unbelievable endurance of electricity?

The palpable animal *something* that seemed to radiate off every man in this town?

She'd forced herself to ignore it all, to explain everything away as having been caused by a concussed brain, the stress of captivity, and logic. But here before her sat irrefutable scientific evidence. It was impossible to speed up the human body's healing process, which meant that....

This was real.

Exhaling forcefully, she staggered backward a step, her gloved hands fisted at her sides. She met Dev's eyes, liquid mercury in a bottle. Incredible. *Impossible.*

Dev smiled, showing his...his.... "Yep, you got it now, don't you?" he said. "Finally, Toni. Gotta be some kind of record."

"No." She snapped off her latex gloves and threw them on the floor. "No!"

She turned and fled.

CHAPTER TWENTY-FOUR

"What now?" Jaćken grumbled at the sound of someone knocking on his bedroom door. He still had a mountain of paperwork to fill out about their clash with Lørke. Not exactly a sit-at-your-desk kind of guy, he'd procrastinated the job, and didn't want to be dealing with anyone's bullshit. Hoisting himself up from his chair, he stalked across his bedroom and yanked open the door. *Ah, crap.* He dropped his brows into a dark scowl: Toni and Vinz.

"What happened?" he bit out. Had Lørke attacked again? Usually, that dickhead needed some recovery time after taking on the voltage he had, not to mention several knife wounds, but Jaćken wouldn't have been surprised if Toni's strong scent had motivated Lørke toward more inhuman feats of dick-headedness. Besides, she looked really upset.

"She's having some kind of freakout." Vinz's tone was calm, although a subtle something in his expression suggested he'd rather be fighting a horde of Om Rău than dealing with a woman in a *mood*. "She took off like a bat out of hell from the hospital, and I gave chase. She claims she wasn't trying to escape, and," he shrugged, "I believe her. Such a move would've been too stupid for a woman like her."

"What set her off?"

"Beats the shit out of me."

"I'm standing right here," Toni remarked churlishly. "You can ask your stupid questions directly to me."

Vinz shot Jaćken a look. "She, um, insisted on talking to you."

He raised his eyebrows. *Me*?

"Yes." Toni took a step closer to the door. "Right now, Jaćken."

"Ah, okay, then…." Vinz backed up. "You've got her, then, sir. Right?"

No—*shit,* no—he didn't *have* her. He'd spent most of the last three days making all kinds of threats to himself not to get stuck alone with Toni again, especially in a bedroom. But Vinz was already heading off and—*double-shit*—Toni was pushing past him into his room.

He cursed in an undertone, then shut the door and leaned back against it. "Okay, so what's up?"

She faced off with him from the middle of his room, feet braced, hands planted on her hips, her eyes fiery with the kind of stubborn determination that never seemed to work out well for him. His stomach did a slow roll over and he fought against the urge to swallow. Last time she'd worn that expression, he'd ended up spilling his guts about why he liked old movies. Yeah, this had *bad* written all over it.

"I need to see your fangs, Jaćken."

He straightened with a snap, the tips of his ears flaming. Jesus, "bad" did not begin to cover just how *not good* this was. "No, Toni. *Hell no*, in fact."

"Jaćken—"

"Go." He jerked open his door again. "Out of my room. Right now. This isn't up for debate."

She paused a moment, then briskly crossed his room.

Thank God. She wasn't going to put up a fight. He almost sighed in relief over the unexpected gift, although a part of him felt an odd disappointment, too. He was starting to get used to her pushing him, kind of felt like he...needed it on some level, to be more himself. Most days, it was just too easy to remain locked behind the hard shell of anger he'd erected around himself too many years ago to remember.

The last three days especially, he'd been on a downward spiral. He'd thrown three knives at his own father and gotten into a knock-down-drag-out brawl with the man, and even though he hated the bastard, he was never sure how he was supposed to feel about shit like that. So, he just didn't. Numbness was even better than anger.

Yeah, he didn't have to be Dr. Phil to realize that this habit was a throwback from his Oṭărât days, where he'd just walked through life on autopilot, numbly waiting for the next fist to fall, the next insult to be slung, the next disappointment to crash down on him. He'd learned to stop bothering with things like hope or with trying to find moments of joy or fun.

Until Fađe would draw him out.

If anyone could relate to what it was like to be born from one of the town's biggest assholes, it was Fađe.

Lørke was a huge asshole, no doubt about that; as one of the last two pure-bred Om RăU males in the world—the other being, Jøsnic, his co-leader of Oṭărât—Lørke redefined concepts like merciless and ruthless. But somewhere in Lørke and Jøsnic's fucked-up Om RăU brains they at least recognized the value of the women, especially the Dragons, and focused their brutality on the men.

Not Bøllven.

He was the cruelest, most vicious son of a bitch in Oṭărât when it came to the females, preying on them in particular...and Fađe was his daughter. Her upbringing had been about as brutal as Jaćken's, and somewhere in the violence of their lives, they'd fostered a relationship out of their shared misery. It was probably no exaggeration to say that, if not for the care of Fađe and his mother, the two women in his life, Jaćken would've disappeared so far behind his defenses there would've been no coming back.

And now here was Toni—infuriating, funny, smart, so damned beautiful—the only woman in a long time who could make him want to do stupid, asinine shit like just talk. A woman he was forced to push away. A woman who was leaving right now....

Toni grabbed the door out of his hand and slammed it shut, her eyes glinting defiantly. "Here's the thing, Jacken. I think I believe all this stuff about vampires and demons now. Okay? All right? But I need more evidence; I *want* more. Are you listening to me? And everyone says you're the only one who can control his fangs voluntarily."

Oh, he was feeling something now. Everything. Too much. He parted his lips as he stared down into Toni's eyes, feeling their probing effect deep in his belly. He did want to unsheathe his fangs in front of this woman, wanted it more than life, to relish the throbbing hunger he'd feel, the raw pulse of desire. Which meant he was heading up shit creek fast *sans* paddle. "Look—" He edged around her and crossed to his wet bar, putting some much-needed space between them. "It's a bad idea, Toni, I'm telling you. Fangs...showing you my fangs would be like an intimacy between us."

"Oh, for Pete's sake. Your fangs extrude when you fight, don't they? That's not intimate."

"It's different with a woman. Just because I *can* elongate my fangs without the usual stimulations, doesn't mean I don't feel anything." *Especially* with you.

She crossed her arms tightly in front of her and glowered at him for a small eternity. When he didn't budge, her lips moved in a silent curse. "Fine." Spinning around, she grabbed the doorknob. "I'll just go ask one of your brothers to show me."

He didn't know what happened. One second he was watching her pull open the door, and the next he was *at* the door, slamming it shut to keep her from leaving his room to go find one of his punk-ass brothers. He stared down at her with burning eyes, his breath rushing in and out of his nostrils like steam hissing from an overheated pot. A raw possessiveness he'd never felt before ate a hole straight through the bottom of his stomach.

"It's okay," she assured him quietly, *she* all of a sudden the calm one. "I'll be very clinical about it." She peeled his hand off the door and led him toward his desk. "The total doctor at all times." She placed her palms on his shoulders, pushing him down into his desk chair, then stepped between the vee created by his splayed thighs.

A low, guttural growl broke from his throat.

"It's okay," she repeated, and bent over him, her blouse gaping open to gift him with the most spectacular view of full, soft cleavage that existed on earth, making everything most-fucking-definitely *not* okay. The armrests of his chair were shaped like a cello's neck and he curled his fingers around the fancy swirls, gripping them hard. He wasn't going to make it through this.

"Tilt your head back," she directed, ducking her own head at the same time to peer into his mouth.

A rivulet of sweat glided down between his shoulder blades.

"I'm going to touch you now." She edged his upper lip back with her thumb.

The gentleness of her touch rocked him down to the seat of his pants. He slid his eyes away from her, his heart trying to break past the cage of his ribs.

She straightened a bit, checking eyes with him, her fingertips resting at his lip. "They're hollow."

He had to swallow twice before he could speak. "They're supposed to be hollow. That's where the Fiinţă comes from."

"Oh. Yes, that makes sense." Her breasts moved up and down beneath her blouse. "Can you elongate them now?"

A sensation crept up the back of his tight throat. He wasn't sure what it was: eagerness, fear, anticipation, alarm…lust? *Definitely* that, for blood. For *her*. "I think…I'm back to thinking this is a bad idea." He latched his gaze onto the long, elegant vein in her neck, counting each pulse beat there.

"Do you want to smell me," she asked softly, "to make it easier?"

No. His heart thumped. *Yes.*

Without waiting for an answer, she lifted her wrist to his nose. He went rigid as the perfume of her blood slammed into him like brass knuckles to the stomach, a deep moan spilling out of his chest. He'd been somewhat safe from her scent ever since she'd started wearing the mud, able to tolerate her...barely. But this close she smelled *exceptional*, like life's essential elements, tangy earth and sweet water and crystal air.

Turning his head toward her, he nuzzled the soft skin of her inner wrist, pulling her scent deeply into his lungs then exhaling it past his lips. He began to shake with the feverish urge to feed on her. And then there they were. His fangs slid out of his gums slick as ivory, pulsing to the steady drumbeat of his heart. No...*hers*.

"Oh, my God," she gasped. She leaned in closer, somebody help him, and gently parted his lips. Exploring one of his fangs with her thumb and forefinger, she tested how deeply rooted it was, how sharp.

She tried to be clinical, he'd give her credit for that, but there was just no getting around the effect her touch had on him. Her hand was electricity itself, the crackling heat of it passing right from her into him, racing the length of his limbs and then landing in his crotch. Thunder roared in his ears as blood rushed in the direction of his cock. *Oh. Fuck.* He braced himself against the inevitable agonizing back-surge that would come when that river of desire hit the dam which was built into every unmated Vârcolac's plumbing.

When it hit, the pain of it forced a short howl out of him. He'd never felt anything so awful—and good—in his life.

Toni straightened and stared down on him.

He stared back at her, breathing as heavily as if he'd just been fighting for his life with an Om Răul. His body burned with a dangerous combination of lusts: blood hunger and the primitive desire to pound savagely between her legs. He flexed his fingers around the armrests of his chair to keep from grabbing for her.

One bite, *one*, and then he could be inside her.

"Your fangs are *real*." She looked at him like, yes, Santa Claus did exist, but he and his elves really made Snuff Films in their workshop instead of toys. She spun on her heel and marched for his wet bar, plunking her elbows on the countertop and then burying her face in her hands.

He stared at her profile for several long seconds. "What...now?" Chrissake, was that his voice? It sounded like he'd dredged it up from a dungeon.

"I need a drink." She abruptly walked around to the other side of the bar and crouched down, rummaging noisily through the cupboards. "Damn it, don't you have any booze around here?"

"There's, uh, beer in the mini fridge." He shifted carefully in the chair, very aware of the blood still loitering in the vicinity of his cock.

She thrust rigidly to her feet, her hands landing on her hips again. "That's *it*?"

"I don't drink hard alcohol."

She scowled at him. "Life as I know it just sort of went *sayonara*, Jaćken. I need something a little stronger than beer."

Yeah, okay, from here on out, he'd keep an emergency bottle of J&B stashed away because this totally sucked. She—

Whoa, something just happened to her expression. She was eyeing him with distinct speculation in her gaze now, her eyes aimed right at his...his *mouth*! He gave in to a spurt of alarm. If he'd had any hair on his body, every follicle would've been standing on end. As it was, his neck hairs were at full salute.

"You know what," she mused. "If I'm heading down the booby hatch, anyway, I might as well go all the way, right?" She started toward him at a rapid clip.

He leapt to his feet, the chair crashing to the floor behind him, his feet tangling in the rungs as he scrambled to get away from her. He backed up at a near run.

She matched him step for step, pursuing him right into the corner.

He pressed his spine into the wall, even going up on his toes to get as far away from her as possible.

"Do you mind telling me," he croaked out, "what's going on?"

"Bite me." Not as in, *screw you*, but in the good way.

His mouth went slack.

"The Dragons said that Ființă gives pleasure, and I want to know what it's like."

Sweat rolled into his eyelashes and he blinked at it, struggling to make some kind of coherent sound come off his vocal chords. A denial would be good at this point.

"Do you realize how long it's been since I've felt any sort of pleasure?" she came at him in a tone that sounded accusing, like *he* should be in the penalty box for that.

"I haven't had a boyfriend," she went on, still hard and attacking, "for a year, and I had to *fake* with him!"

Did he want to know about that? No. Maybe a little. The suck-o part, at least.

"Jaćken—"

"Stop talking," he barked at her. "Vârcolac don't have flings, Toni. I can't just…give you pleasure without bonding to you. Permanently." Never had a single word sounded so fatal.

"Okay." No sooner had she spoken than her cheeks pinkened. She looked like she wanted to glance over her shoulder to see who'd actually said that.

His mouth, meanwhile, had dropped into full fly-catcher mode again. "Have you gone insane?!"

She offered up a laugh that cracked at the end. "I think we've already determined that."

"Jesus, even if I wanted to take advantage of your temporary idiocy, I couldn't." He worked his jaw once. "I've taken a vow of celibacy."

"You've taken a…? *Why*?" She stared at him with a whole lot of *you dolt* showing in her expression.

He clenched his teeth briefly. "Because that was the only way I could stay in Ţărână, that's why. Half-Rău bloodlines like mine don't mix well with Vârcolac DNA—or with Dragons', either, for that matter. Peak 12 skyrockets in both situations. So we three Brun Brothers were allowed to live here only if we promised never to let our tainted lineage into the community. We took the damned vow, of course."

"But...?" Her blonde brows closed in on each other. "Can't you just agree not to have children?"

"Mistakes happen, even with Vârcolac males, who can scent their mate's fertile time. And vasectomies screw up our testosterone, for some weird-ass reason that even Dr. Jess can't figure out. So, that's it." He chopped his hand through the air. "No women."

She hesitated still.

He could tell that she was trying to be brave about it and accept what he was saying, but her eyes gave her away. Their blue depths were clouded with such an unbearable disappointment that now *he* wanted a bottle of J&B. Not to drink, but to crack over his head and escape this totally fucked situation.

He glanced away, his voice dropping into his chest. "You once accused me of hating women. I *don't*, Toni. Not by a long shot. But because I can never be with one, it's just too painful to be around them." He looked at her again. "Can you understand that?"

"I—" A small contraction of pain crossed her features and her voice dropped to a near whisper. "Very well. I won't bother you again." She grabbed the knob, but then just stared at the back of the door for a long moment. "You know, the same life of loneliness stretches ahead of me, too, Jacken. You may not think so, but it does." Her eyelashes moved against her cheeks. "I don't have anyone to love, either."

His throat filled with lead. He made himself say it, though. He had to concentrate like hell to form the words, but he did it. "There are tons of other men in this community, Toni, great men, who—"

"No." She turned her head to look at him, her eyes filled with such a tender ache that the floor dropped away from beneath his feet. "No other men." She walked out and closed the door gently in his face, leaving him with nothing to do but stare at the spot where she'd just been, his soul screaming the loss of her with a sudden, debilitating defeat.

CHAPTER TWENTY-FIVE

The scene was unreal.

Toni stood with her toes squishing in the sand and took it all in, feeling like she had no idea where she was, and not for the first time since her arrival in Ţărână. A tropical jungle and water cliffs in the middle of a cave half a mile beneath the earth's surface? *Come on.* How much more was she expected to take, really?

A beautiful white sand beach spread out before her, complete with palm trees, ferns, tropical plants, and moss covering a panoramic out-cropping of the cave wall. This lush greenery, all fake, of course, provided the backdrop for a spectacular array of waterfalls, fountains, and slides splashing cheerfully into pools of various shapes and sizes. Off to the right, several mini geysers spurted periodically, much to the delight of a group of squealing children. The whole scene could've been photo-shopped right off of a travel agency poster for the perfect Rio de Janeiro vacation, including the gorgeous, half-naked people frolicking about. Although the display of dragon tattoos among the blondes also gave it a new wave, live art exhibition feel.

Toni still couldn't quite get used to how incredible those

tattoos were. The dragon adorned the entire span of the back, shimmering green scales on the body and wings, red scales on the belly, claws, and mouth. The head arched over the left scapula, the wings extended out over the right, the tail curved down to the lower back, and the feet extended out to the left of the spine. The dragon had a fierce look to it, with its claws and teeth bared, but also elegance, the creature giving the impression of graceful flight.

"Amazing, huh?" Kasson popped up at her side, having just finished spreading their picnic blanket out on the sand. Shirtless, he was dressed in a pair of Reef flip-flops and a Billabong bathing suit. The outfit, along with the cowlick in his light brown hair, turned him into the epitome of the California surfer dude. Even his skin tone was surprisingly honey-colored, the result of being a Dragon rather than a Pure-bred, from what she understood.

"Maggie designed the Water Cliffs," he went on. "You know, the curly-haired one? She's the horticulturist. "

"Yes, I know Maggie."

"And her husband, Luken, built it for her…for the community. That's another one of the cool things about living here, Toni. When you put your skills to use, everyone really appreciates everything you do. Hey, look"—Kasson pointed toward the water—"there are the Costaches."

Toni turned. The whole family was by one of the kiddie pools. Beth was talking to a four-year-old girl, who was laughing and splashing in the water, while Arc, wearing green Hawaiian print trunks that perfectly matched the dragon on his back, was encouraging their two-year-old son to stick his toes in.

"See Beth's bathing suit?" Kasson's voice was suddenly right next to Toni's ear.

Uh, oh. She knew where *this* was going. Kasson had been so disappointed when she'd shown up for their lunch date at the Water Cliffs in nothing more exciting than a utilitarian one-piece Speedo and a sarong. Beth, on the other hand, was wearing a bikini of the kind Daisy Duke might've worn: faux jeans hot pants on the bottom and red-and-white checked mini halter on the top. The suit itself was sexy, but the body wearing it was what really made it hot.

"She might have another one of those in her shop," Kasson murmured.

Toni cut a sideways glance at him. "I wouldn't look as good in it as she does."

"Ho," Kasson enthused, dropping his gaze to her boobs, "yeah, you would."

She poked a finger under his chin to lift his attention back to her face. "I'm wearing the mud now, Kasson. You're supposed to be able to behave yourself."

His smile was boyishly charming, though the heated glitter in his gaze cancelled any illusion of immaturity. "That doesn't change the fact that I'm young and horny."

She exhaled a small laugh. "Direct and to the point. Commendable."

"Ah, well, then I should also tell you that I'm at least ten years younger than Dev. I have way more staying power, for sure." Kasson bobbed his eyebrows at her. "That's a good quality to have in a mate, right?"

"Okay, now you're just being rude." It was an effort to smile. The last thing she wanted to think about was a potential *mate*. Her heart was still tangled up over one man in particular…the one who'd snubbed her.

He was posted to one side of the Water Cliffs. Dressed in his black warrior gear and armed with the typical array of knives, Jacken was standing in parade rest, with his hands locked behind his back and his legs set in a wide stance, his head swiveling on his thick neck as he continuously scanned the vicinity. He looked like a boulder falling on him would merely bounce off. Up close, she knew that all of those hard muscles gave off more warmth than a cozy eiderdown quilt.

A rush of heat swamped her belly, followed by a stab of pain. Not in a million years would she have thought she'd end up wanting one of the men here, especially not Hard Face. Had she learned nothing from her long run of bad date choices? Evidently not, because here she was falling for the *one* man in Țărână who wasn't stumbling around on three legs after her. Or couldn't have her because of some foolish vow of—

Pop, pop, pop.

She startled at the strange noise. "What was—?"

"Get down!" Kasson tackled her to the ground and pancaked on top of her.

She *omphed* and cursed. "Jesus, what's going on?"

People started screaming.

Blowing sand out of her face, Toni craned her head up and scoured the Water Cliffs, her breath catching when she spotted an unfamiliar young man high up on one of the rocky overhangs. He was holding a rifle. Shirtless, he was sweating profusely, and—

An icy cold washed through her. Dear God, the guy had a creepy black flame tattoo on his jaw. Up close would he also have a sprayed pattern of dotted scars on his chest?

Her insides quailed. Good God, that was the guy from the murder scene two weeks ago with John Waterson. The *dead* guy!

Two more men materialized next to the supposedly-dead kid, one with spiky black hair, the other a tattoo-covered shaved head. Both were bare-chested, as sweaty as the kid, and also carrying rifles.

The maniac kid propped his rifle back against his hip and swept the crowd with another hailstorm of bullets like he was Scarface.

Pop-pop-pop-pop-pop-pop....

Bodies began to jerk and fall. Shouts rose to shrieks as Țărână's angelic family outing at the Water Cliffs turned into a panicked mob scene.

Kasson hopped off her body and pulled her to her feet. "Let's get to the mansion!" he yelled, urging her into a run toward—

Pop-pop. Two hits to the back and Kasson plowed face-first into the sand.

Toni screamed and dropped into a crouch next to Kasson, checking his injured back. There wasn't any blood.... The sound of pounding feet brought her head up. The spike-haired man and the bald one were racing at her, *directly* at her. Holy crap! This time she didn't hesitate as she had with Lørke. She leapt to her feet and raced for the gates of the Water Cliffs, picking up speed as she left the sand behind.

She barreled onto Main Street, running faster than she ever had in her life. Her lungs were soon on fire, the muscles in her legs screaming, but the sound of pursuit kept her feet moving even when she couldn't feel them anymore. *Jesus, please, just a few more—*

She cried out as something bit into the back of her leg. She tripped, righted herself, then went down hard, scraping her shins as she skidded onto her belly. Bright lights sparkled before her eyes and shards of electricity spiked under her skin. Groaning, she cranked her head around and looked at her leg. A dart was sticking out of her hamstring. Poison? She slumped back onto her face. *Oooooh.* Something weird was happening. Her body jerked and her brain clunked, like a car popping out of gear, control slipping from the driver.

A man's rough hand landed on her shoulder. And then she was being rolled over....

CHAPTER TWENTY-SIX

"Nyko!" Jaćken yelled into the mic of his headset. "Do you copy!?"

Only an ominous dead static answered him back. *Damn it to hell!* His brother was one of the warriors on guard duty today, but hadn't squawked a single heads-up warning about this incoming furball. Maybe for a really bad reason.

Growling, he forced his mind into a necessary blankness as he hurdled another of a growing pile of bodies in the sands of the Water Cliffs. Even if all these people were dead, his brother, too, he sure as shit couldn't think about it now.

He angled hard to the left, trying to cut off Skull from a headlong charge at Toni. Yeah, *Skull*. He recognized the prick who'd tried to punch his brains into La-La Land at Scripps Hospital, the guy Thomal had stabbed in the throat and supposedly killed. Jaćken rounded the corner onto Main Street and—

Spike Boy was pointing a rifle at Toni. Horror flipped a circuit in Jaćken's brain, switching everything to slowmo, the action before his eyes fragmenting into dozens of individual movie frames; Spike Boy pulling the trigger; a dart appearing at the back of her leg; Toni hitting the ground hard; Spike Boy grabbing her by the shoulder....

"You crotch stain! I killed your asshole buddy, now I'm gonna kill you!"

Spike Boy froze in the act of turning Toni over, his black eyes latching onto the man who'd just snarled that at him.

Fucking A! Jaćken almost shouted in relief. It was Thomal, roaring down from the sloped face of the cave wall.

Spike Boy's eyes flashed red and then he was up on his feet and launching himself at Thomal.

Thomal did his fast Dragon-thing, the image of his body blurring with his inhuman speed. And suddenly, he was whaling on Spike Boy with his fists. No knives, good man. Thomal remembered the Topside Om Rău bled acid.

His chest heaving, Jaćken slid down onto his knees next to Toni and rolled her over. Her eyes were slitted and glazed. *Crap!* What was in that dart?! "Stay with me, Toni," he panted.

Her pupils wiggled strangely, then her eyes snapped clear and stared fixedly at him.

"Just hang in there. I'm going to—"

She missiled herself against his chest, her legs clamping his waist and her arms linking around his neck.

He choked on his next breath. He couldn't have been more shocked if she'd just asked him to paint a daisy on her ass.

"Rën!" Skull shouted as he ran toward Spike Boy. "You ballsed it up, you chuffin' wanker!"

Jaćken staggered to his feet. "Holy motherfucker!" he hissed when Toni stuck her tongue in his ear. With no time to figure out what this newest shit-storm was, Jaćken just took off for the mansion, Toni locked firmly in his arms.

He didn't know how fast he ran; he wasn't aware of his legs anymore. The feel of Toni's luscious breasts jammed so closely against his chest that there wasn't a breath of space between them pretty much eclipsed every-damned-thing else in the whole world.

Thomal was soon tight on his heels.

Halfway there, a sexual purring noise started to come out of Toni that curled every little hair in his ear canals. He ran faster, the purring sound scaring the ungodly shit out of him.

"Hurry!" he shouted as Thomal took forever dicking with the key code box into the mansion. By the time he was blasting into the Main Parlor, Thomal right behind him, he was in a dead panic.

"Whoa!" Dev raised his hands when Jacken almost mowed him down. "Slow down, sir, I got a SITREP for you, okay. Things are chilling. The townsfolk are stuffed in the Drawing Room and the kitchen, upset but—"

Toni bit his earlobe, and his panic spiked to the ceiling. If she drew blood he was screwed to the hilt.

"Nyko's checked in through the main phone lines," Dev went on, oblivious to Jacken's frantic efforts to pry Toni off. "We're assholes and elbows with men down, but none are dead, only knocked—"

Something garbled came out of his mouth.

"Apparently, those guns were shooting *pellets*, not bullets. Our men chased those Topside Om Rău shitheads back into the Oṭărât tunnels to—"

He hauled in a huge breath. "*Get her the fuck off me!*" he belted out on the exhale.

Dev stopped talking, his mouth hanging open mid-sentence. The dipshit just stood there, though, he and Thomal both, staring like a couple of cows. Were they blind?

"Toni's been drugged and she's trying to—*ah!*" Air left his lungs in a rush as Toni started to grind her hips against him, forceful pelvic thrusts that made the polyethylene-like bathing suit she was wearing feel like nothing at all.

Dev shifted into high gear at that, leaping forward and grabbing Toni under the armpits. He tried to pull her off, but only managed to get the top half of her semi-levered loose. Her fingers were fisted firmly into the front of Jacken's shirt and her legs were locked around his waist like he was a runaway horse.

"Peel her hands off!" Jacken yelled at Thomal, staggering

forward as he was hauled about in the Dev-Toni tug-o-war.

Thomal didn't make it in time. Jaćken's shirt ripped, splitting all the way down the middle.

Toni made a small sound of pleasure at the sight of his bare chest, and then she did let go…but only long enough to turn and punch annoying Dev right in the face.

"Ow!" Dev barked, blood squirting from his nose.

Toni rounded on Jaćken again and charged.

Jaćken backpedaled crazily. "Get Dr. Jess!" The carnivorous look in Toni's eyes meant that he was in deep shit and heading deeper. "Have him bring a tranquilizer or—*Jesus!*"

Toni jumped on him, slamming against his chest and fastening onto him again. He went flying backward, his feet slipping out from under him until the backs of his knees hit the edge of one of Roth's dainty parlor chairs. His ass came down hard on it and—crack!—the chair split in half, dumping the two of them onto the Turkish carpet with a bone-jarring thump.

Toni didn't waste any time. She climbed up his body and latched her lips onto his.

He muffled a call for help as he grabbed her shoulders and pushed. Somewhere in the back of his mind he was aware of Thomal thundering out of the parlor and Dev trying to pull Toni off by the waist. Otherwise the blood pounding against his temples made it difficult to attend to much of anything but the overpowering feel of Toni's hot, eager lips devouring his. A guttural sound boiled up in his chest. He'd never been kissed on the mouth before, and having his first time be like *this*, with a wild and passion-crazed Toni, was the equivalent of trying to light a cigarette for the first time with a blowtorch instead of a match. It consumed him entirely with heat.

"Damn it, Jaćken," Dev ground out, "what do you want me to do? I can't get her off you, not unless I hurt her."

Like he could answer that? Toni's tongue was in his mouth, slipping deep inside to swirl and explore, to taste him in a way he'd never been tasted before, in a way he'd never even thought possible. Lust hit him like a thunderbolt right between the thighs, the honey-sweet caress of her warm, moist tongue against his own sending a tidal wave of blood rushing hectically toward his crotch. He went tense all over and drew in a torn breath. *This one's going to be a bitch....* The blood slammed against the stop-dam in his cock in an excruciating collision.

He tore his mouth from Toni's on a bellow. "She's killing me, Nichita!"

"Shitfuckpiss." Dev pulled on her hard this time.

Jaćken hissed as he and Toni were yanked up together, the grip of her legs around his waist unbreakable. He was jerked up onto his knees, then sent falling all the way over on top of her, his face planting helplessly between her ample breasts. He wanted to scream—in both frustration and ecstasy—as Toni dug her fingers into his hair to hold his face in place and pumped her hips up against him.

"Good heavens!"

Yeah, *this* was the scene Dr. Jess dashed into along with Thomal. And that, along with Dev's bloody nose....

The doctor just naturally assumed it was Jaćken who'd blown the fuse.

"No!" Jaćken rocketed upright onto his knees, Toni finally sprawling off him, and glared at the syringe dangling from his arm. "Not me, you idiot! *Her!*"

Jess blinked owlishly. "Oh." Then he blanched, his eyes going saucer-wide on Jaćken. "Oh, dear, what have I done?"

Jaćken's body jerked as a burning sensation roared through his veins, oxygen howling in his lungs like a high wind. Oh, shit. What *had* Jess done? He felt his muscles start to pump full of iron, growing heavy. Powerful. *No—no, no, no.* The tranquilizer was making him go Ră999u. He gritted his teeth, molars grinding. *Fight it, fight it.* He concentrated on the texture of the carpet, the scent of rug shampoo, the sound of—

The parlor splintered into a dozen puzzle pieces. *Ah!* He grabbed his head, swaying on his knees. The *crackling* filled his ears first, then the red haze unfurled over his vision. He shook his head, but couldn't clear it. His skull felt big and weighted as a mastiff's. Through the static in his ears, he heard a breathy whimper. A female. He raised his eyes, glaring up from beneath black brows. There she was. The female. Hair, tousled and fiery, lips, red and swollen. Beach skirt dipped between her parted knees. He made a low *snuffling* sound, an animal picking up a scent. The female was aroused. For him. Instinct reared up and clubbed him.

Bite her.

Mate her.

Nostrils flaring wide, he grabbed her under the knees and yanked her forward, locking her thighs around his hips and shoving her beach skirt up to her waist.

One of the other males in the room ground out a nasty curse.

With another whimper, the female arched her pelvis up to him, showing him the panties of her bathing suit. *Wet.* His chest vibrated. The fragrance of her was a sweet essence in the air. His fangs pierced down into his mouth, pulsating, heavy with a load of Fiinţă. He flung back his head, the cords in his neck flexed, and howled his possession. *My woman.* A glass hurricane on the coffee table shattered, a bulb in a standing lamp burst.

Frenzied shouting echoed in the room, voices intermittently making it through the *crackle* in his ears. "Hurry…and go…Nyko!"

He turned again to the female, breathing roughly through his open mouth, a bead of saliva dripping off a fang.

Her head was lolled back on her neck, her lids half-closed.

He threw himself on top of her soft body, crushing her beneath him as he went for her throat.

A brawny arm locked around his neck in a chokehold, the weight of a male pressing his spine.

"Jaċken, no!" The arm squeezed. "…need to…the hell off!"

A feral, killing growl rumbled in his chest. A primal warning. *My woman.*

"Jaċken…me, Dev! Get…!"

Reaching behind him, he grabbed his attacker by the scruff of the shirt and tossed the body off, a mere jerk of the arm sending the large male hurtling across the room as if he weighed no more than a rag doll. The male crashed through the center of the coffee table in a hail of splinters, the scent of blood oozing into the air from the male's nose and now his shoulder.

Fangs throbbing brutally now, he rammed himself harder between the female's legs and lunged for her throat again.

A hand in the back of his hair wrenched him to a stop.

He snarled and snapped. There was an even larger male behind him now, twisting him into a full nelson—both arms pretzeled behind his neck.

The new male hauled him off his woman. "Get her...of here!"

A blond male leapt toward his woman, and a noise came out of the deepest part of him. A low vibrato of evil. The inhuman and threatening sound of Rău.

The blond came to an immediate stop. "...gonna kill me, Nyko...you're...only one who can...without getting...."

The male by the coffee table lurched woozily to his feet.

The female was standing now, too, breathing unsteadily, staring at him with glazed, greedy eyes. She wanted.

He wanted.

There was nothing but the violent rule of need.

With another shattering howl, he drove his attacker backward, throwing all of his weight into propelling the large male into the far wall. Plaster boomed into a meteor shower of white and a painting hopped into the air then hit the floor, stiff-walking from one corner to the other before whacking over. A breath was forcefully exhaled and the arms around him slackened. He thrashed past his attacker's hold and charged for his woman.

"Put her down...linen chute!" The large male was chasing after him.

A doctor came huffing into the room, still round-eyed, another syringe in his hand.

The two other males scooped up his female and heaved her down a hatch.

Bellowing, he plowed viciously through coffee table debris after them. Those males had touched his woman! His vision hemorrhaged a deeper shade of red. The taste of murder wet his tongue.

"Shit!"

"Holy—!"

The males dispersed rapidly, but the larger one stayed right beside him, reaching a hand out....

But no. The only thing that could stop him now was an oncoming train.

And that's exactly what he got.

A palm on his shoulder spun him around and then a fist going the speed and power of a locomotive landed square in the middle of his face.

A hailstorm of stars burst apart before his vision, drifting, drifting.... Then everything shriveled to black.

CHAPTER TWENTY-SEVEN

Toni stared sightlessly at her bedroom ceiling, the blue glow from her muted TV flickering across the antique brass light fixture above her. Sixteen light bulbs on it. She'd counted them over and over by now. She ran her tongue slowly over her upper lip. Moisture. Smoothness. A little arch. Everyone was gone now. Finally. Some peace. She shifted slightly on top of her lavender duvet as the musical *whoo-whoo* of wind drafting through one of the cave's wormholes floated through the room, defining the quiet rather than disturbing it. Her butt ached from so many hours spent lying in bed.

Her mind was a mélange of images. Pictures from her "unfortunate episode" with Jačken—Roth's phrasing, not hers—continuously tumbled through her mind, no matter how much she tried to stop them. A vision of her standing before Roth in his library-office after she'd recovered from the drugging was one of the most prominent.

Jačken had been posted at his usual position to the side of Roth's desk, both of his eyes blackened, a white strip of bandage covering his nose—clearly it'd been broken—and bruises circling his wrists, suggesting that at some point he'd been shackled. Oh, what a hoot that must've been for the man.

"What occurred between you and Mr. Brun wasn't real," Roth had tried to reassure her. "I hope you and he can derive some measure of comfort from knowing that. You were both under the influence of alternative forces, after all."

She'd felt a tic pulse in her cheek even as she'd watched Jaćken's jaw harden to the near shattering point.

As usual, Roth was dead wrong.

She didn't know how she'd done it—maybe something about her Dragon blood—but she'd maintained a certain level of awareness during the "episode." It was like her brain had split in two during her sex-attack, one side utterly beyond her control, yes, intent on screwing Jaćken for no other reason than a force inside her was making her. But the other side of her brain had been very aware that the man she was touching and kissing was, in fact, *Jaćken*. She'd been vividly aware of everything she felt for him, and not only had it been very real, but it'd been the hit-the-wall head-banger of all lust. Way more than the little tingles down below or the slow surge of wetness she'd felt with other men.

"...equally sorry about the harm you endured, Dr. Parthen," Roth had continued to intone. "Nothing like this has ever happened before. Clearly, our new enemy is blah, blah...very formidable...afraid you're going to have to remain in the mansion until the situation can be blah, blah, blah." It was pretty much what she'd expected: Rapunzel-in-the-tower for the rest of her young life.

She'd taken to her bed right after that meeting and hadn't moved from it in the last seventeen hours.

Her withdrawal had thrown the community into a bit of an uproar. Dr. Jess had come by to try and rouse her, then her mate-choices, then some of the Vârcolac women of the community. Finally, Jaćken. He hadn't yapped at her like the rest. He'd merely peered down at her for a quiet moment, then set something on her nightstand. When he left the room, she'd turned her head to see what it was.

The African Queen DVD.

She'd spent the next few hours crying, her heart breaking over and over. *I'm in love with a vampire.* God, it sounded like the worst B movie title. But there it was: the truth. If she hadn't been certain about it before, she was now. "Unfortunate episodes" like the one she'd shared with Jacken had a way of solidifying such matters for a girl. God, where was a sack of pebbles when she needed them? She blinked hard at the light fixture and her lips quivered. Maybe if she slept on a bunch of rocks again, Jacken would realize how strong her feelings were for him, and then he'd set aside his vow to Roth and love her back.

There was a soft knock at the door. "Hey there, it's us," Beth said, poking her head around the jamb. "How are you?" She entered, the four other Dragon women following her inside, Maggie, Ellen, Hannah, and Kimberly.

"Oh...hi." Toni reluctantly hoisted herself to a sitting position. "What's up?"

Beth gave her a maternal look. "You doing okay?"

"Okay enough, I suppose." Although she probably looked like Janis Joplin on a bad trip. She dragged a hand through her messy hair. "Uh, so...what're you all doing here? I mean, I appreciate you coming by, but no offense, I'd prefer to be alone right now."

Kimberly came forward, a grocery sack in her arms. "I know you're feeling crappy, Toni, but since everyone is leaving you alone right now, it'd actually be a good time to go."

Toni blinked. "Go?"

Kimberly smiled triumphantly. "We received a package from your brother that'll get us out of here."

"What?" Toni's mouth dropped open. "*Alex?*"

"That's the one." Kimberly set the sack on the bed next to Toni. "Your genius brother hacked into the community's email system and contacted Beth. She—well, both of us—wrote back and asked for help with the key code boxes. He sent this to Beth's PO box topside." Kimberly pulled a small metal box out of the sack, a couple of electrical wires dangling from it. "Alex says this will read the code and open the doors."

"You're kidding," Toni breathed.

"Nope. Cool on your bro, huh?" Kimberly stuck Alex's box back in the sack. "I'm sure it feels like bad timing, but actually now *would* be the best time to escape, like I said."

Escape. Toni's pulse jumped in her throat. How long had she dreamed of an opportunity like this? And now here it was, so weighted with oppressive sadness because it meant that she'd be leaving Jacken. What was the alternative? Risk more instances of throwing herself at him, like the "show me your fangs" day in his bedroom? She'd come embarrassingly close to begging, and she doubted her ego could stand much more of that. She forced herself to her feet. "Actually, it's perfect timing. What's the plan?"

"We head down to the basement exit," Kimberly explained, "which leads to the garage, and from there we grab one of the community's cars and head up on the elevator. Simple."

Toni lifted her brows high. "It can't be that easy."

"No? I'd be willing to bet big money that the code boxes are the only form of security they have against us." Kimberly smirked. "Just one of the benefits of being underestimated by the men around here."

Beth sat spine-straight in the black antique chair set before Roth's desk, her hands gripped tightly in her lap.

Roth was drumming his fingers on his desktop, his retinas hard and shiny like polished metal.

Along the wall of bookshelves, the Dragons' husbands were lined up. Pedrr, Ellen's husband, was the most difficult to read; Beth couldn't even begin to guess what was going on behind his stoic expression. Brainiac architect Luken, Maggie's mate, generally approached everything in life with logical precision, and today's crisis appeared to be no exception. Sedge looked to be in a mood of resigned acceptance, as if he'd known something like this was going to happen at some point. The surprise factor was shy and gentle Willen; he was clearly very pissed. But then his wife, Hannah, was nearing the end of her pregnancy, and a protective male Vârcolac never liked to be far from a mate, especially when she was carrying his child.

Jacken, standing to one side of Roth's desk, also looked like he wanted to eat Beth's head.

She twisted her hands into a harder knot, fear and nervousness sitting like vinegar at the back of her mouth. She'd never had to face this kind of intense anger before; people just didn't get mad at pretty girls, especially not *men*. Swallowing hard, she glanced to the side at her husband and managed to regain some of her calm.

Arc was standing with his muscular arms crossed over his chest and his booted feet spread in a distinctly aggressive posture. As perturbed as Arc was with her for the stunt she'd pulled with the Dragons, he wasn't going to let anyone just roll over his bonded mate.

Her chest shrank in on itself, and she let her eyes drift closed, feeling her lashes tremble against her cheeks. She'd volunteered to remain in Țărână and be the go-between because she'd known full well the backlash she'd have to endure, and dealing with it would force her to quit being such a sap. And now here she was already relying on Arc's strength. For the love of Pete, did she *never* plan on becoming a grownup?

Roth stopped drumming his fingers. "How did the Dragons get past the key code boxes?" he asked in a cutting tone.

Beth set her shoulders and steadied her voice. "I'm sorry, but I'm not at liberty to discuss that." *There*. That sounded like something Kimberly would say, lawyerly and stalwart and—

Roth snapped his chair upright, his brows lowering. "A most heinous breach of our security has been committed, Mrs. Costache. It is paramount that we be allowed to assess the damage you've inflicted on the poor innocents of this community."

A sudden, thick tension blanketed the office, dark and full of blame.

Beth opened her mouth, but, to her shame, only a small squeak came out. Somewhere in her mind, she knew that Roth was deliberately trying to make her feel guilty, but, yes, dear God, it was working. She'd never forgive herself if anything bad happened to the people here. "N-Nothing bad will...will.... We didn't tell about the entrances. How could we?" She repeated Kimberly's rationalization. "We don't even know where they are ourselves to—"

"Tell whom?" Roth's words dripped ice.

Beth's mouth worked, her heart hammering into her throat.

Rage darkened Jaćken's complexion.

"Beth," Arc urged quietly. "Who did you tell about us? This is important."

She passed trembling fingers over her lips. The words backed up in her throat for another moment. "Toni's brother, Alex, who's some sort of computer genius, hacked into our system and sent me an email, asking about Toni. Kimberly and I described the key code boxes to him"—she heard Sedge exhale a short breath—"and then Alex sent a small machine to my topside PO box that could read the code. But *that's all* we told him. So...so, everyone's safe."

"Everyone's *safe*?" Jaćken growled her words back at her. "Jesus Christ, I've never heard anything more screwed in the head. Toni's unmated!" Jaćken pounded over to Beth and leaned right into her face. "Do you have any idea what you've done?! Even the faintest clue how much danger Toni's in up there!?"

A blast of adrenaline sped Beth's heart into an erratic rhythm. "I-I-I..." she stammered.

Arc stepped forward, and Jaćken bolted his eyes up to him. "Please, Costache, take a swing. It would *so* fucking make my day."

Beth took advantage of the distraction to scramble out of her chair and back away from the men. "Toni knew the risks she was taking by leaving here and she willingly took them." She firmed her chin to keep it from quivering. "I stand by my actions."

"Do you?" Jaćken glared at her, fury rolling off him in

boiling waves. "So the thought of Toni staked out on a bed and being repeatedly gang raped by a bunch of Topside Om Rău is just peachy keen with you?"

She felt herself going pale. "She's with her brother." Her control stretched like a taffy pull, thinning and thinning. "I have every confidence that she—"

"Ah, that's okay, then." Jaćken sneered. "Because a computer genius milquetoast can keep her *so* safe from those Topside Om Rău when they decide to make another move on her."

She pinched her lips together. "Well, I can't see how Alex could do a much worse job protecting her than you've been doing, lately, Jaćken."

"*Beth*," Arc hissed.

Jaćken canted back as if he'd been struck, a snarl seething past his lips.

"Stars and bats!" Willen exhorted. "Where are they, Beth!? Just tell us, please."

"I-I don't know." She backed up another few steps. "I'm only here to receive messages."

"Unbelievable! This is the most—"

"—something should happen to the women?! It's daylight—"

"E-everyone stop yelling at me. I'm sick to death of being blamed for something that's not my fault." She pointed an unsteady finger at Roth. "You're the one to blame for putting innocent women in a repopulation program, and you warriors"—she accused Sedge and her own husband—"for actively participating in the kidnappings when you knew they were wrong. "And *you*," she dared, facing Jaćken. "You have only yourself to fault for Toni being gone. I saw the way she looked at you at the Water Cliffs. She wanted to be with *you*, Jaćken, but you weren't man enough to go tell Roth to shove his vow of celibacy in the toilet. That's why she left!"

A dark noise rumbled out of Jaćken, his eyes going demon black.

"Be quiet, Beth!" Arc warned.

She shook her head, her hair seething around her. "Every

man in this room is at fault! The Dragons tried to warn all of you about their unhappiness, but you just preferred to stuff cotton in your ears." She threw her arms wide. "Well, are you listening now?!"

"Enough!" Roth bellowed, surging to his feet, his eyes steely, his brow thunderous. "Mrs. Costache, for your unutterable breach of our most sacred rules of our security, you are hereby stripped of all your clearances."

She staggered backward. *What*? Her adrenaline abandoned her in rush, leaving her knees weak and her breathing faltering in her lungs.

"You will no longer be permitted use the Internet or receive mail from your topside PO box," Roth continued through a set jaw. "Nor will you be able to—"

"No!" She gripped her throat. Oh, God, she was going to throw up.

Arc quickly took her in his arms and hugged her close. "Ssh, baby, don't worry," he said softly into her ear. "Everything's going to be fine, okay. I'm not going to let you lose anything."

She buried her face in his chest, tears gushing down her cheeks.

"Beth's pregnant," Arc said to Roth, his voice going hard, "which means she has to have contact with her mother right now, and I'll be damned if I'm going to let that be taken away when she needs it the most. You know, it's bad enough that she's only allowed to see her mother and sisters on birthdays and Christmas. She hates that, but she puts up with it because she loves me and this community. We're lucky to have her, damn it, and she deserves better than *punishments*, I don't care what the hell she did with the Dragons." She felt Arc tense. "Anyone tries to make a prisoner out of my wife, and I'll tear this cave down with my own fists to get her out, you can be fucking sure of that."

Beth bit into her bottom lip, her tears quieting to sniffles. She couldn't believe Arc was saying all of this. She'd never heard anyone stand up to Roth before.

Arc's chest expanded on a large breath. "With all due respect, Roth, repopulating our species isn't just about giving birth to live babies. It's about creating happy families to raise those kids, and every day it seems to me like you're getting further and further away from that goal." Arc's hand caressed the length of her back. "I didn't get it before. I wasn't listening, either, but I'm sure listening now." Keeping an arm around her shoulders, Arc started to lead her toward the double doors. "I suggest everyone in this room start doing the same."

CHAPTER TWENTY-EIGHT

Toni, Hannah, Ellen, Maggie, and Kimberly stashed the Pathfinder they'd stolen from the community in a mall parking lot, then Alex picked them up. It took three trips to get all twelve of them—five women and seven children—to the Mission Beach bungalows they'd rented, but hiring a van or taking a cab wasn't a smart option for women going into hiding.

Toni cried in Alex's arms as they stood in the doorjamb of one of the bungalows while the four other women bustled about getting their children settled into bed, since it was actually nighttime for them. Her mood was the lowest it'd ever been. She was never going to see Jaċken again. Escaping Ţărână made that official. The other Dragons would go back, but she wouldn't. She would move out of California, far away from those who sought to hunt her, and try to heal the huge emptiness that threatened to consume her. She'd do it, although it'd take some time. Say, an eternity or two.

Alex, being Alex, just let her cry in silence, even though he probably had a million questions. After she'd wept herself dry, she took a long, hot shower, then curled up in a chair next to a window with a view of the sea, a mug of hot cocoa cupped in her palms. With the other Dragons arrayed around the room, on beds and a couch, Toni told her brother the whole amazing story: her kidnapping from Scripps Hospital, the town of Ṭărână, the circumstance of her being a Dragon—probably Alex, too—blood graphs, tattoos, glowing eyes, Fiinţă, Om Răitu. And the vampires, of course. Alex took it all in silently, just absorbing, while Ellen, Hannah, Kimberly, and Maggie eyed him carefully. By the end of it, Toni felt utterly spent. She couldn't believe she'd only been gone for eighteen days; it felt like months. A lifetime.

Toni set her empty mug on the small round hotel table that stood between her and her brother and rubbed a weary hand over her face. It was dusk now, the setting sun turning the ocean into a lake of molten gold. God, how she'd missed sunsets. But then…she knew she'd also miss the clean, earthy smell of the air in Ṭărână, the low, singing sough of wind through a few special wormholes, the shiny black lava rock that decorated some of the cave walls, and…other things.

She reached up and snapped a lamp on. "So do you think I'm crazy?"

"No, actually…." Alex shook his head, then even laughed. "Truth is, nothing has ever made more sense to me in my life."

Maggie pulled a small tin box out of her tote bag. "He *is* being suspiciously calm."

Alex smiled. "Yeah. In fact, check this out." He jumped to his feet and crossed to his duffle bag, rummaging a book out of it. "Something told me I should pack this. Now I'm glad I did." He set the book on the table in front of Toni.

She peered down on it, and, "Wow." She'd never seen anything like it. The cover was grainy and tan-colored, a blue crescent moon and star shimmering on it like an ethereal deep-sea creature.

"Open it," Alex said.

She did as the other four women stood and gathered around to look, too, and "Wow," again. A replica of the dragon tattoo was right on the front page, Roth's mansion on the next, though looking more like a castle, and people, drawings and drawings of gorgeous people, all of whom looked vaguely familiar.

"That's them, isn't it? The vampires?"

"Yes, although not exactly." They were probably the ancestors of the people currently in the community. "And they're called Vârcolac." Had she just corrected her brother on the terminology for a real, live vampire? Toni pressed a hand over her eyes and groaned. "Christ, Alex, this is just so.... Are you sure I'm not insane? Deep down, I've been hoping I was." Her brother chuckled, and she looked at him again. "It's all true, isn't it?"

He gave her a lopsided grin. "Looks like it."

She blew out her cheeks. Yes, she'd known that already, hadn't she?

"Don't feel bad," Maggie said, crossing to Alex and holding out the tin box to him. "It took me till my first bite to truly believe. Want a cookie?"

Alex adjusted the set of his glasses as he peered into the box. "What kind?"

"Macadamia chocolate chip."

"Oh, definitely." Alex took one.

Hannah plopped back down on the couch, looking drawn and pale. It was clearly taking a toll on her to leave the community she so adored. "I knew right away. All of the Vârcolac exude a kind of animal essence, don't you think?"

"Yep," Ellen said, sitting next to Hannah. "That's what got me, too."

Toni was still skimming the pages of the strange book. "How did you find this anyway, Alex?"

Alex sat down with his cookie. "When I was fifteen, I pried up a floorboard in my bedroom to hide my reefer stash from Mom. The Book was just sitting there, like, *shazaam*, it'd been patiently waiting for me to find it."

She arched her brows, but that was her only reaction. She probably wasn't allowed to think that scenario was weird, considering her recent experiences. She ran her fingers over the strange lettering on the page. "Do you know what language this is?"

"Utter gibberish from what I've been told. But," he lifted a single shoulder, "I can read some of it. Before today and your story, though, it never made much sense to me. I mean, when I read that you and I were Dragon royalty, I really didn't understand the—"

"Wait." Kimberly held up a hand. "What? Did you just say *royalty*?"

Alex smiled widely. "Yeah...get this. According to The Book, Toni and I are both descended from some royal lineage of the ancient Dragons." He brushed cookie crumbs off his hands, then reached across the table to flip to a different page. "See?"

Ellen, Maggie, Kimberly, and Hannah moved to hover over Toni again.

Toni studied the page. "My God, these people kind of look like us, Alex."

"Bizarre, huh?" Alex pointed to one of the pages of gobbledygook language. "From what I've been able to gather, there were two main lines of Dragon monarchy, which came into being because their bloodlines were able to stabilize the population, erasing a lot of genetic problems that were starting to show up. One line went off to breed with the Vârcolac, the other with humans, which ended up making people like you and me. Apparently, we're very rare." He glanced at her curiously. "Did the others know the full extent of your genealogy?"

"I doubt it." She couldn't imagine Roth not using information like *royal bloodlines* to try and pressure her further into reproducing with his people.

Kimberly sucked in a sudden breath. " This is great! You're the answer to our problems, Toni."

Toni frowned. She didn't like the sound of that. "What do you mean?"

"Vârcolac culture only allows those of royal lineage to hold positions of authority, right? So with your royal bloodlines you could become co-leader of Țărână with Roth. Ha!" Kimberly clapped her hands together. "The Dragons would finally have representation." Kimberly swung around to look at the other women. "We don't need to negotiate any more than that, you guys. Once Toni gets into power, she can take care of the rest."

"Hold on a minute," Toni butted in. "It was never the plan for me to go back with all of you."

"I'll go with you." Alex said quietly.

She whipped her head around and gaped at her brother. "For the love of God," she bit off low on her breath, "now who's the insane one?"

His expression sobered. "I think you'd agree that, outside of you and Mom, my life has been damned empty so far. Yours, too, from what I can tell. I don't want to go back to it."

She pressed the heels of her palms against her forehead and let out a long moan. Why was everyone so determined to screw up her plans?

"Think about it," Alex went on. "Our whole lives, both of us have been the square pegs in the round holes. We've never fit in. Me, with all of my strung-out rebellions, and you...do you have any close friends at all, even one?"

She dropped her hands and lowered her head, the familiar pain of that relentless loneliness throbbing in her chest.

Hannah stepped closer to Alex. "You'd feel like you belonged in Ţărână," she promised him.

"I bet she's right," Alex aimed the comment at Toni. "We're not part of this world, sis. That's been the problem all along, we just never knew it. We belong in *theirs*."

Hannah added another two cents. "It's the same thing we've been trying to tell her."

"Just give her a moment," Kimberly said.

"For the love of God," Toni hissed, snapping her head up. "Do you have any idea what you'd be giving up, Alex? Regular access to the sun, your plants, a successful career, Friday afternoon racquetball with your—"

"All of that's meaningless if I'm alone. Hell, I'd live in zero gravity on the moon if it meant sharing my life with someone I loved. And I'm never going to find that special someone *here*. I'm sure of that now." Alex reached across the table and took ahold of one of her hands. "What do you want, sis, huh? To be just another widget-hematologist up here, or to really make a difference down there? To have a chance at falling in love down there, or to continue to have one meaningless affair after another up here? Or no man at all, which is pretty much what—"

She jerked her hand away from him. "I did fall in love, Alex, that's the freaking problem." She thrust to her feet and paced away from the table, heat building in her face. "You want to go live in Ţărână? Fine. Go. These women will gladly take you there. But I can't survive spending every day of my life living next to a man I want with every fiber of my soul, but can never have."

Hannah brightened. "Who?"

"Jaćken," Maggie answered, putting the lid back on her cookie tin. "Isn't it obvious?"

Apparently not to Hannah. The pleased look fell off the librarian's face, replaced by an expression of aghast incredulity. "*Jaćken?*"

Alex set his forearms on the table, clasping his fingers in front of him. "A man who you can't have, Toni? Nuh, uh, the dude doesn't exist."

She exhaled a frustrated breath, tears springing into her eyes. "This isn't just a matter of me wearing a tube top and hot pants or sitting on him until he cries uncle, Alex. The man is half Om Rău, which means he has an incurable genetic defect. *Incurable* as in, there's nothing I can do about it. Do you understand? I can't just change the laws of science and nature to suit my love life."

"I'm not buying it. You've got a stubborn streak in you a mile wide, Toni." Alex shrugged, his hands still clasped. "If you really want this dude, then find a way to get him."

CHAPTER TWENTY-NINE

The succulent scent of bacon wafted in the air, along with the aroma of fresh baked muffins. Blueberry, too, usually Jaćken's favorite. Today, it tasted like sawdust. Crumbling the muffin onto his plate, Jaćken slugged back another mouthful of coffee, scalding his tongue and not giving a shit.

Activity in the mansion's dining room hummed around him, the soft clink-clank of dishes and silverware, the low murmur of people talking about stuff he couldn't give a shit about. But then there wasn't much he cared two fucks about anymore. He ate, drank, slept, and put one foot in front of the other to keep the machinery of his body working, but that was about it. He was a drone. The worst he'd ever been. His persona in Oțărât had been Giggles the Clown compared to this. Everything was nothing. Food had no taste, music had no rhythm, friendships had no depth, the world had no color, no substance. No vibrancy.

Because it was a world without Toni.

They couldn't find her. Not anywhere. Night after night over the last week, he'd gone topside with a team to search for her, but they always returned without a single lead. No sign of life at Alexander Parthen's house or at Toni's place or at her work.

Not anywhere.

Cleeve couldn't pin her down, either. The last known trace the computer whiz had been able to find of either Toni or her brother was on the day Toni had escaped. A substantial ATM withdrawal had been made by Alex Parthen from near his home. The same day, Jaćken and his men had found the Pathfinder, but since then, nothing. No activity on credit cards, no cell phone calls, not a single thing Cleeve could track. Toni, her brother, and four other Dragon women had all become a bunch of ghosts.

Toni was gone. For good. Like in, never-fucking-ever coming back. *Accept it, asshole.*

Jaćken glowered down at the scrambled eggs congealing on his plate. Jesus H. Christ, if there was a man on this earth stupider than he was, he'd like someone to stand up and name the imbecile. *How* could he have ever thought for even a fleeting second that life might be easier without Toni around? That somehow his existence would be less agonizing if he was spared the necessity of watching her hook up with another man some—

The rapid-fire staccato of multiple footsteps interrupted his thoughts, the strides heading down the outer corridor's polished wood floor toward the dining room. Jaćken grimaced at his coffee mug. More of the community's bullshit to deal with. He was the interim man-in-charge, so when anyone had a problem these days, it was *his* ear they yapped it into. Not exactly known for his people skills, he sucked at the job and liked it even less, but there wasn't a whole lot of choice in the matter. Over the last week, Roth had been progressively withdrawing, to the point that for the last two days he hadn't even left his penthouse. The community was heading rapidly down the john, and nobody seemed to have the first clue how to save it. Jaćken least of all.

The Dragons' husbands burst into the dining room, Pedrr and Willen log-jamming in the doorway before stumbling inside, followed by Luken. Sedge and Arc entered last, more calmly, but still clearly jacked with tension. Everyone started talking at once.

"—received a message—"

"—women want to meet at—"

"Finally! Dear heavens, one more day and—"

"—leave right away!"

Jaćken took a sip of his coffee and didn't say anything, sticking with his whole not-giving-a-shit attitude toward this goat rodeo.

"Cut the noise!" Arc barked at the husbands. Stepping forward from the group, Arc held out a piece of paper to Jaćken. "This was emailed to Beth. *Toni's* the one calling for the meeting, Jaćken. She wants to see you, man."

He surged out of his chair before he was even aware his brain had given his body the command to stand. The dining room went pin-drop quiet, everyone no doubt listening to his heart do the 100-yard dash.

He pushed the single word between his teeth. "Where?"

Stationed just inside the ER, Kimberly was standing at a perfect vantage point to spy on the front door of Scripps Memorial Hospital. "They're here," she said into her cell phone to Toni on the other end. "Roth, Dr. Jess, Jaćken," she named the entering Vârcolac, "and the husbands: Pedrr, Willen, Luken, and Sedge. No Arc or Beth, though."

Her heart did a funny pirouette in her chest as she watched her own husband step onto the hospital elevator. He was moving in that fluid way of his, his shoulders so broad he almost had to angle his way inside. She'd really missed him over the past week. She'd visited her parents while she'd been up here, and that'd been nice, but it was Sedge who now meant home to her.

"I'll be right up," she finished off with Toni. "I'm just going to grab a cup of coffee first." The reverse day-night cycle between Țărână and topside was killing her. She didn't think she'd adjusted, even after an entire week up here.

Pressing her thumb on her cell phone's red *end call* button, she headed for the vending machines.

Toni heard them coming three minutes after the phone call from Kimberly, the thunder of footsteps approaching from the nurse's station stirring a flutter of excitement in her belly.

After the longest week of her life, she was finally going to see him again. Jaćken....

It'd been a roller-coaster seven days, every hopeful idea she'd come up with for creating a life with Jaćken getting shot down by a cold dose of reality, back and forth, until she'd finally put her hematological ingenuity to use and discovered a do-able option—a meaningless option if it turned out that Jaćken didn't love her. Because no way was she going to bond permanently to a man who didn't.

He was drawn to her, she knew that much, and by more than just her scent. They'd shared some pretty intense moments. But, seeing as all those moments had ended with him backing off, she really didn't know for sure how he felt about her. Had he backed off out of pure necessity because of his vow of celibacy, or because he genuinely didn't want her in his life, bugging him? The answer to that, more than her upcoming confrontation with Roth, had her nerves jumping.

"You ready, Toni?" Alex was perched on the edge of a long, oval table. They were in a conference room in the hematology wing, with the other Dragons seated in plush chairs around it at the far end of the room, minus Kimberly, who was still downstairs in the Emergency Room. Their combined seven children were safely tucked away in the hospital daycare. Just tonight, Toni had tendered her resignation at Scripps, but had kept her hospital privileges as an adjunct physician.

She took a deep breath. *Right. Keep focused.* This was hardly the time to get caught up in a love-daze. Much still had to be decided before she earned her Happily Ever After—*if* she earned it. Giving Alex a quick nod, she stepped out of the conference room.

Jaćken was on point, in front of the other Vârcolac, and the sight of him flipped her stomach into a full somersault. *Sweet Jesus*. He looked smokin' hot, from his thickly corded legs in black jeans to the leather jacket that hugged the V-shape of his muscular body, the snug fit of his clothes highlighting his masculinity and power. It made her want to do nothing more than run her hands all over those chiseled bulges. She released a slow breath. Damn, who would've guessed Tall, Dark, and Homicidal was what buttered her bread, but evidently it was.

The rest of the men were well-dressed in suits, except for Sedge, who was wearing olive slacks and a dark mauve button-down left open at the collar. Dr. Jess had also thrown on a white lab coat for good measure.

She was extra glad now she'd taken such care with her own appearance. She'd clipped her hair into an elegant ponytail, which lay shimmering over one shoulder, and had dressed in a newly-purchased black pencil skirt, black sling-back pumps, and a wraparound blue silk blouse which, while totally decent in all respects, had made even her own eyes go a little *zowie* when she'd seen The Girls in the mirror. She'd wanted to look pretty for this, though, and…apparently, she'd succeeded.

The group of Vârcolac slammed to a halt the moment she stepped into the hallway.

"Goodness," slipped incredulously past Dr. Jess's lips, while Jaćken looked like he wished he had a lead pipe to gnaw through.

She strode forward, fighting the urge to run at Jaćken and throw her arms around his thick neck with a *Got any Hershey's syrup and whipped cream handy?* or something equally subtle and coy.

"Gentlemen," she greeted as she came to a stop in front of them. This close, she saw that Jaćken was drawn and leaner, still totally do-able, but definitely a man who looked like he'd been through the wringer. Had this past week been as awful for him as it had been for her? Probably rude to hope so. "Thank you for coming."

Jaćken glowered at her. "Do you have any idea how fucking worried we've been about all of you?"

She paused, momentarily caught off guard by his heated rejoinder. Then she *piffed* a breath. Well, it was nice to know some things never changed, and Jaćken's inability to be diplomatic about anything that displeased him was clearly one of life's constants.

"You're a lovely sight, Dr. Parthen," Roth complimented. "But also a surprising one. Once you rid yourself of us, we never thought to see you again."

"If all goes well with our negotiations, Mr. Mihnea, I plan to return to the community."

Out of the corner of her eye, she saw Jaćken stiffen. Was that a good or bad sign?

"I see," Roth said noncommittally.

"Why don't we all go into the conference room." She gestured toward the door. "We'll have plenty of privacy there."

The seven men stepped inside. Luken, Pedrr, and Willen started for their wives at the far side of the room, but Toni pulled out a chair at this end of the table, prompting them with another, "Gentlemen."

There would be no consorting during negotiations.

The husbands reluctantly sat.

Sedge began to sit, noting his wife's absence with a frown, then shot up again.

Roth had spotted the intruder, too. "We have a visitor, I see."

"This is my brother, Alex," Toni said.

Jaćken put two and two together. "You *told* him about us?!"

"Yes," she replied calmly. She physically turned Alex around and lifted the back of his T-shirt, showing them the significant brown dragon tattoo marks on his back, originally thought to be the aftereffects of a bad sunburn. "He's one of us."

She politely gestured everyone to take a seat. Toni and Alex sat on one side of the table, Roth, Jaćken, and Dr. Jess across from the two of them, with the Dragons and the husbands seated at opposite ends. Perfect positioning for a typical Mexican standoff.

She folded her hands on the top of the table and locked gazes with Roth, blue eyes clashing with gray ones. They weren't in his library-office with her trapped and helpless this time, were they? He damned well needed to be fully aware of that.

Roth broke eye contact long enough to glance around the conference room. "All of this drama doesn't seem like your style, Dr. Parthen."

She lazily lifted her brows at him, adopting an expression of mild curiosity, almost boredom. An interesting opening sally. Was Roth trying to make her feel churlish? Childish? Or get under her skin by making her think he knew her better than she knew herself? She smiled. She wouldn't give him any of it. "You made the dramatic gesture necessary, Mr. Mihnea. You weren't listening to the women of your community down in Ţărână. The hope is that we'll have better luck with you up here."

"Just because someone doesn't concede to another's wishes," Roth countered smoothly, "doesn't mean he hasn't heard them."

"Ah." Toni sat back, her forearms on the armrests. "So you were just ignoring them?"

"Not in the disrespectful way you're suggesting." Roth steepled his fingers together in front of him. "I assure you that I haven't been disregarding anyone's feelings or wishes. There have just been issues of survival at stake."

"We appreciate that you're dealing with your own set of challenges." She paused a moment, tamping down the urge to snark, *spare us that argument, we've all heard it ad infinitum.* That probably *would* come across as churlish. "Our position is this, however: nothing excuses taking women against their will. If you continue to kidnap Dragons, we will refuse to live in Ţărână. That's the bottom line, and it's non-negotiable."

His brows arching, Roth turned to look at the Dragons at the far end of the table. "You plan to leave your husbands and children?"

Toni felt her face tightening, her jaw locking. She and Kimberly had discussed the possibility that Roth would use the

Dragons' love for their Vârcolac husbands against them. Now here he was, being oh-so-Roth-like. "The Dragons have no intention of leaving their children. They'll live topside *with* them."

Willen sucked in a breath. "By darkest night."

"Maggie, my dear…" Luken began.

"The husbands," Toni plowed on before the Dragons could waver, "will be invited topside once a week during nighttime hours to feed." She smiled tightly at Roth. "The Dragon women don't want any harm to come to their men, whom they love dearly."

"No." Jacken snapped off the single word like a curse.

She shifted frosty eyes over to him. "Unless you plan to kidnap us again, and woe betide anyone who tries it," she gritted, "then you can take your *no* and stuff it. The only way to get us back into the community is by agreeing to our demands." She looked at Roth again.

He inclined his head at her. "Nicely played."

"This isn't a game," she shot back, air burning through her lungs. "The Dragons engineered this escape to make sure that you understand they're dead serious about their concerns over Țărână's leadership. I recommend you listen to them, Roth, *for once*."

Roth tucked his steepled hands beneath his chin and regarded her mutely.

CHAPTER THIRTY

Jaċken almost turned to glare at Roth with a silent *Just give her what she wants, you dumb shit.* But he fought off the urge, keeping his eyes locked straight ahead, like a good little damned solider.

A cold knot formed in his stomach, so tight it hurt. If Toni and Roth didn't manage to smoke the fucking peace pipe together, then Jaċken would have to let Toni walk right back out of his life. *Yeah, no prob.* And while he was at it, he'd just barbecue his own heart for dinner. Jaċken turned his gaze to the pitcher of water and four glasses sitting in the middle of the conference table. *Screw it. LEAVE, already. Whatever.* The sight of Toni looking so damned beautiful was making him nuts, anyway.

He shut his eyes briefly and inhaled a slow breath. Christ's sake, it felt like someone had installed new hardware in his brain—and mis-wired it. His thinking was completely warped. One minute he was filled with an elation he'd never known at having Toni back, his blood practically skipping through his veins, and smelling her was…hell. Having her scent back in his head was such a profound comfort, it made him realize just how broken he'd been this past week. Just how much he needed her to make him feel like a whole person. The other side of his schizophrenic madness wanted to drop-kick her to the curb without delay. Because, thing was, he was under no delusions that if she returned to the community, at some point she'd pick a mate.

Would it be Thomal of the Fine Ass? Most-fucking-likely. Or Dev the Schlong, as he'd heard the man called? Yeah, wouldn't that be just jim dandy imagining those two bumping fuzzies every day.

Roth's long exhale jerked Jaćken back to the present.

The leader of Ţărână scrubbed a hand over his face, his expression turning weary, exposing the fatigue Jaćken knew Roth had been feeling all week, if not longer.

Normally, it was impossible to tell the age difference between Jaćken and Roth. Until a Vârcolac became an elder, he or she looked about the same at twenty-one as at one hundred and twenty-one. But at times like these, Roth showed his age. It was in his eyes, the look of a man who'd spent more than a hundred years watching his race die, the look of a man who had an entire species' existence on his shoulders.

"You may not believe this," Roth said to Toni, "but we Vârcolac have always prided ourselves on being the good guys. I've hated that our desperate straits have led us away from that for a time." He looked down at his hands for a long moment. "I can't do it anymore. I just can't bear everyone's displeasure; I'm too tired." He looked up. "I agree to your demands, Toni. No more kidnappings. And if that means our breed must die out, well...." He trailed off.

Jaćken heard the husbands shift in their seats. A heavy pause pushed air out of the room.

Toni's expression softened, the color in her eyes deepening. "I don't want the Vârcolac race to go extinct any more than you do, Roth. If you truly are the good guys, then I'd like to see you have the chance to show that, to be the proud, wonderful breed that you no doubt are. My brother and I have been tossing around a plan to get Dragon women down into Ţărână voluntarily."

The room stilled.

"Can you...truly do that?" Roth asked in a quietly stunned tone.

"I believe we can, yes, but it's going to require a willingness on your part to get out of your comfort zone and loosen up on some security measures. To *change*," Toni emphasized.

Roth closed his eyes for a long second. "I've been insisting we keep to the old ways of being for too long, I realize that. Danger has followed us for so many years, we've already had to lose so much of ourselves because of the necessity of hiding. I've probably been holding onto our culture too tightly because of that."

"I would never ask you to give up your culture entirely." Toni glanced wryly at the other Dragon women. "We know how frustrating it is when someone is forced to do that."

Roth pushed his lips together into a closed-mouth smile.

"By the same token, Ţărână is a town of mixed cultures now, Roth, and the leadership there needs to reflect both sides if you want to have a successful and harmonious community. For one, the humans need democracy; they need representation. On the other hand, I also realize that your tradition permits only Vârcolac of royal lineage to hold positions of authority. That leaves *me* as the perfect answer. I can bring a human perspective to the table, yet my royal bloodlines will allow me to lead beside you without putting Vârcolac noses out of joint."

Jaċken snapped his brows together. *What?*

Toni smiled. "As it turns out, I'm a Royal. So is my brother."

"But...how can that be?" Roth breathed.

Toni looked at her brother. "Show them The Book, Alex."

Reaching into a duffle bag at his feet, Alex fished out a book with a crescent and star on the cover, then stood and leaned over the table, setting it in front of Roth.

Dr. Jess gasped. "Good heavens! It's the Străvechi Caiet!"

Alex sat back down. "Hey, so you know it."

"Stars above, yes. This is the book of our history, both past and future." Dr. Jess stared at Alex in awestruck wonder. "However did you get ahold of it?"

Alex's eyes lit. "Kind of magically, I guess."

A small huff passed Jess's lips. "I wouldn't doubt it. The Străvechi Caiet has been lost to us for a century." He reverently opened the first page of the book, then turned another and another, all the while marveling.

"Can you read it?" Alex asked.

"Of course not," Jess scoffed, "no one can. Not unless you're a…." The doctor whipped his gaze up. "You can, can't you? That's how you know that you and Toni are Royals."

Alex shrugged. "Yeah, some of it. I should be able to read more, I sense that, but…I don't know, something's always just kind of in the way."

"By holiest night," the doctor whispered. "You're a Soothsayer."

Jesus, Alex Parthen might as well have just crapped a brand-new, gold-plated Sigmund-phase piece of lab equipment, the way Dr. Jess was looking at him now.

"A…? Really?" Alex perked up, glancing at Toni. "Hey, that sounds cool, doesn't it?"

"I prefer Know-It-All," Toni returned drolly.

"Ha! Would you listen to that! She's just getting me back for all the times I called her stubborn."

Roth regarded Alex solemnly. "If you don't mind a question, Mr. Parthen, what would be the name of the line you're descended from?"

Alex smiled broadly. "Ah, a test. No, that's cool. Human Dragon royalty descends from King Σoseph of the Flacără line," he rattled off. "The Royal Vârcolac come from Σoseph's cousin, Ællen, of the Seară.

Jacken exhaled under his breath. *I'll be damned….*

"Well." Roth looked a little amazed now, too. "You couldn't have known that unless you'd studied Vârcolac/Dragon history in our community school."

Dr. Jess clapped his hands together. "Do you realize what this means?! The Parthens are more than just Royal—they're Royal *Fey*." Jess beamed at them. "That means you both have enchantment skills, yours, Mr. Parthen, being soothsaying. Although clearly the majority of your power has been confined under centuries of repression. We must figure out how to release it." Jess looked at Roth. "Why didn't we see this before, Roth? They both have red in their hair and...dear heavens, Toni has always smelled different, hasn't she?!"

Jaćken darted his eyes over to Toni. Holy fuck.

Nodding slowly, Roth looked at Toni for an elongated moment. "A co-leader, you say?"

Maggie piped in, "We won't return to Țărână without her."

Roth chuckled. "No need to take a stand on this particular issue. I very much relish the thought of your co-leadership, Toni. I've been in sole charge of Țărână for a very long time now." He stood and held out his hand. "Welcome aboard."

Jaćken's heart played pinball against every bone in his ribcage as he watched Toni rise to her feet and shake Roth's hand. The two had come to an agreement. Toni was returning to Țărână.

"Actually, there's still one minor caveat to me coming back," she said.

Jaćken's elation dropped away like a stone in a deep well. Christ, what now—? Oh, crap. The back of his nape prickled as Toni turned a penetrating blue stare on *him*.

"You and I," she said, "need to settle our disagreement first."

This couldn't be good. "I wasn't aware we had one."

"Unfortunately, we do." She sank gracefully back into her chair. "I want to be your mate, and you keep refusing me like a stubborn ass. I'd say that's a disagreement."

Searing heat slapped him in the cheeks as a raging mass of unpleasant emotions churned through him: anger that she would revisit something so painful to him, awkwardness that everyone was now gawking at him, no one bothering to hide how amazed they were that a woman of Toni's caliber could want him. *Yeah, shut your traps and join the club, people.* And also some kind of bizarre-o childish *gee whiz, hurray, she wants me* feeling that made him want to bang his head on the conference table a couple of hundred times.

"Sorry if my Om Rău genes are getting in the way of your dreams of domestic bliss." Shit, that came out even more snarky than he'd intended.

"Bound by a vow of celibacy, no vasectomy possible, blah, blah, blah. Yes, I remember all the reasons you *can't.*"

He stared at her. *You've got to be shitting me.* "Your blasé understanding of the circumstances is touching."

"The hell if I'm being blasé," she snapped back. "I'm telling you none of that matters. I just need to know if you love me. That's it. The rest we can work out."

The heat was back in his face full-force. He'd never been the type of man to melt beneath a table in embarrassment and he wasn't going to start now. *Tempting,* but fuck, no. "I'm not talking about this with you here." *Or ever.*

"You're going to have to," she countered. "I can't go back to Ţărână until I know."

He gave her a hard look. "Are you threatening the welfare of the community over a—?"

"Jesus, you're not *that* idiotic, are you? I don't want to live down there without you, Jacken, so I need to know if you love me."

Pack sand. Stick it up your ass. And, yes, I love you so much I can already taste you was the psychotic babble that lit off inside his head. Nice to know his sanity was still on a ten.

"It's a simple enough question," she prompted.

His temples were starting to pound. "Nothing about this whole damned situation is simple. We just found out that you're a Royal, for Chrissake. Fuck if I'm going to let you waste those bloodlines on me. I can't have children. We've been over that."

"They're my bloodlines. Shouldn't I get a say in the matter?"

"You don't have anything *to* say."

"Don't I?"

"Not that would change my mind. You're going to make a great mother someday, Toni. I won't steal that from you."

Her throat moved stiffly. "People adopt all the time."

A laugh came out of him that did his demonic heritage proud. "Right. Social Services is just dying to send kids down to Vampire Land to be raised by a half-demon father."

She dismissed that with a wave of her hand. "We could finagle our way around that. Just tell me you don't love me, Jaćken, and I'll leave this alone."

He sat there, painfully mute, unable to lie. "It doesn't mean anything if I do," he ground out.

"It means everything!" Tears collected along her lashes.

He surged to his feet and pointed a rigid finger at it. "Don't you *do* that."

Alex, her brother, started blinking rapidly at him.

"C'mon, man," Sedge said from the side of his mouth, "just tell her already."

A tear tumbled free of Toni's lashes and rolled down her cheek.

"Okay! Jesus! Yes! I love you." He threw out his arms. "You satisfied now, you insane battle-axe?!" He spun toward the window, giving her his back. *Shit, shit, shit.* But what else was he supposed to say, for the love of crap? She was crying! He dragged his hand across his upper lip.

"That's all I needed to know," she said softly. "Because I love you, too, and—"

"Shut up." He slammed his eyes closed.

"I most certainly will not shut up."

He whirled back around and glared at her. "Toni, I swear—"

"Would you just be quiet and listen a minute." She reached under the conference table and produced a black leather briefcase. "While I was away, I did some research. I wanted to see for myself what all the uproar concerning your genes was about. So, I had my brother hack into the community's hospital computer and I ran some experiments with the blood graphs on file. Here are two procreation simulations I conducted." She

228

pulled two sheets of paper out of her briefcase and set them on the conference table. "One is of Jaćken and Beth, compared to one of Dev and Beth." She pointed to a couple of hills on the second graph. "Strength and health came out high with Dev and Beth's offspring, but"—she switched to the first graph—"even higher with Jaćken and Beth's. I'm assuming that's because of Jaćken's Rǎu. But the problem is immediately apparent. Peak 12 is at excessive levels." She glanced at Dr. Jess. "This is why you determined the Bruns shouldn't have children, isn't it?"

"Yes," Jess answered, "exactly so."

Jaćken sharpened his glare on her. He was so happy to be taking this trip down memory lane.

"Then I experimented with my own blood." She pulled out another graph, but held onto it. "You see, when Alex told me I was a Royal, it got me thinking. Maybe my blood is different, too, and look!" She set the third graph next to the other two. "Here's me and Dev."

Roth and Jess leaned forward, Dr. Jess making an interested sound.

"Strength and health increase markedly with this pairing, do you see that? My blood *is* different!"

Dr. Jess's eyebrows popped up.

"That got me wondering how my DNA would pair up with Rǎu bloodlines, so I ran Jaćken and me." She laid down a fourth graph.

Jaćken's heart staggered out of rhythm and he stopped breathing.

"The numbers for strength and health are through the roof, the highest, yet. And here"—she pointed to a small rise on the graph—"Peak 12 is at *normal Vârcolac levels*!"

"Holy goodness!" Dr. Jess gasped.

Jaćken stared at the fourth graph, feeling like somebody had poured epoxy onto his brain, all the gears and mechanisms inside his skull glued into immobility. He *should* understand what was going on, he really sensed that, but everything was just stuck in a shocked standstill.

"Whatever's in my Royal bloodlines appears to completely counteract the negative effects of Jaćken's Om Rău." She shifted her gaze over to Jaćken. "You and I *can* have children, Jaćken. In fact, I think we'd make one heck of a Vârcolac kid, don't you?"

Jaćken stared mutely at Toni, feeling like he was going ten rounds with a telephone pole. This...couldn't be happening. "No," he rasped out. "It's not true. It can't be."

Just run and hide when you see your father coming. His mother gently swept the hair off his brow. *Tomorrow will be a better day, Jaćken, you'll see.* But it never was. So stupid to hope....

"Dr. Jess," Toni said, "could you please confirm my work is correct?"

Jess nodded. "Dr. Parthen has done everything accurately."

"No." Jaćken's stomach sloshed sideways. Clammy goose bumps broke out over his flesh. He reeled backward. "No!" He spun toward the window again and gripped the frame in tight fists. He wasn't letting any of it in, not the impossible dream that Toni could actually be telling the truth, not the bone-deep hunger which had been eating him alive ever since he'd met this infuriating woman. He stared at the stars in the sky until they blurred before his vision and formed the word silently with his mouth. *No.*

"Don't misunderstand Jaćken, okay, Toni?" That was Sedge coming to the rescue. "He's not rejecting you. It's just that, for most of his life, he's had to accept that he'll never have a wife or children, or love. You erased all of that in about ten seconds flat, and...I'm guessing he's feeling a little overwhelmed right now."

Overwhelmed? There wasn't a single solid-feeling bone left in his body.

"Thank you, Sedge," Toni said softly.

Jaćken heard her move around the conference table, coming toward him. He squeezed his fists. The window frame splintered beneath his grip with a soft crunch.

Toni slipped a hand around one of his forearms. "Are you going to make me sit on you until you agree to bond with me, Jaćken? Because I'll do it. You know I will."

He dropped his head, a low, pain-filled groan spilling out of him. She would, wouldn't she? Jesus, he was so in love with this whack-job. He wanted her for his wife more than he wanted to breathe. No more schizophrenia about it. He flat-out *wanted* her. "You're a beautiful and smart doctor, a damned *Royal*, and I'm...I'm...a Half-Rău hardass."

She released an unsteady breath. "Oh, Jaćken, do you have any idea how many pieces I'm in on the inside?" She pressed her forehead against his arm, her voice lowering to a whisper. "You're the only man who's ever made me feel whole."

His heart stopped, then restarted, thudding wildly. Jesus Christ, that's exactly how she made him feel. He turned his head to look at her. Their eyes caught and held, and he saw the truth of her words right there in the depths of her magnificent blue eyes. He swallowed hard and found his voice; it was hanging out at the bottom of his stomach, sloshing around with the acid there, burning his throat on the way up and out. "Holy shit."

She laughed breathlessly. "Oh, that's just the beginning of it, pal."

He straightened. "Why the hell didn't you say anything before, damn it, about your blood graph?"

"I had to know if you loved me first." The color of her eyes darkened. "There might be other royal Dragon women out in the world, Jaćken, I don't know. But as it stands now, I'm the one woman who can be your wife, who can give you a home and children, and I didn't want you to want me for only that."

He shook his head at her. "Haven't you been paying *any* attention *at all* these last few weeks?" He made a grab for her, pulling her into a tight embrace.

She wrapped her arms around his neck just as tightly.

Everyone in the room came to their feet and broke into applause.

"Ah, Jesus." He tucked his face into her throat and inhaled

deeply, allowing himself, at last, the supreme luxury of smelling her as his own. God, yeah, she definitely felt like his, her scent saturating him with such a sense of rightness, it was as if he was finding a long lost piece of his soul in this moment. "Don't you know," he whispered against her flesh, "that every viable feeling I've ever had in my whole life has been about you."

The clapping stopped abruptly.

Jaćken lifted his head.

Toni stepped out of his embrace, frowning at the opening door.

At first Jaćken thought it was Kimberly who was knocking while simultaneously pushing open the door—the woman entering had the same short, bobbed blonde hair as Sedge's wife—but, no, it was some nurse. "Dr. Parthen?"

"Yes, Penny?" Toni's frown deepened as she moved toward the nurse. "I thought I'd asked not to be disturbed."

"Um, I'm sorry, but…." The nurse gave her a distressed look. "The hospital was under strict orders to report it if you showed up."

"What are you talking about?"

Toni's question was answered as the door swung wide. There, standing in the hallway, were two men with guns and badges, one with brown hair, the other Spanish-looking with tan skin.

Penny gestured weakly at them. "This is Detective John Waterson and Pablo Ramirez of the San Diego Police Department."

CHAPTER THIRTY-ONE

Jacken's fist hooked out in a brutal uppercut, slamming into the brown-haired cop's chin to shut that gawping-way-the-fuck-open mouth of his....

All right...no, he didn't actually do it. But he saw the act in his mind's eye so clearly, so perfectly, it was as if he actually had. He also wouldn't mind pulling a Three Stooges on the peckerhead and double-fingering the man's bulging eyeballs back into their sockets. For Christ's sake, Toni might as well be naked, the way the cop was eyeballing her.

Jacken should probably cut the guy some slack, considering Toni did look totally hot. But slack-cutting had never been one of his strengths, and he certainly wasn't in the mood for it now. No, the longer that cop stared at Toni with such blatant hunger in his eyes, the more Jacken wanted to introduce the man to getting his ass kicked Rău-style.

"Toni," the cop exhaled her name. "Good God, you really are here."

"Detective Waterson?" Toni inflected her voice with mild surprise, although Jacken saw her hands flex and release at her sides. "What are you doing here? Is something wrong?"

The cop's expression morphed into something between incredulity and irritation. "You've been a missing person for more than two weeks now, Dr. Parthen, and I've been busting my hump trying to find you, *that's* what I'm doing here." He drew up right in front of her and stared her dead in the eyes.

A growl built in Jaćken's chest, a single *crackle* popping dangerously in his ears. He forced himself to concentrate on the glow of the light over the conference table, the smell of disinfectant, the sound of Sedge shifting his feet subtly into a stance of readiness. The growl exited his lips as a hard breath.

Toni cut him a chill-out glance.

Waterson followed the look around the edge of the door— and his eyebrows shot straight up.

"I think there's been a misunderstanding," Toni tried, but—

The cop wasn't listening to her. He was already shouldering past Toni, his eyes traveling in swift assessment over their group, lingering on Sedge and Jaćken. Looked like the cop didn't care much for their large size and obvious strength.

Waterson's dark-skinned partner followed, then Toni stepped back into the room, her expression strained.

Waterson's brows made another trip toward the ceiling when he spotted Toni's brother. "Well, isn't this interesting?" he drawled. "And here I thought you were frantic with worry over your sister, Alexander. Now you look like you should be having tea with the Queen."

"Yeah," Alex chuckled, "no worries, John. Everything's cool, as it turns out."

"Oh?" Waterson crossed his arms and rocked back on his heels. "How's that, exactly?"

"Ah, well, that's because, um...." Alex's smile skewed off center.

Jesus. Obviously, Mr. Milquetoast hadn't prepped for ways to avoid saying things like "vampires" and "secret, underground community." Jaćken muttered a curse under his breath. He'd be seriously amazed if he managed to get through this without hitting someone.

"Please, Detectives," Dr. Jess intervened, a charming smile aimed at the two cops. "If I might be permitted to clarify matters. I think Alex and Toni Parthen might seem a bit awkward because they're not sure how much they're allowed to say. You see, these past few weeks Dr. Parthen has been going through a rigorous interview process for a position with our Research Institute. We have a highly classified operation, however, so during the time Dr. Parthen was with us, she wasn't allowed contact with anyone outside of our facilities, including her family. We've just recently determined she's passed all of her security clearances, and we've come here tonight to officially offer her the position."

"I see," Waterson responded in the bland tone of someone whose bullshit meter was pinging.

"And the name of this institute?"

Dr. Jess gave Waterson a regretful look. "I'm sorry, but I'm not free to say anything more than I already have."

Waterson looked less than impressed. "Well, that's kind of problematic for me, isn't it?" He turned on Toni. "And you couldn't have told your family you were going to be out of touch *before* you left for this…interview?"

"Of course, and I thought I had," Toni answered, rolling smoothly into this new direction. "I was suffering from a concussion, though, and it had made me a bit fuzzy."

Jacken almost snorted his appreciation. *Good answer.*

Waterson pursed his lips. "I have to admit to feeling a bit fuzzy here, myself." He reached into his breast pocket, his lips slanting when Sedge and Jacken stiffened. The detective pulled out a small notebook and opened it. He glanced at it, then looked back up at Toni. "You wrote numerous emails to your brother stating that you were at a hematology seminar in St. Louis." He flipped the notebook closed with a short swing of his wrist. "Now why would you have done that, if you were really at some super hush-hush job interview?"

"I…didn't write any emails like that."

"They came from your email account."

Toni paused, her throat moving. Whether or not she would've eventually said something brilliant, it didn't matter. The silence was long and telling enough.

Waterson slid his notebook back into his breast pocket. "All right, here's what we're going to do. You two big boys are going to turn around and place your hands on the wall, making sure to act all nice and cooperative for my partner here. Nobody else moves—even sneezes—while I take Dr. Parthen into the hall for a private chat."

Jaćken narrowed his eyes on Waterson. He knew exactly what the cop was thinking: that Toni was really in trouble, but she and her brother were being forced to play along like everything was fine by two threatening "big boys," or someone else in the room. The assumption was reasonable. Unfortunately, Jaćken himself wasn't feeling especially top-heavy with reasonableness right now. In fact, Hell could freeze an ice palace up his ass before he'd allow this horny bastard to be alone with Toni.

"No." Jaćken clipped the single word.

Waterson smiled coldly. "Now how did I know *you'd* be the one to put up a fuss about that, champ?"

The dark-skinned cop slid a hand inside his coat.

Waterson jerked his chin at Jaćken's black clothes. "You're not a doctor with this Research Institute?"

"I'm with security."

"Ah. Well, then, you'll certainly understand my need to see your ID, won't you?" The chill in Waterson's smile worked into his eyes.

Jaćken felt a sneer start to pull at his upper lip. *If you don't mind me feeding it up your ass through a tube.*

Tension crackled in the air between them.

"You have very unusual eyes." Waterson's bland tone was back.

"My mother was French," Jaćken responded, just as mildly.

"That explains it. The ID?"

Jaćken reached for his wallet, moving slowly for the sake of the dark-skinned Cisco Kid over there with the itchy trigger finger. He pulled out one of Cleeve's manufactured business cards and held it out. "This is the contact information for the government agency we work for. We answer to *them*, cop, not to you. So any more questions you have can go through that number."

Waterson looked down at the business card and—

The cop's hand shot out, grabbing Jaćken by the wrist and yanking his arm forward. He shoved the long sleeve of Jaćken's leather jacket up to his elbow, exposing the teeth tattoos he'd spotted showing at the cuff of Jaćken's jacket. "Some unique tats you have here, sport."

Jaćken curled his free hand into a fist, but didn't slam Waterson's head down the chute of his neck like he wanted. The barrel of a gun had suddenly appeared at the side of his vision, pointing directly at his face. Waterson's partner had drawn his pistol.

"Oh, God," Toni groaned out.

"I was once in a gang," Jaćken squeezed through set teeth. "Now get your fucking hands off me."

Toni's lids sank closed. Not exactly the chill-out from him she'd been hoping for, probably.

"I think I'm going to choose option number two on this one, chief, and bring you down to the station for questioning. Men with tats like yours are wanted in connection with the attempted kidnapping of a teenage girl, as well as various other crimes around the city." Waterson pulled a two-way radio off his belt. "This is Detective Waterson," he spoke into it, "I'm going to need back up at—" Words stopped coming out of his mouth.

The Cisco Kid was disarmed and lying unconscious on the floor.

No one had even seen Sedge move.

"Oh, man," Alex Parthen breathed, "that was so cool."

"Restate your position, Detective Waterson," a voice crackled from the radio. "Your last transmission was—"

Jaćken grabbed the two-way out of Waterson's hand and

then, *pop*, one quick hard squeeze sent springs, buttons, and internal hardware flying in all directions.

A hammer would've normally been needed to achieve the same results, but Waterson didn't so much as blink an eyelash. *Damned impressive.* Jaćken almost hated to mess the guy up now. *Almost....* Lightning quick, he grabbed Waterson by the throat and hauled the man off the floor, feet dangling.

"Oh, my God," Toni gasped. "Please, don't hurt him."

Waterson strained bugged-out eyes in Toni's direction. "I'm sorry," he rasped.

"No," Toni said, "really, it's not what you—"

But the cop had already turned his attention back to Jaćken.

Jaćken had to hand it to Waterson, the man was a cool cucumber. Even with a roadway of veins sticking out along his forehead, the detective managed to look more peeved off than scared.

"I'm going to...kill you...for hurting her."

Jaćken snorted. "That's some piss-poor detective work, asswipe. Last thing anyone's going to do is hurt her."

"Just let him go," Toni pleaded, "please."

Jaćken cut her a look. "You want me to tuck him night-night into bed and give him a lollipop, too?" What was Toni thinking? Waterson wanted to take them all to jail.

Waterson bared his teeth in a grimace of pain. "This isn't...over between us."

"It is for me, Hoss." Jaćken lowered Waterson into striking range then smashed a fist into the side of the man's head.

Toni watched Waterson drop to the floor, stared at the cop for a count of two, then swung her eyes back up to Jaćken. "Are you *crazy*? You just made an enemy out of the SDPD?"

"Do you think I really give a—?" Jaćken spun around, bringing his fists up as the conference room door crashed open.

Kimberly stumbled inside. "Sedge! God, where's Sedge?"

"I'm here." Sedge leapt forward, his brow creased with concern. "What's going on, Berly?"

She flew into his arms. "I want to go home! Please! Take me back to Ţărână right now!"

Sedge's mouth dropped open. The man probably would've been more prepared for his wife to ask for a colonoscopy "since we're here at a hospital, anyway," than say that.

"Let's all get the hell out of here," Jaćken ordered, gesturing the husbands to gather their wives, "right now."

Earlier....

Kimberly cut through the ER and headed into the small offshoot room full of the vending machines, scanning the choices. Maybe she'd get a granola bar, too. It was, after all, really morning time to her body. Digging in her pocket, she found a dollar's worth of change and plunked the quarters into the coffee machine, one at a time. A cup dropped down, and Kimberly absently watched the long stream of steamy brown liquid squirt into the cup.

A couple of young women ducked into the vending machine room.

"I can't believe they brought him to *this* hospital," the redhead tittered. "Oh, Gawd, the ambulance is just pulling up."

"He's soooo amazing," the brunette cooed in agreement. "In a sec we're going to get to see him close up. I can't wait!"

Well, this was interesting. Had Justin Bieber hurt himself getting yet another tattoo? Kimberly grabbed her coffee cup and drew up to the young women, peering over their shoulders. "Who's coming in?"

The redhead glanced at her. "Only the Seattle Seahawks' best running back ever."

Kimberly's hand jerked into a clamp around her coffee cup. *The Seattle Seahawks....*

"Tim Armbruster," the brunette provided.

The name descended on Kimberly like the shock of a

misfiring gun, like a hand blown off, too absolute and horrific to be believed.

"Weren't you watching the game tonight?" the redhead babbled on. "He hurt his—"

Kimberly's lips parted and her lungs worked in two short pants before the rest of the oxygen clogged deep in her chest.

"—knee, and—"

"OMG," the brunette squealed. "There he is!"

The ER's sliding glass doors swished open and a gurney was pushed in holding a tall, muscular man.

Yes, there he was. Same dark brown hair and eyes, same square jaw, same athletically perfect body.

Every muscle in Kimberly's body locked up—except for the hand holding her coffee. That began to shake violently, splattering hot coffee onto her fingers. Her brain acknowledged the pain, the blistering of her skin, but she couldn't move. She was stuck, helpless. Powerless. Weak. Vulnerable. Suicidal. Her vision swam as she was thrust back to her college years, some of Tim's choicer comments rampaging through her mind as clear and hurtful as if he were hurling them at her right now.

Will you shut up, if I wanted the opinion of a blonde ditz, I'd ask for it.

And you call yourself a PoliSci major...? Christ, that was the stupidest fucking opinion ever.

Do you think it'd be too much to ask for you to actually move the next time we screw, or is it impossible for you to do anything right?

You're such a little whore...you wanna go bone that guy, is that why you're looking at him?

Bile seared up the back of her throat. And then there was the worst memory of them all...the blood gushing down her thighs.

The Tim on the gurney turned his head toward the vending machine area, and Kimberly slammed back against the wall to hide, her coffee cup slipping from her numb fingers. It hit the floor flat on its bottom and geysered up hot liquid, spraying across the carpet and onto the redhead's pants.

"Hey! What the—?!" The redhead broke off. "Whoa, lady, are you okay?"

Kimberly couldn't answer. Tears gushed silently and uncontrollably down her face. Her limbs gave way, dumping her onto her butt so hard her teeth clacked together.

"Oh, my God!" The redhead whirled on the brunette. "Get a doctor!"

Kimberly's head lolled to one side. She saw Tim disappear from the ER waiting room into the treatment area, and the breath she'd been holding ripped out of her. She sucked in another breath like a drowning woman, and another. "I need Sedge," she croaked. Her husband wouldn't let anyone hurt her. *Never, never, never....*

The redhead bent over her, her expression scrunched with confusion. "Doctor *who*?"

Exhaling a pained breath, Kimberly rolled onto her hands and knees, shook her head to clear it, then hefted herself to her feet and ran unsteadily for the elevator.

CHAPTER THIRTY-TWO

Kimberly slumped on her living room couch, sniffling wetly as she peered through the arched doorway of the foyer into the kitchen.

Her husband was filling a plastic bag with ice.

"The house is a w-wreck," she said through chattering teeth. She wasn't crying anymore, but had a serious case of the shakes.

"Yeah, sorry." Sedge crossed into the living room. "I'm not so great at picking up after myself in the first place, and the week you were gone everything just sort of went to hell." He sat down next to her. "Or I did." Taking her burned hand in his, he gently pressed the bag of ice on it. "That okay?"

Nothing was okay. But she nodded.

"So you did this with hot coffee?"

"Yes. It was an accident."

"Did someone bump into you?"

"No. I just spilled it."

"'Cause, yeah...." He cleared his throat. "You came barreling into that hospital conference room looking really upset." He lifted the ice off for a count of three, then replaced it. "You *were* really upset."

"Well, I'd just burned myself." She wouldn't meet his eyes.

"C'mon, Kimberly. Don't treat me like I'm stupid. I mean, you were begging to come back to Ţârână, for God's sake." He peeked briefly under the ice bag to check her hand. "You can't just leave me hanging about what caused that. *Something* happened."

She glanced aside, imagining Sedge's expression if she confessed the details of her relationship with Tim. Humiliation seared her cheeks. "I don't want to talk about it."

Sedge took the ice pack off her hand and set it on the coffee table. "This burn is going to need some ointment." He disappeared into the downstairs bathroom, then came back carrying a small tube like toothpaste. "If the roles were reversed, you'd want me to tell you what had happened, wouldn't you?"

Oh, dirty pool. "Just leave it alone, Sedge. And don't give me one of your puppy dog looks."

He unscrewed the top off the tube. "Did you see your parents while you were topside?"

Her eyes followed his movements as he set the cap on the coffee table next to the ice.

"Were they mean to you?" He squeezed white, creamy ointment onto his index finger. "I know they can be sometimes."

Her upper lip beaded with sweat. The feel of a python wrapping around her throat, slowly strangling her, pushed tears into her eyes.

Sedge gently took her burned hand again. "Did you run into somebody you used to know, some bitch from school, maybe?" He smoothed the ointment onto her burns so carefully that the tears in her eyes gathered along her lower lashes.

Where were you my whole life? She gulped a breath. *Why couldn't I have found you sooner?*

"Maybe some guy you used to date? You and he had a bad break up that—"

Her hand jerked so hard the spasm made Sedge smear ointment along her thumb. He whipped his gaze up to her face, his lips parting as he watched tear droplets roll off her lashes and onto her cheeks like an avalanche of crystal pebbles.

"Oh, shit," he hissed. "It was a guy."

She wrenched her hand away from him. "Leave me alone, Sedge." She slammed to her feet and stormed into the kitchen.

He trailed after her.

"I told you I don't want to talk about it, and I mean it!"

"I can't help you if I don't know what's going on."

"Well, for your information, I don't need your help." She skirted around the kitchen island and hauled open a cupboard. "I'm just fine, thank you very much."

"You and I both know that's not true."

She grabbed a water glass and headed for the sink.

"This is about more than just a bad breakup, isn't it? I can see it on your face."

Her fingers convulsed. The glass fell and shattered on the kitchen floor. "Fuck!"

"Oh, Jesus. Kimberly—"

She dashed toward the other side of the kitchen island, aiming for the stairs. She was going to bed and wouldn't get up for a week!

"Damn it, would you quit running away." Sedge reached out to take her arm, moving with the same swift, aggressive grace he used when bearing down on an Om Rău.

His body heat hit her, tripping panic buttons in her brain. Sedge himself disappeared; she could only see a wide, looming chest coming at her, large flexed biceps. She screamed and flinched away.

Sedge froze with his arm outstretched, her scream echoing away into nothing but the sound of her heavy breathing. Several weighted seconds stalked past. He dropped his hand, very slowly, dawning realization spreading over his face. "The guy hurt you."

She gave her head a violent shake. "No," she rasped out. "Don't make me tell you about this. I *can't*."

Emotion simmered off him. "I'm your husband, Kimberly. This is something I need to know."

A lump grew in her throat like a malignancy. "You won't l-love me anymore." There it was! Out loud! "You'll think I was weak for letting it happen." She *was* weak!

"No way," Sedge came back instantly. "No fucking way. That's impossible."

She just stood there, acid in her throat.

"Tell me." Sedge stepped up to her.

"Don't—" Her chest clutched painfully, memories smashing through her mind like falling boulders.

"I promise I won't—"

"Stop it!" she cried. "Stop talking to me! Don't...don't even look at me!" She smashed her eyes shut and turned aside. "I don't want you to, do you hear!"

"Okay." She heard him back off. "Okay."

Tears seeped out from under her lashes. Her lungs compressed and her heart was beating so fast it felt like it might fly out of her chest. After a long moment, she heard Sedge pull out a kitchen chair. She opened her eyes to see what he was doing

He met her gaze somberly. "I'm going to sit at this table and not move, all right." He sat. "See? And"—he transferred the salt shaker from the middle of the table to a spot right in front of him—"I'm going to stare at this the whole time you talk. I won't look at you, like you asked." He settled his hands on either side of the salt shaker and gazed steadily at it. He waited, but when she didn't say anything, he asked quietly, "So will you tell me what happened?"

She swiped at her eyes with her fist and drew in a fractured breath. Her stomach was in a macramé of knots and the hot taste of vomit sat at the back of her tongue, but somehow she had to force her way through this. Because Sedge was right; he was her husband and deserved to know this.

"I saw an ex-boyfriend in the ER tonight at Scripps," she admitted miserably.

"All right." A ripple of tension passed through Sedge, but he did a pretty good job of not letting much of it show. "And he...he was the one who used to hurt you?"

"It didn't start out like that," she came back defensively. "He was very charming and charismatic, you know, and I was...so young. I was still in college when we first met and easily swept off my feet by his good looks and stardom." She hesitated, and Sedge nodded, encouraging her. "The bad stuff began as only these...little things, like he'd take my dessert away from me in a restaurant and laughingly say he was saving my poor hips from becoming battleships. Or he'd make me change clothes before we went out, saying I'd be thanking him later for saving me from *that* near disaster."

Emotions pressed in on her chest, that familiar hateful sense of worthlessness. "And then one night we were at this frat party and I made some remark, a joke, I guess...I don't even remember what I said. Everyone laughed, and, well.... He must've thought they were laughing *at* him because when we got back to his apartment afterwards...." Her throat swelled and narrowed, trying to shut off her next words. "He slapped me across the face, hard enough to knock me to the floor, and told me if I ever said anything like that again he'd beat me until I bled from every fucking pore."

Sedge stiffened, his nostrils flaring.

"I...Jesus, I was stunned. I'd never been struck before in my life, and I didn't know what to do. I thought about breaking up with him, *of course*, but the next morning, he was so apologetic. He brought me flowers and a diamond tennis bracelet and swore he'd never do it again." Her voice faded to a whisper. "And I believed him."

She swallowed, trying to bring moisture into her mouth. "He did hit me again, and again, but, *God*, he was always so regretful afterwards and so nice to me for a while that I.... I was so confused, and somehow I just ended up staying with him." Her hands started to tremble. She flexed them into fists, then stretched her fingers open. "But then his apologies stopped altogether and the real nightmare began: his joking comments turned into outright insults and his slaps became punches."

Sedge's fingertips dug into the top of the table.

"Over the two years we were together, he told me I was fat, stupid, lazy, and accused me of being a whore any time another man looked at me, no matter that *I* never provoked it. He bloodied my nose countless times, blackened my eyes, knocked out one of my molars, cracked my ribs, broke my wrist, mutilated two of my toes under the heel of his boot, and bruised my body in too many places to count."

Sedge was sitting rigid as steel at the table now, his chest jerking up and down.

"By this time, I was desperate to get away from him," she choked out, "I swear I was, but I was terrified. He'd threatened to kill me if I ever left him, and I knew he would. I didn't think I could manage it alone, either." Shame settled over her, as leaden and dark as despair. "I felt so dumb and useless and oafish by that point. I couldn't do anything without him. And…and then…." A strangled sound escaped her lips. She couldn't say this part! The memory was still a jagged piece of glass in her heart. "Oh, Sedge," she cried softly.

He shot out of his chair in a heartbeat, his chocolate brown eyes ravaged with pain for her.

But she held out a trembling hand to hold him off, the terrible words falling one after the other from her mouth. "One night he came home to our apartment drunk, and attacked me in bed, rough and impatient, and I…. I couldn't say *no* to him, for the love of God. I wasn't able to get my diaphragm in and I ended up…getting pregnant."

Sedge stood riveted by the kitchen island, his face a tight, grim mask.

"I was so scared to tell him about that, but then he was … okay with it. Surprised at first, yes, and I thought maybe…maybe…." An hysterical noise bubbled out of her. "But no, stupid me. A couple of nights later he came home drunk again, raging that the baby wasn't his, screaming that no way with a whore like me the baby was his. He—" Her lungs strained, ached. "He took me by the throat, rammed me against the wall, and started punching me, over and over." She exhaled raggedly. "Right in the stomach."

"No," Sedge moaned.

Anguish ballooned in her chest, the remembered pain, the feel of warm blood gushing down her thighs as the baby inside her died. "You can't blame him, though, Sedge." Silent tears rolled steadily down her face, drenching the front of her shirt.

"Oh, Jesus," Sedge croaked. "Don't say that."

"I should've *left him!*" she cried out, wildness stirring behind her breastbone.

"Kimberly, no—" Sedge stepped forward, reaching for her again.

She shoved his hands away. "If I hadn't been too weak to leave him, then…then my baby would be…." *Alive.* The balloon burst: all the pain, the sorrow, the guilt, the self-hatred. *Everything.* She threw her head back and screamed, long and loud and throbbing, her throat searing raw.

Sedge stumbled forward and pulled her into a fierce embrace, his arms trembling as they wrapped around her.

She pounded her fists against his muscled body, still screaming as guilt tore her insides to ribbons. "No! No! No!" She tangled her fingers into the front of his shirt, pulling and jerking at the material, driving herself into a coughing fit. She started to gasp and wheeze.

Sedge hurried her over to the kitchen sink, scattering through the broken glass on the floor.

That was good thinking. She bent over the basin and threw up.

When she was done, he pulled her against the protective strength of his chest again.

She sagged boneless against him, her eyes sore, her throat like sandpaper.

"Don't you *dare*," his voice vibrated around the word, "blame yourself for anything that bastard did to you, Kimberly. Do you hear me?" He smoothed a palm over her short hair, the gesture comforting, even though his hand was shaking.

"That prick systematically destroyed you. He started out with those little jabs at your self-esteem, right? Small shit you would've felt ridiculous calling him on, but that picked away at your confidence, all the same. And once he had your defenses knocked down, the fucker terrorized you with violence, knowing he'd made you helpless." He pressed his cheek to the side of her head. "He *broke* you, honey. How can you even remotely think you could've left him under circumstances like that? Any woman would've had a tough time with that."

She blinked rapidly and chewed her bottom lip, trying just to let her husband's words wash over her like a balm. He wasn't...judging her.

"You're not weak," he went on. "There's nothing you wouldn't do for anybody, Berly. I've seen that with my own eyes. Like rallying the Dragons into mutiny—and don't try to tell me you weren't the genius behind that. You knew the community would be pissed as hell about it, but you did it anyway, to right a wrong." His voice lowered. "And it was the same with your baby, I bet. Right? It's one thing for your asshole ex-boyfriend to beat the crap out of you, but let him harm your child...." He trailed off.

She nodded, her eyes moistening again. "Yes," she whispered. "As soon as I could get out of bed after the miscarriage, I called a shelter. After that, I ran away to the Peace Corps to hide from him."

He inhaled-exhaled. "So much about your unhappiness makes sense to me now, honey. You've always got this huge, invisible weight on your shoulders. Or in your heart. You're just not satisfied unless you're saving the whole world, and it's not right. You're too frantic about it. I think...it's because you're so relentlessly *punishing* yourself for what happened to your baby, feeling like you should've somehow been able to save your kid. You run around saving everybody else to make up for it, keeping yourself so crazy-busy that you never take the time to just...live for yourself. To be happy." He kissed her hair. "Our whole marriage I've been killing myself trying to figure out how to make you happy, but now I see you've been refusing to let me."

That was probably partially true. She pulled back a little and looked up at him. "Let's not discount the kidnapping thing, either, Sedge."

His lips lifted in a rueful smile. "I think you know I've never done that."

"And don't forget that I've been deprived of the work that I love."

"That's going to change, too, I promise. If Toni doesn't see to it, I will." He brushed a tendril of hair from her eyes. "You missed the big face-off in the conference room. Everyone's listening to you Dragons now. No more kidnappings and Toni's going to be co-leader of Ţărână. You won, Kimberly."

She blinked once. "I won? really?"

"Yep." He chuckled. "Now come on, I'm going to take you upstairs and remind you how a man is supposed to treat a woman. A hot bath, a cup of tea, those smelly candles you like, maybe a little massage action."

"Oh, boy." She gazed into his eyes, taking in all of the love and safety he had to offer her, letting it wrap around her. "Believe me when I tell you that I'm all yours, hubby."

He swept her into his arms and headed up the stairs.

CHAPTER THIRTY-THREE

Toni kicked off her slingback pumps and crossed to the lamp on her bedside table, turning the brightness down to something more romantic. Her blood sang with anticipation, that special kind of giddy excitement a girl only felt when she knew she was about to get laid by a super sexy guy. Maybe later she'd do a victory moon walk.

Nearly chuckling, she scooped up the bottle of Châteauneuf-du-Pape sitting next to the Contessa phone on her nightstand. What would Dev say if he knew she was about to use his gift of one of his finest French reds to seduce another man out of his clothes?

"Hey, Jaćken, why don't you grab a couple of wine—" She cut herself off.

The object of her lust was standing with his back pressed flat against her locked bedroom door, his eyes unblinking, his lips parted around short, shallow breaths.

Here was a new sight: Jaćken on the verge of an all-out panic.

She held up the bottle, slowly, carefully. *No sudden movements around the virgin, ladies and gentlemen, we don't want to scare him off.* "I thought we could enjoy a glass of wine first."

"No." He cleared a scratch from his voice. "I mean, no, uh…thank you. I'm good."

Politeness? Oh, this was worse than she'd thought. "Are you sure?" She couldn't help a small smile. "You look a little nervous."

"Yeah, I'm…feeling a bit boggled."

"Boggled?" She laughed as she set down the bottle. "That doesn't sound like a word you'd use."

"Fucking boggled, then."

She rolled her eyes, even though she laughed again. "Our children are going to be such potty mouths, Jaćken, I swear to God."

The shell-shocked expression returned to his face. "Children," he repeated hoarsely. "Jesus, Toni, I can't believe…this just can't be real." He shoved both hands back through his hair, then stood with his fingers gripping the base of his neck, his elbows spread wide. The stance served to display and augment the magnificent bulk of his body to perfection, his biceps curled up thick, the massive range of his shoulders and lats tapering down to a flat, board-like belly and narrow hips, his solidly muscled legs planted apart in his typical posture of confidence and power.

The sight sent a bolt of pure lust shooting straight through her. "You've got such a great body. You have no idea how long I've wanted to see you naked."

His arms fell back to his sides. He blinked, then snorted. "Yeah, well, I might have a clue about that on my own end."

She strode up to him with a heavy-lidded look. "Well, then, why don't we start making everything feel a lot more real?" She tugged the shirt from his waistband.

He exhaled a burst of air and jerked sideways away from her.

She arched her brows at him. "Running away? That's what boggling does?"

He flushed. "No. I just…I don't…."

She stepped back. "Let's take a short station break. How much do you know, exactly? Are you aware of the whole penis-in-the-vagina thing?"

"Jesus," he hissed, his face turning a deeper shade of red. "Yes, of course. We all took sex ed in school, and...I watched part of a porno once."

Eee-yikes. "Um, well, those aren't exactly the best training videos for what women like. So maybe it'd be best if you just follow my lead."

"No...I mean, yes, following you is fine. It's just.... It's hard to get used to the idea that I'm allowed to do this, Toni, okay?" He held up both hands, showing them to her. "I've never been allowed to touch you. At all."

"Oh, honey," she murmured, her heart warming. "Keep reminding yourself that I'm yours now, okay?" She grabbed his shirttails again, but paused. "I'm going to just do my thing, all right? If I move too fast, you be sure to let me know." She hauled his shirt off over his head, catching a glimpse of the twin dark patches of hair under his arms. In his armpits and on his head seemed to be the only places on his body he had hair. And...her eyes strayed to the front of his pants. *There?*

She forced her eyes back up, and smoothed her palms over his tattooed chest, feeling his muscles tense beneath his flesh. "Let your hunger for me guide you," she whispered. "Don't think of anything else." His skin was warm and surprisingly soft over the hard contours of his muscles. *Satin over steel....* She swept her thumbs along the ridges of muscle underlying his pecs. A small sound escaped her lips as the raw virility of him sent heat spiraling through her, desire pooling hot and liquid between her thighs.

Jacken slammed back against the door, a *crack* of wood, his nostrils flaring.

She gave him a sultry smile. "That's me. I'm so wet for you, Jacken."

His eyes opened wider.

"Touch me, too." Wrapping a palm around the nape of his

neck, she pulled him down for a kiss. "I want your hands on me so much," she said against his lips. Taking one of his palms, she placed it on her breast.

A breath ripped out of him and rushed into her mouth. He tried to pull away, but she wouldn't let him. She locked her palm solidly over the top of his hand at her breast and slanted her lips passionately over his, plunging her tongue deeply into his mouth, delving and exploring, making him kiss her back. God, it was so much better than that drugged-out day in the mansion's main parlor. Everything was so vivid this time. His tongue was sweet velvet against her own, and the taste of him was like having living fire inside her mouth, with all the burn and none of the pain.

She arched against him until finally, *finally*, he gave her boob a single, cautious squeeze. Her nipple peaked against his palm, and she moaned low in her throat, the need between her thighs growing hotter, wetter.

Jaćken tore his lips from hers, a long, hissing breath threading between his clenched teeth.

She didn't want to stop, but it was impossible not to notice that the noises he was making weren't entirely pleasure-filled. "Jaćken," she breathed, "what's wrong? Are you in pain?"

"Jesus, yes. I need to claim you, Toni." He tunneled his fingers into her hair and tilted her head to one side, his eyes latching onto her throat with glinting hunger.

She looked at his elongated fangs, brilliant white and wickedly sharp, and an unholy thrill curled up her spine. Who would've guessed the prospect of being bitten would be such a turn-on, but she'd never wanted anything so much in her life. "Yes, I'm ready."

"Thank God," he groaned. He pulled her close and dropped his face to her throat, one hand cradling the back of her head and the other pressing the center of her spine. He nuzzled her flesh, the rush of his breath tickling her as he drew in several deep lungfuls of her scent. She felt him shudder, and her heartbeat picked up its pace.

"Your scent's already so deep inside my head. Damn...." A low growl rumbled out of him, the animal quality of it spraying gooseflesh up her arms. He latched his lips onto her neck and sucked eagerly at her skin, the pull of his mouth drawing a corresponding tug out of the depths of her womb. Her nipples ripened and puckered, her breathing speeding up. A pulsating power *hummed* from his fangs, sending a shiver of anticipation through her belly. Suddenly she couldn't hold her head upright any longer.

Jacken lifted his own head. "Toni." His voice was heavy with desire, deep and silky. "Do you know about the first bite hurting?"

"What?" she mumbled.

"Shit," he cursed softly. "Toni, open your eyes." His grip on her hair tightened, keeping her head from lolling off her neck. "I need you to listen to me."

It took a Herculean effort, but she pried open her eyes a little, peering at him through the slit of her lids.

"This is going to hurt," he told her. "I'm sorry, honey. The first bite always does. Just...hang in for five seconds, then the Fiinţă will kick in and you'll be fine."

She nodded drowsily.

He hesitated still. "After you've got Fiinţă running regularly through your body, then it'll never hurt, okay?" His hand at the small of her back urged her snugly against his body.

"It's all right," she murmured.

But, no. It wasn't all right.

As his enormous shoulders hunched over her and his hard jaws snapped closed around her throat, her entire body jerked in pain and shock. *Holy Mother of—*! What she'd thought would be no worse than a couple of immunization shots felt instead like two daggers plunging into her vulnerable carotid. She cried out, fear rocketing through her.

Blood gushed out of her artery, filling Jacken's mouth, bringing such a noise of shattering pleasure out of him, her panic deepened. He sucked harder, and instinct for survival seized her. "Jaċken!" She struggled against him. "Stop!"

He only held her tighter, one arm wrapping around her waist like a steel band, the other hand tangling around a fistful of her hair.

A fear unlike any she'd ever known roared through her. Her eyes flared wide and she hauled in a sharp breath. The sound of Jaċken's greedy swallowing and his constant rumblings of elation filled her with the absolute certainty that he was going to lose control and drink too much.

He was going to kill her!

CHAPTER THIRTY-FOUR

Toni gasped as Jaćken drove her down to the floor, his heavily muscled body crushing her into the carpet, his fangs still working relentlessly at her throat. "No, Jaćken!" *Damn him*! She struggled harder, bucking and heaving. "No-oooooh." Her protest sputtered into a moan as she went utterly limp.

The pleasure was impossible. Fist-sized starbursts of heat were lighting off all over her body, gradually melding into a single large pool of fantastic sensation that—Oh. My. God. Her back spasmed into an arch on its own as the tide of warm molasses ecstasy glided lazily through her extremities, seeped into the trunk of her body, then gathered with mind-altering magnificence right in her crotch. She dug her fingernails into Jaćken's shoulders, the sultry heat flooding the folds of her sex. She swelled and clenched and...dear God, she was sopping wet. *Yes. Oh, yes*. Her vagina started to throb with pre-climatic pulsations.

She was panting urgently enough to hyperventilate when that fool man of hers withdrew his wretched, wonderful fangs. "Don't stop," she moaned.

He reared above her onto his knees and threw his arms wide.

Flinging his head back, he howled in utmost savage glory.

She gaped up at him, stunned rigid.

When he looked down at her again, his eyes were stained unfathomably black with lust. "*Fuck*, you taste fantastic." He dropped his gaze to her heaving breasts, then surprised the hell out of her by grabbing the front of her wraparound blouse and yanking hard. Like a special effects tear-away blouse, it came off in one pull, bra and all.

"J-Jaċken," she stuttered, "my God."

He paused a moment to stare in fierce-eyed admiration at her best feature, then with a low, almost purring snarl, he clamped his hand around her bare breast. He massaged and molded it, clumsy and too rough, but her nipple hardened anyway, and in the next breath, his face was pressed between her cleavage. He kissed her there, his breath warming her flesh, then moved to lap at one of her nipples. She dug her fingers into his hair, encouraging him. He latched onto the tight bud with his lips, suckling her with such strong pulls a low groan pushed passed her lips.

Immediately, he jerked off her.

"Don't stop," she protested again. "It's so good."

"Holy shit." His voice was a deep rasp of amazement.

She followed the direction of his gaze down to the front of his black pants. The crotch was bulging outward.

With unsteady hands, he unclasped his belt, then slowly undid his button fly. *Pop...pop...pop....* Boxer briefs came into view, actual ones, not workout gear.

Her mouth went dry. It looked like a lead pipe had been stuffed down the front of his underwear.

"Yeah." He eagerly pushed his briefs down his hips, his erection springing into view. "*Shit* yeah."

A pleased sound broke from her throat. She'd never seen such a fine a piece of male equipment in all of her dating years. He was in possession of both length and girth, and...beautiful. No bulging veins marred his length, as was so often the case with this part of a man, and the top of him wasn't some purple, bulbous head. He was impeccably smooth, pure white marble from his thatch of black hair—hair!—all the way out.

"That," she breathed, "would've been a waste of some fine male apparatus if I hadn't come along." She wrapped her fingers around the jutting appendage.

"Hell!" His body convulsed, and he wrenched her fingers away. "I need to come inside you to complete the bond between us, Toni, not all over this damned room."

"*All* over the room?" She pushed up onto her elbows, lifting her eyebrows high. "Wow. Is there something about the Vârcolac male's trajectory abilities I should know before we—?"

Her sentence gasped to a halt when Jaćken towered to his feet, pulling her up with him. "Get undressed," he ordered her.

The command was clipped curtly and the way in which he'd just helped her up was rather abrupt, but she didn't complain. The high voltage of power emanating from him suggested a discussion about his manners wouldn't have been prudent just then.

"Okay." She slipped out of her pencil skirt, letting it drop to her ankles, then shoved her panties down and kicked both garments aside. She stood before him naked, the wash of air over her body keeping her aroused nipples crinkled into erect points.

Jaćken pinned blazing eyes onto her triangle of curls. "Blonde," he said on a resonant growl. "I thought the hair down there was supposed to be darker than what's on your head."

Her laugh was a little uneven; understandable, considering she was the only one completely naked in the room and her private area was being all but devoured by a pair of black eyes. "Well, I don't dye my hair, so my *down there* matches my—"

"It's pretty. Get on the bed." He gestured brusquely. "I want to look at it."

Her heart stumbled to a standstill. "You want to…to…?" *Look at it?*

He plowed forward, giving her little choice but to hurry over to the bed and hike herself up onto it or risk being run over. She scooted to the middle of the mattress and settled back on her elbows, her legs crossed at the ankles.

Jaćken kicked his boots aside, then nearly ripped the seams of his pants hauling them off. Her lips parted as she watched his muscles ripple and bulge with the task of stripping himself down to buck-gorgeous-nakedness.

The mattress dipped as he planted a knee on it. "Lie back." He climbed toward her. "Bend your knees."

Shivering even though it wasn't cold, she did what he asked, swallowing hard as he bore down on her. Excitement dizzied her senses and—how unexpected—her belly quaked with a little nervousness of her own.

Jaćken placed a hand on each of her bent knees and pushed them apart. A breath slid out of him. "Look at that." His eyes drank in the sight of her. "You're so pink."

She made a tight noise in her throat, her core giving a little pulse. Who knew being inspected could be so arousing and—

Yipe! Her body lurched violently when he swirled his fingertips through the little curls covering her mons, his touch sending an avalanche of sparks tripping through her pelvis.

He jerked his hand away. "What just happened?"

"That," she gasped out, "felt good."

He regarded her strangely. "*Just* that?"

She gave him the best droll look she could muster just then. "Would you like me to touch your hair down there, Jaćken?"

His lips slanted. "Point taken." He reached for her again, his fingers trailing along her sensitive inner thigh, sending more shivers racing through her body. He hunkered down between her thighs to get a better view, his broad shoulders forcing her legs wide. *Oh, God, what's he going to—*

A moan of sheer pleasure erupted from her throat as he slicked a finger along the length of her moist cleft. The biggest shudder yet wracked her body.

He made a fascinated *humph* noise, and involved several more fingers in his examination. He gently explored every pink, dewy fold of her, spreading her lips and—*oh, sweet death*—discovering her clitoris.

"J-Jacken," she stammered out, her thighs starting to quiver. "Jacken, please...."

"Damn, you *are* wet."

She stared fixedly at the familiar sixteen-bulb light fixture overhead with an unholy mix of profound embarrassment and gut-punching arousal when he leaned in close to her opening and inhaled a deep breath. "Smell good, too. Hell, woman, if you could bottle and sell this scent, you'd make a mint." He pushed the tip of his finger experimentally into the entrance to her body.

That's it! "Jacken," she gulped out. "Honey...sweetheart." She could hardly breathe her heart was beating so fast. "I need you to come up here to me."

His head popped up above her hips, a concerned look on his face. "Is something wrong?"

"N-no. I just need you inside me, is all." *Too fast*? Was she going too fast?

"I'm not done. I want to touch you all over." He bared his teeth in a grin that showed his fangs. "Taste you."

She actually gulped. That would kill her right about now. She grabbed hold of his arms and urged him up her body, settling him between her legs. "You can touch me later."

"But—"

Reaching between their bodies, she grabbed his sex and positioned him at her entrance. She felt him stiffen, heard him make a surprised noise. "Right now"—she gripped his butt—"you're driving me crazy." She pulled him in, *hard*.

A guttural, roaring shout erupted out of him as he landed deep inside her, his shaft gliding easily on her slippery wetness. She moaned and arched her spine in pleasure, wanting more. He was a fulsome weight inside her, hard and powerful and throbbing, the size of him stretching her sheath in a promise of fantastic friction once he got going.

If he got going.

Right now he was frozen above her on quaking arms, his lips slack, his eyes huge.

"It's all right," she assured him breathlessly. "It's *so* good, honey."

He remained frozen in place. A bead of sweat lazed out of his hairline and down his temple.

"Try moving, okay?" She lifted her hips toward him in encouragement.

He gave a small, experimental thrust. An enormous shudder rocked his body, and he slammed to a halt. "I can't," he hissed. "It'll end."

"Then we'll just do it again." She touched his arm. "And again and again. We have the rest of our lives to make love together."

He squinched his eyes closed, a vein pulsing visibly in his forehead.

Oh, boy. This wasn't working. "Why don't you lie on your back?" She nudged him over with a hand on his shoulder, making sure they didn't separate as she settled on top of his lap, her legs straddling his thighs. Her lips slackened as a surge of sensation crested in her. His thick sex was penetrating her more deeply in this position, the tip of him kissing a pleasure spot immersed within the farthest reaches of her core. The raging need to feel every long inch of him burned through her. She slowly lifted up on her knees, sliding off his shaft to the ridge of his head, then sank back down. A small cry tumbled past her lips.

He shouted again, his hands clamping her waist to still her movements.

"No, Jacken." She pried his fingers off. "This is where you need to keep your hands." She raised his arms above his head, the tattoos on his chest undulating, and made him wrap his fingers around the bottom edge of the headboard. "Don't let go."

He gave her a dark, panicky look.

"You want me to have my pleasure, too, don't you?"

Apparently that convinced him. He didn't interfere this time when she started to rock her hips against him, slowly setting a rhythm. She tried to maintain a moderate tempo, she really did, but he just felt too good inside her, and before she knew what was happening, she had her chin tucked to her chest, her eyes squeezed shut, and her palms planted flat on his chest as she slammed up and down on top of him, so vigorously it was as if she had some perverse need to knock her cervix into her stomach. An endless string of pleasure-noises spilled out of her.

"Oh, yes!" A knot in her womb started to loosen. *God*! It'd been so long since she'd climaxed, she'd almost forgotten how the beginnings of it felt. "Jaćken," she panted, "I'm going to come, just…just…."

He was clutching the headboard for dear life, his head arched back into the mattress, teeth and fangs gritted, the veins in his neck straining against his skin. "*Toni.*" Her name was a gnashed warning: he couldn't hold on any longer.

That was fine; she was done. The taut coil inside her snapped loose, sending wave after wave of unbelievable pleasure thundering through—A surprised *whoop* burst out of her as the Fiinţă still coursing through her veins grabbed hold of her orgasm and spun it off the charts. Her entire body convulsed and jerked in an explosion of unbelievable ecstasy, bright sparklers dotting the sides of her vision, her sheath clutching at Jaćken's penis in an impossibly tight grip.

"Ah!" His body strained so hard off the bed at that, he almost bucked her off. She threw her hands against the headboard to brace herself as a primeval roar of rapture erupted out of him, a noise that went so far beyond human capacity for pleasure, she had no idea where inside him it could've possibly come from.

Wet heat throbbed inside of her, her womb flooding with warmth as Jaćken shuddered to the end of his very first orgasm.

"Ho-holy fuck," he gasped, sprawling in heaving shock on the mattress beneath her.

Fighting for breath, she fell forward against his chest,

holding him tight as she listened to the wild beat of his heart and the loud, panting grabs for oxygen his lungs were making. As she calmed, she ran a hand idly over his torso, enjoying the contrasting sensations of smooth flesh over thick bones and ridged muscles, discovering a puckered scar near one of his ribs. When the storm inside him finally passed, she lifted her head and peered at her new husband. "So…?" she inquired. "Was it any good?"

She felt him go still. Then his chest rumbled, the vibrations starting out as a small chuckle that grew into full-throated laughter.

"My God." She gaped at him. "I didn't even know you were *capable* of laughter like that, Jaċken."

He shook his head at her, his eyes bright. "Woman, you seriously need to expand your vocabulary if you think 'good' even *begins* to cover what just happened between us."

She gave him an intimate smile. "Yes. For me, too."

His lips settled into a tender, close-mouthed smile of his own. Raising his hand to cup her cheek, he threaded his fingers into the side of her hair. "Hey, you," he said quietly, his gaze filling with such deep affection that her insides scurried about with frantic joy, aimless and bonking into stuff like a wind-up toy. How long had she yearned to see him look at her like that?

"Hey back," she whispered.

His thumb swept the curve of her cheek in a gentle caress. "Have I told you how much I love you, Dr. Toni Parthen?"

CHAPTER THIRTY-FIVE

Somewhere along the way, the mattress beneath Jaćken had turned into a pile of soft feathers. He was sunk deeply into it, *engulfed* in the bed, it seemed, his muscles gelatinous, his bones just…washed away under the effects of satiated exhaustion. He'd never felt more relaxed in his life, never so content. His mind was a desert oasis. No memories of Oṭărât were banging on the door to his brain, no grumblings about the crap circumstances of his existence were yapping in his ears. Those were just blurry images at the back of the stadium. Hard to believe just a few short hours ago he'd been moping over scrambled eggs about the endless misery of his life.

He heard Toni puttering around in the bathroom, the soft padding of her footsteps and water running. He smiled and stretched languorously, the sinews in his right shoulder popping. *Maybe there's a God, after all.*

There sure as shit was a Heaven, that was for damned certain, and it lay right between—to be unavoidably crass about it—the legs of a certain strawberry-blonde doctor he was completely nuts about. *Fan-fucking-tastic.* That's what sex was. How else to describe the indescribable? He'd been utterly

265

unprepared for the whole show. Not that an assload of imaginings hadn't gone into picturing what making love to Toni would be like, but the reality of having her mount up his cock and giddy-up him to within an inch of his life still had him reeling. He broke into a broader grin. Ten out of ten points for taking a guy's virginity in a way that was totally cool, though.

"Jaćken," Toni sang out from the bathroom, "could you come in here for a sec?"

What, he had to *move*? Stupid question. Damn right he did. Because when hot blonde wifey called, then recently laid male—whose awakened cock was really fucking excited to lend new meaning to the term eager beaver—came running. Or maybe he should say *frigging*, seeing as the events of the last few hours had turned him into a husband. He should probably try to tone down the potty mouth.

He sauntered into the bathroom on deliciously weak knees. "Yes, dear?" he drawled.

Toni was standing near the tub, her body wrapped in a plush white towel and her hair piled on top of her head in a messy bun. He was brought up short by the sight of her exposed neck. *Shit*. The skin where he'd bitten her had already purpled into a nasty bruise, the twin puncture marks an angry red. Yeah, he knew the first bite always went rough for a newbie, but it still rankled that he'd hurt her.

"I thought we could take a bath together," she said.

Behind her, both faucets were jetting water into a tub large enough for four men. It was a tub fit for royalty—which worked out really well for *her* now, didn't it?—the basin enclosed by a wide, semi-circular ledge of white tiles, about every fifth one painted with a blue fleur-de-lis. The ledge ascended in steps to a pedestal at the back where a vase of silk flowers about the size of a small child sat. Short mirrors, bordered in gold curlicue frames, and already fogging up from the rising steam, surrounded all sides of the tub.

"I wash you," she went on, "you wash me." She slanted a smile at him. "I did say you could touch me later, after all."

He scratched the back of his head. "Did you? Ah. That must've been around the time you were taking my dick in your eager little fist and ramming it inside you." He reached for a back tooth with his tongue. "I might've been a bit distracted."

She planted her hands solidly on her hips, huffing at him. "Okay, so maybe I went a little too fast, but I was extremely horny, buster. Are you really going to stand there and complain about that?"

"Nope. I actually think there're probably some awesome perks to having a tartlet for a wife."

"A—?" Her lips twitched before she could stop them. "Well, this bath isn't about sex, bub. All right? It's about touching *only*. Do you think you can handle that?"

"Sure. Easy as pie, Doc. I don't want to have sex with you at all."

"Excellent."

"You pretty much wrung me dry on that last one."

"Well, hop in, then." She dropped her towel to the bathroom floor and gave him a saucy look.

Oh, damn me.... His gut went buttery as he raked his gaze over her body: her high firm breasts with those rosy nipples that poked out at him as impudently as the woman herself, the sweet nip of her slender waist flaring into softly rounded hips, the apex of her thighs where gold—in every sense of the word— nested. It whacked the air right out of him. He had to flex his toes into the tiles to keep from flying at her and frantically scrambling his hands all over her goodies like she was an exploded piñata.

Her eyes sparkling sassily, she stepped into the tub and sank down into the water with a sinuous movement that kicked the flow of his blood into high gear. He inhaled a deep, groaning breath. Christ, that felt so good now. Ever since he'd fed on her, it was as if every vein in his body had become a super highway conduit for blood, pushing feeling everywhere it needed to go. Especially right into his—

"You will be careful with that thing, won't you?" She cast

his hard member a sideways glance as she cranked off the faucets.

Yeah, yeah, so he was a big fat liar. And here was Lesson One of all the things he needed to learn about the male-female relationship; the woman would always hold the upper hand, no bones about it. Right, sue him for not caring.

"I'll try not to knock anything over," he remarked dryly as he started for the tub.

Her smiling gaze remained on that part of him sticking straight out from his body and bouncing along like a divining rod seeking out damp, warm places that were the Mount Everest of happy places to be.

He joined her in the tub, and she straddled him again, this time high up on her knees, and began to lather shampoo into his wet hair. He groaned as her massaging fingers did exactly what she'd set out to do: open up a whole new world of touch for him to just about die over. His eyelids kept trying to sink closed, but he forced them to stay open. There was just too much good stuff to look at right in front of him.

"Your body rocks," he murmured, watching foamy soap suds slip off the bud of her nipple.

She smiled. "Duck under to rinse."

He did as instructed, breaking back through the surface to find her with a bar of soap in her hands. She lathered up her palms, then smoothed them over his shoulders, up his neck, and down his chest. Ecstasy abated slightly here, as the *mode* in which his tattoos had been applied had left his chest semi-nerveless. Then pleasure rocketed right back up as her hands dipped below the water to wash his—

His head slumped back on his neck, his eyes spinning up into his skull as she took hold of his arousal and stroked him from tip to base, then back up. His fangs, already half-extended, stretched into his mouth on a near-painful surge. Her hand moved down again, and then he was panting short, tight breaths through his teeth because her hand slid all the way down to his balls. She cupped them and tested their weight, her fingernails lightly scoring the underside of his sac. He moaned low. Here again, was something really fuc...frigging new. Previously not much more than a pair of lead weights hanging between his thighs, his balls were now doing a real number on him, tingling and aching and...being very insistent about what needed to go down next.

Abruptly, she stopped and pressed the bar of soap into his hand. "Your turn."

He flipped his lids open.

Steam was drifting in hot clouds around her, coiling loose strands of her hair against the moisture on her throat. She looked like an enchanted mermaid.

He curled his lips back from his teeth in a wolfish smile. "I can wash you anywhere, right?"

She sloshed backward from the sight of his fangs, although the glittering heat in her eyes contradicted her retreat.

"Oh, payback's a bitch, sweetie pie." He rose to his knees, water cascading off his body, and came at her.

A husky laugh tripped past her lips, her gaze dropping to watch him work the soap into a lather between his hands.

"I wonder where I'll start. Hmm, maybe your—"

It hit him like a Monster Truck. With an *umph*, he lurched forward and fell against her, his forehead clunking against her chest. The soap tumbled from his lax fingers as a raw, primitive sound tore out of him.

"Jacken?" Her arms came around him. "Dear God, what's wrong?"

His mouth fell open and hung there.

"Jacken?"

"Your...scent." Turning his face into the upper swell of her breasts, he rubbed his open lips over her skin. "It's changing." He drew deep, gulping breaths of her newly emerging aroma into the back of his throat, the shifting power of it swirling through every cell in his body, holding him in thrall. He could do no more than stay as he was, his arms wrapped around her body and his lungs voraciously taking in every aromatic morsel of her. "I'm...bonding to you...Toni. Oh, Christ...." A hard shudder shook him, then another rocked him to the core of his being as the biological process worked at transforming him into what he'd be for the rest of his married life: a fully bonded male.

After several mind-blowing minutes, he drew a last, fractured breath, Toni's scent making its final descent into all the small fissures of his brain. He'd never smelled anything so good *in his life* as Toni smelled to him now. Damn, he'd heard other bonded males rave about The Change, but he'd just never believed it could be this powerful. Toni was his now, he felt it completely. The territorial Vârcolac in him stretched and roared. He straightened off her, the Phoenix rising from the ashes, and stared down on her with ruthless possession. "*Mine*," he snarled at her.

Her eyes sprang wide. "Uh, oh."

Eye-blink quick, he hefted her out of the water and tossed her onto the surrounding ledge of tiles. "I've got an idea. Why don't we do that tasting-thing I also missed out on?" Grabbing her ass with two hands, he tipped her hips up, the maneuver forcing her to fling her arms behind her to brace herself.

"Jaćken!" she gasped as he went down on his knees before her.

He shoved his face between her thighs, needing her new taste down his throat right fucking now. Thing was...he didn't exactly know what he was doing. He was only able to poke his tongue and nose around the area a bit at first, too stupefied by the intoxicating mixture of her newly mated aroma and the scent of her arousal to do much more than grunt like a Neanderthal. Then he caught on to *licking* as the best way to experience her, and here he was in his element; the folds of her sex were the softest skin he'd ever felt.

He would've been happy enough just to spend the next week lazily running his tongue all over their slick contours. But he was paying attention to Toni, the noises she was making and the ebb and flow of tension in her body, and although she definitely liked her folds tended to, stroking her clitoris was what really spun her top. The thing must've been packed full of more nerve endings than he'd realized, based on what he was able to do to her. Giving it a little suckle had earned such a noise out of her, her pelvis straining up so hard into his face, that he'd nearly laughed for joy. Still.... He couldn't seem to spend all of his time there.

Because whenever he really got going on that knot of nerve endings, the entrance to her body would squish full of more of her juice, and, damn, the stuff was frigging amazing. Like honey in consistency, and just as sweet, it tasted as good as her blood, and *that* was saying something. He just had to get down there and lap it up.

He was down there now, pushing his tongue into her opening to chase more of it down—a move which ramped up the noises she was making, a bunch of *uh-uh-uh, oh-oh-oh* shit in his ears that nearly brought him to his own explosion. She reached between her legs and dug her fingers into his hair, frantically twisting up fists of it. A message that she was done with his messing around? Her folds were plumped up like a biscuit and a series of broken gasps were hissing between her gritted teeth, so yeah, he probably needed to give her a break. Curling his hands around her legs, he spread her thighs wider and really latched on good to that jewel of hers. With his lips and tongue and jaw all working together, he got down to the serious business of sucking on—

He was rewarded almost instantly. She yelped once, then settled into a high keening cry as her thighs clamped tight around his ears, and—the best part—her feminine core pulsed rhythmically against his chin. His New and Improved Balls got off on that big time, pulling up tight against his body and—*Oh, shit.* A droplet of liquid leaked to the tip of him. He reared back from her with an anxious expulsion of air. He was going to come.

He heaved unsteadily to his feet, bringing her with him to the next highest step of tiles. "I have to get inside you." He probed around her silky wetness and just about ended himself right there. *Damn...damn.* He looked down between her splayed legs to aim better. Another huge mistake. That secret place of hers was a deeper pink than before, the petals glistening and fuller. So ready for him. With a ragged groan, he just drove his hips forward...only to succeed in shoving her backward along the slippery tiles. He growled in frustration.

"Pull me toward you at the same time you push." Her voice sounded heavy and breathless.

His hands were trembling with the force of his need, his fingers no doubt digging too roughly into her skin as he grabbed her by the hips and hauled her forward and upward into his next thrust. An incoherent noise burst out of him as he plunged deep inside her this time, and—*ah!*—the hot petals of her sheath closed around his shaft like a velvet fist. He jerked forward from the intensity of it, *bonking* his head on the mirror behind her.

A muffled sound of amusement escaped her.

He gulped for air. *Yeah, laugh it up, lady.* See how well you do after thirty-odd years of deprivation.

"Are you okay?" she asked softly.

"I just can't seem to get used to...how good you feel."

Her fingers caressed the length of his spine. "Do you want me to get on top again?"

"No." He licked his lips and swallowed. He didn't think there was time for adjustments. "I got this covered."

Right. He felt like an oaf as he started to surge between her thighs. He tried to be proficient about it: straight in, straight out, nice and smooth. But she was such a tight glove of torturously squeezing muscles that, time and again, imminent danger would rise up through his testes and tighten the muscles in his lower back, making his strokes go all sloppy and uneven, his frigging knees banging into the side of the tub.

But then...why should he care, if she didn't seem to? Each deep thrust inside her body, whether unskilled or expert, earned a corresponding groan of pleasure from her, so he must've been hitting something good in there. Her legs were wrapped tightly around him, too, her head thrown back, the picture of a woman in the throes of passion.

Saliva filled his mouth as he hungrily eyed the elegant stretch of throat, bloodlust rising up to join the action. Without warning, he lunged for the unblemished side of her neck and sank his fangs in with one clean stroke, her resilient flesh giving way with a satisfying *pop*.

She jumped only slightly this time, then melted beneath him into a pile of groaning jelly.

He gulped her quenching blood down his throat drunkenly, wondering if he'd ever get used to the incredible taste of it. The power and energy it gave him. How it filled him with—

He went rigid as his climax came at him full throttle, as unstoppable as a bullet. Yanking his fangs out of Toni's throat, he flung his head back and shouted in pure barbaric ecstasy, the blood-Fiinţă combo pouring through his system back-loading his orgasm with staggering force. A bolt of lightning sheared his balls in two and blew the top of his cock off. Shuddering again and again, he pumped hot liquid into his wife's body in what seemed an endless stream, the convulsions of her sheath around him as she found her second orgasm damn near pushing him into a dead faint.

Gasping for breath, he sagged forward, utterly spent. He planted a hand on the mirror behind Toni to keep from collapsing on top of her, and hovered there for the small infinity it took his climax to finally lose some of its grip on him. Hell…shit, if there was anything better than an orgasm in this whole wide world, somebody needed to write an airplane banner about it.

He gazed down on her, still struggling to get his heart back into his chest and his lungs to a place where they could fully inflate again. "All right," he panted. "That one might've been a little 'good'."

She exhaled a laugh. "Boy, howdy," she agreed, and the hazy, satisfied look in her eyes made him want to spike the ball in male triumph.

With a contented sigh that cranked up his *I-was-a-stud-horse-in-bed* success even more, she wrapped her arms around his neck and pulled him down for a hug.

He moved to embrace her, his arms a little unsteady as—

His jaw unhinged in naked shock. When he'd swept his palm through the steam on the mirror just now, he'd opened up a visible patch of reflection behind her, and there on her back was—

"*Holy shit!*"

CHAPTER THIRTY-SIX

The Rec Room was in an uproar.

Alex was laughing so hard he started hiccupping, and the villainous-looking one called Dev Nichita was really gone, rolling on the floor, his arms clutched around his middle. Male model dude, Thomal Costache, was trying to help Dev up, but was stumbling around so much from his own hysterical laughter, he kept missing Dev's hand. Kasson Korzha had tears running down his face, *super* male model dude Arc Costache was close to needing CPR, and that one with the bull skull tattoo on his arm, Gábor Pavenic, was shaking so hard across the shoulders, he might as well have been convulsing.

Holy Christ, but it'd been one hilarious afternoon so far—or middle of the night to Alex, but he was having too much fun to feel tired. He'd always wanted brothers to screw off with, and these warriors were proving capable of degenerating into a pack of unruly frat boys with the right provocation. Like when man about town Roth Mihnea had passed out top-shelf bottles of scotch to Dev, Thomal, and Kasson as consolation for their loss of Toni. The three men had shared liberally with the rest of them, and now they were all pretty thrashed...which had naturally inspired Alex to teach everyone how to do blue flamers.

Yeah, *light farts*.

Alex laughed louder, his ribs starting to ache. Shit, man, there wasn't anything funnier than a mighty blue flamer. The position a dude had to Gumby himself into just to complete the light-off was comical enough: ass scooted to the edge of a chair, knees jacked back to the ears, hand doing a reach-around so that a cigarette lighter could be held near the ol' bunghole, not too close or else a dude risked catching his pants on fire.

Then, *fwapp*, let one rip and watch the spurt of blue flame.

Seriously, he'd never seen men—anyone—laugh so hard as when the warriors had started taking turns. Kasson had yelped like a girl for burning his sphincter, Gábor had nearly crapped his pants for pushing so hard to get a fart out, then Nyko Brun, the most serious body Nazi of all them, had come up to bat. The man had exploded such an Aurora Borealis out of his butt that the current near-seizure-like laughter had promptly taken them all out. Jesus, if they all didn't quit soon, they'd—

"What the *hell's* going on in here?"

Jaċken was standing inside the doorway of the Rec Room, staring at them all like they were a bunch of headless zombie chickens.

Alex's new brother-in-law was dressed only in a pair of hastily-donned black sweat pants, leaving bare what was one Holy Mackerel of a tattoo-embattled upper body. *Daaaamn*. Alex wished Jaċken had been his brother back when he was thirteen and wearing his first pair of eyeglasses. That way, when eighth-grade bully Bobby Knudson had knocked Alex's new specs askew with a hard slap to the face and a sneering, "Hey, poindexter, nice coke bottles," Alex could've said, "Oh, I'm sorry, haven't you met my brother, Bad Ass?"

Tonî was at Jaċken's side, her pink T-shirt on inside out, her pajama pants hanging low on her hips, and the bun on her head damp and unruly from whatever she'd just been doing with Jaċken. *Grody!*

Nyko was the first to recover from his laughing fit. "Well, hey, look, it's my new sister-in-law." He smiled broadly at the newlyweds. "What a breath of fresh air you are now, Tonī. Jaćken obviously did his job well."

The room broke into applause and whoops.

Yuuuukkkk!

"Hell, Jaćken," Arc gasped out, still trying to control his laughter, "what're you doing coming up for air so soon? We didn't expect to see you till—"

A lamp crashed to the floor as Dev staggered drunkenly to his feet.

"Smooth move, bumblefuck." Gábor snickered.

"Would everyone shut up! I need you to check something out." Jaćken pulled Tonī closer.

"Oh, shit." Thomal covered his eyes with one hand, peeking out the edge of it at his brother, Arc. "He wants to show us that he knows how to bang a chick now." He cleared his throat. "Yo, chief, it's really not necessary to—"

"Now, hold on a minute." Dev swiped some magazines off the coffee table. "The table here's clear."

Someone chortled.

"Assholes." Kasson planted his hands on his hips. "The woman's brother is sitting right there."

"I said everyone *shut up the fuck up!*" Jaćken roared. "This is important."

He turned to the Felix Ungar of all doctors, Jess, who was deeply ensconced in a worn leather armchair, an indulgent smile wreathing his flushed face.

"Can you take a look at something?" Jaćken pulled Tonī against his body, her front to his front so that her back was facing the room.

"What is it?" Dr. Jess rose smoothly from his chair, moving with studied grace even though he'd downed just as much scotch as the rest of them.

Jaćken yanked Tonī's T-shirt up in back.

Jess came to a shocked halt. "Goodness gracious!"

"Shit...."

"Damn...."

"Wow...," and the like, came out of the rest of the men.

"It's fantastic," Jess breathed, hurrying forward.

Alex moved to huddle around Tonĭ with the rest of the men. *Daaaamn*, again. Spread across the length and breadth of his sister's back was the same dragon tattoo Alex had seen on Thomal's back earlier, brilliant scales and all. Instead of green and red, though, it was—

"Why's it blue and red?" Thomal asked.

"That's the color of the Fey," Dr. Jess answered.

Kasson was frowning at Tonĭ's lower back. "Is her dragon missing a foot?"

Dr. Jess looked again. "Ah, yes. She had it lasered off."

"What's that thing?" Gábor stepped forward and pointed a finger at the lightning bolt in the upper left quadrant of Tonĭ's—

Jaćken's fist flashed out.

Alex gaped as, impossibly, the punch sent Gábor flying out of his boots and soaring across the Rec Room. He landed ass-first in the middle of the foosball table, skid-bumped across the top, then flipped to the opposite side, bringing the table crashing down on top of him with a splintering *thwack*.

The rest of the warriors threw up their hands in an I-surrender pose and quickly backed up several yards.

Alex just stood there, still gaping.

Dr. Jess pulled him back with the rest, murmuring, "It would be best not to get too close to Tonĭ and Jaćken at present."

"Damn it to fuck!" Gábor scrambled out from under the table, roughly swiping little hockey men off him. "What the *hell* is a newly bonded male Vârcolac doing in general population, anyway?!" He staggered sideways, blood leaking down his forehead.

"Your own fault, dickhead." Thomal snorted softly. "You got too close to her."

Nostrils flared aggressively, Jaćken rounded on Jess. "Is Tonĭ okay?"

"Of course," Jess replied hastily. "She's better than okay, I'd say. She's fully Fey; she'll get her power now. That mark Gábor indicated designates her enchantment skill—although I haven't the foggiest notion what a lightning bolt signifies." The doctor paused thoughtfully. "What activated this?"

"My Ființă, I think. The tattoo popped up after the second bite."

"Hey!" Alex came back to life. "Could this Ființă stuff boot up my enchantment skill, too?"

Everyone turned to look at him. Except for Tonĩ, who was cuddled sleepily in Jaćken's arms, and Gábor, who was kicking debris out of the way and pouting.

Alex went on, "I could read the Strǎvechi Caiet Book, then, right?"

Dr. Jess's cheeks flushed redder in excitement. "Oh, holy Heaven. Yes, just so."

Alex adjusted the set of his glasses, his excitement growing along with Jess's. "All righty, then. Just tell me what I need to do and point me in the right direction."

Laughing, Dev gave Alex a staggering whack on the shoulder. "Well, okay, human. You just have to fall in love with a Vârcolac female and be willing to spend the rest of your life with her. Nothing too major, right?"

"Actually…" Alex smiled. "That's exactly in line with my plans."

Dev's silver eyes brightened. "Ho, shit, wait! I need to introduce you to my sister, Luvera."

"Screw that, Nichita," Kasson inserted hotly. "I've got four sisters who—"

"Would somebody get Jaćken the *fuck* out of here?" Gábor growled. "And a damned bandage might be nice."

"Yes," Tonĩ murmured, "let's go back to bed, Jaćken. I want to…" She stretched languidly and gazed up at her new husband with sleepy adoration, her smile slipping sideways. "You know what a blow job is, right, honey?"

All eyes snapped over to the couple.

Crimson heat shot into Alex's face as Jacken bolted from the Rec Room with Tonĩ at ass-on-fire speeds.

Aw, man…. Now he needed to take a shower or something.

CHAPTER THIRTY-SEVEN

"I need to know how to fight these guys, Tonĭ."

Tonĭ slanted a glance at her husband as she unwrapped two pounds of ground beef. "Yes, well…I wish you luck with that." She plunked the meat into a large mixing bowl. "Make sure you slice that green pepper into small pieces, okay?"

Jaćken gave her a perturbed look from the other side of the kitchen island, a large Chef's knife poised in his hand.

"You're not chopping…." She sighed, then laughed. "What do you want me to tell you, Jaćken? Those Topside Om Răuseem pretty damned immortal to me." She cracked an egg into the bowl. "You saw shave-headed guy die, I saw the young, creepy one as a corpse." She shook in salt and pepper. "Yet, they both looked really alive when they showed up at the Water Cliffs."

"They wouldn't be immortal by nature." He started cutting up the green pepper with quicksilver speed; the man definitely knew his way around a knife. "They'd have to be under the power of an enchantment, and what can be enchanted can damn well be *un*enchanted."

She *plunked* down the salt and pepper shaker. "Why do I

281

keep letting these things surprise me?" she asked rhetorically, then gave Jaćken a droll look. "Enchanted?"

"Certain Om Răd and Fey have the ability to manipulate power through rituals."

"Not you?"

"I wish." He snorted. "No, only Pure-bred Om Rău." One side of his mouth hooked upward. "But you. Soon."

That much was true. She'd felt strange power surges inside her ever since she'd gained her Fey status two weeks ago. Nothing she knew how to use or control, yet, though.

Jaćken scooped up the diced pepper and dumped it in the bowl, then glanced around the counter. "What next?"

She pointed at the can of Progresso Bread Crumbs.

His brows shot up. "Bread? In *meat*?"

"It's meat loaf, and, yes, you'll like it." She handed him a measuring cup. "One cup."

She hid a smile as she watched him measure out the bread crumbs with unnecessary exactitude, once again tickled by how enthusiastic he got over all things domestic.

It was a Brave New World for her husband, though, now that they were tucked away in Țărână's white picket fence neighborhood in a house next door to Arc and Beth. Before that, he'd lived his entire adult life in Roth's mansion. He'd never needed to contend with life's banalities, washing a load of laundry or shopping at a grocery store for more than beer and snacks, or cooking a meal, and now that he had a home of his own, he wanted to master it all. Anything that needed doing, no matter what it was, he wanted to do it with her. And ridiculously enough, she found herself racing home after work to do mundane chores, like make dinner or fold underwear or show Jaćken how to pick out a ripe melon. Because mundane stuff turned into fun stuff when they did it as a couple.

Tenderness filled her heart as she watched Jaćken upend the cup of bread crumbs into the bowl. If she thought she'd been in love with this man before, the last two weeks of marital bliss spent getting to know him, the real him, available to her now that his iron defenses were down, had catapulted her right to the top of Guineas Book contenders for the most in-love girl ever. A state of emotions which was having an unexpected effect on her.

It was putting her into a state of outright, unadulterated fear.

For the first time ever in a relationship with a man, she was truly, deeply in love. Never before had she felt like she had so much to lose. If something ever happened to Jaćken, if she lost him or he left her, it would throw her into such a deep, dark pit of despair and loneliness it would make her former life look like a big sorority blowout. She'd been wracking her brain for ways to get past this fear, but had been drawing blanks, which had succeeded in keeping her at a low simmer of panic.

"Anything else?" Jaćken asked.

"Um...." She closed her eyes for a moment to banish the thoughts from her head. "Ketchup."

She watched him open the fridge and take out a bottle of Heinz from the side shelf.

"Hasn't Cleeve been able to find out anything?" she asked, steering their conversation back to their original Topside Om Răua topic.

"Nothing that's frigging helpful. Only a complaint lodged last year by the bar manager of The Blarney Stone about some chick with a black flame tattoo on her belly. Apparently, the woman ripped a guy's arms out of their sockets during an arm wrestling match."

She gave him an arch look.

"Yeah, sounds pretty Rău-like, doesn't it?" He handed her the bottle of ketchup. "And weird shit like that going down is dangerous for all of us, you know. It starts the police asking too many questions."

She hesitated in the middle of squeezing Heinz into a measuring cup. *Police....* "Oh, God, I'm just remembering the night the police called me in to consult on the murder investigation for that creepy corpse. The kid was wearing some kind of strange ring."

"Yeah? Strange, how?"

Shrugging, she finished filling the cup. "I guess it gave off some kind of an electric shock if anyone tried to remove it."

"Holy shit, I think that's it." Jacken planted both hands on the kitchen island. "That's how those assholes are achieving their immortality. Their *rings* are enchanted. That's right. Skull was wearing a ring the night he tried to steal you at Scripps. I remember because it tore a strip of skin off my face, here"—Jacken drew an invisible line high up on his cheek with the tip of his index finger—"when the fucknut punched me."

She set down the ketchup. "Well, good, you have it figured out. Now you can help me mix the meat loaf." She bobbed her eyebrows at him. "It's the funnest part."

"Oh?" His expression lightened as he strode around to her side of the kitchen island. "Why's that?"

"We get to do it with our hands." She stuck her fingers into the bowl.

He drew up behind her, extended his arms on either side of her body, and put his hands in the bowl next to hers. She began to knead the ingredients together, and he copied her, resting his chin on her shoulder.

"Doesn't it feel good." She chuckled. "All that stuff squishing between your fingers?"

"It feels great," he said, making it clear what he really meant when he pressed his hips forward against the curve of her rump.

"Jacken. For Pete's sake, we're making dinner." She tried to sound scolding, but it was difficult to be convincing with a long, hard phallus prodding her buttocks.

"Last I checked, sweetie pie, we were grownups. So I think we can have dessert first if we want." He lowered his lips to the curve of her throat and kissed her, the tip of a fang grazing her skin.

Excitement spun through her tighter than an over-wound top. Groaning softly, she rolled her head to the side, giving him more access to her neck, blatantly inviting him to take a vein.

"You're shameless," he murmured.

"Very true." Marriage to a Vârcolac was proving to have

more than its fair share of magnificent perks, but being fed on was definitely the humdinger. The intimacy of the act itself was a total turn-on, Jaćken's need for her life-sustaining blood something indescribably special, but she'd be a huge liar if she didn't admit to really getting off on the Holy Moly ecstasy Fiinţă gave her. By itself, the stuff was an Elixir of the Gods, but an orgasm-Fiinţă combination was like sending her whole body, especially her vagina, on a rollercoaster ride through Nirvana, Mount Olympus, Heaven or any other celestial sphere where pleasure was unutterably fantastic. Was it any wonder she was always game?

She laughed softly as Jaćken nipped at her collarbone, then ducked away from his teasing lips. He wouldn't feed on her tonight; every two to three days was about the schedule he kept, and he wasn't due. "Enough now, husband. We have to get this blob of food cooked."

They scooped up the meat loaf mixture and patted it into a loaf pan.

"Stick it in the oven, would you?" she said, washing her hands. "I have to go to the bathroom." She dried her hands and tossed the dishtowel on the counter, then headed into the bathroom at the base of the stairs. She plopped down on the toilet, her body still humming with desire, but...there was also a strange, hard twist in her belly. She stared forward, absently unwrapping an O-stick. Rule Number Something of marriage to a Vârcolac male: *test ovulation cycle regularly*. She urinated on the stick, then checked the results.

"Hey," Jaćken called to her. "How long should I set the timer for?"

She stared at the O-stick another second, then tossed it in the trash. She rose from the toilet, pulled up her jeans, buttoned them, refastened her belt, her movements mechanical. She washed her hands, then exited the bathroom.

"One hour," she told Jaćken as she entered the kitchen.

The punching bag was gashed open from top to bottom and gutted, cotton stuffing littering the floor mats like baby synthetic snowballs. Large pieces of steel were joining the puffs as Sedge systematically ripped chunks of metal frame out of the middle of the bag.

Three other warriors were training inside the gym along with him, all of them pretending to work out while they really kept a wary eye on him.

His body ran with sweat, his hair soaking wet by now, and his muscles quivered like undercooked egg whites. He'd been going at the bag for hours. As soon as he'd put his wife to bed, he'd sneaked out of the house and come here to empty himself of his rage. But it wasn't working. His mind was a seething mass of pictures he couldn't shut down or control. It wasn't working! Sedge cranked back his head and let out a sharp yowl.

Okay. No one was even pretending to train now.

"Yo, Stănescu." Dev approached, although he stopped at a safe arm's length away from him. "What's going down, man, you all right?"

Breathing heavily, Sedge lurched forward and hugged the punching bag like he was an exhausted boxer, which he was. "I can't get the images out of my head, Dev." He staggered sideways, swinging slightly on the bag, his feet sloppy beneath him. "I'm trying, but—fuck!—I can't. I keep seeing him beating on her, breaking her little bones, punching her in the stomach until she...she...." He jerked backward, snarling, and ripped out another hunk of metal, snapping it in two and hurling it aside.

There was a beat of stunned silence.

"Who?" The dark syllable came out of Vinz.

Sedge panted. "Kimberly's ex."

"Holy fuck," Arc hissed. Married, too, Arc was probably the only one who could truly relate to why Sedge was spinning off the flywheel.

Now Dev moved close enough to place a firm hand on Sedge's shoulder. "Listen, Stănescu, you erase those images from your head right now, you hear me? Because I'm *guaranteeing* you that we'll find this dickhead so you can go a few rounds with him." He gave Sedge's shoulder a hard squeeze. "We clear?"

Sedge bared his teeth. "Kimberly won't tell me the bastard's name. She's afraid I'll kill him and end up in jail."

Arc swiped a towel over his face. "Hell, I bet Cleeve or Alex could track down the scrote on the 'Net with just a little information."

"Exactly," Dev agreed. "We'll get you through this. Whatever we need to do so you can avenge your mate, *we'll do*. You need to hear me on this."

Sedge nodded shortly, his throat spasming. "Yeah. Yeah, okay, I hear you."

"All right." Dev whacked his shoulder. "Now hit the showers before you fall over and break your—"

The gym intercom squawked. "This is an all-warrior call!" Cleeve's tinny voice rushed out of the small speaker. "Emergency at the Brun household!"

Sedge, Dev, Arc, and Vinz weren't the first warriors on the scene. Thomal and Breen were already circling the couple who was rolling around on the street and grappling, Toni screaming and kicking at Jaćken, Jaćken tearing at her clothes.

Sedge stopped dead in his tracks at the sight, unable to believe his eyes. This wasn't…Bonded couples never fought physically. Male Vârcolacs were wired to protect their mates; if one ever got it into his mind to hurt her, his cells would pull him to a screeching, and painful, halt.

"Help us!" Thomal shouted. "Tonī ovulated and now Jaćken's glazed out!"

Oh, shit, *glazed*…that was why. But, wait, that still wouldn't explain the level of violence Jaćken was—

Breen darted into the fray, trying to grab hold of Jaćken, but was thrown back with a bloody lip.

Thomal swore. "That chemical change has made him go Răd. Shake a leg!"

Sedge lowered his chin. Shit, Jaćken was in the middle of a combo Ră-fit and procreation glaze-out? They could write off stopping him, then.

"Stănescu," Arc barked. "You grab Tonī and get her into lockdown. The rest of us—blitzkrieg!"

All five warriors leapt on top of Jaćken at once.

Sedge launched himself forward, grabbing Tonī under the armpits and dragging her out from the dogpile.

A vicious snarl coiled out of Jaćken.

Holy crap! Sedge hiked Tonī into his arms and raced for the mansion like a cherry bomb was jammed in his butt crack. Behind him, it sounded like Jaćken was roaring loose from his captors.

Oh, damn me. He really wished he hadn't just exhausted himself at the punching bag.

CHAPTER THIRTY-EIGHT

Raymond set his Courvoisier on the edge of the billiards table and racked a set of balls. He chalked his cue stick lazily, feeling quite relaxed in this, his den, the only room which was truly his own in the Rancho Santa Fe mansion he shared with what felt like a shedload of other people. Entrance into his masculine haven was by express permission only, and tonight he'd deigned to invite his partner, Boian, to join him for a game of Snookers.

"You break," Boian said, puffing on a Cuban.

"Very well." Leaning over the table, Raymond sighted along his cue, then broke the rack with a hard hit on the head ball. Narrowing his eyes, he watched the red balls whiz around the green tabletop.

There was a knock on the door.

Both men turned their heads sharply toward the sound.

Boian jerked the Cuban out of his mouth. "Damn it all to hell," he snarled in what sounded like real anger.

Raymond slid a sideways glance at his partner. Was it any blooming wonder Boian's progeny always seemed to spring directly from Yavell's womb in a nasty temper?

Raymond was tempted to ignore the knock, but someone would have to be completely insane to disturb him for any reason other than mortal danger. "Enter," he called.

Pändra stepped inside, dressed in her typical shagbag inelegance, her frock a see-through red mesh piece that showed off a matching red bra and knickers.

Jesus wept.

"It's about Tonï," the girl wisely announced immediately.

Raymond propped his cue stick on the floor and leaned on it. "Explain."

"The private investigator you assigned to follow Shannon Parthen, Mr. Rathburn, just rang. Tonï is out in town tonight with her mother."

Raymond lifted a single eyebrow into a pleased arc. "That *is* important news, my pet." He turned back to the table and placed the white cue ball for his second shot. "Send the lads out to fetch her."

The Field Irish Pub, located on 5th Avenue in the heart of San Diego's bustling Gaslamp district was always hopping, and tonight was no exception. At eight o'clock, the Happy Hour crowd was in full swing. Tonï was amazed she and her mother had found a place to sit, but they'd managed to snag one of the cozy, dark wood booths near the bar. Both strawberry-blonde women now had a frothy Guinness, Tonï having forgone her usual martini tonight, "when in Rome" and all…or Ireland, as was the case here.

Odd that such a hip young place was one of her mother's favorite hangouts, but Shannon Parthen, née O'Rourke, loved all things Irish, and this pub was one of the most authentic in the city. The walls were covered with enough Irish paraphernalia to make any Dubliner feel right at home, and there was generally a lively Irish ditty playing.

"He's teaching me to play golf." Shannon was talking about her latest boyfriend, laughing lightly as she added, "if you can imagine *me*, of all people, trying to—"

Shannon stopped speaking, her mouth falling inelegantly open and her eyes widening to their fullest.

A strange burp of silence rolled through the crowd next, an almost imperceptible pause in noise and action before everything resumed normal activity.

Oh, crap. Tonĭ didn't need to glance over her shoulder to know who'd just entered the bar. Such a total crowd reaction could've only been brought about by the entrance of too-gorgeous-to-be-true men. "Damn," she grumbled. "Remind me to punch Alex in the face the next time I see him." How else could she have been unearthed among hundreds of bars in San Diego if not for a certain rat fink brother?

"Oh, my," Shannon breathed shakily as Arc Costache came to a stop at the edge of their table.

Gábor Pavenic headed to the bar, lounging negligently against it on one bent arm, his bull skull tattoo bulging. A statuesque brunette smiled cautiously at him, and his return cockeyed grin nearly sent her sliding off her stool. Thomal, meanwhile, was being mobbed by a gaggle of simpering co-eds. Jacken wasn't with them, and a small pain speared through Tonĭ that made no sense. The moment she'd finished her two-day stint in lockdown, she'd come up here for a weekend escape with her mother in order to get a break from him. Right?

Tonĭ swept a gesture back and forth between Arc and Shannon. "Arc Costache," she introduced, "my mother, Shannon Parthen."

Shannon cast Tonĭ a quick *you know this man?* look before offering her hand to Arc. "A pleasure."

Lavishing a grin of roguish charm on Shannon, Arc shook her hand. "I can see where Dr. Parthen gets her good looks. May I?" He used his hold on Shannon's hand to slide her over in the booth, his smile remaining annoyingly in place as he sat down. "You'll excuse me for barging in on your girl time, but I work at your daughter's new place of employment, and—"

"Oh, the Research Institute?"

Arc's smile grew; if his lips spread any more, Mr. Charm would be showing his fangs. "That's right. You see, ma'am, your daughter, since she's new and all, must not have realized that she needs to get *clearance* before she can leave our facilities."

"I'm afraid you're the one who's confused," Tonĭ returned with a frigid look. "The Institute is run differently now. I'd think you'd know that, Mr. Costache, as you *were* present at the meeting where that was explained."

Tonĭ's first stipulation as co-leader had been that no woman would ever be held in Ţărână against her will. As a part of that new guideline, Hannah, Ellen, Beth, Maggie, and Kimberly had been called in front of the leadership and individually polled: Did they want to stay or go? It had been a matter of form—all of the Dragons had agreed to stay, of course—but it'd been important to acknowledge their choice. Roth had even gone a step further and gathered the warriors together so all of them could apologize on behalf of the entire community for kidnapping them.

A muscle in Arc's jaw bunched. "Maybe I should say I'm astounded, then, that you'd run out on your husband, when you know—"

Shannon's eyebrows flew up. "Husband?" She gaped at Tonĭ. "You're *married*?!"

Tonĭ blasted Arc with a heated, thank-you-very-much-you-butthead glower. "I was going to tell you tonight, Mom."

Shannon's hand went to her throat, her fingers twining in her necklace. "Was there a wedding or...or...?"

"No, Mom. If there had been, you would have been invited. Please, don't feel hurt. The whole situation has been...rather unconventional."

"Well, can I meet him?" Shannon asked, still flustered. "He's my son-in-law, after all."

Arc sniffed, the edge of one nostril lifting. "Tonĭ's husband isn't feeling too chipper right now, ma'am."

Tonĭ moved her eyes over to Arc's face and felt something

in her chest begin to squeeze, a bad feeling stirring in her belly.

"Jaĉken needs his...medication." Arc's gaze sharpened on her. "And you know you're the only one who can give it to him."

Tonĩ's cheeks went cold, then numb. But that didn't make sense. Pure-bred Vârcolac could last five to seven days without blood, Mixed-blood Dragons up to ten. Surely a Half-Rău—

"Men of your husband's unique heritage," Arc went on, correctly assuming she needed clarification, "require their meds every three days. Today's the third."

Her stomach bottomed out. Dear God, that meant by tomorrow Jaĉken would be in a blood-coma. She pressed a hand to her mouth, then her cheek. "Where is he?" she asked in a frayed voice.

"We've got him holed up nearby at a Doubletree Hotel on Front Street. Nyko's babysitting him." Arc's mouth compressed into a tight line. "He's pretty bad off."

"Jesus, stop looking at me like that, would you? I'm not a monster. I didn't know something like this was going to happen to him."

"It wouldn't exactly have been an issue, if you'd kept your ass planted at home where it belonged, now would it?" Arc jerked forward in his seat, his eyes blue steel. "You got problems with your husband? Then fucking man-up and fix them, Tonĩ, because everyone's getting sick and goddamned tired of you running away."

Bracing the heels of her palms on the edge of the table, Tonĩ pushed her spine against the back of the booth. Arc's words cut like a knife, spilling blood, opening her up to the infection of guilt. Tears sprang painfully into her eyes.

Arc's gaze dropped. "Shit." He rubbed a hand over his face. "I'm sorry. I saw what Jaĉken did to you, Tonĩ, and, yeah, it was really damned bad." He exhaled a long breath through his nose. "But you're one of the leaders of our Institute now. You can't deal with your marital issues like this. It sets a bad example."

"No, I suppose not," she admitted stiffly.

Shannon was staring at her Guinness, but Tonî could tell her mother was listening intently to everything.

"Look, I know there's a lot of stuff you still haven't been told yet. Everyone thought you knew about the O-sticks, but—"

"I do know."

Arc's brows came down, his narrowed eyes searching her face. "Then why—?"

"Just let me say goodbye to my mother, okay?" Tonî cut in. "I'll meet you in the parking lot."

Arc paused a moment, then nodded. "Yeah, sure." He scooted out of the booth and shook hands with Shannon again. "It was nice meeting you, ma'am." He smiled. "Sorry for all the weird." He jerked his chin at Gábor and Thomal, and the two men joined him on their way out the door.

Tonî watched the three Vârcolac leave, her stomach so heavy it felt like it was full of lead. She smiled faintly at her mother. "Well…um…I'm sure you have a ton of questions about all *that*."

"Just one." Shannon's eyes darkened with concern. "Are you all right, Tonî?"

Oh, God. Toni planted her elbow on the table and slumped her forehead into her palm. Her mother thought Jacken was a full-on power-and-control wife beater. "Mom, listen, I don't want you to think…. What my husband did to me wasn't awful, like Arc said, I mean, it wasn't his fault, so…." She expelled a breath. "I don't want you to think ill of him, okay. He's a great man." *He's just genetically challenged.*

Shannon smiled gently. "I don't mean to kick you when you're down, honey, but your choice in men in the past hasn't exactly been spot-on."

Tonî flipped over a cocktail napkin, changing it from a shamrock to a leprechaun. That was, unfortunately, a valid point. "I can't explain all the reasons why things are different now, but they are. I've chosen well."

Shannon tilted her head to one side, her eyes moving over Tonî's face. "You love him, don't you?"

A rush of emotion flooded Tonī's heart. "Yes, I do," she pushed through a suddenly tight throat. "Very much."

Shannon nodded. "Well, that's the problem, then."

Tonī felt a frown pull at her features. "I don't…. What do you mean?"

Shannon's blue eyes softened. "Tonī, honey, ever since what happened with that Brad Flannigan boy you've been a changed person…more closed. I just don't think you've ever forgiven yourself for it."

"That's not true. I understand now why I slept with him." Oddball that she'd been in high school, having no way to understand about being a Dragon, it'd been irresistible to have a handsome, popular jock show her attention, even though it turned out he'd only been pretending.

"I'm not talking about having sex with that boy." Shannon gave her a meaningful look. "I'm talking about what happened afterward."

A spasm of pain gripped her body. "Mom, no. I don't want to talk about that."

"Of course you don't. You'd rather go through your whole life pretending the consequences of that Homecoming night with Brad never happened. But the problem is that every part of your heart knows it did." Shannon drew a breath and exhaled a rush of air. "Ever since your senior year of high school, you've been living in a kind of preemptive strike mode, Tonī, pushing away anyone you started to care about, or who cared about you, before they could leave you." She glanced down. "Alex might've been an exception, but I certainly haven't been."

Shock tripped Tonī's pulse out of rhythm. "You think *I'm* the one who's been pulling away from *you* all this time?"

"Yes," Shannon answered somberly, "you have been."

Tonī put a hand over her mouth, tears stinging her eyes again. Had it really been her?

"And now I'm guessing you're doing the same thing to this man of yours," her mother said. "You're running away from him, not because of whatever this not-awful thing is he did to you, but because you started to love him too much. And you got scared." Shannon set both palms on the table, a loving ache entering her eyes. "You need to stop beating yourself up for the choices you made back then. You didn't do anything wrong. You did everything absolutely right." Grabbing her purse, Shannon reached inside and pulled out a photograph. "Here"— she set it on the table in front of Tonī—"it's time you took this."

A tear slipped from Tonī's eye and rolled over her fingers. She didn't look at the photo. She didn't have to.

"I've kept it all these years," her mother said softly, "knowing you'd want it someday."

"I don't." Tonī reached out to shove the photo away, inevitably glancing at it. The paper was curled at the corners and yellowing around the edges, but the picture in the middle was startling clear. Acid lurched into her throat.

"Take it, Tonī." Shannon gently pushed the picture back to her. "Show it to your new husband and tell him about it. When you see nothing but loving acceptance in his eyes, then maybe you'll finally realize you *didn't do anything wrong*."

Tonī stared blurrily at the photo. "Oh, Jesus," she moaned low, "Mom."

Shannon reached across the table and gripped Tonī's hand, holding it firmly while Tonī cried, her chin ducked to her chest and tears dropping steadily into her lap. She couldn't believe she was crying in the middle of a bar, but there was nothing she could do about it. That photo had torn open an unhealed wound, and there was no getting around the excruciating anguish of something that had been festering within her for so many years.

When Tonī's tears had finally eased to sniffles, Shannon patted her hand. "You okay, baby girl?"

Nodding, Tonī wiped at her eyes with the palms of her hands. "I...I should probably go, though."

"Yes," her mother agreed. "It sounds like your husband needs you."

Tonī pushed unsteadily to her feet, feeling utterly drained.

Her mother put some money on the table, then stood, too,

handing Tonĩ a tissue. "So when do I get to meet this man of yours?"

"Probably Christmastime. Sooner if I can arrange it." Tonĩ blew her nose. "I should warn you, though, he's…kind of scary-looking."

"Is he?" Shannon laughed. "Okay." She hugged Tonĩ tightly. "Email me, baby girl. I miss you so much."

"I will." Tonĩ squeezed her mother back. "*A lot.*"

The two women exited The Field, parting at the door. Tonĩ headed for the parking lot, spotting Arc, Gábor, and Thomal standing next to the community Pathfinder. Thomal made a pained face when he saw the evidence of her tears.

She came to a stop right in front of Arc, clutching the photo to her chest. "You don't know anything about me Arc Costache," she said, barely keeping a quaver from her voice, "the experiences I've had and the pain I've suffered. So I'd appreciate it if you'd keep your damned judgments about me and my marriage to yourself."

"All right." Arc shocked the devil out of her by pulling her into a quick brotherly hug. "Sorry, Doc."

CHAPTER THIRTY-NINE

Tonĭ made it all of two steps inside the Doubletree Hotel room, then slammed back against the door, her mouth gaping open on a frightened gasp.

Jaćken was coming at her like a Howitzer.

Arc, Gábor, and Thomal scattered in all directions, while Nyko leapt to Jaćken's side and grabbed him by the arm, pulling him to a halt. "Jaćken—"

Jaćken snarled and curled his lip at Nyko, showing his brother a pair of rapidly lengthening fangs.

"Listen to me," Nyko enunciated clearly, sounding amazingly unfazed. "You don't want to scare your wife again, do you?" His voice dipped an octave. "Just let me talk to her a second."

A sinew in Jaćken's jaw shivered ruthlessly, but he nodded and stayed where he was.

Nyko let go of his brother and looked at her. "Please don't be afraid, Tonĭ, all right? Jaćken's not Rău, and he's not going that way. He's just three days without blood and screwy. I imagine the last thing you want to do is let him feed before you've had a chance to talk things out, but—"

"No, it's fine," she interrupted. Dear God, her husband was a mess, his black hair sticking up all over his head like lacquered broomsticks, his eyes wild and bloodshot, his skin zombie pale. Huge sweat rings marked each armpit, while more perspiration painted a wide racing stripe down the middle of his pecs. "He just startled me at first, is all. I'm not afraid."

"Okay," Nyko said, "good, that's good. I'm going to leave this cell phone here for you, though, just in case." He set it on the nightstand. "Press number one and it'll automatically send out an emergency call to every warrior."

"I won't need it."

"Of course not. It's just to make you feel solid about things." Nyko gestured the other men out. "We'll be down in the lobby bar."

The four Vârcolac left, the door shutting softly behind them.

She exhaled raggedly. "I'm so sorry, Jacken. I had no idea this was going to happen to you."

He rushed over to her, his arms wrapping her in a shaky embrace. "I...." He gave her a turbulent look. "I don't want to be too rough, but I'm...."

"You won't be." She grabbed his head and pulled his face down to her throat, every loving instinct in her just wanting to make him better.

With a groan, he plunged in his fangs, his jaw pumping hard against her throat as he sucked like a starving babe at the breast. His body shook, and again.

Her lips parted on a breath as Fiinţă swam through her, heat and pleasure beginning to—

Abruptly, Jacken jerked out his fangs and collapsed onto his knees at her feet. "Oh, shit." He clutched her around the middle, his cheek pressed to her belly. "Tonĭ, I...I'm the one who's sorry. Jesus, if...." He sank all the way to the floor, hunching over, and grasped his head between his hands. "If I could let you divorce me, I would. I swear it."

She knelt down beside him, her knees feeling a little squishy from that bolus of Fiinţă in her bloodstream. "I don't want to divorce you."

He lifted his head, showing her haunted eyes. "I *hurt* you," he wrenched out. "I would've forced myself on you if the warriors hadn't—"

"You were glazed-out and didn't know what you were doing, and I...have to take my own share of responsibility for what happened." She gently touched his sweat-soaked hair. "That night we cooked meatloaf, I'd just checked an O-stick. I saw I was heading into my fertile time, but I came out of the bathroom anyway.

Surprise flexed the skin across his face. "You did it on purpose?"

"Partly subconsciously, I think, but yes. I certainly didn't know you were going to go Rău when I ovulated, but I think somewhere in my mind I was looking for any excuse to run away."

He blinked hard, once, in confusion.

"Will you...sit with me for a minute while I try to explain?"

His brow cleared. "Of course." Pushing to his feet, he moved slowly over to the bed with her and sat.

She picked up her purse from the floor, pulling out the photo her mother had given to her. She handed it to Jaćken, peering over his shoulder as he studied it, seeing what he saw: a blonde girl in a hospital delivery room, painfully young-looking, a bundled newborn baby in her arms. The expression on the girl's face was something between amazed shock and anxious desperation. Tonĭ knew exactly what was going through the girl's mind; that she was going to have to give up something soon that she deeply wanted to keep.

"That's me," she said around a lump in her throat.

Jaćken looked up from the picture and met her eyes.

She smiled weakly. "When I was a junior in high school, I had a stupid crush on a guy that led me into making an even stupider mistake, which got me pregnant." She pointed to the baby in the picture, the lump in her throat nearly choking her. "I held my son for three minutes, thirty-two seconds, then never saw him again." Tears flooded the corners of her eyes. "Ever."

"Toñi...." Jacken took hold of her hand.

"I know I did the right thing by giving him up for adoption. I was in high school and couldn't have taken proper care of him. Other girls, maybe, but I was really immature and had low self-esteem. Now I understand that it was because of being a Dragon. My mother found a very good home for him, too, so I know he...he's had a good life." He'd be about sixteen by now. Was he good at sports like his dad? Did he like chocolate chip mint ice cream like she did? A cold, hollow feeling opened in the pit of her stomach like an echo. "Problem is," she continued on a rasp, "even though my logical mind tells me all of that, my heart doesn't agree most of the time." The tears in her eyes tumbled down her cheeks. "I feel like I abandoned that little boy, just like...just like...."

"Just like your father did to you," Jacken filled in for her.

"Yes," she sobbed.

"Ah, honey." He drew her against his body and held her close. "I don't know your father's reasons for leaving, but I do know that he was an *adult* when he walked out on his wife and kids. In my eyes, that makes him a selfish bastard. Whereas you gave up a baby you obviously adored for *your son's* welfare. That's the furthest thing from selfish there is." He gave her shoulders a squeeze. "You're nothing like your old man, okay? You shouldn't feel anything but proud of yourself for making what was probably the biggest and hardest sacrifice of your life."

She pressed her face into his thick, sweaty shoulder, nodding mutely. She cried harder, though—really hard, sobs wrenching her chest and clutching at her throat.

"Toñi, it's okay, really." He was probably completely freaked out by her breakdown, but, God, she was stripped so raw, she couldn't help it. "You're such a caring person, honey; look how much you've done for the community and the Dragons in just two weeks. You gotta remember that about yourself."

She gulped and sniffled, bringing herself back to some

semblance of calm. "M-my mother says I've been pulling away from people ever since I gave up the baby, and…I think she's right. Somewhere in my mind I must've decided that anyone I loved would eventually be lost to me, like my father, and then the baby, so I needed to leave first before I got hurt." She leaned back and looked at her husband through swimming eyes. "I love you *so* much, Jaćken, more every day, and as idiotic as it sounds, that's why I left you. I'm just so afraid of losing you, and…and being destroyed."

He exhaled. "Okay, first off, that's…uh, probably the best thing anyone's ever said to me." He ran a hand down the side of her hair. "Secondly, are you *insane*? Leaving you is an absolute impossibility, you have to know that. Besides the fact that I'm biologically bonded to you, I'm batshit crazy in love with you, too."

"I know you wouldn't leave me on purpose, but…well, you could die."

He snorted. "I'm not going to die."

"You don't exactly have a desk job, Jaćken."

"Tonĭ, I'm not going to—"

The door exploded open with a thunderous crash, hitting the wall with enough force to send the doorknob bulleting off and splinters rupturing from the frame.

Tonĭ screamed as the Topside Om Rău she'd come to know as Spike Boy barreled into the hotel room with a rifle in his hands.

Jaćken threw his body in front of her.

Spike Boy lifted the weapon, sighted….

And shot Jaćken in the head.

CHAPTER FORTY

Spike Boy launched himself at Tonī, and she screamed again, scrambling backward, her heels digging into the mattress. Fear rocketed adrenaline through her, and her heart sped into an impossible beat.

Spike Boy seized her by the ankle and dragged her across the mattress.

With a sharp, discordant breath, she kicked Spike Boy's hold off, the side of her shoe scraping a patch of skin off his hand.

"Shite!" he snarled, white liquid oozing from his cut. "You bloody diesel!"

She rolled onto her hands and knees and clambered to the bedside table, grabbing the cell phone Nyko had left there, and—

Spike Boy threw himself on top of her.

The cell phone slipped in her grip, dangling precariously from her fingertips.

"Now, now, no scarperin' off, Tonī love." Spike Boy yanked the phone out of her hands and hurled it against the wall.

Her heart drummed a pattern of panic in her chest. She'd managed to plant her thumb on number one, but had it been long enough to send a signal?

Rearing above her, Spike Boy planted a knee in the small of her back and wrenched her arms behind her.

She struggled and yelled, her stomach heaving into her throat.

Spike Boy zipped a plastic spot-tie around her wrists, then flipped her onto her back and stuffed a ball gag into her mouth.

No! She hissed a breath from her nostrils, her eyeballs flexing in terror against their sockets. A scream pounded against her larynx. Jaĉken! But her husband was knocked out on the floor. Not dead, *thank you, God*—Spike Boy had used pellets again—but certainly in no position to help her.

Spike Boy hefted himself off her, pausing to rake his gaze over her body. "Fuck me ragged, but you're a right fine piece." His black eyes glittered. "It's goin' to be a bit of all right knobbin' you, especially between the—"

The sound of the hotel door opening brought Spike Boy's head whipping around.

The Vârcolac were entering the room—they'd received her call!—but they were coming in slowly and cautiously, no doubt figuring they'd be arriving in the middle of a marital spat.

Spike Boy had plenty of time to move into ambush position.

Thrashing her legs, Tonĭ tried to scream a warning around her ball gag.

Thomal was first through the door, his eyes jerking wide at the unexpected presence of an Om Rău.

Spike Boy grabbed Thomal by the throat and testicles. "Another 'round with *you*, is it?" He tossed Thomal across the room, sending him smashing through the fourth floor window in an explosion of razor-edged glass.

"Thomal!" Arc shouted. He pulled a Crouching Tiger, Hidden Dragon across the room after his brother, flinging his body halfway through the broken window just in time to catch Thomal by the forearm. The two men dangled there as Spike Boy snatched his rifle off the hotel table and swung toward—

Gábor let fly a knife.

The blade sliced deep into Spike Boy's shoulder, white acid

spraying. The Om Rău yelled and dropped his weapon.

Nyko surged in behind Gábor, hissing when he saw Tonĩ trussed up like a prize deer, and Jaćken sprawled out on the floor. He reached for a knife on his belt—

Another Om Rău—Skull—appeared behind Nyko in the hotel doorway, his own rifle up. *Sh-zip*. He took out Gábor.

Eye-blink quick, Nyko spun around and snatched up the barrel of the rifle, ramming the stock back into Skull's face, driving the man's nasal bone into his brain. Skull's face tilted skyward, flat as a plate, white acid fountaining in all directions. As the Om Rău timbered over like a felled oak tree, Nyko snatched the rifle out of his hands, whirled, and shot Spike Boy twice. *Sh-zip, sh-zip*.

The pellets splatted harmlessly against Spike Boy's leather jacket. He laughed. "We're immune to the enchantment, tosser. Why else do ye think we swan about with these pellet rifles? They can never be used against—"

Nyko rushed him.

Spike Boy stomped on the butt of his own rifle, flipping it up into his hands. *Sh-zip*. "—against us."

Nyko dropped to the floor.

Spike Boy turned, saw Arc still dangling, and pegged the blonde warrior with two pellets.

Arc crumbled out of the window, falling four stories down with his brother to the street below.

Tonĩ let out a strangled cry.

Spike Boy sauntered over to the bed and stared down at Tonĩ with those shiny black eyes of his. "Well, shite, Sunshine, looks like everyone's catchin' a good forty winks now." His lips pulled back from his teeth in a mockery of a smile. "No rescuin' for you today, love. What a bleedin' shame."

CHAPTER FORTY-ONE

Sedge Stănescu rolled his shoulders to settle the blazer into a better fit across his body, grimacing as he did. The monkey suit was annoying the hell out of him. His thick, broad body just wasn't made for pulling off "businessman" comfortably, but he had to look the part of a reputable, up-and-coming newscaster for this performance. Although his overall "look" probably wasn't being helped much by the insane rage pouring off him in scalding waves.

Damn it, the dick-breath was *late*.

Sedge started to pace again. What kind of unprofessional piece of shit couldn't manage to—

A knock sounded at the hotel door.

Dev Nichita swiveled his head toward Sedge, his silver eyes lighting up with savage Pure-bred fire. Dev's lust for violence was nearly as heated as Sedge's.

"Do you think maybe you can ratchet down the psycho killer a bit, Nichita?" Sedge said in a low tone. "You look like a vampire right now, and one who's totally pumped to disembowel a guy."

With a quick lift of his brows, Dev said, "Have you taken a

look at your own face in the mirror, Stǎnescu?"

"Yeah, I know." Sedge drew in a deep, calming breath. "Let's both put a lid on it, okay? I don't want to blow this."

Dev nodded, inhaled his own chillax breath, then crossed to the door. Putting on his best grin, he threw open the door. "Tim Armbruster!" he exclaimed, reaching out and pumping the football star's hand vigorously. "It's a real pleasure, man. Over a thousand yards rushing, eight TDs this season.... You're my favorite running back of all time."

Armbruster smiled broadly. "Hey, thanks, fella, it's always nice to meet a fan." The tall, built athlete stepped inside, limping only slightly from the knee he'd strained over two weeks ago. He clapped Dev on the shoulder as he passed into the room. "You look like you could do some damage yourself. You ever play?"

"Nah, nah, not really," Dev lied. "Just spend a lot of time in the gym."

"Ah, well, not everyone can toss the pigskin around, right?" Armbruster chuckled, the sound filled with arrogance.

Dev sliced a look at Sedge.

Yeah, *fucking poser*. The guy was going to make this even easier than it already was.

"Not as good as you, at least," Dev drawled.

Sedge stepped forward. "Mr. Armbruster, I'm Bob Haywood." He shook Armbruster's hand, gritting his back molars together to keep from pulverizing the man's bones right then and there. This hand had committed unspeakable acts of violence against Kimberly. "And you've just met my cameraman, Chip Landon." He gestured to Dev, dressed in chinos and a polo shirt, lucky bastard. "Thanks for coming out to do this segment on running backs. As I mentioned in my email, I'm a brand new broadcaster at ESPN, and having a man like you on the show will really help give me a leg up."

Armbruster chuckled that obnoxious chuckle again. "Hey, an all-expenses paid trip to the Hotel del Coronado,.Bob? Who can say no to that? "

Sedge bared his teeth in what he hoped was something close to a smile. *Bob. Did I say you could call me* Bob, *asswipe?*

Armbruster glanced around. "So...." He sniffed. "Who else you got coming in?"

"Chris Johnson from the Tennessee Titans is lined up for tomorrow. Right, Chip?"

"Day after."

"Ah."

Armbruster crossed his arms, some of his arrogance slipping. "Johnson's good. Top of his game right now."

Better than you, loser. "We only picked the best for this segment," Sedge said smoothly, amazed the words didn't sound as gritted as they felt.

"Yeah...." Armbruster nodded, puffing up again. "Makes sense."

The muscles in Sedge's hands tightened into preemptive fists. "Why don't you come on in and get settled." He led the football player past the large camera on its tripod, set up just for show, although it was tempting to record what was really going to go down. Sedge wouldn't mind having it for posterity. "We'll discuss how this is going to run."

"Jesus," Armbruster exclaimed as he spotted the array of photos laid out on a rectangular table across the room. "Look at all this." He stopped at the long side of the table and inspected the pictures. Some were action shots, others of him at parties or events.

Sedge took up position at the short end of the table, kitty corner to Armbruster. "Great, huh? We're going to use these for publicity."

"Some go back to my Huskies days at the University of Washington."

Sedge checked for reaction on Armbruster's face. The man's gaze passed dismissively over the photo of himself and Kimberly leaving some after-game party, her in a beaded gown, young and so pretty, her yellow hair long. It was if she was nothing. Less than nothing. Sedge wrapped his fingers around the edge of the table.

Dev came to stand at the other short end, across from Sedge. "Wow, man." He whistled under his breath. "You never lacked for some serious beauties on your arm, did you?"

Armbruster chuckled again, the sound making Sedge grip the table harder. "I've never suffered in that department, fella, that's for sure. And they weren't always on my arm, but generally on their *knees*, if you get what I mean." He winked at Dev, the gesture dripping with superiority.

Dev smiled, just short of showing his fangs. "Ho, yeah." Anyone who didn't know the warrior wouldn't notice the *I-can't-wait-to-see-your-face-get-fucking-ripped-off* in the expression, but Sedge did.

Sedge nodded subtly at Dev. *Let's do this thing before I snap the table in two.*

Eyes glinting, Dev's smile took on a nasty edge. "Actually, I think Bob knows one of these women." He gestured at the photos. "Don't you, Bob?"

"In fact I do, Chip." Sedge moved to the long side of the table, directly across from Armbruster. "Her." He pointed to the picture of Kimberly. "Do you remember this woman, *Tim*?"

The football player went still, a tic of muscle pulsing in his jaw as he *surely* felt the hostility Sedge was allowing to seethe off him now.

Armbruster's eyelashes flickered, as if he'd involuntarily conducted a searching glance of the room. *Not gonna find any friends here, pal.*

"Or," Sedge went on, his voice a low drawl of menace, "have you just abused too many women during your days as an asshole to keep count of them all at this point?"

Sedge could almost see the cogs and wheels in Armbruster's brain turning as he contemplated his next move. The running back finally lifted his head, meeting Sedge's cold stare with a frosty one of his own. "What the hell is this?"

"Take a wild guess."

"You're not an ESPN newscaster, are you?"

"Quick of you."

Armbruster stepped back from the table, tension visibly tightening his muscles. "You've wasted a lot of time and money then, big guy. I remember Kim, yeah. She's a crazy bitch, if you haven't already figured that out. Whatever she said about me isn't true."

Fury seared the back of Sedge's throat and hazed his vision. "Excuse me, but did you just call my wife a *bitch*?"

Dev crossed his arms over his chest. "That kind of confirms a lot about this schmuck, doesn't it, Bob?"

"You scumbags don't know shit," Armbruster snapped back. "You only know her side of the story. Betcha she told you I killed her unborn baby, right? That's total crap. She *miscarried*, all on her own, but she never got over it, that's the problem. She went completely loopy, talking smack about me and shit. I finally had to break up with her, *me*, and now she's feeding you the same pile of bull."

Sedge ducked his chin, his nostrils flaring. In his own kitchen, he'd witnessed Kimberly confess the story of her relationship with this monster. He'd sooner believe the sun was going to rise from beneath his scrotum tomorrow than what Armbruster had just said—even without the additional evidence that hacker god, Alex Parthen, had unearthed for him. "A guy like you doesn't have any balls at all, you know that. You have to beat on and terrorize someone smaller and weaker than you to feel like a man. It's pathetic."

"Right," Armbruster sneered. "You're going to believe that little cunt over me because she's your source of pussy. Not surprising, but it doesn't make it right."

"Jay-sus," Dev flared, "the way this guy talks about women is really starting to bug me. How 'bout you, Bob?"

Sedge narrowed his eyes on the football player. "Definitely."

Dev lifted a manila folder off the edge of the table. "Yo, douche-nozzle, what's your explanation for what happened to your other girlfriends, then, huh? This file here is filled with hospital reports about at least half a dozen other women you dated."

Armbruster didn't react. His silence was really fucking telling, though.

Scenting the kill, Dev laughed low in his chest, the sound hair-raising. "Do you know what it's like to feel helpless, Armbruster?"

"He's going to find out," Sedge promised darkly.

"Yeah, all right. Whatever." The running back squared his shoulders. "So how we doing this? Both of you at once? One at a time? Whatever it is, bring it, fudge-packers. I've handled worse."

Dev settled his hip on the edge of the table. "I'm just here to enjoy the show, *fella*. This is totally Bob's deal."

"Just one of you?" Armbruster laughed scornfully. "Why, this is almost going to be too easy."

"I'm thinking, not so much." Dev smirked. "How's that knee, anyway?"

Sedge was over the table lightning quick.

CHAPTER FORTY-TWO

Toni's pulse was nearly pounding out of her mouth by the time Spike Boy pulled his car up in front of a sprawling Mediterranean-style mansion. She flexed her bound hands behind her back and shivered. Jesus, what *was* this? Blazing porch lights chased back the night to reveal a red tile roof, terracotta walls, white-slatted shutters, and subtropical landscaping. She'd thought she was going to be brought to a "crib."

Inside, the house was just as stunning. She was led through a domed foyer to a spacious living room done in blond wood with cathedral ceilings, then down a long hallway floored in Spanish tiles. The place reeked of quality and class and money.

Whose house was this?

Spike Boy headed to the last door on the left in the hallway, pulling her inside a large bedroom. Intricately paned windows were strung across the opposite wall, the outside shutters currently closed, and there was a large skylight above, displaying a panorama of twinkling stars. The furniture was expansive and beautiful, but the place was disordered, the bed half-made, clothes strewn about, its occupant clearly sloppy.

Something low in Tonĩ's stomach pulsed. This was Spike Boy's bedroom.

"You should be waitin' for Raymond to get home with Videön and Hütch, Rën," Skull said, planting himself in the doorway. His nose was still mashed out of shape, but other than that all bruising and white acid were gone. "He doesn't even know we've nicked her, yet."

Spike Boy—Rën—flung his leather jacket onto a chair. "Raymond wants me to impregnate her, Mürk. I don't see how the old man would girn about me gettin' to that task straight away."

Tonĩ went dry-mouthed with shock and fear. *Impregnate!* She stumbled sideways, the two emotions colliding within her until she couldn't tell one from the other, the chaos nearly shutting down her mind. Without thought, she darted for the door.

Amazingly, Mürk stepped aside to let her pass.

Rën seized her by the bound wrists and jerked her backward. Pain screamed through the small bones in her wrists, and she gasped around her ball gag.

"Raymond will spit tacks if you hurt her," Mürk warned.

"Then she'd best be docile and sweet as a lamb, hadn't she?" Rën pressed wet lips to her ear. "Hear that, Tonĩ, love? You need to please me, right. Leave me a very satisfied man." He ripped the cord from her wrists then yanked the ball gag out of her mouth.

She coughed and cried out, sucking in a ragged breath.

Rën tugged his T-shirt over his head, exposing an upper body strewn with scars; Gábor's knife wound was fresh and red. His eyes took on a venal glitter as he toed off his boots, the way he looked at her making her skin crawl.

She shot a desperate glance at Mürk, her belly knotting into a hard tight ball.

Mürk's gaze skidded from her to Rën.

"You want to have an ogle at us, mate, while I'm slippin' her a length, is that why you're dossin' about?" Rën crossed to the bedroom door and shoved Mürk out into the hallway. "Right sick of you, old sod." He slammed the door shut and rounded on her. "Get your kit off, Tonĭ, now."

A wracking shudder shook her spine. She stood frozen in place, unspeakably terrified. Oh, this situation way out-trumped the day she'd been kidnapped by the Vârcolac. She'd been scared that day, without question, but right from the start, the men of Ţărână had treated her with nothing but absolute respect. She'd quickly learned that no one was going to do her bodily harm.

Not so here.

"I have a brother named Videön." Rën spoke offhandedly as he unbuckled his belt. "Now he likes it when a girl cries and carries on while he's fuckin' her, see. He's the real radgie one. But me?" Rën shrugged. "Either way's fine with me. Savvy?" He shoved his pants down, stripping himself naked.

Tonĭ's pulse beat thundered up into her head, the sight of his large, thick penis slamming another layer of horrible, inescapable reality over this appalling situation. His organ probably wasn't any bigger than Jacken's, but the circumstances made it seem dangerously enormous. In a few short minutes, this man was going to try and shove that thing inside her when she wouldn't be—*couldn't be*—anything but bone dry.

"There's...." She cleared her tight throat, opening up a channel for speech. "There's no reason for doing this, Rën. I'm already mated to a Vârcolac, which means I can't get pregnant by any man other than my husband. That includes Om Rău."

"I can think of two reasons," he said, leering at her breasts. "Any road, my brothers and I aren't like the sheep-shaggin' Underground Om Rău you're used to dealin' with, love. We're half-Fey."

"The rule still applies." Although truth was, she wasn't sure about that, but it seemed prudent to add it.

"As bang-tidy as you are," he came back lazily, "it'll be worth the experiment."

"Worth incurring this Raymond's—?"

"Get undressed!" he roared, "*now*, or I'll do it for you."

Jumping at his shout, she jolted backward, her eyes darting around the room. The walls were closing in on her, time running out, options disappearing. "C-can't...please, can't we do this with my clothes on? You know, j-just the first time."

His gaze dropped to her breasts again. "No."

Her abdominals cramped around a surge of panic. She could feel the forceful, painful rhythm of her heart, pounding beyond her control, heightening her sense of helplessness. Bile swam up her throat and into her mouth, its acrid taste making her eyes water.

Rën planted his hands on his hips. "This can be a doss for you, Tonĩ, or hard as fuck. What's it going to be?"

Every atom of stubborn pride inside her rebelled against being docile and sweet as a lamb, but as she passed her eyes over Rën's body, she knew she didn't have a hope in hell of fighting him off. She'd seen a lot of large physiques during her time in Țărână, but Rën's was one of the more brutally masculine bodies out there. With his massive muscles carved into curving rock, he looked to be somewhere between Jacken and Lørke.

If she was really clever—and lucky—maybe she could hold him off for a short time, but to what purpose? Țărână's warriors were unconscious, for God knew how long, and even if they should awaken, they had no way of finding her. No eleventh-hour rescue was on the way.

Rën stepped toward her.

It was such a casual step, it left her totally unprepared for his hard slap. Her head whipped sideways and her bottom lip split open, blood rushing onto her tongue and chin, her ears ringing from the pain. She had only a moment to shake the fog from her brain before a powerful arm closed around her waist and hauled her off her feet. She screamed as she was tossed onto the bed, landing in a loose-jointed sprawl.

Rën followed her onto the mattress, one hand snapping shut around her throat, the other tearing at her clothes.

Wheezing and choking, she clawed at the vise-grip around her neck, her throat pumping frantically against Rën's fist. She tried twisting and bucking, but the Om Răŭ, at least a hundred pounds heavier than she, skilled at fighting, and totally unaffected by feelings of morality, had her stripped in seconds.

Terror consumed her. She forgot to breathe, her throat going dry and gritty. Her eyesight grayed at the corners.

Rën let go of her throat—but only to grab her legs and jack her knees back to her ears, tilting her core upward.

The intolerable vulnerability of the position ignited a strange, savage electricity in her. It whirred and whipped, an awesome force. She grappled for control over it, but the power remained just outside of her ability to manage. *Please, somebody, help me! Mürk, that Raymond person, someone!* She inhaled a huge breath and screamed for as long and as loud as she could.

"Shut your face now, girl. It's not as wretched as all that." Rën grabbed his blood-engorged penis and poked around for entrance into her body.

Teeth gritted, she fought like a madwoman, but with her legs hooked over Rën's broad shoulders and the weight of his muscled body easily keeping her folded in half, she couldn't do much more than get her calves swinging furiously. She was utterly helpless. Tears streamed down her face and pooled in her ears. Icy sweat broke out all over her skin, everything inside her cringing against the imminent violation. As a last-ditch effort, she reached between her legs and grabbed Rën's hand, pulling his member aside.

Rën gaped down at their joined hands, an expression of abject shock on his face. "How the buggerin' shite are you touchin' that?"

Touching...? Dear God, she was touching his ring—his *immortality* ring—and it wasn't shocking her!

She wrestled with his hand, gouging her fingernails into his palm to force his hand to open. He was stronger than she was, and started to make a fist—then one of her nails nicked his penis, and in the moment his hand spasmed, she yanked off his ring.

"Bloody hell!" Rën snarled. "Give that back, you fuckin' scut."

She shoved the ring in her mouth, but before she could swallow it, Rën slapped her again, the hard edge of his palm catching the side of her eye. Stars blinked to life in front of her, and she gasped in pain.

Rën jammed his fingers into her mouth and—

The skylight overhead shattered, glass raining down, and one, two, three, Jaćken, Sedge, and Dev smashing down with the prism-like shards. Suddenly Rën was no longer on top of her, but driven to the floor by the juggernaut that was her husband.

Her head spinning, Tonĭ teetered to a sitting position and clawed through the glass on the bedspread for a sheet. Wrapping it around her naked body, she stumbled off the mattress and rushed to the nightstand, wedging herself between it and the wall. She watched through tear-blurred eyes as Jaćken roared above his victim, his eyes flashing the hellfire of Rău red. He punched Rën with a blow that sounded like a plumber's wrench meeting a side of beef. And again. And again.

"Jaćken," she called to him. "I-I removed his immortality ring."

Jaćken paused long enough to notice that, yes, Rën was bleeding normal red blood, not white acid. He had two long knives slicked from his belt in a heartbeat, one in each fist. Fangs bared and dripping, Jaćken stabbed the blades into either side of Rën's throat, then crosscut his arms, slicing Rën's head off with a sickening crunch. More red blood gouted from the ragged stump.

Tonĭ leaned behind the nightstand and vomited. Doctor or not, she was done with this night.

"Tonĭ?" Jaćken heaved to his feet, the front of his shirt plastered to his body with blood, his eyes searching wildly for her. Spotting her in her hidey hole, he raced over and crouched down before her. "Are you all right? Jesus—!"

She launched herself out of her nook and into her husband's arms. "Th-thank God you got here when you did." She trembled against him. "That Om Răŭ almost...almost...."

"I saw," he said in a clogged voice. "I'm so sorry I didn't get here sooner, honey." He leaned back to look at her, brushing his thumb over her split lip. "Shit," he hissed.

She wrapped her hand around his wrist. "How did you get here at all?"

"Dev and Sedge were topside tonight on another mission and received your emergency call on their cells, too. They came to the Doubletree Hotel, roused us, and then we followed the homing signal in your purse."

"My purse?"

"Anyone who goes topside gets wired up with a tracking device. Us warriors have it in our cell phones. It's one of our normal security measures."

"Well, it would've been nice to have known that. I felt really damned hopeless." Tonĭ laid her cheek against her husband's chest, not caring that she was getting herself all bloody. "You guys have to be better about filling in your new co-leader."

Jaćken laughed shakily. "Yeah."

"I want to go home."

"I bet you do." Jaćken's tone was gruff. He kissed her hair.

Arc slipped silently through the broken skylight above, landing on cat feet. He was covered in dirt and grime and his nose was bleeding. "What the hell," he swore, glancing at the headless corpse. "You guys were supposed to save that dick wad for me."

Jaćken came to his feet, drawing Tonĭ up with him. "What that lowlife did to my mate way surpasses what he did to you and your brother, Costache."

Arc's gaze raked over Tonĭ's sheet-clad body, her bloody mouth and bruised eye. He paled a little. "Oh, man, I'm sorry. Tonĭ, are you—?"

The door was front-kicked open by Mürk and the bald Om

Răn stormed inside the room, a rifle jacked back against his shoulder. "Everyone get your hands where I can see them!" he shouted, pinning the barrel briefly on each of them.

Sedge and Dev slowly raised their hands in the air, the smirks on their faces making it a mocking gesture. Arc and Jaćken didn't comply, both of them just glaring.

"Up!" Mürk snarled, "or I drop you."

"Now would be nice." Dev drawled the comment.

Mürk's brows snapped low in confusion, but in the next moment, a belt whipped over Mürk's head from behind and looped around his neck. "Howdy, cue ball," Gabor said, jerking the belt into a tight garrote. "Not fun having someone sneak up behind you, is it?"

Mürk wheezed and reddened.

Dev plucked the rifle out of Mürk's hand. "Gimme that."

Gábor shoved Mürk farther into the room. "You gonna end this guy," he asked Jaćken, "same as that other?"

Mürk angled his gaze to Rĕn's lifeless body, fear rocketing through his eyes and his face staining a deeper shade of red.

Jaćken bent to unsheathe a knife from his boot. "Fuckin'-A."

Mürk fought to get away, the white line of his teeth showing.

Jaćken cupped Tonĭ's cheek with his free hand. "I know it's been one hell of a night, honey, but do you think I could ask you to get Skull's ring off?"

"What?!" Mürk thrashed against Gábor's hold. "No! Bugger off, you piggin' grot!"

"I won't let him hurt you," Jaćken assured her.

Nodding mutely, she clutched the sheet tightly around her body and started forward.

Jaćken kept a steadying hand on her lower back as he led her to a spot in front of Mürk.

Mürk fought harder. "Get her away from me!"

Dev stepped forward and slammed a brutal fist into Mürk's midsection.

As Mürk sagged against the garrote, Jaćken grabbed the Om Răn's arm and forced it up, presenting his hand to Tonĭ.

She swallowed convulsively. "You're going to have to pry open his fingers."

"Oh, please," Arc drawled nastily, "allow me." He seized Mürk's wrist and twisted sharply, breaking it with a brittle snap. Mürk's hand flopped open.

Tonĭ quickly tugged his ring off.

Instantly, Mürk threw back his head and howled in pain.

Jaćken put his knife to the Om Rău's throat, the point pressing against the man's bulging Adam's apple. "Don't watch this," he told her.

"Tonĭ, please!" Mürk begged, "don't let him kill me! Please!" He struggled backward, his thick boots gouging up chunks of carpet. "For fuck's sake, Tonĭ, I'm your *brother*!"

CHAPTER FORTY-THREE

Jaćken rammed a clip into his M-16 rifle, then glanced at Nyko, seated next to him on the passenger side of the Pathfinder. "You ready?"

Nyko had an M-249 "SAW" machine gun propped between his legs, a huge motherfucking weapon for a huge motherfucking man, but as Nyko peered down at it, he frowned forlornly. "I'm much better with knives, you know."

Weren't they all. The warriors had only, er, borrowed these U.S. military weapons from a shipment headed for the Marine Corps Base at Camp Pendleton for the rare times they required firepower. "I just need you to look like a sociopathic Godzilla, Nyko. Point the damned thing at—" Movement in the rearview mirror snagged Jaćken's attention. A black stretch limousine was pulling into the gloomy, underground parking garage. "They're here." He twisted around to glance at the men in the backseat. "You two ready to rock?"

Sedge blew a Bubble Gum bubble and lazily snapped it, his own M-16 cradled in his lap.

Dev had an M-4, a rifle similar to the M-16, but with a shorter barrel, gripped in his hands. His pointy smile spoke volumes.

Jaćken shifted his gaze to the man wedged between the protective muscle in the middle seat. "Roth?"

"Of course," Roth replied. Only two words, but they cut like honed steel.

Yeah, he'd say so, then. Over Dev's shoulder, Jaćken saw four men climb out of the limo. One was that trigger-happy mutt from the shoot-out at the Water Cliffs, black flames slithering up his jaw. The other three Jaćken had never seen before, but they were all black-haired, tall, beefy, and to a man looked like the types who strangled kittens and drowned puppies just for shits and giggles. One's hair was cut into a viciously spiked mohawk—not that he needed help in the menacing department—another had a scar tugging his upper lip into a permanent sneer, and the fourth was sporting black flame tattoos up both arms from his elbows to underneath the short sleeves of his T-shirt. Scar Lip and Mohawk's requisite black flames must lie elsewhere on their bodies, nowhere Jaćken had a need to see, thank you very fucking much.

They were armed for a damned street war, most with Uzis and Glocks; Scar Lip had an AK-47 assault rifle. An interesting amount of hardware to be carrying for a business deal that all parties had agreed would go down "non-violently" as an "act of good faith" between races.

Roth snorted softly. "It appears that nobody trusts anybody."

Roth had that right. "Stay tight on your game," Jaćken ordered his warriors, hopping out of the Pathfinder. "The shit could hit easily with these fuck nuggets."

He prowled to the end of the car and took up a wide-legged stance across from the four Half-Rău, his M-16 held nose-down. Roth stood beside him, Sedge and Dev flanking the two of them a little behind.

They all waited.

The garage was silent as a tomb; no keys jangled, no engines cranked over, no footsteps echoed out. No one was around. Anything at all could go down here and the world would never know.

Scar Lip finally broke the silence. "Bring Mürk." The two words sliced cold and hard, edged with barely-suppressed violence.

"No," Jaćken returned. "We have matters to settle first. Tell your leader to stop sucking down caviar and join the party."

The limousine door swung open again and a well-polished shoe emerged, then a sleek pant-leg, and finally the rest of a man, tall, elegantly dressed. "Debonair," chicks would call a guy like this, or "silver fox" with his thick, silver-blonde hair and steely cheekbones. Jaćken would call him a damned meteorite. The intensity of power coming off him filled the entire garage, an electrical current that surged and ebbed through Jaćken's body as if electrodes had been attached to his 'nads and some kids were fooling around and rapidly turning the switch on and off.

Roth stiffened. Apparently, his 'nads weren't having a jolly time, either.

Mr. Elegant headed across the garage, the heels of his dress shoes tapping sharply on the concrete floor. He came to a stop a few yards away, his blue eyes cold and piercing, his hands clasped loosely behind his back. "Raymond Parthen," he introduced in a cultured accent. "I detest caviar, if the truth be known. Terribly fishy stuff."

Hatred corroded Jaćken's veins. He ached to squeeze the trigger of his M-16 and keep squeezing until this man was a sieve. The look on Tonĭ's face in Spike Boy's bedroom when she'd discovered that *her father* was head of the Topside Om Rău would be burned into his memory forever.

"Roth Mihnea," Ţărână's leader counter-introduced.

"Charmed. My son, Mürk?" Parthen inquired blandly.

Roth swept a fleck of dust from the sleeve of his blazer. "He's here."

"You'll get him back," Jaćken informed Parthen, "when you agree to what we want."

"Which is?"

"Leave Tonĭ the hell alone. I don't want you anywhere near

her again. Ever. You got that? You've hurt her enough to last a lifetime."

"Have I? My, what distressing news. And after I had my lads use pellets to save her the gore of all those killings, too. *Tut*. A wasted generosity. But here nor there...." Parthen flicked a careless hand through the air. "I need my daughter, gentlemen, regardless of your concerns."

"And your douchebag son?"

"You're welcome to keep him. But I daresay you'll risk Mürk learning valuable information about your underground hole, Vârcolac, and for no discernible gain on your part. You see, my dear chaps, the moment I found Rën dead, I changed my entire operation. Murk no longer knows anything about my affairs."

Jaćken curled his lip. "I just might have to shed a man-tear over your fatherly devotion."

Parthen offered Jaćken a smile that didn't defrost his eyes. "Shall we cease this palaver and make a mutually beneficial deal?"

Jaćken shrugged. "As long as nothing you have to say includes Tonĩ. I *daresay* I've already made my position clear on that."

"*Your* position." One golden brow arched upward. "Who are you, might I ask, to comport yourself with such authority on my daughter's behalf?"

Jaćken tightened his grip on his M-16. *Here comes the fun part.* "Her husband."

Parthen burst out laughing.

Jaćken had to fight like hell to keep blood from rushing into his face.

"You jest!" Parthen's gaze made a contemptuous trip over Jaćken. "Dear Lord, has Tonĩ gone barking mad?"

Jaćken showed his teeth. "As father-in-laws go, you're not exactly curling the hair on my balls, either."

Parthen tugged on the cuffs of his dress shirt. "As uncouth as you appear, it would seem. It's bloody fortunate that we shan't be holding the positions for long, isn't it?"

The comment was followed by a deep base note of electricity thrumming through Jaĉken's body. Something that might've been unnerving had Jaĉken not been so caught up in despising this fucker.

"You see, my dear boy, I have long-term plans for my daughter, and those don't include her dipping into the primordial ooze that's clearly your gene pool for her offspring."

Jaw clamped, Jaĉken chinned at the four men by the limo. "And you think those shit-stains have better pedigrees? They're Half-Rău, too, you dingus."

"Half-Rău and half-*Fey*," Parthen corrected. "Bred correctly, this brood of mine will have progeny with active enchantments. Hence the reason my son and daughter are so important to my endeavors. I realize that someone of your suspect intelligence might have difficulty understanding—"

"Yeah, I get it. With their royal bloodlines, Tonĩ and Alex's children will be some of the most powerful."

"Ah! There you go, old tosspot! You're not as much of a gobbin as you appear."

"And you're obviously not as powerful as you appear." Jaĉken broke topside rules and let his fangs show in a smile. "Or else why the need for so much help?"

Parthen made a sweeping gesture with his hand. "It's a mammoth task I've set myself, boy, requiring many bodies in a multitude of different places. I'm taking back everything, you see—land, money, governmental positions, power—regaining the supremacy us Fey folk used to have in this world many years ago, before the regulars came along and managed to snuff most of us." He tilted his chin. "This is a bit of history you Vârcolac should be well familiar with, is it not? Indeed, our two races could join forces in this venture. In all truth, I'd never thought to include you Vârcolac in my plans. With your blood and sun weaknesses, you're worthless creatures, but, after all, there'll be a need for servants and lackeys in the new world order."

Jaćken laughed darkly. What would this egomaniac say if he knew that a few shots of Fiinţă from a lowly Vârcolac could bring *today's* Fey generation into their full enchantments. "Power lies where you least expect it, Parthen. I'd remember that if I were you." Jaćken nodded toward the Pathfinder.

Nyko stepped out into the open from the side of the car.

The four Om Rău across the garage shifted and stiffened, hands going knuckle-white on their weapons. It wasn't so much the SAW they were reacting to, as Nyko. In keeping with Jaćken's request to just look like a sociopathic Godzilla, Nyko had removed his shirt, exposing the full panorama of his body's muscles and…artwork. Yeah, that pretty much did it.

Nyko opened the Pathfinder's rear hatch and hauled Mürk out by his shackles, plunking the man on his feet.

Parthen noticed his son's arm cast at once; he stiffened, just barely, but it was enough.

Roth's voice went flat and hard. "Before instigating a war with us, Mr. Parthen, it would be wise for you to note that we can get your rings off."

More shifting from the four Om Rău, their collective tension like a blast of hot, dense air.

Parthen's eyes turned so glacial, the blue of the irises became almost transparent. He chuckled, the sound equally wintry. "Do you have any notion who you're toying with, lads?"

Sparks of pain shot down Jaćken's arms and deep into the bones of his legs. He kept his face blank, though, knowing Parthen was checking for a reaction.

"I believe," Roth said, sounding remarkably calm, considering he was probably undergoing an internal barbecue, too, "that you're the one misjudging us."

Parthen inclined his head. "It appears we are at an impasse. I shall leave peaceably now, Vârcolac. I'm a man of my word, and there shall be no violence today. But eventually"—he sighed, as if truly regretting what he had to say next—"I'll have to destroy you. Surely you must realize that." With a final, sideways glance at Mürk, he turned and strode back to his limousine.

CHAPTER FORTY-FOUR

SpongeBob SquarePants let out an inane giggle as the cartoon sea sponge made some equally inane remark about Krabby Patties. Jaćken turned his wrist where it rested on his wife's shoulder and checked his watch. Five minutes into the show and he felt like his brains were melting out of his ears.

"We don't have to keep watching this," he told her. "I can call Raln and tell him to un-fuck the programming."

"It's mind-numbing." Tonī shifted closer. She was cuddled up next to him on their living room couch, her legs curled under her. "I kind of need that right now."

"Might I suggest football, then?" He peered down at his wife as she squirmed again, and frowned. "Do you need more pain meds?"

"Actually, yes." She straightened off him. "Would you mind getting them?"

"Of course not." He hopped up, grabbed the bottle of Motrin from the kitchen, then headed back into the living room. "You should've asked Dr. Jess for Vicodin or Percocet."

"It's just some bruises."

Bruises that looked a helluva lot worse the day after

receiving them from Spike Boy. *May the fucker rot in Purgatory.* Jaċken crouched down in front of his wife, and shook three pills out of the bottle into his palm. He twisted his mouth at her. "You know, you never used to look like this before you started hanging out with Vârcolac." And now twice in less than a month.

"True." She gave him one of those warm, wifely smiles that turned his soft spot into absolute goo. "At least I'm not bored."

He set a hand on her knee. "Never again," he said quietly. "You have my solemn vow on that, Tonĭ."

"I know." She moved some strands of hair off his brow with her fingertips. "I feel safe with you, Jaċken, don't worry."

"Good." He hadn't earned that, yet, he knew, but he would.

"What are you going to do about Mürk?"

He braced his forearms on his thighs. "Well, your dear old dad made a good point. Skull *is* pretty damned useless to us. No sense torturing him for information he doesn't have, which leaves us stuck with either detaining him in one of our jail cells for the rest of his life or outright killing him."

"No." Tonĭ sat up straight. "I don't want you to hurt him, Jaċken."

He exhaled a rough breath. "Yeah, I know."

"Can you...? I want you to let him go."

He gently placed the pills in her hand. "Tonĭ, I realize you're weirded-out about him right now, but he's our enemy—"

"He's my half-*brother*." She rested her head on the back of the couch and stared at the ceiling. "Look, you're right; my mind is blown from discovering I have I-don't-know-how-many half-siblings, and I know I'm making an emotional decision with this." She looked up, leaned forward, and touched his jaw. "I just can't deal with the thought of those options you mentioned, no matter how much of a bad guy he is."

He hooked one side of his mouth into his cheek. "Releasing him might come back to bite us in the ass," he pointed out.

"I know, I'm sorry. I'm being stupid."

"No." Fact was, he didn't want Skull to remain in Ţărână,

either. Jail cell or not, the man tainted the surroundings. Plus, Tonĩ had touched his face. "You're the boss."

She slanted a look at him. "Not when I'm on this couch."

He laughed deep in his chest. Yeah, she'd actually been doing a great job of separating out "wife" from "leader" with him. He took her hand and pressed his thumb over the pills he'd put in her palm. "Remember when you gave me those Ibuprofen tablets at Garwald's?"

"How could I forget?" Her eyes sparkled at him. "It was the first time I saw you smile."

"It may have been exactly then," he gently closed her hand around the pills, "that I fell in love with you."

She cocked a brow at him. "It wasn't during the letter opener incident?"

He chuckled. "Maybe a little then, too." He kissed her closed fist. "Two against the world, Mrs. Brun. You and I. For always and forever."

"Ah." She bent forward and brushed her mouth over his, the best kiss she could manage with her split lip. "I like the sound of that."

Raymond lounged back in the cushioned deck chair on the terrace of his new Fairbanks Ranch mansion, his legs crossed, his palm cupping a snifter of Louis Royer Old Grande Champagne cognac. It was a luxurious libation, costing him nearly five hundred dollars a bottle, but he was in an unbearable mood at discovering it was going to be such a considerable chore getting Tonĩ back. He bloody well needed the palliative.

Sipping his cognac, he watched the sun make steady progress toward the horizon. Behind him inside the house, servants moved briskly about unpacking boxes, and then a presence arrived at his back, one he recognized.

"The prodigal son returns," Raymond said dryly.

Mürk moved to the other cushioned chair and sat.

"How did you find me?" Raymond asked, watching the

orange ball of the sun sink into a gauzy nest of clouds.

"I borrowed a cell phone and called Pändra's secret line." Mürk held up his casted arm. "I'm going to need another ring."

Ah, yes, he'd just dash off and do that straight away. "I can't imagine you escaped the Vârcolac's lair."

"The cockheads just let me go." Mürk shrugged. "Must've been something you said."

After only one day, too. Those blood-consuming beings showed some aptitude for appreciating logic, then. "Any weaknesses to report?"

"No." Mürk kneaded his brow wearily. "They kept me shut away in a prison cell the whole time."

Jorgé, the Parthen butler, appeared on the terrace. "May I get anything for you, Master Mürk?"

"Jesus suffering fuck, a beer would be bostin for this sodding headache."

"Yes, sir."

Mürk dropped his hand and looked at Raymond. "There's something you need to know."

Raymond drifted the snifter back and forth under his nose, enjoying the rich smell of the cognac. "My breath is bated, son."

Mürk allowed a dramatic pause to develop, which was rather cheeky of him. "Toni's the one who took our immortality rings off."

Raymond turned his head toward his son, a stillness enveloping his body.

"She's acquired her enchantment power," Mürk added unnecessarily. Because, what else?

The piece of information he didn't have, however, was by what means. "How, pray tell, was she able to do that?"

Mürk slouched deeper into the chair. "I haven't got a baldy notion."

Raymond turned back to the sunset and took a long sip of his drink. The sky was streaked a beautiful, brilliant tangerine. "That's something," he murmured, "I most assuredly need to discover."

Jorgé moved like a ghost onto the terrace, setting a jar of beer and a small dish of peanuts at Mürk's elbow. He disappeared just as unobtrusively.

Mürk picked up the beer and took a gulp. "What are you going to do?"

"Reacquire her, of course." Raymond gestured negligently. "Kill every last Vârcolac, if need be. No more hospitable pellets."

"So we're at war with them?"

Raymond set down his snifter and folded his hands in his lap. "Yes, son, we're most definitely at war."

CHAPTER FORTY-FIVE

Three months later, June.

Beth stepped into her kitchen, a book clutched to her breasts, and stopped short.

Arc was perched on a high stool at the kitchen island, the heel of one boot hooked on a rung, the other foot planted on the floor. He was wearing her favorite jeans, Levi's 501 button flies, and a tight blue T-shirt that set off the color of his eyes to perfection, as well as the sleek bulk of his muscles. Reading the sports page with an open Coke bottle at his elbow, he was the absolute picture of sexy masculinity.

She ran her tongue across her lips. God, why were her horny monkey hormones still raging so intensely into her fifth month of pregnancy? Honest to Pete, couldn't she just be like other pregnant women and get nauseous and exhausted?

"Hi, baby," Arc glanced up at her. "What's up?"

"Um, I brought home your suit for the cocktail party. It's in the living room." Shock of shockers and miracle of miracles, eight new Dragon women were being brought into the community next week—Tonī had dangled some big money carrot in front of them, or something—and upon arrival, they would be introduced to some of the town mucky-mucks at a shindig in the mansion's Garden Parlor. What a gas. Beth just loved parties, especially the dressing-up part. "You're going to look great in it."

He chuckled. "Well, yeah, my wife's the best fashion designer ever."

She stepped up to the island, letting her eyes drift to the curved muscle in his thigh. Heat shimmied in her belly. "Try not to look *too* good."

He gave her a smile of overblown arrogance. "Not possible, babe." He noticed the book she was holding. "What's that?"

"Oh, I went to the library and picked out an idea for our classic."

"Hey, cool." Arc set aside the sports page. "Let's see it."

The warmth in her belly turned into something tender. Arc was trying really hard to have a deeper relationship with her. In the last few months they'd talked about all kinds of different topics, and recently he'd even agreed to read a classic novel with her and then discuss it. It was so touching. Probably wasn't fair what she was about to do, but.... Straight-faced, she laid out her choice on the kitchen island in front of him: *War and Peace* by Leo Tolstoy.

Arc's brows shot up. "Jesus God, Beth." He reached out and flipped to the last page. "This is 1296 pages!"

"And," she stipulated, holding up a finger, "we can't have sex until we've read it all and discussed it."

"You've got to be shitting me."

She crossed her arms. "You won't read it without proper motivation, Arc. I know you."

"I so totally will."

"Ha! Maybe over the course of two years."

"C'mon, Beth, be reasonable." He rubbed a hand along his jaw. "All right, how about this: we can have sex after we've read and discussed each chapter?"

"That would be every night."

"Ah." His eyes glinted.

"Arc!"

"Okay, okay, here's another idea." He opened a drawer in the kitchen island and pulled out two paperbacks, setting them next to hers: *Animal Farm* by George Orwell and *One Day in the Life of Ivan Denisovich* by Alexander Solzhenitsyn. The first was about a hundred pages, the second barely over two hundred. A couple of tug boats compared to her Titanic. "We could read one of these."

She planted her hands on her hips. "You're such a stinker! What did you do, go to the library and ask Hannah for the shortest classics she could find?"

"They're supposed to be good books, and one's a Russian author, same as yours." He smiled at her, obviously proud of himself.

She latched her eyes onto his smile, his mouth. "Well...." *Shut up, horny monkey*! She reached out absently for one of his books, her eyes remaining pinned on his white teeth, his alluring canines. "I always have wanted to read *Animal Farm*. But, um, no sex till we're done reading it."

He sighed. "Yeah, all right."

"Okay, then." She edged around the kitchen island. "So...." She bit her bottom lip as she maneuvered in front of his stool, positioning herself between his thighs. "That means we should probably have sex now, you know...." She slid her hands slowly over the hard contours of his shoulder muscles. "Just to tide us over."

He was on his feet so fast the stool clunked over behind him. Grabbing her by the waist, he whipped her around and set her on the island, his hands warm and eager as he shoved up her skirt.

She spread her legs, arched her head back, and moaned. "God, I'm such a pushover."

"No, babe," he bent his lips to the curve of her throat. "I am."

Kimberly threw open the door to her house and barreled into the living room. "Sedge!" she called out. "Oh, hey—!" She skidded to a stop. "What the hell's this!?"

Sedge was standing by the coffee table with a huge smile on his face, several candles lit and a bottle of champagne chilling in a silver bucket. "Whoa, now, Mrs. Stănescu. You need to watch your language now that you're a junior associate with Bitterman, Zanhunch, and Pickett."

"Tonī told you already? That blabbermouth." Kimberly laughed as she said it, not at all upset, of course. If it wasn't for Tonī Parthen insisting that a lawyer was needed to see to the community's ever-growing investments and financial interests topside, Kimberly might still be unhappily writing unpublished papers or contemplating rock gardens. She glanced down at her watch. "I was offered the job all of an hour ago."

"Well, yeah," Sedge said, "but I needed to get another matter cleared with Tonī related to topside, so I pressed her for the info." He picked up a fluted glass of champagne and held it up to her in toast. "Congratulations, Berly. You did it."

"Yeah, I did. Boo-yah!" She pumped her briefcase up-and-down over her head. "I actually wasn't sure I could pull off a power interview anymore, but I guess I impressed them." Bringing a high-dollar client to the table in the form of the, *ahem*, "Research Institute" hadn't hurt her chances. Crossing to Sedge, she set down her briefcase and accepted the champagne. They *clinked* glasses and she took a sip. "So what's the other topside matter?"

"Oh, no.... We don't need to talk about it now. Let's celebrate."

She set her flute down. "C'mon, spill."

He cleared his throat. "Yeah, okay. Um...now that you're going to be spending so much time topside, I've been looking into the possibility for you to, uh...."

When nothing else came out of her husband's mouth, Kimberly arched a brow. "What's with all the weird, Sedge?"

He exhaled a *whooshing* breath. "Here's the thing. Roth has a sister-in-law named Karrell who lives and works topside, and I think she's someone who—"

"A *Vârcolac?*"

"Yes. Roth keeps it quiet because he doesn't want anyone else thinking it's okay to live outside of the community."

"Perish the thought," Kimberly drawled.

"Kimberly—"

"No, really. I can't friggin' believe this, Sedge. For three years I've been trying to get Roth to let me live topside, and all this time—"

"Karrell doesn't come and go—just like *you're* not going to—so it's not a security issue."

Yeah, Kimberly was being required to live up top Monday through Thursday for work, spending nights in a small apartment, and the rest of the time, she'd be with Sedge in Ţărână. Not optimal, but that was the only way Tonî could get prickly Roth to agree.

Kimberly rolled her eyes. "Whatever." She didn't want to waste her energy on Roth. He wasn't ultimate emperor around here anymore, and she supposed baby steps were better than no steps; Rome wasn't built in a day, after all. "So what's the deal with this Karrell?"

"Karrell's a...a therapist."

"A—huh?"

"Yeah, I...I was hoping, you know, I was thinking it'd be a good idea for you to talk to her." Sedge lowered his voice to the tone of a cowboy trying to calm a twitchy horse. "You could tell her about what your ex-boyfriend did to you, Kimberly. And Karrell's Vârcolac, right, so you wouldn't have to censor yourself. You could also talk about me, if you needed to, about what a pain in the ass I can be sometimes."

"You're never a pain in the ass." No, he was the sweetest man on earth, still trying to help her with the Tim thing.

"You're *not* crazy, okay." He made an adamant downward gesture with his hands. "I don't want you to think I'm saying that. And I'm not trying to insult your intelligence, either. It's just that what your asshole ex did to you was really rough, Berly, and I think that maybe you need some help getting over it." He picked up his champagne glass, but then set it right back down. "So, what do you think?"

"I think..." she stepped forward and wrapped her arms around Sedge's neck, "that you're the best husband a girl could ever ask for."

His hands came to rest on her hips. "You're not mad?"

"No."

His eyes turned all puppy doggish. "And you'll go?"

Truth was, she hadn't been doing the best job getting over it by herself. "Yes." She eased back and kissed his cheek. "I'll go."

He smiled at her. "Good."

She stepped out of his hold. "Speaking of my ex." She crossed her arms firmly beneath her breasts. "When I was topside, I saw a news report about him. Apparently both of his knees have been damaged beyond repair. They're not saying how, but the scuttlebutt is that his career in football is officially over." She narrowed her eyes on her husband. "You wouldn't happen to know anything about that, would you?"

Sedge met her gaze with saucer-eyed innocence. "How could I? You never told me his name, remember?" He picked up his bubbly. "He's a football player, is he?"

She snorted. "Nice maneuvering, slick."

"I really don't know what you're talking about."

"I'm sure not."

"Shall we get back to celebrating?" He downed his champagne. "You want to go out to dinner?"

"Actually...." She flipped her eyes meaningfully toward upstairs. "I was thinking more like a game of hide the salami."

He barked out a laugh.

"What, have I already worn you out?" It was amazing what happiness could do for a woman's sex drive. As soon as Tonī had told Kimberly that the community needed a lawyer, pretty much right after Tonī had taken over, Kimberly had been making up big time for the long dry spell she'd put her husband through.

"Hardly," Sedge drawled.

Yeah, great thing about a Vârcolac male, one whiff of a mate's blood and he was raring to go. Waggling her eyebrows like a villainous lech, she took her husband by the hand and led him up the stairs.

One week later.

"I really don't see why this mission is necessary."

Alex rubbed a hand over his mouth and nodded, trying to look like he was giving Roth's comment serious weight rather than the *you've got to be kidding* he was actually thinking. He glanced around the U-shaped table at the other Council members—a Council being just one of the many great changes his sister had made since taking the co-helm of Ţărână—checking for reactions. Only the primary four had been gathered, Jaćken, Tonĭ, Roth, and Alex himself, due to the urgency of the matter that needed deciding.

Dev Nichita was also here, waiting for the Council to give him the nod for this mission. Or not. He was standing at the open end of the U, his hands locked at the small of his back and his legs planted wide. From the steely cut of his bearded jaw, it was clear what Dev's thoughts were: something along the lines of *quit being a pussy, Roth, and let me do my job.* Jaćken had recently created a Special Ops Topside Team to deal with problems with the community's new Om Rău enemies, and Dev was the man he'd put in charge of it.

Alex shifted his gaze over to Jaćken, but his brother-in-law's thoughts were more difficult to divine. Jaćken was busy eyeballing Tonĭ's throat, the long stretch of her skin exposed by her up-style hairdo.

Gimme a break. Alex almost rolled his eyes. When *wasn't* Jaćken eyeballing Tonĭ with a mind on grody stuff? *Huh*, yeah,

Alex had learned the hard way never to go over to the Brun household without calling first. *Bleech*...although, okay, Alex was admittedly really glad that whatever had made Tonī bolt her marriage three months ago—something she'd never discussed with him, surprisingly enough—had clearly been ironed out. He'd never seen his little sister happier.

Alex glanced down at the table, envy over the intimacy Tonī and Jacken shared stabbing through him. He'd kind of...well, hell, he'd really figured he'd be linked up with someone himself by now. Guess it'd been a mistake to assume his royal-ness would attract a swarm of female candidates for the future Mrs. Parthen. Turned out the exact opposite was true. The Vârcolac women were so star-struck by his status they barely even talked to him.

He'd lived through one month of this ridiculous dating drought, and then Roth had finally grown as fed up as Alex with the situation and butted in to arrange a blind date. Not surprisingly, Roth's mate-of-choice for Alex had been a royal Fey Vârcolac by the name of Jennilīth.

The blind date had gone pretty well, and now the two of them were seeing each other regularly, but...you know, Alex was still waiting for the wow factor to go off in his heart. He wasn't sure why it hadn't yet.

"What's your reticence, Roth?" Tonī asked, bringing Alex back to the present.

His sister was seated next to him along one arm of the U, her head bowed as she re-read the email Alex had hacked out of the airwaves. It was a message from their bigger and better enemy, the Topside Om Rău, to their good ol' everyday enemy, the Underground Om Rău. According to the message, the Topside Om Rău were handing over four Dragon women to the Underground Om Rău at a warehouse in a few short hours. Why any Om Rău would give up one precious Dragon, much less four, was a mystery, but one that didn't require solving for them to act. At least not to Alex's way of thinking.

Not so Roth.

"This mission is too risky for the indefinite benefits it would bring us," Roth argued. "We've brought eight women into the community just yesterday, whereas the four we discuss now are a complete unknown. We don't know if they fit the other required parameters, or if they're even remotely interested in joining us. I say our resources are overburdened enough already."

Alex cleared his throat to call attention to himself. "Thing is, Roth, those eight were the only women off an original list of fifty who accepted our offer." And didn't the town shit a collective gold brick when Alex had unearthed that many Dragons in California. Yet, *finding* Dragons had been a whole different deal than convincing them to spend a year in an underground cave away from their families. "Do we really have the luxury of ignoring any we can lay our hands on? They're the key to the salvation of your race." Yeah, kind of something he hadn't thought he'd have to remind Roth about.

Roth frowned. "Many of those fifty have expressed an interest in joining us at a later date, when the timing in their lives is better." Roth snapped his chair straight. "I assure all of you, I don't underestimate the value of these women. How many years have I lived with the threat of extinction of my own race? But, need I remind you that on this mission our warriors would be facing down members of *both* the Underground and the Topside Om RăU. We have no idea how many men that could be, although I think it's fair to assume that their numbers would grossly exceed ours. We can only spare the barest number of warriors for Mr. Nichita's team. The safety of our current eight is our first obligation."

Alex sighed under his breath. The man did have a valid argument. Țărână's Om Rău neighbors posed a constant threat.

Tonī leaned back in her chair, the look in her eyes that stubborn glint which always popped an *uh, oh,* into Alex's mind. Probably Jacken's, too, if the man had learned anything in nearly four months of marriage. "You bring up all good points, Roth, but here's the thing that's itching at my conscience. Four women are about to be handed over to some extremely unsavory men and we're privileged to *know* that. Do you really feel comfortable just sitting back and doing nothing to save these poor women, regardless of whether or not they bring us a direct benefit? Because I'm not sure I do, not after my own experiences with these Topside Om Răŭ."

Oh, boy. Cranky face Roth.

Dev, on the other hand, looked like he wanted to zip over and kiss Tonĭ.

Tonĭ glanced across the U-shaped table toward her husband. "Can you give us a risk assessment, Jaćken?"

"What do you want me to tell you?" Jaćken snapped. "The pucker factor on this mission's going to be damned high, but as you just said, does it really fucking matter?"

Tonĭ lowered her lashes and flicked her husband a *look*.

Yeah, that hadn't been so helpful.

Jaćken laid an arm on the conference table. "This mission is do-able," he continued in the kind of hard tone that suggested impatience on a level with Dev's. "I wouldn't have put Nichita in charge of it if I wasn't sure he could handle it."

Alex glanced over at Dev, the large Vârcolac's black fatigues barely containing all of the huge, bulging muscles of his body. Alex made a face. Man, he really needed to get into the gym more often.

"And who will Mr. Nichita be leading?" Roth asked curtly.

Dev answered that. "Costache, Pavenic, and Stănescu."

"Only four men total?" Roth turned back toward Tonĭ to give her an astounded look. "You're really supporting this?"

"It's what the warriors train for, Roth," she said softly. "I trust in their abilities." She looked at her husband again. "This is ultimately a decision for the Head of Security, though. It's your men who'll be put in danger, Jaćken."

Jaćken shoved to a standing position almost before the words had stopped coming out of Tonĭ's mouth. "Put your team in the field," he ordered Dev.

"Yes, sir." Dev swiveled an about-face, long strides taking

him from the conference room.

The rest of them scraped to their feet.

"You'll excuse me," Roth said stiffly. "Other matters need my attention."

Alex jammed his hands into his pockets as the rear door closed behind Roth. "He's not going to be the life of the party for a while."

"The hell with him." Jacken's jaw somehow managed the feat of growing even harder. "I hate it when he gets like that."

"I know," Toni said gently. "I'm sorry, honey." She set a hand on her husband's forearm. "I'm working on him."

Jacken checked his watch. "Shit," he growled.

Toni's brow furrowed. "Will Dev's team make it in time to save those women?"

Jacken met his wife's gaze, the line of his mouth grim. "It's going to be tight."

GIFT OPTION

I hope you enjoyed THE BLOODLINE WAR. Word of mouth is an author's Willy Wonka Golden Ticket, and so if you wouldn't mind taking a moment to leave a review, I would very much appreciate it.

In appreciation of your time and effort, I'm offering a FREE short story to fans who leave a review. Send a screen shot or copy of your review to Tracy@TracyTappan.com and you'll receive "Lună Zână," a story about three residents of the town of Țărână who broke a sacred law of the Vârcolac more than thirty years ago. Their wrongdoing will eventually culminate in a revelation that changes one person's life forever, and only fans who read this story will have a clue to this incredible secret.

More gritty adventure and raw passion in
The Community Series

Book 2, THE PUREST OF THE BREED, which focuses on the notorious Nichita family, is coming soon.

Sign up for Author Updates at www.tracytappan.com to be notified.

ABOUT THE AUTHOR

I've always been fascinated by men who make their way by their weapons, from every kind of ancient warrior to modern day soldiers. I suppose that's why I married a man who used to saddle up on an H-60 Seahawk helicopter strapped with Hellfire missiles and spend his days fighting bad guys. Now I put my imagination to work writing about tough, but sensitive, heroes who wield swords, knives, guns, and their bare fists...and, of course, the women who tame them!

After earning a Master's degree in Marriage, Family, and Child Counseling, Tracy Tappan worked in the clinical field before devoting herself full time to writing. She has a fertile imagination, reaching back to her childhood, which has compelled her to write in a multitude of genres. In nearly a quarter of a century of being a military wife, she's lived all over the United States and in Europe, enjoying seven years overseas, first in Rome, Italy, then in Madrid, Spain. She's now settled back in sunny San Diego with her husband, a menagerie of pets, and two children who seem to think they can come and go as they please.

http://www.tracytappan.com